HAYS CITY SHOOT-OUT

Streaming blood, his left eye swollen shut, Hickok lurched against the wall, willing himself to remain on his feet. Instinctively, he reached for the pearl-handled Colt, and as the barrel came clear his rage exploded in a sheet of flame.

The two troopers were abruptly knocked spinning as the Colt roared twice. Stumbling forward, Hickok braced himself against the table and raised his pistol for the finishing shot. Alive or dead, he meant to make certain the troopers would never again regain their feet. But waves of darkness suddenly obscured his vision, and he dropped to his knees . . .

NOVELS BY MATT BRAUN

Wyatt Earp
Black Fox
Outlaw Kingdom
Lords of the Land
Cimarron Jordan
Bloody Hand
Noble Outlaw
Texas Empire
The Savage Land
Rio Hondo
The Gamblers
Doc Holliday
You Know My Name
The Brannocks
The Last Stand
Rio Grande
Gentleman Rogue
The Kincaids
El Paso
Indian Territory
Bloodsport
Shadow Killers
Buck Colter
Kinch Riley
Deathwalk
Hickok & Cody
The Wild Ones
Hangman's Creek
Jury of Six
The Spoilers
The Overlords

The Gamblers

MATT BRAUN

Previously published under the title *Mattie Silks*

St. Martin's Paperbacks

The Gamblers was previously published under the title *Mattie Silks*.

This is a work of fiction. All of the characters, organizations, and events portrayed in this novel are either products of the author's imagination or are used fictitiously.

THE GAMBLERS

Copyright © 1972 by Matt Braun.

All rights reserved.

For information address St. Martin's Press, 175 Fifth Avenue, New York, NY 10010.

ISBN: 978-0-312-96215-9

Printed in the United States of America

Pocket Books edition / September 1978
Pinnacle edition / May 1985
St. Martin's Paperbacks edition / June 1997

St. Martin's Paperbacks are published by St. Martin's Press, 175 Fifth Avenue, New York, NY 10010.

10 9 8 7 6

BOOK ONE

COWTOWN
AND SOILED DOVES

CHAPTER ONE

Mattie Silks stepped from the depot and began walking toward the center of the city. Grasping her faded carpetbag, she walked slowly along South Street, absorbing sights and sounds wholly foreign to one whose life until yesterday had been spent in a backwoods' farm community. Springfield was as far as her money would take her, and already she had the feeling it was a wise choice. After what had happened she knew that things certainly couldn't get any worse. But broke or not, she somehow sensed that this town was to become a momentous turning point in her life.

Though barely nineteen, she was a woman full grown to all appearances, yet she seemed unaware of the reaction she evoked among the throngs of men around the train station. Oh, she was conscious that men found her pleasing to look at, well enough, and vaguely sensed she had the power to transform them into stammering, heavy-handed schoolboys. But she hadn't yet perfected the art of deliberately provoking their admiring glances.

Not unlike most farm girls, she had a natural, unaffected grace. The fluid motion of her trim body brought no less comment in the city than it had in the hinterlands. Small in stature, what the folks back home called dainty, her ripe, full breasts tapered sharply to a tiny waist, then her body flared again in rounded, tempting hips. Her sensual, uninhibited movements were those of an innocent doe, yet the images she brought to men's minds were lustful, if not downright depraved. Flaxen hair nestled softly in curls atop her head, and but for the inquisitive blue eyes her oval face might have been demure. The simple farm dress she wore beneath a shawl did nothing to detract from her delicate features, and by contrast even seemed to emphasize the unspoiled quality of her beauty.

Rough, blustering men, shouldering their way along South Street, suddenly stepped aside and watched with bold, roving eyes as Mattie moved blithely toward the public square. Intent on soaking up the excitement and wonder of the first real metropolis she had ever seen, the young girl simply couldn't be bothered by their stares.

Reaching the square moments later, Mattie suddenly stopped in her tracks, dumbstruck by the bustling, swarming anthill of activity before her. What appeared to be a vast open field was actually a public marketplace, carpeted in a finely ground layer of dust, stretching seventy-five yards in each direction. The four blocks of buildings surrounding the area had been constructed so that every corner facing the plaza was cut back to form the sides of a massive square. The major thoroughfares of the city adjoined this huge clearing at the points of the compass, and wandered off erratically to intersect outlying streets.

Fascinated, Mattie paused to observe the hundreds of people moving back and forth across the marketplace. Tradesmen hawking their wares, farmers peddling produce and livestock, shell-game operators, medicine shows and knots of colored softshoe dancers, each intent on attracting both the curious and the gullible.

Enthralled by the clamor and hubbub surrounding her, Mattie began walking aimlessly along the outer edge of the plaza. Slowly working her way through the crowd, she felt strangely removed from the uproar, like a spectator at a festive county fair. Now and then she paused to look at the fashionable dresses in shop windows, and admire the grand emporiums fronting the square. For a naive country girl, the sophistication and finery was really more than she had ever dared imagine in her wildest dreams. Despite her efforts to meld unobtrusively into the crowd, she couldn't resist gawking at the huge buildings and the milling beehive around her. Excitement swelled in her breast, and try as she might, she couldn't still the fluttering of her heart. Something grand was going to happen in her life. She just knew it. And whatever it was, it would be a thousand times better than the cruel world she had just escaped.

Only a week before, Martha A. Silks, youngest daughter of the Reverend Luther Silks, had thought she would be content to remain on the family farm in Indiana for the rest of her days. But overnight that calm had been shattered.

Thinking back, Mattie could understand her father's shock. But she still couldn't believe he'd become so enraged by her harmless little affair with a traveling drummer. Besides, it wasn't as if the drummer had taught her anything she didn't already know! After all, farm boys weren't exactly bashful once they'd cornered a pretty girl in a hay loft. Giggling wickedly, she tried to imagine her father's roar of outrage if he'd even suspected just how many hay lofts she had become acquainted with since turning fifteen. Suddenly disgusted with the whole ridiculous affair, she jerked her mind back to Springfield. Gazing about the colorful scene once more, she resolved that from this moment on she would wrench from life every measure of happiness to be found, regardless of the price.

But in the meantime she had to eat and the few remaining coins in her purse certainly wouldn't go far. Then, as if providence had smiled benevolently on her plight, she noticed a "Waitress Wanted" sign in the window of Delmonico's Restaurant. Making a mental note to inquire about the job that very afternoon, she headed up Oliver Street in search of a decent boardinghouse.

Two blocks west on College Street, a horseman leisurely walked his black mare toward the Metropolitan Hotel. Broad-shouldered and barrel-chested, standing slightly over six feet tall, he had the weathered, tanned face of a plainsman. And from beneath the perpetual squint of a man who had spent a lifetime staring into the sun, glinted a hard, blue-eyed gaze.

His eyes moved constantly, pausing briefly on the faces of men crowding the boardwalk, and the cold intensity of his look had a chilling quality about it. Within the center of his gaze there was something missing, like a hawk contemplating a nest full of fat mice, and it seemed reasonable to suspect that more than one man had averted his eyes from that flat, deadly stare.

But the most striking aspect of his appearance was the amber, shoulder-length hair cascading from beneath a broad-brimmed felt hat. Curling over the collar of a well-tailored black cutaway coat, it seemed cast out as a challenge in the face of the somber, conservatively groomed townspeople. There were some who remembered that plainsmen often wore their hair long, purposely taunting the Indians upon whose lands they poached. But whether this man's flowing locks were mere vanity, or a carryover from some past life, was a question few men dared to pose.

Late of the Union Army, he had drifted into Springfield only a month before. Establishing himself as a regular at the poker tables around the city, he rapidly became known as a skilled gambler, willing to back any play with a hefty bankroll. Seemingly devoid of nerves, his cool, steady manner seemed better suited to an undertaker, and whenever he entered a game, men more often than not became very careful with their hands. And there were some, noting the litheness of his movements and the Colt Dragoons protruding from a red sash around his waist, who quietly wondered if his true profession might not be more akin to the mortuary business than the riffling of pasteboards.

But whatever his line of business, none doubted that he was a man of daring, thoroughly committed to separating the high rollers from their money belts. And he had come to the right place.

Springfield in the summer of 1865 pulsated with activity. Located in the southwest corner of Missouri, only a short distance from the borders of Kansas, Arkansas, and Indian Territory, the city was ideally situated to serve as a center of commerce for the expanding economy of the area. While it had been exposed to savage border warfare during the Civil War, twice changing hands between Confederate and Union forces, the town itself had suffered little during the long years of bloodshed.

Nestled in the foothills of the Ozark Mountains, the city had been a hotbed of conflicting ideologies almost from the moment of settlement. Free staters and pro-slavers battled for political domination of the area even before the war began, and it was hardly surprising that when hostilities ceased, Springfield remained something of an open city.

When the war ended, the population of the town was slightly over four thousand. But the sudden influx of discharged soldiers, both Rebels and Yanks, transformed it overnight into the richest boomtown along the border. To the delight of bankers, merchants, and the South Side's grungy dives, the city now entered a period of violent expansion. Coffers swelled with a seemingly inexhaustible flood of bright, gold coins.

Word of Springfield's growing wealth quickly spread across the border states, and along with the masses of soldiers jamming the roads and trains came a small army of human parasites. Lured by the scent of easy money, a horde of gamblers, prostitutes, and conmen descended on the city that spring. Establishing themselves in the saloons, gaming rooms, and whorehouses that proliferated in the area south of the public square, they quickly created a domain rife with corruption and greed.

But unlike the western boomtowns, Springfield was a settled community with an entrenched citizenry, and this new element was a disquieting influence. Still, graft has a way of reshaping even the most righteous of attitudes, and while the tenderloin was never sanctioned openly, the sporting crowd found the town fathers both tolerant and sympathetic. So long as the price was right.

Among the first to arrive following the cessation of hostilities was the cold-eyed gambler, who had already become something of a legend in the sprawling, riotous boomtown. And as he rode down College Street that warm June afternoon, more than one head turned to stare after him in hushed speculation.

Reining the black mare to the hitching rack, he dismounted and strode confidently up the steps of the Metropolitan Hotel. As he passed through the entrance, the loungers on the porch ceased talking and gave him their undivided attention. Only after he had disappeared from view did their murmuring resume. And as usually happened, their talk centered not around who he was, or even what he was, but rather just how good he *actually* might be with those pearl-handled Dragoons.

Walking through the lobby, the long-haired gambler nodded with square-jawed reserve to the desk clerk, then mounted the staircase to his room.

"Good afternoon, sir," trilled the paunchy little man behind the desk. "Hope you had a nice ride, Mr. Hickok."

The weeks passed with monotonous regularity for Mattie. June had given way to July and as the restaurant simmered in the summer heat, she found herself fretting more and more over the boredom of her job. Breakfast, lunch and dinner, waiting on the same people, serving the same food week after week, with never a respite. But her time in the restaurant hadn't been without compensations of a sort.

Lou Blomger, Delmonico's owner, had become a friend more than an employer. Portly and jovial, Lou always had a good word for everyone, and for that Mattie was thankful. Not that he wasn't like any other man, for it was clear that with the slightest encouragement, he would have gone much further than a few playful swats on the bottom.

But the customers! My God, she thought, how could I ever have considered these people sophisticated? If papa thought my virtue was jeopardized back in Peru, he'd have a stroke over some of the propositions I've been getting from customers. And married customers at that! Thinking back, she had to laugh over her own simple-mindedness that first night on the job.

The dinner rush had been particularly hectic that evening, and Blomger had spent his time scurrying between kitchen and dining room, supervising every detail. He kept an especially close watch on Mattie as she bustled from table to table. While she was pretty enough, it was obvious that she had only recently scraped the manure off her sturdy farm shoes. The way she nervously slammed plates down in front of customers made him fear he had hired a real bumpkin. But Mattie had been oblivious to the critical eye of her employer, completely caught up in the excitement of Springfield's most resplendent eating establishment. The dapper men and finely dressed ladies had fairly taken her breath away with their charm and gaiety. Watching them, listening to their sophisticated chatter as she served the meals, Mattie had thought them the most cultivated, enchanting people she had ever encountered.

What a joke! Especially on her. They were cultivated all right, like a hog that had learned to swill from a bucket instead of a trough. And as for their charm! Well! The propositions she'd been getting lately certainly weren't any different than the whispered invitations she had received from field hands back on the farm. These Springfield dandies might be sophisticated, but their minds still slithered around in the same gutter. And she was damned fed up with the whole beady-eyed lot! The way they mentally undressed her with their smirking, come-hither looks. She might as well be serving tables stark naked!

But she could handle these lilac-scented clods well enough, and somehow she could even manage the sheer boredom of the job itself. The real problem was the gauntlet of drunken lechers she had to run every night after work.

From the restaurant to her boardinghouse on Oliver Street was slightly over two blocks. But in the pitch black of a summer night it might as well have been ten miles. Each evening the public square was jammed with roving bands of ex-soldiers, generally just drunk enough to convince themselves that they were the answer to every girl's prayer. Nightly, she found herself rushing at an ever-faster pace in an effort to elude the clutching, grabbing hands. Short of plugging her ears with cotton there was no way to avoid their filthy suggestions, even though she had managed to leave a few of them with bruised shins and punctured egos. And the infuriating part was there was no end in sight!

Mulling it over, Mattie wondered why she couldn't meet a good man. Not a decent man necessarily, just a good one. A man who would be kind to her, and provide the affection her Teutonic, unemotional family had been incapable of giving her.

Papa just wasn't a loving man, she thought. He was too choked up with the wrath of God, and obsessed with making their farm the showplace of the county. In his harsh, unforgiving mind, her affair with the drummer had scarred the family name beyond repair, and as a man of God, he could do no less than cast the offender from the fold. And poor mama! After so many years she had become just like him, withdrawn and cold, waiting dumbly for the Almighty Jehovah to reach down and snatch her soul into that paradise in the sky.

Well, I want more than that, she fumed. I want a man that'll love me and look after me, and won't be ashamed to show his real feelings. Now, Bill Hickok, there's a man who has a lot to give a woman. Maybe he doesn't lavish affection on a girl in public, but you can tell from the way he caters to that green-eyed hussy of his that he treats her right. Abruptly, her mind drifted back to a night some weeks past when she had first seen Hickok and his current mistress, Susanna Moore.

Shortly after the courthouse clock struck six, Hickok had walked through the front door with a stunning brunette firmly attached to his left arm. Blomger had moved quickly to greet the newcomers, escorting them with great deference to their usual table. Upon entering Delmonico's for the first time, shortly after arriving in Springfield, the gambler had informed Blomger he would require a table in the rear of the room, against a wall. While the request seemed a trifle strange, the ingratiating host was only too happy to oblige. The following day Blomger had learned that the man who introduced himself as James Butler Hickok was in fact none other than the famed scout and gunfighter, Wild Bill Hickok.

After seating Hickok and his consort on Mattie's first night at Delmonico's, he had cornered her in the kitchen. "Now listen, girlie, there's a man and woman sitting at your back table, and I want you to make damn sure they get good service." Fixing her with a stern look, he concluded, "The man is Wild Bill Hickok."

Mattie restrained a laugh. *"Wild Bill!"*

"Yes, Wild Bill! And for your information, Miss Towhead, he's killed at least three men in pistol duels, and no telling how many during the war. So if I were you, I'd make goddamned certain he wasn't displeased with the service. Do I make myself clear?"

She ducked her head contritely. "Yes sir."

But as she pushed through the kitchen door, a mischievous smile lit her face. How amusing it would be to wait on a wild man, she thought, wondering if he ate with a knife and fork or just scooped the food up with his bare hands. Then she turned into the dining room and pulled up short, transfixed by the most piercing blue eyes she had ever encountered. Startled, she stood for a moment returning the stare, absorbing every detail of the long wavy hair, the sweeping mustache, and the handsomest face she had ever seen.

Regaining her senses, Mattie marched straight to the table. With a saucy curtsy, she said, "Good evening, Mr. Wild Bill. What would you like for supper?"

Glancing at Susanna, the corners of Hickok's mouth

broke in a slight smile. "Well, I'll tell you, missy. Just for openers I'd like for you to start callin' me Mr. Hickok. Only the newspapers call me Wild Bill." His eyes narrowed, and he slowly surveyed her figure from top to bottom. "Course, my friends just call me Bill."

"Oh, I can tell that you're a man with lots of friends, Mr. Hickok," Mattie said innocently, darting a look at Susanna. "Like my daddy always said, a man is known by the company he keeps and the friends he supports."

Chuckling, Hickok glanced back in time to catch a withering look from Susanna, then turned to the menu.

Reflecting back over that first night, Mattie remembered how impressed she'd been with Susanna's poised beauty. Jealous would be a better word, she thought. *Just might as well be honest about it. There's a woman that really knows how to make a man toe the line. And the clothes she wears! Those dresses must cost him a fortune. Of course, he's a gambling man, and papa always said they were the worst kind. But what the hell does papa know about life anyway? Plowing fields and rutting around on mama like an old boar hog is the only world he knows.*

Pausing, her brow wrinkled as she chewed over a sudden thought. Come to think of it, that Susanna hasn't been in here with Bill the last couple of days. And unless I'm going loony, he's been a lot more pleasant without her around. *I wonder. . . .*

Walking from the dining room, Mattie pushed through the kitchen door and found Blomger supervising an ancient Negro cook. Sweating profusely from the heat of the stoves, the darky was butchering a side of beef as Blomger scrutinized his every move with utmost care.

"Lou," she inquired abruptly, "how is it that Mr. Hickok's harlot hasn't been with him at supper the past few evenings?"

"Now listen, Miss Smart Britches," Blomger thundered. "If you want to get yourself in a pot full of trouble by calling that woman a harlot I don't mind in the least. But goddamnit, don't go around shouting things like that in my restaurant. Do you understand?"

"Why, Lou, honey," Mattie purred. "You're the one that's shouting, not me. Now don't get so testy. All I wanted to know is what happened to Susanna Moore."

"Well, I don't suppose it's any secret," Blomger responded huffily. "John, hurry up and get that beef butchered before the supper rush starts."

Pulling Mattie to the other side of the kitchen, the restaurant owner glanced around, lowering his voice in a conspiratorial tone. "Now, the way I heard it is that Dave Tutt stole Hickok's girl with a bunch of jewelry and set her up in a big suite of rooms at the Lyon House. But anyone that's got brains enough to fill a teacup sure as Christ better not bring the subject up in front of Hickok."

"But who's Dave Tutt?"

"Oh, he's some hardcase gambler from Arkansas. Bill's been beating him at poker sort of regular, and what with Tutt being a Southerner and Hickok a Yankee it just makes the situation all the more galling to Dave. If it hadn't been for that he'd probably never even noticed the girl. Everyone knows he only stole her to get back at Bill. But listen, as sure as God squats to do his business like regular folks, Bill Hickok will kill that man before the month's out."

"You mean Bill will go after him with a gun?" Mattie demanded.

"No, Bill's too smart for that," Blomger informed her. "Somehow he'll make it look like self-defense. But if you got any loose money laying around go bet it on Mr. James Butler Hickok. Cause even if he don't know it, *Dave Tutt is a walking dead man!*"

With a strange sense of dread, Mattie returned to the dining room and tried to distract her mind by preparing the tables for the evening rush. But the harder she worked the more troubled she became. And for some reason, a mist of tears drifted over her eyes.

The evening of July 26 was oppressively sultry. The sweltering kind of night that left a man's clothes stuck to his skin like a fresh mustard plaster. Flashes of lightning were visible in the ridge of mountains far to the south, and the people of Springfield, stifling in the muggy stillness, could only hope that the cooling rains would reach town before morning.

Fortunately, the players hunched around a poker table in the Lyon House were considerably more comfortable than the rest of the city's panting masses. The high-ceilinged, dimly lit saloon served to retain whatever coolness there was in the atmosphere, and the game proceeded without comment concerning the sticky night.

A low, overhanging lamp cast distorted shadows over the five men seated at the felt-topped table. The gaming room had emptied shortly after three in the morning, and a pre-dawn stillness hung over the saloon. The weary bartender stifled a yawn as he listened with bored disinterest to the players' terse conversation and the muted calling of their bets.

Dave Tutt stared across the table at Wild Bill Hickok, trying to fathom the plainsman's last raise. Reluctantly, he concluded that Hickok wasn't bluffing and tossed his cards on the pile of coins in the center of the table. Disgusted, the stocky gambler lit a cigar, hunched his bull neck deep in the collar of his ruffled shirt, and sullenly contemplated the situation.

Hickok was winning and if his streak continued it could be disastrous, particularly since Tutt was personally backing two of the other players. Figuring that the three of them could easily best Hickok and the fifth man, a half-drunken former army officer, Tutt had arranged for his cronies to enter the game one by one as other drowsy players called it a night. But Hickok's phenomenal run of luck was something he hadn't bargained on. With his bankroll now residing on the opposite side of the table, he grimly concluded that luck needed a helping hand.

As the man on his left began shuffling, Tutt nudged him with his foot. Glancing up, the man hesitated momentarily then began riffling the deck with a practiced touch.

Aware of the risk he was taking, Tutt calmly puffed on

his cigar and smiled through the blue haze, wondering if Hickok was really as fast with those Colts as everyone claimed. The thought of actually testing him was a bit unsettling, but Tutt wasn't about to spill any whiskey over it. He had fought savagely for the Confederacy, killing more than his share of bluebellies, and to his way of thinking Hickok was just another goddamn Yankee. One whose reputation was probably more rumor than fact. Besides, he thought, I've buried a few hardcases in my time, so what's to worry about a long-haired bag of shit like Hickok.

Slowly, almost imperceptibly at first, the tide of the game began to change. Curiously, Hickok's run of luck came to an abrupt halt, and his gleaming stack of coins began to dwindle at an alarming rate. Where before he had been winning consistently, the cards now seemed to fall in the other direction and the pile of money gradually but steadily shifted to the opposite side of the table. Lady Luck was a capricious bitch, as every gambler knew, but this sudden switch in the play had about it the stench of a rigged game.

Seething, Hickok folded what appeared to be a winning hand, and lit a cigar. Somehow he was being cheated, but so far he had been unable to detect any subterfuge. Casually, he watched Dave Tutt shuffle and begin dealing. Again he was unable to perceive even the slightest irregularity in Tutt's handling of the pasteboards. Whenever it came his turn to deal, Bill unobtrusively began checking the cards for pin pricks or shaved edges, but to his complete bafflement there was no indication of a crooked deck.

Goddammit, Tutt has to be cheating! For the last hour he had drawn good betting hands, the kind of cards that called for raises and seeing the other man down the line. But invariably, Tutt or one of his cronies had beaten him with a hand just good enough to win. Even as he fumed, Tutt dragged down another pot, and it suddenly occurred to Hickok that he was now well over five hundred dollars in the hole. Reflecting back over the nights he had cleaned Tutt at the poker table, Hickok knew for a certainty that the stocky gambler would never be his equal in a straight game.

Ultimately, the breaking point came. The man on Tutt's left was again dealing, only this time his deft fingers slipped for a fraction of a second, and Hickok's eyes came alive with grim satisfaction. After drawing three kings, and calling repeated raises, he laid his cards down only to watch Tutt spread a hand revealing four deuces. Tutt smugly scooped in the pot, gloating over the slick ease with which they were trimming the arrogant bastard. This was easier than he had thought, and as his mind drifted back over previous games, he began berating himself for not having sluiced Hickok down the drain long before this.

Suddenly his reverie was broken as Hickok smoothly jerked one of the Colts from his waist sash and laid it on the table. Fixing the startled dealer with a cold, malignant stare, the plainsman gently fingered the pistol. "Someone in this game is dealin' seconds, and if he don't stop we're gonna be forced to take up a collection for his widow."

Dropping the deck as if the cards had suddenly turned molten, the dealer cast a furtive glance at Tutt and then carefully placed his own hands in plain sight on top of the table.

Gazing across the table at the grizzled plainsman, Tutt felt a gut-wrenching instinct that told him Hickok wasn't bluffing. While the three of them could doubtless kill him in a shootout, Tutt was only too well aware that Hickok's first slug would catch him just above the brisket. Suddenly the prospect of pushing the matter any further lost its appeal. There'll be another time, he thought, and the sonovabitch will never know what hit him.

"Why, Bill, you must be mistaken," he intoned smoothly. "This boy ain't no card sharp, and besides, he'd never think of cheatin' a friend of mine."

Hickok stared at him for a moment, then holstered his gun and kicked his chair away from the table. Glancing at Tutt through the haze of smoke, his mouth twisted in a sardonic smile. "You've been mighty lucky tonight, Dave. Leastways I guess you could call it luck."

Tutt blinked at the veiled challenge, and his voice was tinged with sarcasm. "What would you call it, Mr. Hickok?"

"Don't rightly know. Suppose some men might call it cheatin'. But then I recollect you just told me you don't cheat friends." Hickok's gaze narrowed and a cold glint appeared in his eyes. "Course, a man given to cheatin' might have a hard time figurin' just who his friends are. You had that trouble lately, Dave?"

"Bill, you're talkin' hogwash, and you know it," Tutt stated calmly. "You're tryin' to rile me for some reason, but I'm just not gonna take offense."

"Why, that's real charitable of you," snapped Hickok. "Regular little gentleman, ain't he? Frankly, Tutt, I've often wondered just what the hell it would take to rile something like you. What's the matter, don't you have enough of your boys around the table to make the odds suit you?"

"Goddammit, Hickok, don't you talk to me like that," Tutt said, rising from his chair. "You're not sore because I beat you at cards. You got your ass up in the air because I swiped your whore right out from under your nose." Waving his arm toward the door, he shouted, "And everyone in this town knows it too!"

"You sheep-humpin' sonovabitch," Hickok snarled. "Let's just see if you're as fast with a gun as you are with your mouth."

"Oh, no, *Mr. Wild Bill*," Tutt laughed derisively. "I ain't playin' into your hand. Nothin' would suit you better than to have me pull a gun so you could run tell the law it was self-defense."

Leaning across the table with startling swiftness, Hickok backhanded the stocky gambler a smashing blow to the mouth. Tutt's lower lip burst open like a ripe melon, and he fell backward into an adjoining table.

"Being a tinhorn is bad enough, Tutt, but you're a goddamned coward to boot. You're not safe around me anymore, so go armed at all times." Glaring around at the other players, his eye fell on the money stacked before them. Reaching across the table with his left hand, he began stuffing his pockets with gold coins. "Reckon I'll just take back what I lost in this *friendly* little game. And maybe a couple'a hundred extra for interest. Unless you gentlemen got any objections. No? Well, maybe some other time."

Backing across the room, never taking his eyes off the stunned gamblers, Hickok stepped through the door into the sultry night.

Pushing himself from the table, Tutt wiped the blood from his lips, wincing with pain as a malevolent grin spread slowly across his face.

Concealed behind a pillar of the Greene County Bank, Dave Tutt's vigil suddenly came to an end. Stealthily he observed Bill Hickok enter Delmonico's. He had been waiting here since late afternoon, certain that the plainsman would eventually show, and now his strategy had paid off in spades.

Since last night's humiliation in the Lyon House, his anger had smoldered into a simmering rage. But with jackal-like cunning he had restrained himself from making any precipitous mistakes. Throughout the day members of his gang had shadowed Hickok from a discreet distance. Using extreme caution, they made sure that the gunman had never once become aware of their presence. From all outward appearances Hickok had maintained his normal daily routine. Either he didn't believe Tutt capable of retaliation or else he just wasn't troubled by the possibility. Either way it infuriated Tutt that Hickok considered him something less than a formidable adversary.

Well, that bastard's time is near, he thought, and when it's over we'll see if he's still got a sneer on his face when they nail him up in a pine box. Pondering the situation carefully, Tutt concluded that the best time to catch Hickok unaware was when he had a full gut. Preferably in a public place where he least expected a showdown, and would be lulled into a false sense of security.

Scanning the square with the eye of a hungry predator, Tutt's gaze came to rest on the courthouse. Located on the extreme northwest side of the marketplace, this Gothic structure was the hub of activity in the city. Momentarily his attention was distracted by the intense brilliance of the sky above the courthouse. Suddenly he realized that the sun would be dipping into the western horizon just about the time Hickok came out of the restaurant.

Looking toward Delmonico's again, he quickly calculated that when Hickok emerged from the restaurant he would either walk toward his hotel, or else cross the square headed east. Whichever way he heads, Tutt reasoned, the sonovabitch will have to look dead in the sun if someone fires on him from the courthouse. Chuckling venomously, he signaled three of his gang, who were loitering opposite the restaurant, then began crossing the square toward the courthouse.

Delighted with his own craftiness, Tutt gleefully visualized Hickok's panic when caught in a crossfire between the four men. The strategy took on even more appeal when he considered that with Hickok staring straight into the sun the chances of him hitting an opponent at a distance of fifty yards were practically nil.

Gloating, he laughed aloud, and walked on through the carpet of dusty soil.

Moments before, Hickok had walked through the door of Delmonico's on the stroke of six, holding to a routine that hadn't varied since the day Mattie met him. Supper, then a cigar with coffee, and afterward a brief stroll around the square before settling down for a night of poker. Like most men, Hickok was a creature of habit to a great extent. With one essential difference. Whenever it suited his purpose, he could cannily alter his routine to advantage in a given situation.

Last night he had deliberately goaded Dave Tutt, belittling him in front of friends. These things had to be handled just right to avoid any trouble with the law, and he had coldly provoked the arrogant Southerner, hoping to push him into a reckless assassination attempt.

Hickok had known many men like Tutt. Blustering, rough-talking, full of bullshit and beans till the chips were down. Then backing off so their dirty work could be done in the dark, or while a man's back was turned. Certain that

Tutt would choose some skulking plan, the plainsman had spent his day in the normal leisurely manner. Breakfast over the lunch hour at Delmonico's, a long afternoon's ride in the countryside on his black mare, then a refreshing drink in the dimness of the Metropolitan Bar. Afterward, a cool bath in his hotel room followed by an early supper at the restaurant.

Understandably, the attack hadn't come during the daylight hours. Though Bill had given a bushwhacker plenty of opportunity, he really hadn't expected any open move that afternoon. Trailing Blomger to his table in the back of the restaurant, he mulled the problem over once more. Backshooters like Tutt had a fondness for the dark, and the most likely time for him to strike would be in the early morning hours when Hickok was returning from a gambling dive. Being a pragmatic man, he reasoned that there was little he could do besides wait, and beware of dark alleyways. Dismissing the matter from his mind, he turned his attention to the menu.

"Good evening, Mr. Hickok," said Mattie, standing at his elbow. "Or have I earned the distinction of calling you just plain Bill?"

"Well, little lady, you've been askin' that question nearly every night for a month, and my answer's always the same. Are you a gamblin' woman?"

"And my answer is always the same too, Mr. Gamblin' Man. What game do you have in mind?"

"Hah," he laughed, delighted with her saucy retort. Then a shadowed expression passed over his face. After a moment he resumed in a more serious vein. "Now listen here, Mattie. You're too young to get hooked in the traces with an old buffer like me. Like you said, I'm just a gamblin' man, here today, gone tomorrow. And besides, your folks might think I'm a mite too old for you. Why, come November I'll only be a year shy of thirty. Leastways if I live that long."

"Oh, my folks are back in Indiana, and they wouldn't—" Suddenly she stopped in mid-sentence as the import of

Hickok's words dawned on her. "My God, that's why you've been kidding with me. Everyone in town is saying you and Dave Tutt are going to shoot it out at any moment. You knew you might get killed and you didn't want . . ."

"Whoa!" Bill silenced her with his abrupt tone. "Slow down a bit. You're takin' a lot for granted, missy. I might want to get in harness with you, but for the moment I got a little unfinished business to settle." Smiling, he reached out with a brown leathery hand to squeeze her chin. "There's one thing you can be certain of though, Dave Tutt sure as hell ain't gonna stop me."

"Oh! Oh!" Stamping her foot in exasperation, Mattie ran toward the kitchen. Watching her, Bill shook his head at the strange ways of females, and pondered again the remarkable talent they had for complicating men's lives.

Within a matter of minutes Mattie returned, once again her normally spontaneous self. Slamming a huge, sizzling steak in front of the astonished gambler, she admonished, "There! Keep your strength up, and make damn sure your aim's good."

Stepping from Delmonico's, Bill puffed contentedly on his cigar, reflecting on the evening's turn of events with Mattie Silks. *She may be a mite young, but she sure as Christ knows where the goodies are buried. Wouldn't be surprised but what them farm boys taught her some tricks the South Street madams would even admire knowin'. And she's gutsy as hell! Not many women'd have the starch to fill a man's belly and then send him off to the wars smilin' like a chessy-cat. Yes sir, once I get Dave Tutt's hash settled, why I believe I might just explore a few things with that little fire-eater. Course, the first thing to do is give that double-crossin' Susanna a solid boot in the ass, and send her packin' for parts unknown.*

Sensing that Mattie was still watching him from inside the restaurant's front window, he stepped off the boardwalk and started across the square toward the Lyon House. Just might as well brace the wolf in his own den, Hickok thought, particularly since he ain't got balls enough to draw on a man face to face.

Striding across the open expanse of ground, he failed to notice that three hard-eyed characters had joined a group of drunks coming up from South Street. Losing themselves among the staggering crowd, the three men stealthily worked their way to the opposite corner, directly to Hickok's rear.

Nearing the Lyon House, he suddenly sensed a stir of excitement among the loungers on the porch. Watching them closely, he saw that their interest focused on something across the square, in the direction of the courthouse. Alert now to some unseen danger, he spun to the left, jerking one of his Colt Dragoons in the same movement.

Through the hazy brilliance of a late evening sunset, he spotted the indistinct shape of Dave Tutt. Standing on the street in front of the courthouse, Tutt raised his arm, sighting along the gleaming barrel of a large-bored pistol. Even before he heard the report of the shot, Bill saw a puff of smoke issue from Tutt's gun. Crouching, he flinched imperceptibly as the slug whistled through the air beside his shoulder.

Extending his left arm, Hickok quickly laid the Colt's barrel over his forearm, then dipped his head to obscure the blinding sun with the brim of his hat. With cold deliberation, he took careful aim and fired a single shot. Somewhat like a grotesque, flapping scarecrow, Tutt staggered backward, flailing the air with his arms, and dropped dead in the dust.

Mattie's scream from the direction of the restaurant pierced Hickok's eardrums. Whirling, he dropped instinctively into a crouch. While the situation was anything but amusing, Bill couldn't help but laugh at the rather incredible scene which greeted him.

Spinning in crazed circles, one of Tutt's cohorts was desperately trying to throw Mattie to the ground. Astraddle his back, clinging with her legs like a golden-haired leech, Mattie alternately choked him with one arm and scratched his face with the nails of her free hand. Standing sheepishly to one side, the other two henchmen fingered their holstered guns while casting baleful glances toward Hickok and the somewhat absurd predicament of their comrade.

Almost as if a burlesque troupe had suddenly brought theater into the streets, the crowd of boisterous drunks began laughing and cavorting around the wild melee. Stewed to the gills, they urged Mattie on, convinced that someone had graciously staged this entire farce just for their benefit. Retracing his steps across the square, Bill fired a shot into the air, which instantly brought the festivities to a halt.

Disheveled, locks of hair streaming down her face, Mattie released her captive and gingerly slid to the ground. Tears welling up in her eyes, she ran to Hickok, sobbing. "Oh, Bill. I saw them from the window and I could tell they weren't drunk like the rest of those men. And then when you drew your gun they started reaching for theirs. And I couldn't think of anything to do but scream. And then I came running out here and . . ."

Covering the frustrated assassins with his Colt, Bill drew the hysterical girl to him and squeezed her shoulders gently. "Easy little lady. It's all over now. Besides, these meatheads never had a chance against you." Restraining a laugh, he pressed her tear-stained face to his chest. "Why, you little hellcat, you had'em outnumbered all by yourself."

Ordering Tutt's accomplices to drop their gunbelts, Hickok left Mattie to the solicitous care of Lou Blomger, and marched the three men toward the courthouse. Passing Tutt's body, he glanced down with a detached sense of pride, noting that the slug had mushroomed squarely through the gambler's heart. Not bad shootin', he mused, not bad at all. 'Specially with the sun starin' straight down your goddamn throat.

Herding the dejected gunmen into the sheriff's office, he charged them with attempted murder, then made a statement relating the incident in its entirety. The sheriff somewhat nervously informed him that he would doubtless have to stand trial for murder himself. A mere formality, he hurriedly stressed, but nonetheless necessary. With the lawman's assurances ringing in his ears, Bill was released under his own recognizance, and walked from the courthouse into the deepening twilight.

Crossing College Street, headed back to the restaurant and Mattie, he looked west into the final, diffused rays of a retreating sun. *Adios, Mr. Dave Tutt. You squirrely sonovabitch, you should'a known I'd get you!*

CHAPTER TWO

~~~☙~~~

Indian summer had spread across the rolling fields of southwest Missouri. Springfield basked in the September warmth, and for the most part the townspeople had all but forgotten Hickok's spectacular duel with the gambler from Arkansas. Fulfilling the sheriff's prediction, Bill had stood trial for murder, but the jury deliberated less than ten minutes before returning an acquittal. Moments later he stepped from the courthouse a free man. That evening Wild Bill Hickok and his latest mistress, a fetching young blonde by the name of Miss Mattie Silks, were the guests of honor at a dinner in Delmonico's, celebrating his exoneration.

Mattie had taken up residence in Hickok's hotel room the evening of Dave Tutt's abrupt demise. As befitted the paramour of a successful gambler, she hastily retired from the table-waiting profession, assuming her new role in life with the exuberance of a cuddly puppy. In a sense she had become the toast of Springfield, the golden girl who had won the hearts of both the influential elite and the South Side underworld with her brash display of courage. Over the ensuing weeks, the young heroine and her stern-faced lover had become a familiar sight on the streets of the city. Arm in arm, they strolled the square after dinner each evening, browsed through the more expensive shops outfitting Mattie in a resplendent new wardrobe, and toured the countryside every Sunday afternoon in the finest buggy available at Murphy's Livery Stable.

While the handsome young couple was separated from the gentry by an unbridgeable social chasm, they were nonetheless patronized to a certain extent by the town leaders. And in the still, drowsy moments before she drifted off to sleep each night, Mattie often reflected that for a simple farm girl she had come a long way in three short months.

She was deliriously happy with her audacious lover, whose curious ways made him seem more Indian than white man. In public he remained stoic and reserved, displaying an aloof, taciturn manner to those they encountered. But in the privacy of their room, beneath the downy comfort covering their bed, his husky voice came alive with the inner thoughts and uncertainties he kept hidden beneath those cold eyes. Mattie alone was allowed to enter this secret world, and the emotion and sensitivity she discovered there would have astonished his cronies in the South Side dives. Strangely, considering his rough-hewn exterior and the mercurial violence of which he was so capable, Mattie found him to be a surprisingly gentle lover. Patient, unselfish, and tirelessly inclined to the most shocking experiments.

Widely versed in the more exotic forms of the game, he had discerned within her a deep, simmering well of sensuality. Slowly, as the nights passed in ardent embraces, it required less and less coaxing for her to join in his abandoned approach to lovemaking. Soon, Mattie found herself casting modesty aside, openly reveling in the delights of their passionate explorations.

Sensing the even rise and fall of Bill's chest next to her, Mattie sleepily mused that there was really only one facet of his character she would change. Within him lurked some throwback of predatory savagery, and it was this single fault she had come to fear so greatly. When affronted by another man this ungovernable ferocity came raging to the surface, and in that moment of explosive anger, he seemed to Mattie an unchained animal run amuck.

The day after his acquittal of the Tutt killing, the publisher of *The Missouri Patriot* had run an editorial castigating the jury for their verdict, openly accusing Bill of premeditated, cold-blooded murder. After kicking in the door of the newspaper office, Hickok dragged the cringing journalist into the center of Booneville Street and methodically beat him into a blubbering hulk. Since the publisher was too terrified to press charges, and the authorities generally agreed that the punishment suited his slanderous remarks, Bill was never brought to account.

Purely by chance, Mattie had been in a dress shop across the street when the savage encounter took place. Gripped with shock and a tinge of revulsion, she found herself unable to reveal her presence to Bill, and they had never spoken of the incident. But she was saddened by what she had witnessed and shaken by a presentiment that Bill's unbridled hostility would one day lead him into a situation from which there would be neither glory nor escape.

Turning, she slid her arms around his corded shoulders, pulling him close. Even in the flickering intoxication of sleep she was aware that the love he had released within her left no room for condemnation, and she drowsily dismissed the subject from her mind.

Walking along the square, Mattie and Bill filled their lungs with the crisp, invigorating breeze borne on the north winds. Delmonico's had been stifling, packed with noisy, high-spirited revelers celebrating Thanksgiving, and the forced gaiety had finally become too much for Bill.

Lou had outdone himself in serving a traditional holiday dinner, and the young couple had all but gorged themselves on wild turkey, bread stuffing, and rich giblet gravy. But the moment arrived when Mattie sensed that her man had tolerated the festivities long enough. After congratulating Blomger on a superb meal they hurried outside into the bracing air, wandering aimlessly in the direction of the Jordan River.

While Bill was normally reserved in public, Mattie had noticed over the past week that he was strangely silent even when they were alone. Tactfully, she had refrained from broaching the subject in the hope that it was only a passing mood. But the effects of Lou's devastating holiday punch had now loosened her tongue. As they neared the river, she brazenly decided to approach the matter directly.

"Bill, honey," she prompted, "if there's anything wrong, or you're worrying over something, I certainly wish you'd tell me about it."

"What're you talkin' about?" he countered a bit too quickly. "I thought everything was goin' along just fine."

"Well, yes, I guess it is," Mattie admitted. "I mean your gambling winnings have been real high, and of course, you dress me like I was a duchess or something. . . ."

"And you should be dressed like royalty!" His arm tightened, squeezing her waist in a bearhug. "Cause that's what you are to me. Pure grain, uncut royalty."

"Oh, you just don't know how much it means to me when you say things like that." Standing on tiptoes she placed a kiss on his weathered lips. "And God knows I love you, too. But that's not what I'm getting at. I'm talking about how withdrawn you've been the last week or so. Almost like you were unhappy, or maybe your mind was off a thousand miles somewhere."

Absently, Bill picked up a rock and chunked it across the rippling surface of the river. Watching the rock sink, he hesitated, as if mulling over a thought which resisted being put into words. Glancing at Mattie, he lowered his eyes to the ground, then stared pensively toward the mountainous ridge-line on the western horizon.

Shaken by his reluctance to speak, and the obvious emotional quandry with which he was struggling, Mattie remained silent, waiting for him to resolve the conflict in his own way.

Finally, he drew a long breath and nudged a rock into the

water with his foot. Only then did he lift his eyes to hers
once more.

"Mattie, I'm not sure I can tell you what's wrong. You
know I'm not much good with words, and even if I was I
don't rightly know if I could make you understand anyway.
I guess I feel trapped, sorta like an old bull with Indians
ridin' all around him, forcin' him back in the herd. Not
leavin' him any room to run." Pondering the clarity of his
analogy for a moment, he stared grimly at the river. "One
way or another I been out on the plains or up in the high
country for somethin' over ten years. 'Bout the only time I
spent in towns was to revittle or do a little hell-raisin', and
even then I'd got a bellyful of civilization in a month or so.
Now, what with one thing and another, I been in this town
for close to eight months, and I'm beginnin' to feel like it's
closin' in on me."

Placing an arm around her shoulders, he began walking
and they moved silently down the riverbank. The stillness
was broken only by the rush of the water, and the wind
moaning through the stark nakedness of the trees. Mattie
clenched her jaw, aware that he was somehow attempting
to marshal his thoughts. Suppressing an urge to voice the
deep feelings she harbored for this powerful, inarticulate
man, she silently kept pace.

"Towns has a funny way of eatin' away at a fella," Bill
resumed, evidently having found a path through the maze
of what he wanted to say. "Course, I got myself stuck here
waitin' around to settle with Dave Tutt, and then there was
the trial afterwards. But any other time I would've packed
it in right then and pointed that black mare's nose due west.
Truth of the matter is, you're what kept me here and you're
what's makin' me stay. And damned if I haven't come to
feel like a double-harnessed horse bein' pulled in two directions."

Glancing quickly at her, he smiled faintly, and his eyes
softened. "I ain't complainin', mind you, not so's you'd notice it at any rate. I'm plumb satisfied with the arrangement,
happier with you than I ever been with a woman before. And

I ain't tryin' to kick the traces between us, so don't worry about that. It's just that this goddamn town's beginnin' to smother me, and I'm sorta like a dog with a bone hung in his throat. I can't swallow it and I can't spit it up, and by Christ I wake up every mornin' feelin' like it's gonna choke me."

Without looking up, Mattie pressed herself closer to Bill. Nuzzling her head against his chest, she tried to hide the tears evoked by his moving and somehow eloquent plea.

"Bill, listen to me for a moment." Stifling her tears, she tried to summon words to relieve his anguish. "I don't own you and I've never wanted to. If you were the kind of man I could own then I couldn't respect you or love you, and I suppose we'd still be flirting at Delmonico's. I don't want to lose you, but I'm not going to plead or use cheap tricks to hold you here. You see, I really do love you. Enough so that if you want to leave, I won't stand in your way."

Gazing up, she grinned mischievously. "Of course, if some big, long-haired gamblin' man happened to invite me along, I'd be tickled to death to go wherever it is he has his mind set on."

"Sweet blue Jesus," he laughed. "Wouldn't you be some-thin' in buckskins, squattin' around a buffalo-chip fire? Why, I bet we could sell tickets to ever Injun within a hundred miles just to take a peek at that." He chuckled for a moment, then resumed in a grave tone. "Naw, Mattie, it just wouldn't work. Where I'm talkin' about is no place for a white woman, 'specially one with blonde curls. Actually, it's a poor life for any woman, white or red, and I sure as hell wouldn't drag you into that."

Hesitating, Bill drew a deep breath, then rushed on with the thought he had nervously been skirting. "The army needs scouts what with the Injuns raidin' in Kansas and the territories, and I been thinkin' I might sign on for a few months. Just long enough to get my lungs aired out, you understand. But look here, why couldn't you stay in Spring-field, sorta wait on me? And after I've made a few scouts and drunk a bellyful of mountain water, why then I'd come on back for a while. That is, if you feel disposed to wait."

"Oh, you big lummox, you know I do. It breaks my heart to think of your going, but you could win a lot of money by betting I'd be right here waiting when you get back." Smiling with a gaiety she hardly felt, Mattie brightened. "I'm sure I could get my old job back at the restaurant, and if you weren't gone too awfully long why I suppose I could think up something to make the time pass faster."

"Now, that's one thing I won't allow," Bill growled. "You just aren't goin' back to work in that greasy spoon of Blomger's. I been thinkin' on this whole business for quite a while now, and I figure if you and me could work out somethin' personal like, why I'd set you up in some sorta business. Maybe a dress shop. You got a good head on your shoulders, and I sure as Christ can't tote all the gold I won on horseback. So we might as well invest some of it and be partners . . . or somethin'."

"Bill," she exclaimed, "that's a marvelous idea! I know I could make a success of a business, and while you're gone I could be banking plenty of money so you'd have a big stake to start gambling with when you return. Oh, I'm so excited!" Dropping her head, Mattie grew silent for a moment, then glanced up at him. "There's only one thing though: I definitely don't want to open a dress shop."

"Well, that's all right by me," he conceded. "What kind of business do you think you'd like to have?"

"You'll probably be surprised," Mattie began apprehensively. "But don't fly off the handle till you've had a chance to hear my idea. Now, I've been observing what goes on in this town pretty closely, and while the dress shops and stores make good money, it's obvious they don't do near as well as some of those South Side businesses. People have to eat and they need clothes, but if they had to choose between a square meal and a good time it seems pretty clear they'd decide in favor of a little hell-raisin', as you call it. I've heard Lou talk about it and he says that when money's tight, and people won't even go to a restaurant for supper, they'll still go down to the South Side and spend their last nickel in one of those joints."

Determined that he wouldn't interrupt her rapid-fire chatter, she drew a deep breath and quickly plowed on. "People are going to have their fun even if they have to wear patched trousers and walk around with grumbling stomachs. You may see the shops on the square go begging for business sometimes, but those South Side dives are packed to the rafters every night with people just climbing over one another to throw away every dollar they own."

"Sure, but—" Hickok tried to interject. Mattie held up a determined hand, forestalling his objection.

"Now, just wait until I'm finished," she demanded. "Anybody that's not blind, or too thick-headed to see it, knows for a certainty that those South Side joints drag down the majority of dollars spent in this town. And I'm sure you're well aware of it since you've spent *at least half your life* in places just like that. Of course, there aren't too many businesses on the South Side that a woman could operate. But like I said, I've been observing what goes on down there very carefully, and I'm convinced that the best investment in the city of Springfield is a whorehouse."

"A whorehouse!" Bill exploded, visibly recoiling at the thought.

"Yes, a whorehouse!" Mattie retorted. "And don't act so shocked. You've undoubtedly been in enough of them to realize that they're an extremely lucrative investment."

"Just what the hell you been doin' in the afternoons while I was out ridin'?" he rasped. "And what goddamn idiot has been pumpin' you up with all this banker talk? Lucrative investments, my ass!"

"Your ass has nothing to do with it, Mr. Hickok," she snapped. "But that particular portion of the anatomy on a dozen young girls could very easily make us wealthy in a couple of years, or less. No doubt you've heard the rather coarse expression that every young lady is sitting on a gold mine."

"Great crippled Christ," he groaned. "If that don't beat all I ever heard of. *A whorehouse!* And you not even twenty years old yet. How in the name of God do you think you could run a place like that? They get plenty rough sometimes. And besides, I just don't like the idea of my woman in a whorehouse. Jesus."

"Quit cursing, Bill, and think about it sensibly for a minute," Mattie's smile returned, and a note of persuasiveness entered her voice. "I didn't say I'd work there. I'm your woman and there's not enough gold in the world to make me lay down for another man. I said I'd run it. You know, be the proprietor, or whatever it is they call it."

"The madam," he interposed dryly.

"Yes, that's it. The madam," she echoed. "That has a good ring to it, doesn't it? Like the madame of one of those wealthy gentry estates. Oh, Bill, I just know it would work. And it's not like we belonged to the upper-crust anyway, is it? I mean we wouldn't be harming our social position or anything like that. And I'd make you so proud of me, Bill, I really would. I'd be the most gracious madam on South Street."

"Gracious?" he snorted. "Well, that would be somethin' new on South Street for certain. Mattie, I wanna do somethin' for you, and I sure as hell can't dispute that whorin's a money-makin' pastime. But are you sure this is what you wanna do? Once you jump in there's no turnin' back, and the nice folks won't even look at you, much less invite you to join their church."

"Yes. I'm sure," she responded. "I don't give a tinker's damn about being accepted by those bankers and merchants, and if religion is what made my papa the way he is then I'll be thoroughly content never to be invited into a church."

Mattie had some time past related the details of her departure from the Indiana homestead. Remembering, he nodded agreement with her harsh judgment of churches and their sanctimonious brethren.

"All right then, little lady," he agreed somewhat reluctantly. "If that's what you got your mind set on, why we'll just put you in business. And God help them other South Street madams. Knowin' you, you'll end up with a house

so almighty elegant it'll drive the rest of 'em crazy as a parrot eatin' sticky candy."

"Come in, gentlemen. Make yourselves at home," Mattie
called. "Girls, make these gentlemen comfortable and look
after their *every wish.*" Smiling she walked from the parlor leaving five giggling young girls, each in low-cut revealing gowns, to determine the pleasure of the three men.

"Dora," she called to a slim Negro maid coming down
the stairs with a trayload of empty glasses. "Get those men
a drink and make damned sure they pay when they're
served."

Christ, she thought, how long are those dimwitted
drunks upstairs going to take? Now there'll only be two
girls left in the parlor if more customers show up. By God,
eight girls just aren't enough. Blomger promised me he'd
scout up more girls, and tomorrow morning that smiling tub
of lard gets a fire built right under his britches.

"Hey, blondie," declared a voice from the parlor door. "I
don't like any of them girls in there. But I sure enough like
you. How about you and me traipsin' up them stairs arm in
arm? Have a little party, huh?"

Turning, Mattie found herself the object of a leering
smirk from one of the men she had just escorted into the
parlor. Returning his look with poised indifference, she reflected that no matter how many pretty girls she had in the
parlor there was always some joker who wanted to exhibit
his virility by conquering the madam of the house.

"Mister," she laughed, "your money's good here anytime. But if you robbed the Greene County Bank tomorrow you still wouldn't have enough to get me in bed. I don't
work here; I own the place. Now, I tell you what. Have a
drink on the house and do your best not to wear my girls
out. They have a long night ahead of them."

Grinning at this allusion to his potency, the man watched
Mattie walk into the small cubicle which served as her office.
Shrugging good-naturedly, he stepped back to the parlor,
dragging a large-breasted redhead onto his lap.

The last four months had been hectic for Mattie. Displaying her usual zeal and determination, she had gone searching for a suitable location the day after obtaining Bill's permission to become a madam. Stumbling onto a somewhat dilapidated two-story, brick house on South Ally Street, she immediately visualized its possibilities and dragged Bill along to conclude rental arrangements with the owner. Situated a few doors off South Street, and only one block from the square, the house was ideally located in the heart of Springfield's tenderloin district. Moreover, it held the potential of attracting a clientele from both sides of town.

Aware that the Christmas season was hardly the time to open a whorehouse, she shrewdly employed a promotional gambit. Spending the month of December completely refurbishing the inside of the house, she invited the entire South Side to a much-publicized gala opening on New Year's Eve. The establishment was an instant success. And even before the doors were opened, the name of Mattie Silks, Springfield's youngest and most devastatingly attractive madam, had become a topic of conversation throughout the entire city.

Enlisting the aid of Lou Blomger, who maintained a somewhat enigmatic alliance with the South Side's more disreputable element, Mattie and Bill had arranged weekly payoffs to both the police and city hall. Hedging all bets, they also concluded a pact of peaceful coexistence with the underworld kingpins long before the New Year's opening. While it was never once even casually alluded to, Hickok's reputation with a gun had a singular cooling effect on those South Side denizens who resented anyone, especially an amateur, forcing her way into the rackets.

Reluctant to depend solely on his reputation for Mattie's protection, Hickok had toured some of the sleazier South Side dives auditioning strong-armed bullyboys for the position of bouncer. After numerous encounters, which wrecked three saloons in the process, Bill found what he was looking for—a thick-browed, ham-fisted throwback to the stone age.

Towering over those around him, Mattie's new protector, Thomas Fitzpatrick Mulhaney, insisted on trailing behind her diminutive figure like a docile mastiff. Known simply as Fitz throughout the tenderloin, the burly giant seemingly withered before Mattie's charm, carrying out her wishes with unquestioning devotion. Awed by her daring, Fitz's manner left few in doubt as to his willingness to shield her from danger. And his mere presence was enough to give most men second thoughts about becoming belligerent.

What with Blomger's underworld contacts, and the fame of her establishment spreading throughout the city, Mattie found herself swamped with hopeful young aspirants seeking to further their careers as courtesans. By the last week in December she had recruited eight charming young ladies, each a stunner and only slightly more refined than an alleycat in heat. Following the riotous grand opening on New Year's Eve, the house continued to attract a nightly flow of lusty high rollers. Exceeding her wildest expectations, Mattie had banked sufficient profits by the end of January to offset a major share of the money invested in redecoration and furnishing.

While she had been accepted into the hierarchy of the tenderloin, which was a dubious distinction at best, Mattie purposely limited her outside contacts to Bill and Lou Blomger. Social amenities could wait, for she was like a woman possessed, and over the coming months her remarkable ambition centered wholly on creating the most elegant parlor house in southwest Missouri.

Seated around the kitchen table, Mattie, Bill, and Lou Blomger conversed in low tones over coffee. The house was closed for the evening, and the weary girls had retired for a well-earned night's rest. Business was booming, threatening to corner the market in the tenderloin. And just as Hickok had predicted some months past, the South Side madams were beginning to grumble about Mattie's spectacular success.

Sensing that the situation had all the earmarks of a

potential rift with the underworld clique, Hickok had called a meeting to discuss alternative measures. Like the board of directors of a thriving but tenuously structured corporation, the three friends were vitally concerned about their fledgling enterprise.

"There's one thing for certain," Hickok was saying. "Some of these madams are backed by the biggest crooks in the tenderloin. And when you dip in their pocketbooks you just might as well figure you've got a fight on your hands."

"Bill, I think you're being a little hasty in your judgment," Blomger said. "Sure some of the madams are screaming and pitching fits, but that doesn't mean anything will come of it. The bosses down here know Mattie is pretty well protected, and any kind of violence would be bad for the whole South Side."

"Maybe. Maybe not," Hickok grunted. "When you start tinkerin' with people's livelihood you're talkin' about somebody that'll cut their nose off to spite their face. Why, I recall a beaver man on the Yellowstone that went up against a whole passel of Hudson Bay boys just—"

"Bill," Mattie interrupted gently. "This is a different thing entirely. We're not out West where people kill each other over a few beaver skins. We're dealing with businessmen, even if they are crooks, and they would much rather talk a problem out than resort to violence. Besides, no one has said the first word to me about our business hurting the other houses."

"That's just what I mean! The time to be on the lookout for Injuns is when you *don't* see 'em!"

"But we're not dealing with Indians," Mattie cried in exasperation. "This is Springfield!"

"You're just foolin' yourself," Hickok snorted. "These South Side boys could teach Injuns a few tricks about how to put a man under. You mark my word! There's trouble brewin'! Talk's going around, and we got to head it off before these bastards get their courage sucked up."

"So what do we do?" Mattie asked dryly. "Strap on a gun and go out and shoot up the South Side?"

"Now that you mention it, that's not a bad idea. If I winged a couple of the bosses the rest'd probably fall ass-over-teakettle in the rush to skip out."

"Oh, Bill! We're trying to avoid a fight, not start one. And besides, you seem to be the only one that's heard any of these threats."

"Now, Mattie, that's not exactly the fact of the matter." Blomger's somber tone jerked their heads around. "Truth is, I've heard a few rumbles here and there. But I wouldn't go so far as to say anyone's going to get rough about it."

"In a pig's ass!" Hickok growled. "They might start out talkin', the way Mattie says, but if you don't see it their way they'll get tough fast enough."

Glancing around, Blomger's eye fell on Fitz, who was sitting silently in a corner. Paring his nails with a wicked-looking jackknife, the burly ruffian was completely oblivious to the conversation, concerned only with keeping a watchful eye on his dainty charge.

"Fitz, what do you think about all this?" Blomger inquired. The Irishman's head swung around and he stared blandly across the room. Clearly he failed to comprehend either the question or its meaning.

Blomger tried again. "Fitz, what I'm asking is if you think Miss Silks is in any danger from the bosses here in the tenderloin?"

Fitz puzzled the question for a moment, dimly aware his advice was being sought. But not quite sure of the answer expected. Inspecting his fingernails critically, he announced calmly, "Anybody fucks with Miss Mattie is gonna get his head pinched off."

Mattie blushed, restraining a giggle. Blomger simply shook his head, staring at Fitz as if he were studying a specimen in a zoo.

"By Christ, I can pick 'em, can't I?" Hickok laughed uproariously, slamming his fist on the table. "He ain't worried about who's right or wrong, or even who's doing the fightin'. Just knows, by God, that anybody comes near Mattie ain't gonna walk away." Grinning Hickok's eyes flickered with unaccustomed warmth. "Fitz, you're bull of the woods, and that's a fact. I got an idea the two of us could clean out this whole goddamn tenderloin without even workin' up a sweat."

Fitz grunted agreeably, nodding his head as if a minor truth had been stated, and went back to paring his nails.

"Now that would just be grand, wouldn't it?" Mattie's tone was caustic, laced with sarcasm. "You two hooligans out demolishing the South Side when what we're trying to do is find a way to head off trouble.

"*Head it off?*" Hickok thundered. "Christ, I must've been talkin' to myself. I didn't say nothin' about making peace. Goddamn, when you run up on a snake you cut its head off. What I'm sayin' is, we've got to move fast. Get them bastards before they get us!"

"Bill, I still think you're being too hasty," Blomger said. "These South Side bosses just can't afford any real trouble. Oh, they might talk rough and toss around a few threats, but they're not about to start an open war. The townspeople just wouldn't stand for it."

"Horseshit!" Hickok blurted. "The people don't run this town. It's that lard-assed pack of scavengers at city hall that calls the shots."

"Exactly," Blomger agreed. "And that's why the South Side boys won't start any real trouble. If violence erupted in the tenderloin people would stay away in droves, which means that business would drop off to nothing. And the politicos uptown wouldn't hold still for their payoffs being jeopardized. They may be lard-assed, as you call 'em, but they're not dumb."

"So what could city hall do? Close down all the dives? Lou, you talk like a man that just crawled out of a poppy den."

"Bill, you're looking at it all wrong. The uptown bunch wouldn't close down the dives. They'd just escort the current crop of bosses to the city limits and find another group to take their place. Within forty-eight hours it would be business as usual, and don't think for a minute the gang leaders down here aren't aware of that fact. They exist only so long as city hall allows them to exist, and they're not about to do *anything* to rock that boat."

"Not even a quiet little killing, or two?" Hickok taunted. "Just enough to get rid of Mattie, or scare her out of business?"

"Come on now, Bill. Use your head. Mattie's a celebrity! Why, even the gentry think of her as a glamorous courtesan of the old school. There's not a man in the tenderloin stupid enough to harm Mattie personally. He'd be dancing at the end of a rope so fast the police wouldn't even have time to get him booked."

Hickok studied Blomger for a long, still moment, half-convinced but still not certain that his own way wasn't best. Then his eyes fell to the table, distracted by the thought that he had somehow been outflanked with slick words in a situation that demanded action.

"Bill, honey," Mattie prompted gently, "don't sull up like an old bull. Lou just happens to be right this time. If things should get worse, why you and Fitz could still go out and crack a few heads."

"You seem to forget I planned on ridin' west before long," he countered. "What happens if all hell breaks loose while I'm gone?"

Mattie's eyes took on the look of a wounded doe, reminded again that his departure was growing closer with each passing day. The stillness thickened, and the only sound in the room was the grating noise of Fitz scraping his pared nails. Finally Blomger sighed heavily, glancing first at Mattie, then back at Hickok.

"The only certainty in this life is that we're all going to end up six feet under. One way or another. But I will promise you this, Bill. I'll put the pressure on the boys at city hall, and unless I'm dead wrong they'll see to it that things stay peaceful on the South Side."

"Blomger, if you are wrong you might just end up that way." Hickok's voice was cold, menacing. "As of right now, you've got ten percent of the action in this operation. Just a little somethin' to keep you on your toes. But if anything happens to Mattie while I'm gone, I'm givin' you fair warning. You'd better have a ticket on an outbound train, and hope to Christ it ain't punched for the hereafter."

Lou Blomger's face blanched, but he met Hickok's stare with an unwavering gaze. While he knew that the plainsman's warning was far from an idle threat, he was not a man easily intimidated. Lifting his coffee mug in a mock toast, he smiled engagingly.

"As flies to wanton boys are we to the gods. They kill us for their sport."

Hickok frowned, and his brow wrinkled ominously. "Now just what the hell does that mean?"

"Nothing, Bill. Nothing at all. Merely a pungent observation on life from the immortal bard. Something to the effect that we survive solely on the whim of the Good Lord's sense of humor."

"Amen!" Mattie added hastily. "Since we're all partners in this little venture now, suppose we break out a bottle and have a real toast."

"Goddamn if that's not the first tolerable idea I've heard all night." Hickok's eyes lost their coldness, and he seemed relieved the discussion had ended. "Fitz, hitch that chair on over here and let's get down to some serious drinkin'. All that high-toned talk gave me a powerful thirst, and I got an idea we're gonna howl tonight."

Dragging Mattie onto his lap, he poured a drink and downed it in one gulp. Fitz snapped his jackknife shut and took a seat at the table, wondering in his own brutish way if Hickok was a madman or just a damn fool.

The damp, fragrant scent of a spring dew hung in the dusky hours before dawn as Mattie walked toward the Metropolitan Hotel. Like a devoted watchdog, Fitz shadowed her footsteps with a shuffling, loose-limbed gait. For the last four months Mattie had traced this same route each night after closing the house, guarded diligently by her semi-retired hooligan. But this was to be their last pre-dawn excursion.

The winter snows had disappeared from the plains, and Hickok would depart on his long-delayed western pilgrimage shortly after sunup.

Operating a South Side bordello had wrought a noticeable change in Mattie's character during those blustery winter months. For one thing, she had turned twenty, and the addition of a single year somehow brought increased confidence to her manner. Confronted with the necessity of providing supervision and guidance for her "lady boarders," she had won their respect with firm, sympathetic treatment. And while many of the girls were older both in experience and years, they willingly acknowledged the authority with which she ruled the house.

Greeting a steady stream of customers in the vestibule each night, she rapidly discerned that there was an art to handling the "johns," whether drunk or sober. And she soon developed the subtle finesse which moved them into the bedrooms and back out the front door in the shortest possible time, with the least amount of trouble. Occasionally, she found herself faced with a belligerent drunk, but the heavy hand of Fitz unfailingly resolved the issue. Generally it ended with a battered and somewhat wiser drunk being unceremoniously dumped on the street outside. Dealing with tradesmen, merchants, and graft-hungry police had also contributed to her maturity. Unexpectedly, she had discovered a latent talent for wheeling and dealing, which left them slightly in awe of both her beauty and agility of mind.

While the change in Mattie was evident it had no marked effect on her outward dealings with others. Primarily, it was manifested in a cool assertiveness which hadn't been so apparent in the past. But still clearly visible were the warmth and gentleness of her fleeting girlhood. All in all, Mattie was rather pleased with the way she had handled the operation thus far. Though she detected a note of cynicism creeping into her thoughts occasionally, she chalked this up to broader exposure to the avarice and lust of her fellow men.

Still, supervising the sordid details of a brothel hadn't

been without its emotional toll. Having known only gentle lovers in her life. Mattie's naivete had at first provoked a wave of nausea toward the brutish rutting which took place upstairs each night. But she felt an even deeper shock at the callous venality of her lady boarders.

While the girls were attractively young, and possessed certain charm, collectively they bore the manner of a shrewd, greedy fish merchant. Hardened by a lifetime devoted to mere survival, they viewed the men who briefly shared their beds as unfeeling brutes—faceless, bovine puppets to be briefly manipulated for whatever gold they possessed, then dismissed once the shabby transaction was consummated. Witty and gay while entertaining gentleman callers, the girls more often than not reviled the johns with gutter invective as soon as they were alone.

Unsettled and troubled in the beginning, Mattie slowly came to accept both the customers and the girls for what they were, rather than what she had imagined them to be. Shortly she had rationalized her own position as that of an entrepreneur. She was simply a middleman, providing a service the public demanded.

Talking with the girls over coffee one afternoon, Mattie had gained a disturbing insight: delicate beauty can often belie insensitive bitterness. Spellbound by their comments on the previous evening's customers, her education as a madam was advanced drastically when one of the girls revealed the bizarre logic of a whore. Jennie, oldest and most experienced of the group, had been caricaturing a particularly offensive john. Heedless of appearing callow, Mattie found herself unable to resist posing a question which had been on her mind for weeks.

"Jennie, maybe you can straighten me out on something," she began obliquely. "If you girls dislike these men so terribly, why in God's name do you stay in the business? Why don't you find a decent man and settle down with a family?"

"Why should we bust our ass for one worthless bastard," Jennie snapped, "when we can get rich wigglin' it for a few

dungheads every night? Mattie, them horsesbutts think
they're screwin' us, but they're not. We're screwin' them!
And they don't even know it. They pay us a wad of money
and think they've bought us heart and soul. But you want'a
know something—it's like they never even touched us."

Mattie had set aside such thoughts tonight, however. For
her man was departing within a matter of hours, riding west
toward the savage plains, and there was room for little else
in her mind. Turning onto College Street her pace quickened as she drew closer to Bill's waiting arms, and the
measured tread of Fitz's footsteps on her heels somehow
seemed to toll the hour she had so long dreaded.

Upon reaching the hotel room, Mattie hurriedly undressed and slid silently into bed, snuggling close to the muscular warmth of Bill's lean frame. Awakening, he twisted
around, circling her body with his powerful arms. In whispered declaration of all they had shared over the last year,
they joined, seeking to slake a passion aroused to the fullest
by their imminent separation. Afterward, having satiated
one another, they clung together in the intimate communion
of spent love.

Leaning over her, Bill's tousled hair brushed softly
across Mattie's breasts and his penetrating gaze traced the
symmetry of her face. Kissing her gently, he nuzzled close
to her ear. "Every night I'm gone, no matter how far away
I'm camped, I'm gonna stare in the fire and see you. And
wish to Christ I was right here beside you."

Willing herself not to spoil it by crying, Mattie bit her
lip and pressed desperately to his chest. But the taste of salt
formed in her mouth even as she struggled against the tears.
Sniffling, she raised her face into the sinewy muscles of his
shoulder. "Oh, Bill, please don't let anything happen to
yourself in that wilderness. I love you so much and there's
just no life for me without you."

Holding her close, he became aware of the first rays of
sunlight filtering through the window and, with one final
caress, slipped from the bed. Dressing quickly in buckskins and boots, he strapped on his gunbelt and moved

soundlessly back to the bed. As they embraced her lungs filled with the strange, smoky scent of his buckskins. Then, without speaking, the door closed softly and he was gone.

Moving to the window, she saw him appear on the street below as the liveryman brought around his black mare and a packhorse. Mounting, he reined the mare about and rode west out of Springfield.

"Look after yourself, gamblin' man," Mattie called quietly. "And please come back."

CHAPTER THREE

A brilliant orange glow edged over the horizon as the two men warily moved their horses through the scrub undergrowth. Indians had passed this way within the hour, leaving an obscure trail in the shortgrass and brush. Cautiously, the horsemen worked their way toward a cottonwood grove lining the steep banks of a creek.

Eyes riveted to the ground, Bill Hickok scanned the faint trail left by the Indians' unshod ponies. Raising his head, he spit a stream of tobacco juice and peered intently toward the stillness of the distant tree line, now less than a hundred yards away. *Too goddamn quiet, but there's sure as hell only one way to find out what's in there.*

Glancing at the trooper next to him, Hickok silently cursed the military for their ignorance about the plains' tribes. Often he had commented that having a soldier along on a scout was about as much use as tits on a boar hog. Doubtless this poor bastard wasn't even aware that they might get their ass skewered when they tried to cross that creek. Well, if they did jump the Cheyenne maybe the soldier would at least have sense enough to hightail it back to warn Captain Brady.

Thinking of Brady and the troop of cavalry a mile or so behind sent his mind back to the beginning of the campaign. *And that asinine general!*

Assembled at Fort Larned, under the command of Major General Winfield Scott Hancock, the expedition had moved west across the prairie in early April. Comprised of the Seventh and Tenth Regiments, the expedition was charged with persuading the Indians that it was no longer prudent to make war on the white man. Assigned to the Seventh Cavalry, commanded by Brevet Major General George Armstrong Custer, Hickok had followed his bewildering orders without comment at first.

Directed to seek out large concentrations of Indians, Hickok leisurely scouted the vast plains while the expedition marched in circles. The Indians weren't fools, as he was well aware. They simply broke up into small bands, fleeing before the advancing cavalry, much like water rushing away from a hand thrust into a bucket. Then, when the troops moved on, the scattered bands calmly regrouped in their wake, slightly inconvenienced but no worse off for the experience. When General Hancock's saddle-sore command finally returned to the fort they had marched over a thousand weary miles. And not once during their sojourn in the wilderness had they encountered a single hostile.

Far from being intimidated, the plains tribes casually resumed their savage raids, thoroughly unimpressed by the parade-ground campaign they had witnessed.

The next month had been a nightmare for the cavalry, scurrying to and fro across the countryside in response to the bloody depredations. Settlers, railroad crews, and wagon trains bore the brunt of the mounting raids. And the army stewed in the juices of its own frustration. Rarely did the cavalry even see the savages, much less engage them in battle. Upon reaching the scene of the latest attack they were greeted by the stench of smoking ruins and mutilated corpses, but no Indians. Even on those few occasions when they were able to run the raiding parties to earth, the hostiles simply split forces and vanished without a trace.

Hickok and the other scouts had been amused at first. There was something grimly humorous about the army flapping across the plains like a headless chicken. But the futility of chasing Indians instead of attacking them soon wore thin, and the disgruntled scouts became openly vocal. Undaunted by their arguments, General Hancock rigidly stuck to the West Point manual, and the troops proceeded to plod ineffectually after the will-o'-the-wisp raiding parties.

Not even Custer, who supported the scouts in their recommendations, could make a dent in their hidebound commander. The youthful general's flamboyance was in direct contradiction to Hancock's stuffy arrogance, and the Seventh Cavalry rarely had a chance to test the brash schemes of the man known only to the Indians as Yellow-hair.

Still, there were times when scouting almost seemed worthwhile. Only yesterday a rider had slid his lathered horse to a stop before headquarters at Fort Hays, where the Seventh was now stationed. Leaping from the saddle, he left the wind-blown animal heaving for breath and raced inside. Within minutes Custer sent a runner to fetch Captain Silas Brady and Hickok. Reporting to headquarters, they found the general excitedly pacing the floor.

"Come in. What the hell took you so long?" Custer demanded. "Now listen closely. The Kansas Pacific track crew has been raided just west of Round Mountain. The foreman spotted the Indians before they attacked and sent this man for troops. That means they're less than twenty miles away, and if we move fast we might be able to catch the red bastards for a change. Brady, get your company mounted with field rations and be ready to march in ten minutes."

As the officer turned to leave, Custer fixed Hickok with a defiant stare. "Bill, you've been bellyaching for a real fight. Here's your chance. Get on their trail and stick to it like a leech. And don't come back till Brady and his boys have skinned a few of those devils. That's an order."

"Gen'ral, I'll show 'em Injuns all right," Hickok retorted.

"After that we'll just have to see how handy they are at skinnin'."

"That's all I ask." Flashing a wide smile, he clasped the scout's shoulder. "You just put them in a fight and I'm quite confident they'll know what to do from that point on."

Nodding, Hickok hurried toward the stables, elated at the prospect of seeing action. The boredom of the fort had grown stifling over the past few weeks, and a bit of gunsmoke was just the thing to clear his head. Minutes later the cavalry troop had pounded out the front gate, primed for bear. Glancing at Hays City in the distance, Hickok suddenly remembered that Mattie was due to arrive sometime within the next few days. But the exhilaration of an impending fight quickly reasserted its grip, and his thoughts focused once more on the road west.

Late that evening they had trailed the war party to the north fork of the Solomon, where the tracks turned northeast in the direction of Prairie Dog Creek. By now Hickok knew they were trailing Cheyennes, and since they weren't running for home, it seemed clear the Indians hadn't expected any stubborn pursuit. Or else they had gotten cute and planned a little surprise somewhere up ahead. With any luck, the scout had informed Captain Brady, they should jump the hostiles sometime next morning. To himself he silently added that it might be the other way around.

Hickok had moved out at first light, accompanied by a trooper who would return to alert the cavalry once the Cheyenne were sighted. Now, crossing the last few yards of open ground leading to Prairie Dog Creek, Hickok's nerves stretched taut with a sense of unseen danger.

Still, there was only one way to find out. Nudging his horse, he entered the dense grove of trees lining the bank. As they eased their mounts down the slight incline the scout's eyes darted through the trees, then across to the opposite bank. Suddenly, from the corner of his eye, he caught a slight movement. But before he could yell, the twang of a bowstring splintered the stillness.

Wheeling his horse, Hickok was aware of the trooper

tumbling to the ground with a feathered shaft buried in his chest. Leaning low in the saddle, he gigged his horse savagely. But even as the animal responded it stumbled from shock as an arrow cleaved its heart. Shuddering, the horse ran a few steps, then fell to its knees, catapulting Hickok out of the saddle. Rolling as he hit the ground, the scout hung on to his Henry Repeater and began crawling back toward the thrashing horse. Instinctively, he shot the animal in the head and threw himself behind its protective bulk as a hail of Cheyenne lead churned across the glen.

Their ambush spoiled, the infuriated war party set about killing him in no uncertain terms. Listening to the slugs chunk into dead horse, Hickok glanced over the animal's flanks and saw two braves running toward him. Waiting until the last moment, he rose slightly and snapped two quick shots, dropping both warriors in mid-stride. Then a wrenching blow numbed his left shoulder, and as he slid behind the horse a bloodstain spread over his buckskin shirt.

Once they get behind me, I'm dog meat. With the thought came a solitary moment of terror that he might be taken alive. He had seen what the Cheyenne could do to a man over an open fire, and he sensed that his only chance lay in restricting their movements to the grove of cottonwoods. Ignoring the pain in his shoulder, he jerked one of the Colts and emptied it in the direction of the trees. Hastily reloading, he forced himself to measure powder and tamp the balls with calculated speed.

Darting a glance over his barricade, Hickok's regard for the Indians' daring went up a couple of notches. Mounted on ponies, two braves were circling him at that moment. Outflanked and pinned down, he wouldn't have the chance of a snowball in hell when the main party attacked dead-on. Staying low, Hickok edged his rifle across the withers of the fallen horse. Aiming carefully, he swung the barrel in an arc and fired. Grinning, he saw the Cheyenne slump, then tumble backward off the pony. Twisting, he grabbed the Colt and looked up to see the second warrior bearing down on him from a distance of less than thirty yards.

Even later he couldn't remember hearing the report from the Indian's old trade musket. But he clearly recalled the smoke, and the searing pain as the ball ripped a gaping furrow through his right thigh. Shoving the pistol to arm's length, the scout fired twice and watched the warrior's face disappear in a crimson blotch as he pitched over the pony's back.

Blinded by exquisite pain, Hickok swallowed hard on the rancid gorge in his throat. Thrusting the Colt over the horse's flank, he emptied it into the Indians emerging from the trees on the far side of the creek. Staring in shocked fascination, he watched as they continued across the stream. Death itself seemed to mock him, for he had missed the Cheyenne gut-eaters with every shot. Slowly, as though he hadn't a care in the world, Hickok pulled his second Colt and methodically thumbed slugs into the pack of warriors hurtling toward him. The lead brave stopped, as if impaled on a bolt of fire, and soundlessly crumpled forward with his head on the creek bank. As he fell the remaining Indians skidded to a halt. Staring intently at something in the distance, they hesitated only a moment, then turned and began running back toward the woods.

Cheyenne sonsabitches, Hickok chuckled madly to himself, ain't got the guts to finish the fight even when they got me cold. Resting his head on the horse's bullet-scarred flank, the scout struggled to catch the notes of a distant bugle as his mind drifted into swirling darkness.

Distracted by a grating piano from Tommy Drum's saloon, Mattie pushed the books aside. Her mind refused to concentrate, and besides, the emporium's monthly bill never seemed to tally with her own records anyway. An abnormal calm had settled over the house, and she could hear Fitz snoring peacefully in the parlor. Middle-of-the-month doldrums, Mattie called it, when the soldiers had squandered

most of their pay and the few callers were mainly hide hunters and teamsters.

Farther back in the house she heard the girls talking and
giggling in their bedrooms. *That ungodly giggling! Don't
the little scatterbrains ever have a serious thought in their
heads?* Forcing her attention back to the books, Mattie
smiled ruefully. Judging from their foolish extravagance in
Fine's Emporium, it was doubtful that among them, the girls
had ever put two serious thoughts back to back. *Well, why
not? Hays City sure as hell isn't Springfield, and even
whores are entitled to a few pleasures.*

Staring absently at the books, her mind drifted once
more to the discordant music. Silently she contemplated
how much Bill would win tonight. Often she found herself
wishing he weren't such a skilled gambler. *If he lost more
he wouldn't be so damned independent. Then maybe I
could get him to toe the mark, instead of coming and going when the mood strikes him.*

Tommy Drum's saloon was only a few doors up Main
Street from her house, and anytime Hickok wasn't on
patrol he could be found hunched over the gaming tables.
Lately he had pursued dame fortune with a passion that
increasingly left Mattie in a fit of jealousy. *After coming
all the way out to this godforsaken wasteland,* she fumed,
*and nursing him back to health, you'd think the big lum-
mox would be more appreciative.* Mulling the thought over
with a vengeance, her mind wandered back to that first terrifying day in Hays City.

After two years of separation, broken only by Bill's in-
frequent visits to Springfield, they had at last arranged to
be together. Or so it seemed. Bill had written that spring,
urging Mattie to pack girls and baggage and come west.
Fort Hays had been erected on the Smoky Hill River two
hundred and fifty miles due west of Kansas City, and according to Bill it would be a goldmine for a ladies' boardinghouse like hers. Overnight, Hays City had sprung up within
the fort's shadow, and when the railroad arrived the village
shortly became a wilderness oasis for troops, hide hunters,

and freight caravans. Thrilled by the thought of ending their long separation, Mattie had wired back promising to start west as soon as she could arrange the details.

Two weeks later, covered with soot and grime, she stepped from the train at the windswept K&P station house. Unprepared for the single dirt road and the ramshackle buildings, she was appalled by her first glimpse of Hays City. It was like a shantytown, dusty and coarse, and certainly not what Bill had described. Suddenly the west was stripped of the glamour she had imagined, and the realities of operating a bordello on the frontier became very real indeed.

But there was no turning back now, and on second thought not even Hays City could be as bad as it looked, so long as she was with Bill. Composing herself, she led Fitz and the girls down South Main, toward the white clapboard house Bill had described in his last letter.

In the weeks prior to her arrival, Bill had set carpenters to building additional bedrooms on the back of the house. Slowly it rose like a white elephant on the dusty plains. Overnight Hays City was electrified with the news of its first full-scale brothel. While the few saloons had provided backroom cribs in the past, even a foul-smelling hide hunter occasionally winced at the hags who plied their trade on the frontier. Most men required a liberal sampling of their favorite rotgut before they were up to visiting the backroom. So it was that talk of Mattie Silks's forthcoming arrival swept through town on the fires of rekindled lust. Already men were pouring from the saloons to gape at her tittering retinue, and if their hungry stares were any indication, they would be storming the doors before nightfall. Shepherding her flock into the house Mattie had sent Fitz to the fort to inform Bill of her arrival.

Toward sundown Fitz barreled through the door with his features set in a grim frown. Hickok had just been dragged in on a litter and talk around the fort had it that he was mortally wounded. Skirts flying, Mattie raced up the street and turned north toward the fort, oblivious now to the town or its grungy inhabitants. Inquiring directions, she pushed past the guard at the front gate and burst into the post infirmary.

Gasping, she stood frozen in terror at the grisly scene revealed in the flickering lamplight. Bill lay ashen-faced on a crude table, breathing shallowly. Smothering a cry, she watched helplessly as the post surgeon slowly extracted a lead ball from an oozing wound in his shoulder. Sinking against the doorjamb, Mattie's brow suddenly went cold with sweat. Silently she thanked whatever god it was that had allowed him to sleep through the brutal probing.

Leaving an orderly to bandage Bill's shoulder, the surgeon ripped a filthy rag from the scout's leg. Mattie again stifled a cry as she stared at the jagged furrow along his thigh. Gently swabbing caked blood from the wound, the surgeon clucked appreciatively to himself. But for a few inches the musket ball would have severed the femoral artery.

Finished, the doctor turned to an officer with pale, shoulder-length hair who had been standing silently in the shadows. "General, I'll tell you straight out. If those troopers had put him on a horse, instead of making a travois, Wild Bill Hickok would be a dead man. As it is, he's lost a lot of blood, but I'd say he's got a fighting chance."

Unable to restrain the tears any longer, Mattie buried her face in Fitz's broad shoulder and sobbed uncontrollably. Sheepishly, Fitz glanced around at the curious officers. "This here is Hickok's woman."

Stepping across the room, the long-haired soldier gently touched Mattie's arm. "No need to cry, ma'am. You heard the doc. He's going to be all right."

Lifting her head, Mattie tried to speak, but the words caught in the back of her throat.

When she failed to respond, the officer paused for a moment, then resumed. "Allow me to introduce myself. I'm George Custer. And you must be Mattie Silks. I've heard Bill speak of you often." Mattie's eyes widened as two orderlies lifted the unconscious scout and placed him on a nearby cot. Custer glanced around, then smiled reassuringly. "Now, don't worry that pretty head. Why, he's tough as buffalo leather. And the Indian doesn't live that could kill Bill Hickok. I know. I've seen too many of them try."

Later, after Custer had left, Mattie sat silently beside the cot, staring hopefully at Bill's haggard features. Around midnight his eyes opened and he looked about uncertainly. Pallor still covered his face like chalk, but the flinty gaze seemed as clear as ever.

"Hello, gamblin' woman," he said in a drained voice.

"Hello yourself, gamblin' man." Kneeling beside the cot, she put her cheek next to his and stroked his amber hair. "Now don't try to talk. Just rest. I'll get you home and have you well so fast you'll be chasing me around the bed before breakfast."

With a muffled chuckle, Bill closed his eyes and once more lapsed into a profound sleep.

Over the next month, Bill had slowly recuperated in the white house on South Main, openly reveling in being pampered and clucked over by so many women. Gradually, he began moving about the house, and taking short walks up the street. And finally the day arrived when he was once more spending virtually every waking hour in Tommy Drum's saloon.

Mattie's spell was broken as she came full circle to Bill's incorrigible love of gambling. *Damn him anyway! If he's not out getting half-killed by Indians then he's holed up in some gambling dive. And he expects me to sit here with my thumbs crossed. Well, that's going to change. Gambling is one thing, but chasing off after Indians is just too much!* Groping for some means of bringing Bill to heel, Mattie started as the door suddenly opened.

"Well, looka here," Bill roared happily. "The little mistress of the house guardin' the door like a goddamn toy bulldog."

"Thanks for the comparison, lover," she retorted.

Bill maneuvered carefully across the room and sank stiffly into an armchair. Watching him, Mattie concluded that the whiskey supply in Drum's saloon had been reduced appreciably. "Since you're drunk as a lord it's obvious you must have lost tonight."

"Oh, I ain't so drunk, but you're right about my losin'," he agreed cheerfully. "Lost my ass and my shirt buttons, too. So I decided to see just how much tangle-foot it would take to make a grown man forget his troubles." Grinning like a wolf, he snickered. "Wanna know somethin'? I left Bill Cody and Tommy Drum glassy-eyed as polled shoats. Drunk 'em both clean under the table."

"Bravo! The courageous scout emerges victorious again." Her mocking tone brought his head around. "Honest to God, Bill, you're such a little boy sometimes I get to feeling like a *wet nurse*."

"Well, you're sure as Christ the best-lookin' mammy I ever saw," he howled, attempting to rise. "Why don't we just trot off to bed and give Billy boy some nourishment."

"Later, Romeo. First, I wanted to talk to you about something." With a firm grip on her temper Mattie resumed in a more engaging manner. "Bill, honey, we've got to do something about getting you out of the army. Why, look at you. You're still limping and your shoulder looks like it's been worked over with an axe. We've just got to find you a safer line of work."

"Well, little mama, you can just quit your frettin'. I'm way ahead of you. The army ain't what it used to be, and that's a fact. All this talk of peace treaties and kissin' the hostiles' ass. That ain't for me. No siree, it ain't. As of today I have plumb resigned from the scoutin' profession."

"Oh, Bill!" Mattie exclaimed. Bounding across the room, she threw herself in his lap and hugged him fiercely. "That means you'll stick to gambling and be here all the time."

"Hey, don't break my neck, you little fire-eater," he said, quickly disengaging her arms. "Now, I didn't say anything about hangin' around Hays City all the time. Matter of fact, I've been offered a real fine job. Meant to tell you about it, but it just kept slippin' my mind. Anyway, your old Billy boy is about to become Deputy US Marshal."

"Marshal!" Leaping from his lap, she stood over the plainsman like an angry bantam. "You mean a lawman? One of those underpaid fools that goes off chasing robbers and bandits?"

"Well, yeah, somethin' like that." With a crooked smile he reached for Mattie in an effort to calm her.

"Don't touch me, you Judas!" she exploded. "Oh, Jesus Christ, Bill Hickok, you're impossible." Reduced to tears, she ran down the hall and slammed the door to her bedroom with a force that rattled the entire house.

Somewhat dumbfounded, Bill rose in an alcoholic haze and headed for the front door. Just then Fitz entered from the parlor, rubbing his eyes in a sleepy stupor.

"Heard some yellin', Bill. Anything wrong?"

"Fitz, there ain't a goddamned thing wrong except that females should of been born with three tits instead of a tongue." Without pausing to clarify this cryptic observation, Hickok stormed out the door.

Rubbing his scarred brow, Fitz puzzled the strange ties that bound his mistress and Wild Bill. After a moment he gave it up and walked with a lumbering tread toward the more inviting certainty of his bed.

Wearied after fourteen hours in the saddle, the two men sat their mounts stiffly. Since dawn they had ridden over a hundred miles, fording the Smoky Hill and the north fork of the Walnut as they followed a trail which skirted west of Fort Larned. Wandering brokenly at times, the trail held to a southwesterly direction, and it was clear to both men that the tracks were almost sure to cross the Arkansas River. From first light they had clung to the clearly marked trail of fifteen newly shod army horses. Skillfully reading the tracks they knew that five of the horses carried men. While they hadn't spoken of it, they also knew that the thieves would switch to fresh mounts throughout the day in order to maintain the ground-eating pace.

Upon reaching the Walnut late that morning they had lost the trail briefly as the tracks seemed to end at the water's edge. Suspecting a ruse, they rode west along the banks, looking for a spot where the horses had again taken to land. An hour later their hunch paid off when the tracks emerged from a small tributary, once again angling off to the southwest. While the thieves' final destination was uncertain, it was now clear that the horses were being hazed toward the Arkansas. All of which was a great deal more than the lawmen had known the night before.

Pounding on the front door had aroused everyone in Mattie's house shortly after four in the morning. Mumbling curses at whorehouses and amorous drunks alike, Bill groggily rolled over as Mattie slipped from bed and padded toward the front of the house. Like some grotesque apparition, Fitz raced down the hall in his nightshirt, moving in front of her just as she reached the door. Drowsily, Bill heard subdued voices in the hallway, and moments later Mattie returned, shaking him awake. It was Bill Cody, she said, with an urgent message from the fort.

Cursing fluently now, Bill had crawled from bed and stumbled toward the parlor. Speaking rapidly, Cody related that five enlisted men had deserted during the night and stolen fifteen horses after beating the stable guard unconscious. Custer wanted them caught and had aroused Cody, ordering him to alert Hickok so that they could be on the trail by dawn. Shaking his head, the new marshal observed that outlaws ought to have more respect for a man's sleep. Pondering the injustice of it all, he trudged back to the bedroom and began dressing for what promised to be a long and dirty job.

Hickok and Cody had often teamed as scouts for the army, and after wrecking most of the saloons west of Kansas City it only seemed natural that they would remain partners. Shortly after Hickok was appointed Deputy Marshal, it came as no surprise that Bill Cody also signed on as a federal man. While he had developed some reputation as a buffalo hunter, Cody wasn't yet known as a manhunter. But that would change soon enough. With Hickok as the professor, the local wits were fond of saying, it didn't take a man long to cross over the line.

When Hickok returned to the parlor he avoided the worried look in Mattie's eyes and kissed her hurriedly. Her hangdog expression irritated him. It was his job, and women ought to know better than to mope around when a man had work to do. Mounting the horse Cody had brought along, he led the way back to the fort and began searching for tracks. Spotting the deserters' trail only moments after first light, they had struck off toward the southwest.

Now, evening was settling over the prairie and the lawmen decided to make camp for the night. After hobbling the horses, Hickok began gathering dried buffalo chips for a fire while Cody broke out their rations of jerky and coffee. Later, they leaned back against their saddles, upwind from the smoldering buffalo chips. Twisting a few weeds together, Cody held them in the fire for a moment, then touched the flame to Hickok's cigar before lighting his own pipe.

Appears to me those boys are headed for Colorado," Cody commented, puffing on his worn pipe.

"You know, I never was much for second-guessin' what a bunch of dungheads will do." Hickok flicked an ash from his cigar. "But I got a strong hunch them birds mean to join up with our old pal, Major Smith."

"Jediah Smith?"

"That's the one. You might recollect that after he was cashiered last fall the forts started losin' horses and mules hand over fist. Rumor has it he's got himself a gang of hardcases somewhere down around Trinidad."

"What you're sayin'," Cody mulled aloud, "is that Smith got those boys to desert and bring along a few horses in the bargain." Staring into the fire, he puffed thoughtfully on his pipe for a moment. "Unless I'm wide of the mark, you figure they're gonna leave a trail a drunk Cheyenne could follow . . . straight to Jed Smith himself."

"The thought had crossed my mind." Taking a final drag,

Hickok tossed the cigar in the fire and watched the flames consume the stub, "Reckon you know we're gonna be outnumbered five or six to one if we do stumble on their hideout."

"Offhand, I'd say that sounds just about right," Cody grinned. "Is that why you brought the scattergun?" Nodding, he indicated a sawed-off shotgun hooked over the pommel of Hickok's saddle.

"Might reduce the odds a little now that you mention it."

"You know something, Bill?" Cody's face suddenly went solemn. "I've never killed a white man in my life, just buffalos and Injuns. Never even been in what you could rightly call a real gunfight."

"It ain't a particularly rewardin' experience." Hickok stared at the dancing flames, lost in the remembered smell of gunsmoke and the stench of men's bowels loosed by death. Turning to the younger man, his eyes narrowed. "When it comes, make sure you aim for the bellybutton. A gutshot takes all the fight out of a man, and if he's drilled dead center then you're lookin' at cold meat."

Nodding, Cody studied his friend's grizzled face for a moment, then shifted his eyes to the fire. The conversation waned, and after a while the two men curled up in their blankets. Staring at the vast, cloudless sky, Cody contemplated the older man's advice and suddenly recalled a grim joke making the rounds. *There's no law west of Kansas City and no God west of Fort Scott!* Chuckling, he mused that folks might be shocked to learn that west of Fort Hays the rule of law and the wrath of God had become the personal property of Wild Bill Hickok.

The morning of the fourth day dawned crisp and bright as the two lawmen inched their way along the floor of Pinon Canyon. Upon reaching the headwaters of the Arkansas late the day before, the tracks turned sharply south, headed toward the craggy slopes outside Trinidad. Roughly paralleling the Purgatoire River, the trail had led them to a crude cabin some miles downstream.

After spotting smoke a mile back they had quickly hidden

their horses and begun a cautious approach to the cabin. Shortly they were near enough to make out something over thirty horses in a log corral just north of the house. Within moments they realized the chase had ended. Almost every animal in the corral bore a US brand high on its flank.

Separating, Cody crawled to the left, taking cover behind an outcropping of rock. Stealthily working his way up an arroyo, Hickok halted less than twenty yards from the shack. Suddenly, the door opened and four men stepped outside, walking to a shallow stream which emptied into the river. Laughing at something said by a heavily whiskered member of the group, they proceeded to relieve themselves in the running water. Waiting until the men were well into their morning ritual, Hickok rose slightly and yelled, "Hands up!"

For a moment the tinkling sound continued, then died with the suddenness of a spring shower as fear gripped the men. Without thought to their predicament, they spun in unison, drawing their pistols in the same motion. As they turned the double roar of Hickok's shotgun reverberated off the canyon walls, magnifying the blast as if thunder had been loosed within the narrow corridor.

Staggering backward under a hail of buckshot, two of the men were dead even as they pitched headlong into the stream. The bearded outlaw clutched at his stomach, then slowly sank to his knees and toppled over, staining the earth a rich, muddy brown. Untouched, the fourth man raised his gun, drawing a bead on Hickok.

At that moment Cody joined the fight. With the sharp crack of his rifle the man lurched drunkenly and crumpled to the ground.

Crouching in the arroyo, Hickok jerked one of his Colts and drove two slugs through the cabin door as it slammed shut. The shriek of a wounded man twisted Hickok's mouth into a tight smile, and he peered cautiously over the edge of the gully.

"You sonsabitches got about one minute to come out of there with your hands over your head." He paused to let the message take effect. "If you don't, we'll burn that goddamn cabin and fry your asses like a piece of side-pork."

Allowing a few moments to pass, he demanded, "What's it gonna be? I'm not gonna fart around all day waitin' for you to make up your minds."

Slowly the door edged open and a man nervously poked his head into sight. "Don't shoot, mister! We're comin' out unarmed."

The trapped men stepped through the door one by one, lining up in front of the cabin as they squinted into the early morning sun. Calling for Cody to keep them covered, Hickok ordered the outlaws to turn their faces to the cabin and place their hands high on the wall. Crawling from the arroyo, he walked forward and eased through the cabin door, satisfying himself that the shack was empty.

Grabbing two rawhide lariats, he stepped outside to find Cody guarding the gang. Moving down the line, Hickok roughly jerked each man's hands behind his back and bound them securely with lengths of rawhide. After saddling horses, the lawmen helped the trussed outlaws to mount, then hazed the rest of the herd from the corral. Returning to the cabin, Hickok scooped coals from the fire with a pan and dumped glowing embers on the bunks.

Moments later, riding north along the riverbank, the group paused to watch the cabin disappear in flames. Casually returning the outlaws' hostile stares, Hickok informed them, "Boys, we know that big bearded gent was Jed Smith, so there won't be anyone trailin' us to break you loose. We got a long ride and I intend to get every one of you back to Fort Hays." Then his pale eyes went cold as ice. "Course, how you get there is strictly your choice. Any man even looks like he's tryin' to escape, I'll blow his goddamn head off with this scattergun."

Seated around the large dining table in the kitchen, Mattie and Bill were having a late lunch. She preferred dining alone with him, away from the constant chattering of the girls. Since his gambling hours caused him to be a late riser anyway, Mattie had provided a simple solution. The girls took their lunch on the stroke of twelve, and not a moment later. Mattie's rule was law within the confines of the house, and shortly after noon each day she was free to arrange her own cozy luncheon.

Usually she spent part of each morning devising some new and delectable manner of preparing Bill's favorite dish. After so many years in a land devoid of chickens, he had an insatiable appetite for eggs, and never seemed to tire of Mattie's lavish concoctions. On this particular morning she had outdone herself by preparing a huge blackberry omelette, with filet of buffalo hump on the side. Rarely given to conversation while eating, Bill wolfed the food down appreciatively, then sat back to light a thin, black cigar.

"Mattie, the only thing better'n that meal," he said exhaling a cloud of dense blue smoke, "is this-here cigar. I guess them as don't smoke can't understand what the weed means to a man."

"Sweetie, the way you smoke nobody would ever have the slightest doubt." Then she laughed. "Sometimes I think you'd sooner give up cards than go without tobacco."

"Jesus! What a choice." Puffing furiously at the thought, he observed her closely for a moment. "Appears to me you're about as happy as a hog in a cabbage patch. Any particular reason, or is it just that sunny nature of yours showin' through?"

"God, your comparisons are so complimentary." Mattie smiled in spite of herself. "No, there isn't anything in particular. I've got you and I've got a profitable business, and those seem like two very good reasons for a girl to be happy."

Mattie's simple statement concealed an even broader truth. Hays City had grown out of all proportion to the forecast of its founders, spreading west across the rise of ground leading to the military compound. Buffalo hunters, soldiers, and an enlarging farm community had sparked an economic boom unlike anything envisioned by the town fathers. All of which acted as a lure for a host of gamblers, merchants, and saloon-keepers from eastern cities. Main Street now boasted three dancehalls, twenty-two saloons, and four gambling dives, each packed nightly with a swirling mass of coarsely dressed, rough-mannered frontiersmen.

Though most of the saloons and dancehalls encouraged their girls to perform in the backroom cribs, Mattie remained unperturbed concerning the growing competition. Underlying this benevolent attitude was the fact that her brothel on South Main continued to be the only parlor house in Hays City.

Since opening for business, she had run a clean, dignified establishment, one which brooked no rowdyism on the premises. With Bill Hickok as her paramour and the burly Fitz to act as bouncer, the message had fallen on receptive ears, and the rules of the house were seldom violated. Mattie also demanded conduct befitting genteel young ladies from her boarders, and they behaved accordingly. Understandably, such decorum was in marked contrast to the dives up the street. The jaded whores found in the dollar cribs were an unsavory lot at best, and when a man had the money he much preferred the demure, lilac-scented creatures awaiting him in the parlor house.

With some justification then, Mattie felt that she had cornered the market in Hays City. And as the town entered the peak of an economic boom she experienced a sense of well-being that had seldom been with her since leaving Springfield.

These thoughts must have been apparent, for as Bill studied her face he seemed reflective. "Well, I suppose me and this house ain't such a bad deal. Near as I recall though, most girls be wantin' a bunch of babies and a homestead, or somethin'. Don't you ever sorta miss not havin' such things?"

"Why, Mr. Hickok! You fairly take a girl's breath away. Is that a proposal?"

"No, ma'am," he snorted. "We're talkin' about you. I'm happy as a buffalo in a mud waller just the way we are."

"Well, so am I," Mattie responded. "I don't know what

difference a ring would make, anyway. And so far as having babies is concerned, I'm not sure I even want one." Especially, she thought to herself, since I know a baby would drive you straight out the front door.

"How about Hays City?" Bill inquired. "You happy with stayin' here?"

"What is it, Bill? You sound like you're getting restless or bored. Are you trying to say you'd like to move on to a new town?"

"Naw, I didn't mean that. Not exactly, anyway. Course, I been hearin' rumors that a new town east of here is gonna be the biggest cattle center this state has ever seen."

"Well, let me tell you something, Bill. We've got a fine business here, and it certainly brings in more money than your gambling. So if you get the itch to move on just make damn sure it's a place where there's plenty of trade for a parlor house. I don't care where we live, and I'll go anyplace you want, just so long as I have the most elegant house in town."

Before Bill could frame a reply, the hall door burst open and Cody rushed into the kitchen.

"Custer wants to see you," he said without greeting. "And he said to get off your duff and make it over to the fort real quick."

"Well, what the hell's he want?" The message was just a bit too curt for Bill's tastes.

"You know he don't tell people nothing," said Cody. "He just yelled for me to get you up there and be damn quick about it."

With a frown, Bill kissed Mattie lightly and accompanied Cody out the back door.

The set to Mattie's jaw was equally grim as she stormed around the kitchen. *Damn that Custer anyway! Not a day passes but what he's after Bill to start scouting again. Christ, being a marshal is bad enough, but if he goes back to scouting I'll . . . oh, hell, I don't know what I'll do!*

The afternoon passed slowly for Mattie, though every moment was occupied preparing for the evening rush. After organizing the cook, she sent Fitz for a case of whiskey, then turned her attention to the maid's somewhat lackadaisical efforts. On occasion, her mind would drift to the fort, and as the hours passed she began wondering what could be taking Bill so long. Only too aware of Custer's charm, she was worried sick that Bill might let himself be badgered into signing on as a scout. The more she thought on it, the more her mood darkened, and as the afternoon drew to a close, her disposition worsened noticeably. When Bill hadn't returned for supper, her temper grew even sharper, and the girls gathered around the dining table wisely held their giggling in check. After dinner she moved down the hall from room to room, performing the nightly ritual of inspecting the girls' appearance and the fit of their low-cut gowns.

Shortly after sundown the front door opened, and Mattie caught her breath as Fitz greeted Bill from the parlor. Running down the hall, she found Fitz pumping Bill's hand and for a moment her heart stopped as she sensed that something significant had occurred at the fort. Turning, Bill caught sight of her and leaped across the room. Lifting her high in the air, he swung her around the parlor.

"Little lady, it's been a big day for your old Bill," he exclaimed. "A *big* goddamn day!"

"Honey, what is it? What's happened?" she said, forcing a smile. "I've never seen you so excited."

"Well, for openers, Tom Ganlon got hisself killed in a gunfight late last night. Must of happened after I quit playin' cards and came home."

"But that's no reason for rejoicing," she said. "Tom Ganlon was the best sheriff Hays City ever had."

"Was the best, Mattie!" Bill trumpeted the words, his voice rising with excitement. "*Was!* But not anymore. Cause you are now lookin' at the best sheriff Ellis County will ever have!"

"You?" she blurted. "You're the new sheriff?"

"Well, almost. Just as soon as Custer heard Ganlon had been killed he wired Governor Harvey suggestin' that I be

appointed to the job. Harvey finally wired back, sayin' he'd
be glad to endorse me, but he'd prefer to see a special election held. So Custer got the town council up to the fort and
spent the afternoon swift-talkin' them into backin' me." Recalling the afternoon's events, Bill laughed. "I wanna tell
you, when that Custer gets going he's a real ball buster."

"But, Bill, stop and think for a minute. Hays City is no
better than a slaughterhouse. Ganlon was the third sheriff to
be murdered in a little over a year. Do you want to be next?"

"There ain't nobody gonna kill me, Mattie. There ain't
nobody good enough or fast enough with a gun to kill me.
Besides, I have to get elected first, and that won't be till
sometime next week. So stop your worryin'."

"What if they shoot you in the back?" she cried. "And
leave you lying out there in the street like a dog! Then what
good will those damn guns do you?"

"Come on, now. Don't raise such a fuss." Drawing her
into his arms, Bill held her close to his chest and squeezed
her tightly. Staring absently into space, he chuckled. "Yes
sir, that yellow-haired soldier is a real ball buster."

The months that followed saw the crisp autumn winds sweep
down across the great plains, displacing the unendurable
heat that had scorched Hays City throughout the summer.
The nights became pleasantly cool, the days shorter and
less oppressive. But Mattie's thoughts rarely centered on
the change in seasons these days.

Whenever Bill had gone off chasing Indians or outlaws
she could avoid facing the fact that he seldom returned without at least one man having met death at his hands. What
took place on the plains was another world, removed from
the gentleness and warmth of their bedroom. And she could
close her mind to reports of ruthless killings in the barren
wilderness. But what had happened in Hays City wasn't
some distant, impersonal rumor. It was real, brutally real,
and she often had the feeling that the angel of death had
come to rest on her very doorstep.

Without opposition, Hickok had been appointed sheriff
by an overwhelming vote in the special election. Much to
George Armstrong Custer's delight, the community had
fallen into line without excessive pressure, thereby paving
the way for the election of his good friend and faithful scout.
Assuming office with the zeal of a camp-meeting preacher,
Hickok immediately let it be known that the town's random
violence would no longer be tolerated.

Warily, the lawless element drew back, somewhat in
awe of his reputation as a gunfighter. Cautious, but not
overly concerned, they looked on disdainfully as the new
sheriff clamped a lid on the boisterous dives lining Main
Street. Their considered opinion was that Hickok had
bitten off more than he could chew, especially if he happened to turn his back at the wrong moment. Passively,
with the amused detachment of scavengers, they sat back
to await events.

Within a fortnight Hickok grew bored with the unvar-
ied routine of patrolling the town. While he had decreed an
end to rowdyism and lawlessness, the lack of excitement was
more than he had bargained for. Seeking some relief from
the tedium, he once more resumed his chair at the poker
table in Tommy Drum's saloon. Soon gambling again became his main preoccupation, and he limited himself to a
token inspection each evening of the town's gamier honky-
tonks.

But the monotony ended abruptly, shattered by gunfire
in a manner that left the townspeople appalled and gripped
with fear. Within the space of a single month, Hays City's
cold-eyed sheriff killed two men. The first, a local barfly
known as John Mulrey, made the mistake of shooting up
the Lady Gay Saloon. Entering just as Mulrey had emptied
his gun, Hickok calmly shot him above the belt buckle, then
returned to his poker game.

The second killing, if anything, left the town in an even
more pronounced state of shock. Sam Strawhim, an acquaintance from Hickok's scouting days, committed the
unpardonable act of throwing a beer stein at the sheriff.

Enraged, Hickok dusted him on both sides with a chest shot, and left him to die on the floor of Bittle's Saloon.

While both men could have been arrested easily, Hickok had demonstrated that the law was absolute in Hays City and, further, that he would brook not the slightest threat to his position as chief enforcer. Slowly, the town became aware that their vote had loosed the wrath of a Jehovahlike creature within their midst.

But for Mattie the personal impact of the killings was even more devastating. The senseless deaths of Mulrey and Strawhim couldn't be shunted aside as easily as those faceless men Bill had hunted down on the plains. Twice within the last month she had lain awake far into the night. The love she felt for Bill was not easily shaken, for they were bound by something more tenacious than mere lust. And yet she was unable to dispel the thought that the man sleeping so peacefully beside her had casually gunned down two defenseless men in cold blood.

The malevolence she had glimpsed briefly so long ago in Springfield was again exerting its insidious curse on Bill. And this time it had manifested itself in the pitiless death of men who deserved no more than a heavy fine or a night in jail.

Still, he was her man, justified or not, and she would defend him to the last ounce of her strength. But try as she might, Mattie couldn't elude an abhorrent thought. The killings were nothing more than executions, wholly removed from the role of a lawman staking his life against that of a desperate outlaw.

Then, on the morning following Strawhim's death, her revulsion was abruptly replaced by sheer terror. Rumors drifted back to the bordello that there was talk of *retiring* Hays City's overzealous sheriff. Even in her despair, Mattie realized that this was merely the townspeople's quaint way of hinting at outright assassination.

Entering the kitchen shortly after noon, Bill seemed strangely carefree, as if last night's killing had neatly cleansed him of some festering malignancy. Grinning like

a playful wolf, he swatted Mattie on the bottom, then proceeded to devour a gargantuan breakfast of fried eggs, side-
pork, hot biscuits, and apple pie. Lighting a cigar, he shoved
the chair slightly away from the table, rubbing his stomach
with obvious contentment.

Picking at her food, Mattie watched him tensely, waiting for some comment about the hostile mood of the town.
Finally, unable to restrain herself longer in the face of such
cool indifference, she broke the silence.

"Bill, what do you intend doing about the situation here
in town?"

"What situation?" Smiling innocently, he glanced at her
through a thick haze of smoke.

"What situation!" she retorted. "You can't be serious.
Surely you know that the townspeople are up in arms over
what you've done."

"Now, Mattie," he said condescendingly, "just what the
hell is it I've done?"

"Oh, Bill, don't play games with me!" she snapped. "You
know very well you've shot down two men in the last
month."

"So? The bastards were breakin' the law, and they only
got what was comin' to them."

"That's not what they say in town." The words came out
sharper than she intended, but her temper was beginning
to fray.

"Is that so? And just what do them egg-suckers along
Main Street call it?"

"Bill, don't you understand? They're after you. Everyone's saying you've taken the law into your own hands.
That you've become judge, jury, and executioner."

"Bullshit!" The dishes rattled as his fist slammed on the
table. "I'm goddamned if I've ever seen any of them slack-
jawed storekeepers out packin' a gun to keep the peace."

"That's not the point," Mattie said, lowering her voice
in an effort to calm him. "There are only a few merchants
in town and they're mostly neutral. It's the saloonkeepers
and gamblers that mean to get you. They're afraid you're

going to ruin their business by scaring trade away with too much killing."

"Jesus Christ!" Thoroughly amused, he laughed arrogantly. "Are you sayin' that bunch of fat asses is gonna try and gun me down? Why, goddamn, there's not a man in this town that has the guts to pull a gun on me."

"Maybe not. But it doesn't take any guts to shoot a man in the back. And that's exactly what they intend to do. Fitz came to me this morning and said he heard talk all along the street that you were going to be bushwhacked in the dark."

"By Jesus, I wish they would try it. I surely do wish they'd try. It'd give me the chance to clean out a few more of the sonsabitches." Then he grunted, and a contemptuous smile twisted the corners of his mouth. "Don't worry, Mattie, they just ain't got the stomach for it."

"Oh, God, Bill. Sometimes you infuriate me so much I just don't know what to do. Are you just going to walk around like nothing's wrong? Aren't you going to do *something?*"

"Like what?" he demanded. "There's not a damned thing I can do. Except wait and see if one of 'em works up the gall to take a shot at me. Or do you think I ought to saddle up and take off runnin'? If that's the case, then you must think I'm a murderin' sonovabitch just like the rest of them faint hearts uptown."

"No, Bill, it's not that." Lowering her gaze, Mattie stared blankly at the table, afraid he would see too much revealed in her eyes. "It's just that I love you so much, and I'm almost crazy with fear that something's going to happen to you."

"Well, stop your frettin'." Chuckling. he covered her hand with his thorny paw. "The man ain't been born that's big enough to fit Bill Hickok for a box."

Standing at the bar in Tommy Drum's saloon, Fitz slowly sipped a glass of whiskey. He had been nursing the drink over ten minutes for fear his wits would become completely befuddled. *And Mattie wouldn't like that.* Glancing at himself in the mirror, the bemused reflection confirmed that liquor had flowed much too freely for one night.

Couple more and Mr. Thomas Fitzpatrick Mulhaney'll be staggerin' around like a blind dog in a meat shop.

Turning, he leaned against the bar and focused his attention on the card players, trying to forget the glass of whiskey. Fitz had virtually become Hickok's shadow in the last few months, trailing behind him like an out-sized guardian angel. Mattie insisted that he watch Hickok's back and, as usual, Mattie got her way. Still, Hickok resented his presence, and in deference to the gambler's pride Fitz tried to remain in the background as much as possible.

Lately, life had proved a dismal experience for Hickok. It all started the night Captain Tom Custer, the general's younger brother, had gotten drunk and shot up the town. In early October gunfire had ruptured an otherwise peaceful evening. Rushing into the street, Hickok collared the struggling officer and marched him back to the fort. Curiously, the general gave Hickok a severe tongue-lashing. The Custers had done too much for him to warrant such treatment, he declared, adding that the incident would not soon be forgotten. Enraged, the sheriff had stormed out of Custer's quarters and they hadn't spoken since. Afterward, word leaked out that young Tom Custer had sworn to get even for being manhandled in such a humiliating manner.

Less than a month later the regular general elections were held, and Hickok found himself out of a job. True to his word, Custer had withdrawn his support, and the townspeople needed little urging to make it official. Three months of Hickok's brand of justice had been quite enough. Morosely, Hickok boarded the train for Topeka, where he was twice arrested for brawling during a weeklong drunk.

Throughout the winter Mattie watched with unrelieved anxiety as Bill shuttled between Hays City, Topeka, and Kansas City. Gambling for enormous stakes, he sought to forget his humiliation at the polls. But for overbearing men, defeat has a peculiarly bitter taste and Bill's normal arrogance was soon replaced by outright hostility. Like a sheepdog gone bad, he began to see himself as an outcast and those he had once protected now became his prey.

Ever sensitive to his moods, Mattie saw in Bill a growing resentment toward her remarkable success as a madam. Short of closing the house, she could think of no counter-measure that might offset his envy. And on those rare occasions when he suffered heavy gambling losses, their relationship became even more strained. Proud, more aloof than ever, he bitterly resented having to ask her for money, though it was understood from the beginning that half the profits were his without question. Still, there was a stark difference between paramour and pimp, and under the circumstances Bill found it increasingly difficult to make the distinction in his own mind.

Heartsick, aware of the battle he was fighting within, Mattie did her best to indulge Bill's every whim. Blinding herself to his churlish disposition, she strove desperately to restore his wounded vanity and rid him of the hate that now ruled his life. Alarmed that Bill might deliberately provoke violence, she had extracted a promise from Fitz that he would never let the belligerent gambler out of his sight. There were certain factions, as she knew full well, that would welcome the chance of settling old scores. And in Hays City, Bill Hickok could no longer count on the law to back his play.

But the weeks had passed uneventfully, and as Fitz toyed with his glass of whiskey, Mattie relaxed in a rocker on the front porch of the house. Sunday nights, for some reason, seemed to dampen the lust of her customers. Since business had been sparse throughout the evening she decided on a breath of fresh air and had stepped outside after draping a shawl across her shoulders.

She was just on the verge of returning inside when she noticed five soldiers walking slowly down North Main. Something about their quiet, determined manner caused her to remain seated, and as they drew closer she caught her breath.

Etched clearly in the light spilling from Drum's saloon, the firm expression on Tom Custer's face brought Mattie to her feet. Escorted by four raw-boned enlisted men, he covered the last few steps without pause and disappeared through the door of the saloon.

Oh, my God, they're after Bill! And even with Fitz there he won't stand a chance.

Jumping from the porch, she ran along the boardwalk, praying against all odds that she was wrong. Bursting through the saloon door, Mattie saw Bill rise from a poker table just as the four soldiers swarmed over him.

Struggling vainly, Hickok tried to free his arms as one trooper grabbed him from behind while the others began pummeling him about the head. Blood splattered in a crimson fountain as his nose flattened under the rain of blows. Desperately he kicked and heaved, trying to break the vise which bound his arms.

Taken unawares by the suddenness of the attack, Fitz shook his head to clear it of whiskey fumes. Recovering his wits none too soon, he moved across the floor with surprising agility for a man of his bulk. Bellowing with rage, he grabbed one of the troopers by the hair, jerked him around, and drove the man to the floor with a shuddering blow. Reaching into the swirling mass of bodies, his huge hand grasped the shirt collar of a second trooper, whose arm was cocked for another blow at the trapped gambler. Spinning him about, Fitz kicked the man in the groin with all his might. The soldier's scream ended in a sickening crunch as the giant planted a knee squarely in his face.

Terrified by the savagery of Fitz's assault, the soldier holding Hickok released his grip and began scuttling around the table.

Streaming blood, his left eye swollen shut, Hickok lurched against the wall, willing himself to remain on his feet. Instinctively, he reached for the pearl-handled Colt and as the barrel came clear his rage exploded in a sheet of flame.

Backing away from Fitz, the two troopers were abruptly

knocked spinning as the Colt roared twice. Slammed to the floor like broken dolls, they lay motionless as a dense cloud of gunsmoke drifted across the saloon. Stumbling forward, Hickok braced himself against the table and raised his pistol for the finishing shot. Alive or dead, he meant to make certain that the troopers would never again regain their feet. But waves of darkness suddenly obscured his vision and he dropped to his knees, then fell face down on the floor.

Captain Tom Custer had watched with mounting horror as Hickok and Fitz decimated the ranks of his raiding party. When Hickok collapsed to the floor, Custer reached for his gun, now obsessed with an insane need to kill the gambler.

But Custer's murderous intent had not gone unnoticed. Grabbing a whiskey bottle from the table beside her, Mattie closed the gap in a single bound and splattered it against the back of his head. Amidst a shower of glass and blood, Custer slumped to the floor like a poled ox.

Dumbfounded, Fitz stared in mute wonder at the carnage about him. Somehow he still hadn't comprehended that the two troopers had fallen victim to Hickok's gun. Suddenly Mattie was standing before him, slapping awareness into his brain, ordering the bewildered giant to take Hickok back to the house immediately. Lifting the gambler as he would a battered child, Fitz wordlessly followed Mattie onto the street.

Within the hour Hickok had recovered sufficiently to realize the gravity of their situation. Mattie and Fitz were safe enough since they had done nothing more than come to his aid after an unprovoked attack. But his own safety was another matter entirely. After shooting unarmed soldiers it was a safe bet that retribution by the military would be swift and final. Sitting on the side of the bed, his mind raced in circles as Mattie gently swabbed his bruised face. His options were limited and the only move that made any sense was to put distance between himself and the fort. The decision made, he glanced up at Fitz, who was standing in the doorway casually inspecting his skinned knuckles.

"Fitz, you old sonovabitch. I think you just might have

saved my hide tonight." Smiling, he winced as his lips cracked. "Now, do me one last favor before we end up fightin' the whole goddamn Seventh Cavalry. Run over to the livery stable and get my black mare saddled. And for Christ's sake, make it fast."

Nodding soberly, Fitz stepped into the hall and lumbered off toward the stable.

"Oh, Bill." Mattie groaned and slumped against his shoulder. "What are we going to do?"

"You ain't gonna do nothin'." Caressing her hair, he lifted her chin after a moment. "You'll stay right here and smile pretty when they come lookin' for me. After that sell the house for whatever you can raise and then get on the train and meet me in Abilene."

"Abilene? What in God's name is Abilene?"

"It's a railhead about a hundred miles east of here on the Smoky Hill. Word's around that it's the biggest goddamn boomtown Kansas has ever seen. The Texans are drivin' thousands of cattle in every day to ship 'em back East. And if I know anything about Texas drovers there's only one thing they like better'n whiskey. Give you any ideas?"

"What you're trying to tell me, lover," she smiled knowingly, "is to bring the girls and Fitz."

"And when you get there I'll have the finest little parlor house you ever seen, all ready and waitin'. Now, lemme have a big hug before that grizzly bear of yours gets back with my horse."

CHAPTER FOUR

Smoke and cinders floated back over the coaches as the train rattled eastward across the rolling plains. Occasionally, a small hill or a clump of trees came into view, but for the most part the landscape seemed utterly desolate. Seated next to a window, Mattie stared out as if mesmerized by this boundless, hostile land. Though it was only early April the prairie already simmered with heat, and the air rushing through the open windows was permeated with specks of soot.

Absorbed in her own thoughts, Mattie ignored the giggling chatter of the girls. The distasteful business of Hays City was finished at last, and her mind ranged ahead to Abilene. It was a new town, born overnight to meet the demands of a beef-hungry nation. And from all she had heard it was the richest town on the plains. Just the place for a fresh start, both for herself and Bill. With a parlor house they would make out just fine, and all the heartache and killing of Hays would become a dim memory.

While thoroughly accustomed to the frontier by now, she had experienced enough bloodshed to last a lifetime. After the horror of Hays City, the uppermost thought in her mind was to devise some way of preventing Bill from courting danger so recklessly. Gambling would hold his attention for a time, but she knew that eventually he would grow restless and set off in pursuit of some greater hazard. Curiously, it was almost as if he were driven to stare death squarely in the face, and in so doing register his contempt for the fate that other men feared the most. Fretting over the problem, her speculation had hardened into solid resolve. But she still didn't know how she was going to overcome his preoccupation with danger.

Life seemed so grand except for the constant fear that Bill would one night push fate beyond reasonable limits. Operating a parlor house was everything she had hoped for, and more. Often it almost seemed that she had her own family, as though she were the mother to a bevy of squealing, immature young girls who were dependent on her for strength and guidance. Strangely she welcomed the emotional demands of her insecure and ofttimes frightened young charges, and gave of herself unsparingly.

Lately Mattie realized that she had even developed a strong moral obligation toward the welfare of her girls. While she had never sold her own body, she had witnessed the loss of self-esteem which gnawed on the vitals of any girl on the line. And being there, seeing it happen before her eyes, she knew that the stigma visited by society on whores was as nothing compared to the mental torture which the girls inflicted on themselves.

Some frontier wit had recently coined a homespun euphemism that the newspapers gleefully adopted, and everyone now referred to whores as soiled doves. But the humor escaped Mattie, for she somehow saw each of the girls as defenseless, fragile little birds, harmless, gentle sparrows who had been defiled and corrupted before they could learn to fly.

Sometimes, Mattie wondered if her concern for the girls stemmed from a buried sense of guilt at having provided the means of their downfall. *But was she really to blame? Or were some girls just born to be whores, no matter what?*

If they hadn't become boarders in her house, they would almost certainly have fallen under the influence of another madam. And more than likely one who wasn't nearly so concerned for their well-being. Still, the doubt lingered on.

The greatest uncertainty came when she found it necessary to replace one of the girls. Generally it was caused by fading beauty or an emotional burden that could no longer withstand the daily hammering of a brothel. When no other choice remained, Mattie would prepare the girl for the trip back East, doing her utmost to relieve the anxiety, and sometimes outright fear, of returning to a former life. But the emotional drain was frightening, for it was as if a member of her own family were being cast out, exiled as she herself had once been.

Such incidents were not easily forgotten, and no matter how she drilled her mind to think of other things there was always an abiding sense of personal loss.

Afterward, she would wire Lou Blomger, who was now a kingpin in the Springfield rackets. Before long a bright-eyed young thing he had recruited would step off the train and knock expectantly on her door. Then all the uncertainty and self-recrimination would disappear in the rush of welcoming a newcomer to the family. Sometimes, in solitary reflection late at night, she thought it was like finding a newborn babe on one's doorstep. Where it came from, or what road it had traveled in getting here, was unimportant. What mattered was that it had somehow found its way to the *right* doorstep, and through it the family would survive.

Suddenly, Mattie's thoughts were jarred back to the present as the train began slowing. Glancing out the window she observed a large hotel near the station, and a sprawling hodgepodge of buildings in the distance. Then the train lurched to a halt before the depot and a crowd edged toward the passenger cars. As Fitz assisted the girls down the steps, Mattie heard an appreciative murmur from the gang of men around the train and a delightful tingle swept through her body. *They really are my family. And by God, I'll bet I'm prouder of them than their own mothers ever were!*

"Mattie! Mattie!"

Alighting from the train, she caught sight of Bill shouldering his way through the crowd. Running forward, she threw herself into his arms. "Oh, you no-account gambler, I thought I'd die before this infernal train could get here."

Squeezing her, he grinned in the crooked way she remembered so well. "Good, 'cause tonight you're gonna get plenty of chance to prove just how much you missed me. Or are you out of practice?"

"Maybe out of practice, lover," she teased, "but plenty willing. So watch yourself."

"Christ on a crutch! You're somethin', ain't you. Listen, you little fire-eater, if you mean to tame this child you got a long night's work ahead of you."

"My, how you brag, gamblin' man." Laughing, she kissed him again. "Why don't you stop bellowing and show me where all this merriment is going to take place."

"By God, you're right! Time's awastin'." Glancing around, he waved to Mattie's retinue, now completely encircled by grinning, raw-boned men. "Fitz! Gather them girls up and bring 'em along. And if any of them drovers try to get a pinch for free you bust their goddamn heads!"

Ignoring a moan from the crowd, he grabbed Mattie's arm and began walking down Texas Street at a fast clip. Turning onto First Street, the town's main thoroughfare, he pointed out various business establishments and described the horde of trail hands that took over the town every night. Mattie stopped counting when she realized that the dance-halls, saloons, and gambling dives far outnumbered those in Hays City.

Her impression was that every storefront in town was dedicated to separating the Texans from their money, and later she would discover she wasn't far from wrong. With the exception of two hotels, a mercantile emporium, and one bank, the entire business community of Abilene was devoted to either avarice or lust.

As the procession moved along First Street more and more men began leaving the dives to join the trailing crowd.

Shouting and laughing, they ogled the flirtatious young girls, filling the air with suggestive remarks. Bringing up the rear, Fitz was hard-pressed to keep the drovers from rushing in and mingling with the girls. But an occasional scowl from the burly watchdog forced them to back off a few paces.

Abruptly, Bill halted before a pleasant frame house with a covered front porch. Unlike any of the surrounding buildings, it was set back off the street and bordered by a low picket fence. But its most striking feature was that the house had been painted a lurid shade of yellow.

Staring at it in bewilderment, Mattie was almost afraid to ask the obvious question. The throng of trail hands crowded closer, watching her face expectantly. Glancing at Bill, she offered a silent prayer that it was only his crude idea of a joke. Smiling weakly, she waited, hoping they would once more resume their walk up First Street.

"Mattie, I had it built specially for you." Looking around the crowd, Bill's eyes lighted with pride. "There ain't nothin' else like it in Abilene!"

"No, I'm sure there isn't." Darting a baleful glance at the gaudy structure, she searched desperately for something further to say.

"Mattie, what the hell's the matter?" Bill lowered his voice almost to a whisper as the drovers edged closer, straining to catch every word. "Don't you like it?"

"Oh, Bill. How could you?" She shuddered slightly as the house glared back at her. "Yellow. And such an offensive shade, too."

"So! You don't like it!" Facing their enthralled audience, he fairly bristled with mock indignation. Certain the story would be retold in every town, he was determined not to come off the fool. "Ain't that just like a woman? You break your ass to please 'em and no matter what you do it ain't enough!"

"Bill, please don't get mad," she pleaded. "I love the house! It's just that it's so . . . yellow."

"Don't let him throw you, lady!" one of the Texans yelled

from the edge of the crowd. "We like it, and the mercantile store is already callin' that color their whorehouse yellow. Ain't that right, boys?"

The Texans roared good-naturedly, thoroughly delighted with the obvious consternation of the famed Yankee gun-fighter.

"Shut your goddamn mouth." Hickok jabbed his finger at the man who had spoken, then glared around the crowd. "This here's a private conversation, and you cow prodders'd do well not to butt in."

Flushed with anger, he turned to find Mattie staring at a small frame structure across the street. Noting the curious expression on her face, he stated matter of factly, "That's the local schoolhouse."

"*Schoolhouse!* My God, Bill, how could you build a brothel right across the street from a school?" Shaking her head wearily, Mattie opened the fence gate and stepped through, motioning to her soiled doves. "C'mon, girls. We might as well take a look before the town fathers hustle us out on the next train."

Mattie had an ominous feeling about this meeting. The town mayor couldn't afford to be linked with a madam, and he certainly wouldn't call her in for social chitchat. So that left only official business, and she didn't like the smell of that at all. Something was in the wind, and intuitively she knew it had nothing to do with good will and brotherhood. Live and let live might be all right for most folks, but where madams and mayors were concerned it seldom reared its head.

While she had never met Joseph McCoy she knew his life history, as did everyone in Abilene. He was the town's most illustrious citizen, respected by all and feared by more than a few. Except for him there wouldn't have been an Abilene, not to mention the gold on the hoof the Texans kept driving up the Chisholm Trail. McCoy's vision and bulldog determination were responsible for the Kansas Pacific laying track to the exact center of nowhere. Only then did a town spring from the plains and make ready to greet the thousands of Longhorns plodding northward. Whatever Abilene was, Joseph McCoy had created it out of sweat and sheer audacity. And to no one's surprise, he held a mortgage on the land and most of the souls within the city limits of the West's richest cow-town.

Only three years ago, McCoy had been a down-at-the-heels promoter, living from one windfall to the next. But he had a dream, and more importantly, the brass to make men of influence sit up and listen. Texas was beef rich and money poor, a situation tailor-made for men weaned on the calculated risk. If nothing else, McCoy was a supreme gambler, especially with other people's money. Very simply he proposed to exchange Northern currency for Southern beef. The fact that a railhead didn't exist, or that Texas cattlemen had never heard of Joseph McCoy, deterred him not in the least. Unfazed by such trivialities, he blithely proceeded to lay the foundation of an enterprise which would alter both the character of the West and the men who ruled it.

After a whirlwind courtship of the Kansas Pacific, he rode west along the Smoky Hill River, searching for the spot to found his empire. Topping a slight rise ten miles east of where the Smoky Hill joined the Solomon, he brought his horse to a halt. Spread before him was a broad, rolling prairie, sloping gently toward the timbered bottom land along the river. Limestone bluffs jutted sharply above the opposite bank, rising gradually to blend once more with the distant plains. Over the vast expanse to his front lay a sea of Buffalo grass, broken only by the sluggish waters of Mud Creek emptying into the river below.

Water, boundless stretches of prairie, well situated to the Chisholm Trail. Everything a man needed to entice both the cattlemen and the Kansas Pacific across the hundreds of miles of wilderness separating them from his dream. Confident that he had struck the mother lode, McCoy promptly bought two hundred and fifty acres from the startled villagers of Abilene. This was where he would build his city on the plains. And build it he did.

Since receiving the mayor's summons that morning,

these thoughts and more had been running through Mattie's
head. While the message was politely worded and seemed
casual in tone, it left no doubt that *the* Joseph G. McCoy
wished to see her that very day.

Bill had been skeptical about the whole matter, bluntly
disputing McCoy's right to summon Mattie as though he
were some sort of tin god. At first, he insisted on escorting
her to the meeting, but in his frame of mind she could vi-
sualize where that would lead without even trying. Gently,
she dissuaded him from tagging along, promising that if she
needed help he would hear her yell all the way across town.

But as she climbed the stairs to McCoy's office, her confidence waned slightly, and she found herself wishing that
she hadn't been so hasty in declining Bill's offer. Drawing
a deep breath, she knocked on the door and drew an
unintelligible volley of words in response. Opening the
door, she stepped inside and found herself under the scrutiny of a very small man seated behind a very large desk.

While she knew nothing of men and their complexes, she
had learned that little men often have angry, overbearing
dispositions. The fierce brittle eyes that bored into her now
seemed to fit the mold perfectly, sliding over her as a wary
shopper would gauge a suspect piece of meat. And she had
a sinking feeling that this meeting was already headed on
a downhill course.

"Well, come in, Miss Silks. You are Mattie Silks, aren't
you?"

Mattie nodded, taking the chair he indicated. She was
fascinated by his voice, which was something on the order
of a tiny growl. It was almost as if a Pekingese lap dog were
trying to imitate the gruff roar of a bull mastiff. Absorbed
in the comparison, she had forgotten to speak.

"Come now, am I so frightening?" His mouth quirked
in a small, superior smile, and Mattie sensed that he wanted
to intimidate her. "Or has the cat got your tongue?"

"Neither, Mr. McCoy. It's just that I had never seen you
before and I was curious about the man that built Abilene."

McCoy's smile froze and his eyes were hooded as he

inspected her, much like a snake sizes up a victim to see if it's worth the effort. *She's pretty all right, just like everyone says. And probably smart, too. Or maybe just cunning. In her business a woman has to have an instinct for the jugular just to survive. But then, the smart ones are always the easiest. Figure they've got sex working for them, and bank on anything in pants being fool enough to fall for it.*

Joseph McCoy was neither a fool nor a man ruled by the capricious whims of lust. Empires were his game, and at the moment there was every likelihood that his newly won kingdom was about to explode beneath his feet. Lately his problems seemed to compound, one atop the other and, curiously, this woman appeared to be at the root of his two most serious threats.

But he couldn't afford to offend her, not just yet at any rate. In the last year he had lost two marshals, one run out of town and the other murdered. Staring straight down his throat was another cattle season, with a thousand unruly Texans already headed north. And Abilene was defenseless, stripped of law enforcement like a freshly plucked chicken. Distasteful as the thought might be, Bill Hickok seemed the only man capable of containing the trail hands' destructive urges. But Mattie Silks was his woman, and if in offending her he also alienated Hickok then his little sandcastle stood every chance of being toppled into the Smoky Hill and washed away like so much sludge.

"See anything you like, Mr. Mayor? Or are you just window-shopping?"

Startled, McCoy realized he had been staring at Mattie for some moments. Shifting gears with the mental agility of a born hustler, he directed his attention to the more immediate problem.

"Sorry. Sometimes I get carried away with the trials and tribulations of being a small-town mayor." Hitching forward in his chair, he made a vain attempt at smiling sincerely. "Which brings me to the reason for our little chat. No doubt you've heard of the Women's Christian League. And I'm sure you're aware of their crusade to rid Abilene of all vice. Gambling, alcohol and . . . ah . . ."

"Whores." Mattie threw the word back in his teeth, suddenly taking an intense dislike to this little man.

"Yes, that's right. Although I did have a more charitable word in mind. But my point is this, Miss Silks. The citizens of Abilene, as you have reason to know, are not what one might term moralistic in their views. Quite the contrary. Thus the Women's League needed an issue to arouse the public, and I regret to say you have given them one."

"Me?" Mattie couldn't have been more surprised if he had spit on her. "What have I done? I've only been here a week."

"True. But a week has been long enough it would seem." Mistaking her shock for fear, McCoy's confidence swelled. This might work out all right after all. "The issue I refer to, Miss Silks, is your house. Or more precisely, its location across the street from our local school. As you can appreciate, the Women's League feels this is having an adverse effect on the children."

"Well, I can't dispute—" Mattie had been about to agree, but McCoy overplayed his hand.

"Then, too, there is the question of color."

"Color?" Her tone was no longer shocked, or agreeable.

"Uh, yes." The change in her manner had not gone unnoticed and McCoy's eyes again hooded. "The Women's League called on me yesterday to lodge a formal request that your house be moved to a more suitable location. I'm sorry to say they also demanded that the color be changed to a less offensive shade."

"Demanded, did they?" Mattie's cheeks flushed, and her eyes crackled with anger. "And just who the hell are those old biddies to demand anything of me?"

"Please, Miss Silks. They're only doing what they think best for the community."

"Mayor, this town charges me an outrageous fee to operate a sporting house, and I haven't heard of anyone from the Women's League complaining about my dirty money.

Not on your life! If it wasn't for me, they'd be paying taxes. And they know it."

"But I repeat, we have to do what's best for the community."

"Oh, screw the community! They're nothing but a bunch of sanctimonious old hypocrites. And little men like you, Mr. McCoy, make me sick to my stomach. Always so quick to judge, but you're not above sharing in the loot."

Rising, Mattie stuck her nose in the air and marched toward the door. Turning at the last moment, she leveled a withering glare at McCoy. "Mr. Mayor, you can tell the Women's League you've seen me and my answer is no. And if they don't like it they can parade down there and I'll shove that yellow house down their throats, splinter by splinter."

Spinning on her heel, she slammed the door.

Joseph McCoy rubbed his forehead and wondered where he had gone wrong. For a moment there, he thought he had her number. But just when he was ready to nail her to the wall everything went to hell. Some days a man just shouldn't build empires. He ought to get drunk, or go fishing. But that wouldn't solve anything. He'd still be faced with the Texans on one hand and the Women's League on the other. And at the moment he was damned if he knew which one unnerved him the most.

Walking along First Street, Mattie purposely slowed her pace, breathing deeply in an effort to regain her composure. Wondering if anyone had noticed her flushed face, she tilted the parasol slightly, and tried to drive all thought of Jake Karatofsky from her mind. But it was easier said than done.

It had all started that morning when the cook returned from shopping at Karatofsky's Mercantile. The store tendered bills on the first of each month, and when Mattie opened her statement she was flabbergasted. Staring at the scrawled figures, she was shocked beyond words for a moment.

Kathy, one of her most reliable girls, had managed to charge over three hundred dollars in less than a month.

Instantly, Mattie's thoughts had turned to the handsome young Texan with whom Kathy was currently spending all her free time. From the size of the bill it was clear the girl had somehow converted him from trail hand to pimp.

Mattie didn't even need to ask how it had happened. The boy had bedded Kathy his first night in town and shortly afterward probably lost all his money in some crooked gambling dive. Broke and reluctant to end his stay in Abilene so quickly, the Texan was susceptible to Kathy's arguments. Soon he found himself in the not unpleasant position of being a kept man. Kathy, of course, only wanted someone to cuddle and love, much as a little girl lavishes affection on a doll. The fact that the boy still retained some vestige of gentleness simply made him all the more desirable.

When Mattie confronted Kathy with the bill, her suspicions were confirmed immediately. Bursting into tears, the girl sobbed that the only way she could be sure of keeping the boy in Abilene was to support him. Even then there was always the uncertainty that she would awaken one morning to find he had headed back down the trail for Texas. Unspoken, but silently understood by both women, was the fact that all cowtown whores bore the same cross. Men stuck with whores only as long as they were supported in a style far grander than any they had known before.

Presently, it came clear that Kathy had left nothing to chance. She was supplying him with gambling money, paying his bill at the Drover's Cottage, and even outfitted him in a complete wardrobe at Karatofsky's Store. But the crowning blow was when she admitted charging his new saddle on the store account.

Incensed, yet half-sympathetic, Mattie secured a promise that the affair would end that very day. Thoroughly chastised, Kathy was well aware that failure to keep the promise would result in her being escorted to the first train headed East. Storming from the house, Mattie wondered why the girls never seemed to learn that such men would only desert them once their money was gone.

Still fuming, she proceeded to the store and braced

Karatofsky. Why, she demanded, had he allowed the girl to charge anything but personal items? *Especially a saddle?*

Affronted by her tone, Karatofsky flew into a snit, lamenting the hazards of doing business with whores. The argument rapidly turned into a shouting match, and Mattie lost her temper completely, directing some unladylike remarks at the storekeeper. Unnerved, he ordered her from the store, screaming in a shrill, gibbering voice.

Muttering allusions to his ancestry, Mattie left Karatofsky talking to himself and rushed out. Just as she reached the doorway the storekeeper fired a parting salvo. *She could take her trade elsewhere until she learned how to speak with a civil tongue!*

Crossing Cedar Street, she hurried past the saloons and gambling dens along First. Oblivious to the stares of the sidewalk loafers, she wanted only to reach the sanctuary of her house. Mentally, she continued to curse Karatofsky, eviscerating his very soul. *Pot-bellied little bastard! All that shouting was just for the benefit of those self-righteous old crones standing around watching. He knew the Women's League would spread it all over town how the upstanding merchant threw the wicked madam out of his store. Wonder what they'd think if they knew that horse's ass was soaking me an extra twenty percent for a charge account? Oh, hell, I've got enough trouble without starting another feud.*

Turning in at the gate, Mattie was once again struck by the offensive yellow hue of the house, and its pervasive tones somehow reminded her of Bill. *Jesus, as if I didn't have enough to worry about, now I have to spend my days wondering if he's slipping it to Jessie when my back's turned.*

Suddenly, the weight of her problems simply seemed too great, and she sank down in a rocker on the porch to ponder her overburdened life. *Spendthrift whores with greedy pimps, McCoy and his Women's League, merchants who insult you for no reason. And Bill wearing that damned badge again! God, it's just too much, too damned much. And for what? This glaring monstrosity of a house and a man I'm not even sure I can trust anymore. Goddamn Bill*

Hickok, anyway. If he's balling Jessie I'll . . . I'll shoot him!
No, I couldn't do that. But I could sure as hell shoot her!

Less than a fortnight past, Lou Blomger had sent Mattie
a replacement for a girl who had been sacked and shipped
East. The new girl, Jessie Hazel, was easily the most beautiful of all the soiled doves who had worked for Mattie over
the years. Tall and regal in appearance, the sheen of her
raven hair framed a delicate face and striking violet eyes.
Overnight she became the most popular girl in the house.
Within a week the stunning young harlot had created a
legend among the Texans, one that would endure long after
the fame of Abilene had withered.

Still, Mattie was suspicious of the girl from the start.
Why would anyone so lovely, and with an obvious note of
gentility about her, come West? Such a girl could make a
fortune in the eastern cities, and she was decidedly a cut
above the girls Blomger usually selected for the cowtowns.
Was she running from something? Or just a troublemaker
that other madams had blackballed? Mattie knew from
bitter experience that there were girls like that. Vain, obsessed with their own beauty, driven to play the role of seductress with every man they met. And they always caused
trouble with the other girls.

Mattie had a bad feeling about this one, a premonition
that an ill wind had just swept in from the East and settled
over Abilene.

But the Texans, as it developed, weren't the only ones
susceptible to a pretty face. After a few days it dawned on
Mattie that Bill somehow managed to be in the parlor or
kitchen whenever Jessie was present. Once she even surprised them conversing in hushed tones while seated in
rockers on the porch. Yet her suspicions were aroused to the
fullest by a very simple, and seemingly innocent, occur-
rence.

Bill's taciturn manner had curiously given way to bursts
of witty small talk, and these spells seemed to come over
him most whenever Jessie just happened to enter a room.
Observing his droll performance, Mattie had the feeling she

was watching a battle-scarred rooster trying to imitate a strutting peacock. Never before had the imperious gunfighter groomed himself so carefully, or stooped to enter conversations of such utter banality. But if he fooled anyone, it was only himself.

While Mattie never openly reproached him, she remained fairly sure that his overtures hadn't progressed beyond mere flirting. And yet she wasn't certain.

Then, on April 15, Bill was appointed city marshal, and things started coming apart at the seams. After accepting Mayor McCoy's offer he had returned to the house in a state of boyish exuberance. Bursting with pride, he fully expected Mattie to share his elation. But this time she left no doubts as she unleashed a vicious tongue-lashing, born in equal parts of frustration and fear.

Shouting and cursing, they bitterly assailed one another, dredging up long-forgotten incidents and petty grudges. Finally, Bill stalked from the house in a towering rage. By morning their anger had cooled somewhat, and things seemingly returned to normal. But in the light of later events, Mattie often looked back and wondered if her bitter accusations that day hadn't been the final straw.

Over the next two weeks Bill slowly grew less attentive, and not nearly so demanding in bed. Mattie often lay awake in the night, wondering if he actually was out patrolling the town. *Or was he in bed with Jessie right at that moment? There was a back window, and these days she wouldn't put anything past the sorry bastard.*

Unable to summon the courage to walk down the hall and resolve her suspicions, she tossed fretfully night after night, consumed with fear and jealousy. What lay behind that door might be more than she could bear, something she would regret having seen.

And the doubt was slowly driving her mad.

Hickok's eyes roved the street from one end to the other as he leaned against the wall in front of the Bull's Head Saloon. Drunk and full of devilment, little knots of Texans crowded the boardwalk as they stumbled from one dive to the next. Attired in a black frock coat, red sash, and low-crowned hat, the marshal's frown touched on every movement of the trail hands, much the same as a sullen old bull gazing about his domain. There were some who even thought he resembled the Longhorn on a sign hanging over the Bull's Head door. But they didn't say it.

The saloon was owned by Ben Thompson and Phil Coe, a shifty pair who had arrived from Texas that spring. Thompson, in addition to being a gambler, was a gunman of some reputation and most men walked lightly in his presence. Coe towered over his squat partner, and was noted as a barroom brawler. He seldom carried a gun, preferring to settle arguments with his fists, and it was rumored that he had once stomped a man to death. While they were believed to be cardsharps, it hadn't been proved and as yet no one had been foolish enough to accuse them outright.

Upon opening the saloon, they had hung a sign over the front door displaying a huge Longhorn. But this was no ordinary, garden-variety mossyback, for it quickly became apparent that the bull was endowed with extraordinary masculinity. The Texans thought it was a real gut buster. But the sign created a furor among the townspeople, and that afternoon Mayor McCoy had received another delegation from the Women's League. The ladies failed to see the humor, terming it an obscene exhibition.

Caught in the middle again, McCoy ordered Hickok to resolve the matter by nightfall. When the marshal approached Coe and Thompson, they absolutely refused to alter the sign. It was already drawing large crowds and as far as they were concerned, it could hang there till doomsday. Summoning a sign painter, Hickok stood guard while the bull's remarkable assets were blacked out with a few strokes of the brush.

But with sunrise Wild Bill Hickok found himself the laughingstock of Abilene. Traced in the early morning rays, the bull's undercarriage was even more pronounced in black than it had been originally. Hickok had never been one to appreciate a joke on himself, and he made no secret of his resentment toward the saloon owners. Thompson and Coe openly branded the marshal a bad sport, and what began as a simple joke slowly ripened into mutual hostility. Everyone in town sensed a showdown brewing, and the local gamblers surprised no one by making Hickok the odds-on favorite.

Each night the marshal posted himself in front of the Bull's Head in the hope it would discourage business. But tonight his presence seemed to have no effect, and he finally grew bored with the whole idea. Shoving away from the wall, he crossed the street and began his mid-evening tour of the town. The dives were swarming with Texans, somewhat like an antbed gone mad. Recently, the newspapers had started referring to the drovers as cowboys. While no one was sure of its origin, the Texans bristled at such a sissified term. Used even in jest, it was a surefire way to start a brawl.

Watching them tossing their money away on saloon girls and crooked games, Hickok shook his head in disgust. No matter what they were called, Texans were still the most addlebrained breed he had ever run across.

Every saloon and dancehall along the street shook to the rafters with the strident chords of brass bands and rinky-dink pianos. Smiling brightly, hard-eyed girls in gaudy dresses enticed the trail hands through the doors, where a quarter bought a slug of watered whiskey, or a wild whirl around the dance floor.

Caterwauling at the top of their lungs, the Texans clomped and stomped as the music blared amidst a swirl of jangling spurs and painted women. While the cowboys downed prodigious amounts of their favorite rotgut or popskull, there was rarely a fight that couldn't be handled by the unsmiling bouncers. Gunplay was also rare, and strangely enough, throughout the entire summer the only shootings had been among the Texans themselves. Drunk or sober, they knew who would come looking for them if they perforated an Abilene resident.

And there wasn't a man among them eager to butt heads with Wild Bill Hickok.

The marshal was rather pleased with himself on this uneventful July evening. The Texans remained a bit in awe of his reputation, and with the season half-over he was finding it easier to police Abilene than he had expected. Though the lack of action grew boring at times, the job was not without its compensations. With three deputies to patrol the streets he was afforded ample time for other diversions, and lately he had been busier than a man with the trots.

What with a nightly poker game in the Alamo, and a token appearance on the streets from time to time, his evenings were pretty well shot. But shortly after midnight, things really got hectic.

Like the cat that crept in, crapped, and crept out, he would soundlessly sneak in the back window of the yellow parlor house for a short tussle with the jasmine-scented Jessie Hazel.

Hickok seldom felt even a twinge of conscience over these whispered moments with Jessie. He was a man of varied tastes, with a lusty appetite for women, and he hadn't been faithful to Mattie since their first year in Springfield. What she didn't know wouldn't hurt her, he reasoned, and if a man stood off and looked at it just right she was to blame, anyway. After all, she was the one who brought the girl into the house in the first place, and only a fool would tempt a man with a little sugartit like Jessie. Besides, Mattie was getting too damned possessive lately anyhow. A man had to have room to paw dirt, and sniff fresh meat every now and then. More than anybody, a whorehouse madam ought to know a woman can't snub a man up too short. Not unless she wants her ass kicked.

Standing in the shadows in front of the mercantile, Hickok stiffened as Phil Coe approached the corner of Cedar Street. Only a matter of some urgency could force the Texan to leave his gambling dive in the middle of the evening. Walking rapidly, Coe turned the corner, then proceeded up First Street. There was something here that didn't meet the eye.

Curiosity aroused, Hickok stuck to the shadows and trailed a short distance behind him. Then he halted abruptly, cursing under his breath as he watched the gambler enter the gate and mount the steps to the yellow parlor house.

Coe was one of Jessie Hazel's regulars, appearing like clockwork before the rush started each evening. But a call so late at night was out of character and therefore suspect. While the thought of Jessie in bed with Coe was galling, Hickok had held his peace until now. Mattie was entitled to her pride, even if she was a pain in the ass, and unless forced to it, he didn't want to hurt her. Still, some sixth sense warned him that Coe's presence here tonight was out of the ordinary. Rankled, but unable to fathom the gambler's purpose, he hurried toward the house.

Mattie and Phil Coe were standing in the hall when Hickok burst through the door. Glancing toward the parlor, he caught a glimpse of Jessie seated demurely on the edge of a chair, a bulging valise beside her on the floor. Startled, Mattie opened her mouth to speak, but her throat suddenly seemed very dry.

"What the hell's going on here?" Hickok demanded.

"Bill, I . . ." Mattie's voice faltered.

"Hickok, I've come to get Jessie," said Coe coolly. "And Mattie's agreeable to it so you've no need to be concerned."

"Get Jessie? What kinda goddamn game are you playin', Coe?"

"No game, Marshal." He smiled, clearly relishing the moment. "Jessie's gonna move in with me, that's all. She's willing and I agreed to compensate Mattie handsomely, so you got no call to bother yourself about it."

"Horseshit!" Hickok fixed Mattie with a withering stare. "Appears you ain't above sellin' a girl's soul as well as her body."

"Bill, I just want her out of here." Mattie's voice was weary and subdued. "I just can't take any more, so please don't make trouble."

"Well, ain't that a goddamn shame." Mocking her, he ignored the insinuation. Turning to the gambler, Hickok's eyes went cold and pale. "Coe, you're pushin' your luck. But it's your ass. Bet or check."

"I'm not armed," Coe said, spreading his coat wide. "And I don't think you'll gun me down in front of witnesses."

"Maybe not," Hickok snapped. "But I'll sure as Christ make you wish you'd been shot."

Jerking the Colts from his sash, Hickok turned and tossed them on a chair next to the wall. He rashly overlooked something that was chillingly clear to Mattie. The Texan had him bested by four inches in height and at least thirty pounds of lean muscle. Though skilled with guns, the marshal wasn't much of a rough-and-tumble fighter. His first mistake had been in chucking the Colts. The second was in turning his back on Phil Coe.

As he turned, Coe caught the lawman with a smashing blow just below the ear. Hickok crashed into the door, shattering the framed panel of glass, then dropped to his knees. Like a lobo scenting fresh blood, Coe stepped in to deliver the final blow. Hurt, but still game, the marshal tried to rise, bracing himself against the wall with one hand. Sensing his utter helplessness, Mattie screamed and threw herself around Coe's neck. Amused by the gesture, the powerful Texan laughed and slung her across the hall.

Grabbing a handful of hair, Coe jerked Hickok's head back and brutally drove his fist into the lawman's jaw. Hickok sagged, falling forward, but Coe had waited too long to have it end so quickly. Clutching the gunfighter's head in both hands, he wrenched it upward. Holding it steady, he lifted his knee with savage force into Hickok's face. Soundlessly, the marshal crumpled like a bloody rag, his face a jellied mass. But Coe wasn't satisfied yet. His blood lust had risen now, and he lifted his boot to stomp the defenseless lawman.

Suddenly, the parlor door filled with Fitz's hulking frame. Summoned by the sound of breaking glass, he stood motionless for a moment, dimly attempting to gauge the scene before him. Observing Mattie's disheveled condition, his nostrils flared with brutish anger. Then a roar escaped his throat as the impact of Coe's boot brought a sickening groan from Hickok.

"Fitz!" Mattie screamed, like someone unchaining a vicious dog. "Get him, Fitz! Get him!"

Coe glanced over his shoulder, and any thought of the prostrate marshal suddenly departed his mind. With cold fury, Fitz was advancing toward him. Whirling, Coe shifted uneasily from side to side, measuring the distance for a groin kick. If he failed, he was finished, for the tables had now turned.

Snarling, Fitz leaped in before the gambler could move, consumed with sheer animal rage for the man who had dared to harm his mistress. Grasping Coe's shirtfront, he lifted the gambler as effortlessly as a rag doll and held him aloft with one hand. Pinned in a corner, the Texan struggled desperately to break free. Methodically, like a sledge thumping against a melon, the burly giant's fist splattered into Coe's face again and again. Each blow landed with a mushy crunch, and the gambler's features dissolved beneath a pulpy blotch.

Fitz slowly became aware of Mattie tugging at his arm, screaming that he must stop before the Texan was killed. Releasing Coe, he watched impassively as the battered form slid to the floor, shoulders wedged in the corner.

Though brutally mangled, the saloon owner was still half-conscious. As Mattie began working to revive Hickok, he jammed his arms against the walls, pushing himself erect inch by inch. Standing once more, he stared venomously into Fitz's hard, pitiless eyes. Clearly, the ham-fisted giant would like nothing better than a command from Mattie to finish him off.

"Don't worry, horse," the gambler croaked. "You'll get another chance. And I guaran-goddamn-tee they'll cart you away in a box next time."

"Fitz!" Mattie's order stopped him just as he reached for the Texan again. "Get that sonovabitch out of here, but don't beat him anymore. And send his whore packing with him!"

Motioning Jessie Hazel into the hall, Fitz opened the shattered door and stood aside as the young girl eased past him in a state of shock. Turning, he grabbed Coe by the coat lapels and jerked him out of a corner. Contemptuously, he flung the Texan through the doorway like a rumpled sack of oats. Stumbling across the porch, the gambler plowed into Jessie and spun about, his face contorted with rage.

"Mister," Fitz rumbled, "if you ever come around here again I'll tear yer fuckin' arms off just like you was a fly."

"Get ready, big man," Coe snarled. "Just get ready. 'Cause sure as Christ was spiked to a cross, you and Hickok are dead men."

The star-bright night seemed strangely silent as Hickok crossed Mulberry Street shortly after midnight. Breathing deeply, he savored the crisp fall air for a moment, then exhaled slowly. He liked cold weather, and when the brisk winds swept down over the plains each fall he always felt like a new man. Yet the elixir of frosty mornings and bracing winds had done little to restore his disposition.

Turning onto Cedar Street, Hickok decided to have a drink at the Gulf House, and sauntered on through the chill night. But the saloon was empty, and for some reason he wasn't taken with the prospect of drinking alone. Though it was only early October, the Texans had deserted Abilene in droves following the first cold snap. The once-crowded dives now seemed somehow ghostly and forlorn without them. It was as if the town had been abandoned to the onslaught of winter, and the solitary tread of his footsteps along the boardwalk sapped his spirits even more.

The evening had been a total loss. Brooding and moody, he sensed that on this night Abilene could offer absolutely nothing that would spark his interest. Earlier he had taken a chair in a poker game, but the play seemed sluggish and uninteresting. Unable to concentrate on cards, and bored with the same old faces, his mind turned to the one remaining diversion.

Shortly after Jessie Hazel moved in with Phil Coe, he had met a young chippie in the Planter's Hotel bar and within the hour the action had shifted to her room upstairs. Shallow and undemanding, the girl seemed perfectly content with his brief visits each week. But her simple ways slowly began to grate on his nerves.

Casting about for new conquests, his spirits perked up when the Hippo-Olympiad & Mammoth Circus came to town in mid-August. Traveling from town to town, the circus was owned by Mrs. Agnes Lake, a grass widow whose good looks hadn't yet abandoned her. Figuring ring-dang-doo was where you found it, Hickok began spending part of each evening playing dip-the-wick in her rickety wagon. When the circus rolled out of Abilene two weeks later, the grass widow walked with a decided list, and the marshal was glad to see her go. Cramped bunks in a drafty wagon just weren't his style.

For want of anything better, Hickok again took up with the vapid saloon girl. Yet he seemed to be drawing nothing but busted flushes. Flibberty as an addled squirrel, she was even more tiresome than before.

Whether Mattie was aware of his bedroom sorties had become a matter of supreme indifference to Hickok. He had felt deeply betrayed when she conspired with Phil Coe to remove Jessie from the house and his resentment hadn't lessened over the months. The passionate nights that had once filled their lives were now a thing of the past, and even Mattie's devilish wit ceased to provoke his smile. They slept in the same bed, and as if by habit they still shared the noon meal. But Hickok's brooding silences dominated these moments and his sullen disinterest was driving an ever-widening wedge between them.

For her part, Mattie held her peace and waited. There was little else she could do. Those nights that he did come home he always reeked of another woman's perfume, but she had lived with Hickok much too long not to realize that recriminations would only drive him farther from her life. While she desperately wanted to revive the happiness and love they had once shared, she felt like someone trapped in a quagmire from which there was no escape.

Though the subject of Jessie Hazel had never been broached, Mattie had no illusions as to the source of Hickok's waspish attitude. Things being what they were, she knew there was little to be gained by denouncing him, no matter how well deserved. One thoughtless comment on her part could easily sever the worn thread that still bound them. And at a time when her every instinct cried out to somehow put the past behind them, she employed the utmost tact in dealing with the churlish lawman.

But Hickok's thoughts weren't on Mattie, or her forgiving nature, as he walked along First Street. Even the chill night air couldn't rid his mind of the disgust he now felt for the girl at the Planter's Hotel. By whatever name, her uninspired performance in bed was sheer boredom and he decided he just couldn't be bothered with the simpering little wench any longer. On the instant his mind turned to Jessie Hazel.

Occasionally, he saw her on the street, but she rarely looked in his direction. While it rankled him, Hickok couldn't help but admire her spirited beauty and he often caught himself musing over their abandoned moments in that back bedroom. Once, when they passed on the street, he was shocked by the feeling that Jessie had become even more beautiful under Coe's patronage. The thought made him wince, as if a hot poker had been gouged into a festering wound. What he felt for the Texan was pure, murderous hate. It was like something alive in his guts, ripping and tearing as it fed on his vitals.

While Hickok and Coe had both recovered from the savage battle in Mattie's hallway, their outward scars were as nothing compared to the marks on their souls. They were proud, arrogant men, and each believed himself to be the loser. As summer turned to fall their animosity grew, like a canker sucking life from diseased tissue, and revenge became the core of their existence.

Hardly anyone in Abilene believed that the affair had ended with the fight in the yellow whorehouse. These were men who lived by the law of an eye for an eye, and too much had happened for them to back down now. Barroom discussions usually ended in agreement that a final encounter was inevitable, and when it happened something more lethal than fists would be involved.

Absorbed in his thoughts, Hickok strolled absently along the deserted streets. Idly, he wondered if Coe meant to leave Jessie in Abilene.

While playing poker earlier, he overheard talk that Coe planned to depart for Texas the following morning. With the cattle season finished, the gambler had obviously decided it was time to close the Bull's Head and return to Austin for the winter. Ben Thompson, his gunman partner, had already departed for Kansas City and rumor had it that he wouldn't return. Hickok knew that Coe and a group of twenty cattlemen were even then touring the town's dives, hurrahing Abilene one last time before the long ride down the Chisholm Trail. Apparently the gambler planned to depart without settling their feud one way or the other.

And the thought grated to the very marrow of Hickok's soul.

Wearied with the lethargic mood of the town, Hickok decided to call it a night. Walking in the direction of the house, his thoughts turned briefly to Mattie and he silently hoped that she was already asleep.

Entering the gate, he heard anguished sobs coming from inside the house. Crossing the porch in a single stride, he raced through the open doorway. Bursting into the parlor he came to an abrupt halt, hardly able to comprehend what his eyes beheld.

Fitz lay stretched out on the floor, staring glassy-eyed into space as a bloody froth spurted from his mouth. Breathing shallowly, his massive chest barely moved. Even to the horror-struck girls crowded around him, it was obvious that their gentle companion was near death. Kneeling beside him, Mattie worked feverishly to staunch the flow of blood. Blinded by tears, she swabbed hopelessly at a lattice work of bullet wounds stitched across his chest and stomach.

Fitz's shirt had been ripped open to the waist, and as Hickok moved closer his practiced eye noted that the wounds were mortal. Amazed that a human could absorb so much lead and still live, he silently speculated that there wasn't a man on the plains who was the equal of this soft-spoken giant. Bending, he knelt beside Mattie as she re-placed blood-soaked compresses with fresh rags.

Stirring slightly, Fitz moaned and his glazed eyes focused on the lawman's face. "I wish . . . I wish. . . ."

Then a rush of air escaped his lips, and a look of soft repose came over his face. Unassuming in life, the burly Fitz quietly greeted death in the same manner.

Unable to believe he was gone, Mattie stared hollowly at her faithful watchdog. Leaning across her, Hickok gently closed the sightless eyes and drew the blood-caked shirt back over the dead man's chest. Placing his arm around her shoulders, he drew Mattie to her feet and searched her blank gaze.

"Mattie! Get hold of yourself." He shook her gently as her eyes stared through him. "Who did it? *Tell me who did it!*"

"When they shot him he stumbled back to the porch and fell in my arms. Then he looked at me and said, 'I wish Bill was here. Him and me could've whipped 'em.' "

"Who? Who shot him?"

She was still in shock, reliving the horror again. "We sent for the doctor. But he was out delivering a baby, and Fitz just lay there and bled to death."

"Wake up!" Hickok shouted, shaking her roughly now. "Come out of it and tell me who killed him."

"We were sitting around talking and then we heard men out on the street. They were yelling that they wanted to see 'Hickok's whore,' and dared Fitz to step out on the porch. I tried to stop him, but he just pushed past me and went charging out the door."

She closed her eyes, and a shudder spread over her body as the scene flashed before her mind again. "He ran to the gate and they started cursing him. He didn't say a word. Just opened the gate and stared at them. Then Coe yelled, 'We come with your box, you big pimp,' and somebody else shouted, 'Blast him,' and they all started shooting. He didn't have a chance. He just stood there, looking surprised. Like he couldn't understand why they wanted to use guns instead of just fighting him. And when he wouldn't fall they took off running back toward town."

"Yellow sonsabitches!" Hickok cursed. "Don't worry, Mattie. Those bastards'll get what's comin' to 'em."

Turning, he started toward the door. But Mattie's voice froze him in his tracks.

"Where were you?" she screamed. "Out sacked-up with some whore when Fitz finally needed *you*. Is that where you were, Marshal Hickok?"

For a moment he stood staring at the floor, the silence broken only by the rasping sound of Mattie's breathing. Then he walked into the night without speaking or looking back.

The loading pen east of the railroad station was ringed with a raucous group of idlers. Red-faced with laughter, they shouted encouragement to the sweat-stained, cursing men inside the stout wooden corral. Clouds of dust obscured the action as the men attempted to haze four terrified buffalo up the loading chute and into a waiting cattle car. Snorting with fright, the buffalo would run before the yelling men only to panic after being driven a few steps up the clattering ramp. Swapping ends with incredible ease, for all their clumsy appearance, the monstrous brutes then charged back down the chute as if exploded from a cannon. Scattering, the men scrambled for their lives.

Clearing the pen's high fence for the tenth time in the

last hour, Hickok swore roundly, wondering if they would
ever manage to load the stupid beasts. Roping the buffalo
out on the prairie and dragging them to the pen had been
something of a lark. But after repeated attempts to force
them up the chute, Hickok's patience was rapidly wearing
thin. Still cursing, he jumped to the ground for another try.
If something didn't happen fast, the train would have no
choice but to leave his skittish wards stranded at the siding.

Standing in the shadows at the end of the depot, Mattie
watched the swirling battle of wits raging in the loading
pen. Every now and then she caught a glimpse of Hickok
in the dusty tangle of men and buffalo, and her throat
tightened on a lump which was much too large to swallow. Hugging the wall, she edged deeper into the shadows, determined that her presence would go unnoticed.

After more than an hour had passed, Mattie began to
hope that the train would leave without the buffalo. Though
it wasn't much, at least it would delay Bill's departure for
another day. Then she gloomily admitted to herself that
whether he left today or tomorrow wouldn't alter the facts
one iota.

Over the shouting and pounding hooves in the pen, her
thoughts sifted back through the past three weeks. Dismally,
she wondered if there had been any single incident that
had triggered the final split with Bill. For days Mattie had
brooded over the possibility that she might have been the
cause of their bust-up. But somehow her mind boggled at
taking all the blame. She had forgiven too much, and suffered far too many indignities, to believe that the fault was
hers alone.

Looking back at the heartbreak of those past few weeks,
she saw even more clearly that the night of Fitz's murder
had been the beginning of the end. All too vividly, she recalled Bill stalking from the house without replying to her
hysterical accusation.

With his blood running cold, Hickok had hurried toward
town, knowing that before the hour was out he would kill
Phil Coe. Nearing the corner of First and Cedar, he heard

a volley of shots from the southeast quarter of town. Keeping to the shadows, he raced down a weed-choked alley and entered the Alamo from the rear door. Unmindful of the hushed crowd, he strode across the room, jerked both Colts, and stepped through the front entrance.

Standing in the middle of the street, Phil Coe and a group of Texans were gathered around the body of a dead dog. Drunkenly, they were arguing over who had fired the fatal shot. Unaware that the lawman was now standing on the wide porch of the saloon, the cowboys cursed one another as they disputed who should be awarded the dog's ears.

Taking it slow and easy, Hickok edged away from the lighted windows, all the while watching the rowdy Texans. Somewhere in that group he would find the towering frame of the gambler. Suddenly, Coe's deep voice rose above the quarrelsome shouts, and the marshal had his man.

"Coe!" Hickok's voice filled the street. "Turn around you murderin' sonovabitch!"

An uneasy silence settled over the Texans. Phil Coe casually moved to the edge of the crowd and peered at Hickok's dim outline on the porch.

"Why, what'sa matter, Marshal?" Curiously, Coe seemed contrite. "All we done was kill that old fool dog."

With that, he leveled a pistol secreted by his side and snapped two shots at the lawman. Expecting some trick, Hickok still flinched as both slugs thudded into the wall at his back. Extending his arm, he fired twice as Coe's bulk aligned with the barrel. Grunting with satisfaction, he saw the gambler lurch backward. Bored from stomach to backbone, Coe pitched to the ground in a widening pool of blood.

Then footsteps sounded on a nearby boardwalk, and a man came hurtling around the corner. In his hand was a gun, glinting in the dim starlight. Hickok spun and sent him tumbling to the earth with a single shot. Crouching, he whirled again to the front and emptied the smoking pistol into the Texans' ranks. Switching the second Colt to his right hand, the lawman thumbed shots with a blinding roar as the trail hands panicked and bolted down a side street. Hickok's lips cracked in a tight smile as he watched two wounded cowboys struggle to their feet and hobble off in pursuit of the fleeing Texans.

Puzzled about the man who had blundered around the corner, he walked to the body and flipped it over with a shove of his boot. Startled, he stood gazing at the face for a moment. It was Mike Williams, a drinking crony, who until moments ago had been the bouncer at the Novelty Theater. Sometimes it seemed like a man would be a hell of a lot better off if he just kept to himself and forgot about making friends. Shaking his head, he left the bodies sprawled in the road and headed toward the Alamo for a drink.

Though Hickok's disposition had improved somewhat after Coe's death, Mattie soon realized that it had nothing to do with avenging Fitz's murder. It was simply that the lawman's pride had been restored and there was no longer any doubt about who ruled Abilene.

The weeks following the gunfight passed with oppressive slowness in the yellow parlor house. There was no warmth or intimacy between them, and day by day it became clear to Mattie that too much had transpired for things ever again to return to normal. Still, the greatest barrier separating them was Hickok's certainty that she would always blame him for Fitz's death. Soon he began drinking heavily and gradually grew even more distant than before the killings.

Embittered by her silence, and yet too proud to broach the subject himself, Hickok came to regard Mattie as a thorny reminder of a night he would sooner forget. Still, she hung on, resolutely clinging to the dream that they could somehow salvage a remnant of their life together. But his aloof manner gave her scant hope, and within a fortnight it became only a matter of time until some careless word or action would signal the end.

Strangely, the townspeople finally brought it to a head. They had had enough of Hickok's surliness, and his prolonged bout with the bottle. When the newspaper took up the cry, the town council saw the handwriting on the wall, and voted unanimously to remove the marshal from office. As if the only link binding him to Abilene had at last been snapped, he immediately began making plans for his departure. Storming from the mayor's office after the council meeting, he spent the afternoon exchanging telegrams with various eastern journalists. Their books and articles publicizing his exploits on the frontier had made him something of a national figure, and they were delighted with the scheme he now proposed.

Returning to the house that evening, he found Mattie dry-eyed and waiting, seated in a rocker in their darkening bedroom. Lighting a lamp, Hickok glanced at her uncertainly, not quite sure of what remained to be said.

"Reckon I'll be leavin' in the morning," he commented matter-of-factly. "Suppose you heard the city fathers gave me the door."

"Yes, I heard." Mattie's voice was drained, emotionless. "Where will you go?"

"Oh, I been speculatin' on it for quite a spell. Got an idea of showin' them eastern faint-hearts what the West is really like. Guess I caught the bug from Bill Cody. He's always talkin' about formin' a stage show and gettin' rich in them eastern theaters."

"I see," she said calmly. "What kind of show will you organize?"

"Well, it's a cinch I don't know nothin' about actin'. So I sorta figured to get me some buffalo and hire a few tame Injuns, and let them pilgrams back East see what a real buffalo hunt looks like. Chasin' them across some fair grounds back in New York oughta pay a hell of a lot better than it does to shoot 'em out here."

"Well, lover, you couldn't help but make a big splash back East. So be sure and send me your newspaper clippings."

Recalling that last flippant remark as she watched the caboose disappear in the twilight, Mattie wondered if it had really had any effect on the vain plainsman. Certainly it hadn't changed anything between them. When Hickok had returned from the expedition with the captured buffalo he hadn't come anywhere near the house. Though he remained in Abilene for a week making arrangements for the trip East, it was clear that he had no intention of trying to patch things up.

Knowing he was near, yet separated by ghosts that refused to die, had been a grueling experience. After a week of sleepless nights, she had felt something akin to relief when Hickok boarded the train upon finally loading his buffalo.

Now, unable to summon a tear from a soul wearied with crying, she stared impassively as the train vanished over a distant rise. *So long, gamblin' man. If there is a God, I sure hope he doesn't pay you back in kind.*

Turning, Mattie rested her head against the depot wall for a moment. Then she lifted her chin defiantly and began the long walk through a lonely town.

BOOK TWO

HIGH ROLLERS
AND HARLOTS

CHAPTER FIVE

Wild Bill Hickok was dead. When word came over the telegraph in early August, Georgetown was electrified. Dirty Jack McCall had assassinated the West's most feared gunfighter in Deadwood, Dakota Territory. Shot him in the back of the head while he was hunched over a card table in a cheap saloon. Killed instantly, Hickok had slumped to the floor clutching the winning hand, aces and eights. Already it was being called the dead man's hand, and certainly none would dispute that it had brought misfortune to the foremost man killer of the day.

When Mattie heard the news she went to her room and sat in a rocker by the window. Strangely, she couldn't cry or even feel the deep hurt that she expected. Too much time had passed and her tears had all been used up long before. She always knew that Bill would manage to get himself killed somehow, and just as she had predicted years ago in Hays City, death had come from the back. Staring out the window, she felt a distant sense of loss. But no remorse or even pity. *How very much like Bill, to draw his last breath in a poker game. And holding the winning hand, too! Lord, that must have hurt worst of all. Spent his entire life chasing*

*Lady Luck and damned if she doesn't kill him just when
he's holding winning cards.*

Suddenly it occurred to her that this summer had been a
bad season for old comrades. George Armstrong Custer had
gone under on the Little Big Horn in June, and now Bill.
Yet it was almost like a stranger, or some character in a
dime novel, had died. Nearly five years had passed since she
watched Bill board the train in Abilene, and try as she
might, she couldn't form an image of his face. The hurt had
been too deep then, and all she had wanted to do was forget. Somehow a person had to go on living, and it couldn't
be done by burying your face in a tear-stained pillow every
night. The important thing was to survive, to get through
another day, one day at a time. And when enough days had
passed the hurt became only a tiny throb, until finally you
awoke one day and it was just gone. Vanished, or maybe
erased, like a chalky smudge on a schoolroom slate.

Whatever happened to the grief, it had disappeared in the
Kansas cowtowns long ago. Thinking back, she couldn't re-
member the exact day she had gotten over being jilted by
Bill, but it was sometime shortly after she left Abilene.

The Women's League had finally organized a full-
fledged reform movement in Abilene, but only after joining
forces with the Granger's Association. For once Joseph
McCoy found that even his slick tongue couldn't carry
the day. Women and farmers working together were
more than the town council cared to tackle, and after one
final season, the Texans were no longer welcome. Fences
appeared across the southern boundaries of the country,
backed by the courts and deputy marshals. When the
Chronicle carried an ad warning the Texans to stay clear
of Abilene, even Joseph McCoy packed it in and moved on
to greener pastures.

After that Mattie's recollections became muddled. Cowtowns, trail hands, shootings, a long succession of soiled
doves that didn't even have names anymore. Ellsworth,
Newton, Wichita, Caldwell, Dodge City. They all seemed
fused into one indistinct blur, and Mattie sometimes had

difficulty sorting them out in her mind. The reign of each cowtown had ended abruptly as the railheads moved ever westward, and even the old Chisholm Trail had reverted back to wilderness.

But like a pack of dogs chasing the same bone, the gamblers, whores, and whiskey peddlers simply folded camp and boarded the first train bound for the *new* Eldorado. And leading the pack in search of this elusive mecca were Mattie and her soiled doves. By now they were an institution along the frontier, and for Texans who had trailed north each season it was almost like coming home to plop down on a sofa in Mattie's swank parlor.

While most of what had happened in the cowtowns remained dim and confused, there were some things that Mattie remembered clearly. Mostly having to do with people and events, for the towns themselves were as much alike as a litter of baby skunks. Wichita came to mind only because it was where she had first met Wyatt Earp.

After Ellsworth and Newton, Mattie had opened a fashionable parlor house in the red-light district of Wichita, commonly referred to as Delano. Though many of the brothels were run by madams she had known for years, there was a new one owned by a man and wife only recently arrived on the frontier. Since the shady-lady business had always been rather close-knit, she soon became friends with James and Bessie Earp.

James and Bessie ran one of the dicier houses, catering to the roughnecks who figured that poontang was all the same, whether the tariff was a dollar or a fistful of diamonds. With such clientele, they were frequently hauled into city court for operating a disorderly house. Before long it became a local joke that James and Bessie were giving the red-light district a bad name. But despite their coarse ways, Mattie liked them. She found James and Bessie to be completely unassuming, and their simple manner was a refreshing change from the high-toned madams who held themselves above the crowd. Within the month, she also met their silent partner.

James had a younger brother, who was a buffalo hunter by profession and a drifter by instinct. With an eye for the sure thing, he had observed that brothels were more dependable than banks, and quicker than scat James and Bessie became flesh merchants. After listening to the garrulous couple brag about their young kinsman for some weeks, Mattie actually found herself growing curious. When he came wandering in off the plains one day she got the surprise of her life.

Unlike his low-brow relatives, Wyatt was an astute, fierce-eyed hawk of a man. He was ambitious, cunning, and, as far as Mattie could see, completely unprincipled. In the main, his ambition centered around power and money, and it was devil take the hindmost for anyone who got in his way. But he was also handsome, ruggedly built, and very courtly toward pretty women. And for some reason, possibly because Hickok was out of her life at last, Mattie had never been more radiant.

Within a week they became lovers, and before a fortnight had passed, Wyatt officially took up residence in her parlor house.

While laconic to the extreme, Mattie found Wyatt the shrewdest man she had ever met and quite witty in a dry sort of way. But the most appealing aspect of young Wyatt Earp was that he was a real bearcat in bed. And right then Mattie desperately needed an ardent, moonstruck lover.

Both her vanity and her confidence in herself as a woman had been shattered in Abilene. Such things are not easily restored in a woman approaching thirty, and more than anything else she needed to know that she was still desirable to an honest-to-God man. A week later, when she found herself uncomfortable sitting, and in actual pain merely walking, Mattie figured that what she had to offer must be pretty desirable after all. Thereafter she limited young stud Earp to once a night and was in sheer ecstasy when he raised the roof over having the cookie jar put out of reach.

Eventually, of course, it came to an end. All things on the frontier were transitory, lovers included, and when

Wichita folded as a cowtown, Mattie moved on. Later she heard that Wyatt had become a deputy marshal, and as his first official act forced James and Bessie to close up shop. This bit of news gave Mattie a good chuckle, for it was so characteristic of Wyatt. After all, if a man has ambitions, especially in the political arena, he couldn't very well have a brother running a two-bit whorehouse.

Something over two years were to pass before she ran into Wyatt again. By this time she was operating in Dodge City, which was experiencing its first birth pangs as a cowtown. Wyatt was even more solemn and grim-faced than she remembered. He had killed a man in a gunfight and in the process acquired a reputation as a fast gun. All of which tended to sober any man in a land where every jackass with the price of a pistol was looking to make a name for himself.

While Earp said he was in town to discuss a marshal's job, Mattie suspected there was something more to the visit. Since she was unattached at the moment, he bunked with her for a week. And within a matter of days, he received some very strange callers indeed. Luke Short, Bat Masterson, and Doc Holliday, a deadly threesome even for a cowtown. Masterson and Short were likable enough, but Doc Holliday's cadaverous eyes gave her the shivers, and she was relieved when Wyatt rode out at the end of the week. Some years would pass before she learned that only a select few, herself included, knew of the meetings. And, more significantly, that the four men were cronies long before Earp became a lawman in Dodge.

Shortly afterward, she began hearing stories of the Colorado mining camps, and the vast riches that could be gleaned by women who were willing and able. According to rumor, it was purely a matter of supply and demand, and in Colorado it was a seller's market. She was willing, and her soiled doves were certainly able, so that took care of the supply. After lengthy inquiry, she learned that in a mining camp called Georgetown there wasn't a parlor house worthy of the name. And that took care of the demand.

Cowtowns were beginning to pall on her anyway, and after a decade on the plains that fresh mountain air sounded like the very thing to restore a girl's complexion. Not to mention the gold. With much wailing from the Texans, Mattie and her lady boarders packed it in and caught the train for Georgetown.

Now Bill Hickok was dead—shot down just as she always knew he would be. Rocking back and forth, she stared out the window and reflected on the vicious bitch called fate. Maybe Bill had found what he sought after all. Certainly he had rolled dice on his own coffin often enough. It was funny how hindsight made life's past riddles come clear and shiny bright. Looking back, she saw that Bill's had been a star-crossed path from the very start. *Strange to think of him lying in a box somewhere. Not sad, really. Just strange. How that man loved to be admired. And now he's all alone in that box, without anyone to feed his pride. But you have to give the devil his due. He was a hell of a lot of man!*

Mattie and the girls had arrived in Georgetown just as winter released its grudging hold on the land. Within a week the warm chinook winds swept down out of the mountain passes, melting the ice and snow with breathtaking rapidity. For the next month the streets were axle-deep in mud and slush, which made even a trip to the outhouse something of an adventure. But the sun's warming rays slowly baked the moist earth, and soon it was possible to traverse the town without once wetting a toe.

Georgetown was the offspring of a mother lode, one of the richest silver strikes ever made in Colorado Territory. Located just east of the Continental Divide, the town was founded in a rocky gorge at an elevation of a mere eighty-five-hundred feet. Main Street butted up against a mountain, and as the village grew it acquired a New England flavor, with carved wooden posts and picket fences lining the boardwalks. But unlike their eastern cousins, the miners had no time for the niceties of life, and the town lacked sanitation in any form. In certain seasons this presented no problem. But in the warmer months a stench hung over the town like a cloud. While the natives took it in stride, newcomers found it a most unnerving experience. For the odor was at once offensive to the nostrils and unsettling even to the hardiest of stomachs.

Still, no one thought of leaving, for the inhabitants of Georgetown were of one religion, and held one god in common. Salvation lay within the jealous grasp of the mountains, and those who had made the pilgrimage fully believed that the great god, Silver, would provide all the redemption ever needed.

While Mattie was accustomed to the frontier, and its harsh ways, she was appalled by conditions in Georgetown. Even a decade in the cowtowns hadn't prepared her for the mining camps, and she found herself ricocheting from one shock to the next. Simple things, that seemed only a matter of common sense, were the most disturbing. On her first shopping trip she noticed that the grocers all set their vegetables on the boardwalk outside the stores. Though this made a handsome display, it required only a moment's observation to see that every vegetable in Georgetown was at the mercy of passing dogs.

Collaring a grocer just as a lop-eared hound lifted his leg over a plump squash, she commented acidly, "Mister, the very least you could do is place the edibles above the high-water mark. And if you want any of my business, you'd better do it damned fast." Scratching his head the storekeeper conceded the idea had merit, and promptly built wooden racks for the vegetables. Within days every merchant in town had followed suit and even the dogs seemed to prefer the new arrangement.

But the most frightening part of the mining camps was the violence. While men had killed one another readily enough in the cowtowns, there was at least a trace of honor governing the shootouts. In the mining camps, the only honor was to emerge alive and survival by the most expeditious means was the accepted code. Rarely did a night

pass without gunshots being exchanged in one of the Main
Street dives, and so long as both men were armed there were
few questions asked.

Still, those killed in gunfights were but a tiny drop in
Georgetown's bucket of gore. The local graveyard often
seemed the busiest spot in town and most of its residents
were the victims of robbery and outright murder. Vast riches
were being gouged from the surrounding mountains, and
even men who worked in the mines made a passable wage.
Moreover, with Lady Luck astride his shoulders, a man
could become wealthy in a matter of hours at the faro tables,
or betting on the endless round of foot races, boxing matches,
and rock-drilling contests. Where money flows freely the
jackals are seldom far behind, and at times it seemed to
Mattie that the dregs of mankind had somehow found their
way to this remote mountain camp. But if the holdup men
and thieves were a revelation, the law itself provided her
with a real eye-opener.

The law was visible enough, in the form of peace officers and various courts, and even quick to act if someone
of prominence was harmed. But like everyone else in camp,
the men behind the law had journeyed to Georgetown for
only one reason. While there were some who dug their
wealth from the earth, and others who acquired it by slit-
ting throats, the law gathered riches by the simple expedi-
ent of corruption.

Graft and bribery were accepted facts of life, and on
the whole the community rather envied these men who were
able to line their pockets without dirtying their hands. The
police had a monopoly on the protection racket, extracting
the juiciest plums from whorehouses, gambling dens, and
saloons. But while their exorbitant demands infuriated
Mattie, she was absolutely blessed compared to the jobbing
unloaded on many a mine owner. When a sole judge determined which contestant owned a mining claim worth millions, it was a rare day that justice could counterbalance the
weight of a substantial bribe. Like every mining camp in
the Rockies, the law in Georgetown served the highest

bidder. And judges were considered reprehensible only when they sold out to *both* sides.

Yet there were times when justice was served swiftly and without recourse. Seldom did such events have anything to do with the courts and perhaps only indirectly with the law. But the mighty sword of justice had struck a blow nonetheless, and for a week or so the man in the street felt secure in the knowledge that an eye for an eye remained the most gratifying covenant yet devised.

Mattie's first exposure to vigilante justice came one evening when she heard the roar of an angry crowd on the street. Stepping to the window, she caught a brief glimpse of a mob dragging some poor wretch toward the telegraph poles outside town. Only later did she learn that he had murdered a harmless old prospector for a few ounces of dust. What she never forgot was an article in the *Miner News* which openly sanctioned the vigilantes' brutal methods: "Immediately after his 'conviction' for murder, Judge Lynch arranged to have him telegraphed home."

The more she saw of Georgetown the more Mattie realized that she had embarked on a whole new way of life. These mountain camps were more primitive than the cowtowns at their bloodiest, and with each passing day it became clear that the miners themselves were only one step removed from walking on their knuckles. But there was one salient difference between the mining camps and the cowtowns, and for Mattie it represented the only factor of significance. The mines operated around the clock, six days a week, fifty-two weeks a year. For the madam of a parlor house that meant a torrent of gold, pouring in with the ceaseless regularity of a mountain waterfall. Where the Kansas railheads had boomed only five months out of the year, the mining camps were begging to be plucked night and day, winter, summer, and fall. For those who could stand the gaff. On that basis alone, she decided to stay until she had accumulated sufficient wealth to finance the fanciest, most elegant whorehouse in Christendom.

Though there was much about Georgetown that Mattie

detested, she was utterly fascinated by the Hotel De Paris. Quaint and charming, like a holdover from some opulent era of the past, it had become a landmark in this dingy, isolated mounted village. Louis Dupuy had built the hotel shortly after the strike began, and lovingly devoted himself to creating a small slice of sophistication and grace in the wilderness. French by birth, he was a raconteur and gourmet by choice, and host as well as hostelry had become famous throughout the Rockies.

While shopping one day, shortly after arriving in town, she had decided on a whim to have lunch at the Hotel De Paris. Madams weren't always welcome in the finer restaurants, but she had heard so much about Dupuy's masterpiece that she couldn't resist the temptation. Walking through the dining-room entrance, she suddenly drew up short, literally bedazzled by the refined elegance which dominated this monument of French cuisine. The entire ceiling was a muted pattern of inland wood mosaic, offset by a glistening floor of perfectly matched panels in dark mahogany and light oak. Carved figurines encircled the room at ceiling height, like small, sculpted gods overlooking the chosen few, and a huge crystal chandelier swung in delicate suspension from the ceiling. Old-world etchings and fine engravings covered the walls, and spotted around the room were ornate, carved credenzas and highly polished serving tables.

Mattie felt like a rube, but somehow she didn't care. It was the most cultured room she had ever seen, and even if the other diners laughed she was going to stare until her eyes couldn't absorb any more.

"Does madame approve?" Mattie turned to find Louis Dupuy standing at her elbow, smiling pleasantly. At first she thought he was making a sarcastic play on words. But then she caught the French inflection and realized he was addressing her as one does a lady.

"Oh, yes, I do approve." Still mildly awestruck, she swept the room with her eyes. "It's the most elegant thing I've seen in my entire life."

"*Merci beaucoup.* As an admirer of beauty, may I say

that your presence lends a quality to my humble room that it sorely lacks."

Slightly taken aback, Mattie actually felt her cheeks blush. "Why, thank you. Since I'm obviously talking to a gentleman, you must be Mr. Dupuy. My name is Mattie Silks."

"Enchante, Madame." Bending, the stout little Frenchman took her hand and kissed the tips of her fingers. "But, of course, you are well known here, Madame Silks. As you are throughout all of Georgetown. Our little village has long awaited the arrival of someone like yourself."

"Mr. Dupuy, whether you mean it or not, you could charm the birds right out of the trees. Now why don't you fix me up with a table and tell all about your hotel. Someday I'm going to build an elegant house myself, and I have a feeling you could give me a few lessons in where to start."

Bowing, Louis Dupuy took her arm, and escorted Georgetown's most widely discussed courtesan to his favorite table.

Though Georgetown was a haven for the flotsam of humanity, it also had its elite. In San Francisco, or possibly even Denver, the swells would have looked down their noses at what Georgetown called its high rollers. But in the mining camp, these men had attained an enviable station, and after a day in the grit and slime of the tunnels, any miner in town would have given considerable just to trade places.

This select few, who held dominion in Georgetown, included only a scattering of professional men. Judges, doctors, a lawyer or two, and the local mine owners, of course. By far, the greater membership was comprised of men who lived by their wits, or some extraordinary skill. Among this latter group were the gamblers, drifters, foot racers, prizefighters, and that lonely breed in a singular notch all their own, the gunfighters. While most stuck to the craft best suited to their talents, there were some who aspired to greater fame. Parlaying a rare combination of skill with massive doses of audacity, they grasped for the brass ring,

the good life it promised. With the supreme contempt of the
very arrogant, they disdained the fearsome odds that confronted them. When the chips were down, they were addicted to the game itself, the way a poppy-eater is hooked
on Lotus Land, with never a thought for the consequences.
And among the inner circle of this fatalistic band were two
men who had been watching Mattie with the utmost scrutiny. Cort Thomson and Chalk Wheeler.

As in most communities founded on a lust for wealth,
the men of Georgetown believed that the goodies in life
went to him who got there firstest with the mostest. So it
was that Mattie found herself swamped with offers that
fairly staggered the imagination. Word had spread through
camp that while her soiled doves were for hire, Mattie herself was not to be had at any price. But for Georgetown's
elite this merely added zest to the game, and they quickly
began laying odds as to who would be the first to sink his
dauber in the new parlor-house madam.

Mattie had been amused at first. The doorbell would ring
and a well-dressed stranger would announce he was there
to see Miss Silks. Hair slicked back, smelling of bay rum,
he would then waltz into the parlor, stiffly lower himself
onto a sofa and promptly announce his proposition. And the
offers were often startling. Mining stock, precious gems, a
small fortune in gold pieces, inducements that under less-
strained circumstances might have swayed her judgment.

She was amazed at how solemn these men were about
the whole affair. Without fanfare, or even the slightest attempt at small talk, their offers were made with all the deli-
cacy of a fish merchant. But as the doorbell continued to
ring, and there seemed no end to this presumptuous charade, her mood underwent a remarkable change. While this
type of thing might do worlds for a girl's vanity, there came
a point when she began to feel like a haunch of venison on
the auction block. These men were competing, trying to out-
bid one another as they would for a good dog or a fine
brood mare. And the comparison left her cold.

Still, she knew men, and once their appetites had been

whetted there was no telling where it might lead. The male fraternity hated nothing worse than a high and mighty whore, and many of her best offers had come from prominent, influential citizens. If she insulted them, they might make trouble for her, more trouble than she could handle. And only a fool fouls her own nest. What she needed was a protector, someone the other men respected, maybe even feared. Survival was the first law, even in Georgetown, and to save the golden goose she first had to safeguard the nest.

This was the moment Cort Thomson and Chalk Wheeler had been waiting for. Both men were great believers in the hunch, and instinct told them that Mattie wasn't about to be swept off her feet by a bunch of yokels jangling their pokes. This little lady needed the deft touch of a master, and so far as these two were concerned, that excluded everyone in Georgetown except themselves.

While Thomson and Wheeler knew one another, there was no love lost between them. They weren't enemies, but they weren't friends, either. They avoided each other whenever possible, with the grudging respect that one reserves for a skilled adversary. Both pursued the same brass ring, and like two large dogs on the same block, they were willing to share the spoils, so long as no one got too greedy.

Cort Thomson was a Texan, and at times it was almost his undoing. Swaggering down the street with a cocky little smile on his mouth, he was an open challenge to anyone with a chip on his shoulder. And there were plenty of those in Georgetown. But Cort had two saving graces. Despite his cocksure attitudes, he was a very engaging fellow, with a lusty sense of humor and a rowdy, hard-drinking nature— just the kind of man that appealed to a rough and tough no-holds-barred mining camp.

Never content with merely being good at one thing, Cort took uncommon pride in the fact that he could best most men at whatever game they chose. He was a foot racer par excellence, thriving on the roar of the crowd as he streaked across the finish line to collect a handsome purse. Decked out in pink tights and star-spangled trunks, he was enough to set any woman's heart fluttering. And as he strutted around, flexing his lithe, corded muscles for the benefit of the spectators, many a miner envied his lean masculinity. For make no mistake about it, Cort Thomson was a good-looking man. Sandy blond hair, bold blue eyes, short bristly mustache, and a husky voice slurred with a soft Texas drawl. In or out of his pink tights, he was a man that bore watching.

But while foot-racing was a pleasant pastime, Cort's other endeavors proved considerably more lucrative. Gamblers come and go in a mining camp, yet there were few to match this young Texan's brash skill. Poker was his game, and though many believed him to be the biggest bluffer east of the Rockies, there was seldom a call when he bet the limit. Glib and uncommonly persuasive, he had even been known to talk a man out of a pot. And when prospects at the poker tables turned slow, he wasn't above engineering some slick con game to separate an unwary pilgrim from his poke. Still, Cort liked to brag that he had never once thimble-rigged a man who didn't have larceny in his soul to start with.

All in all, Cort Thomson was something to behold. Convincing, nervy as a gaunted fox, and as slick with a deck of cards as any man who ever came down the pike. In fact, those nimble hands were the second of Cort's saving graces. When push came to shove, there was only a blur of motion before a Colt appeared in his hand, and three men had already met untimely deaths by underestimating his speed. After his last gunfight, a bull-necked miner had convulsed the entire saloon with his puzzled observation. "For a skinny little bastard, he's sorta sudden, ain't he?"

Chalk Wheeler, whose designs on Mattie closely paralleled those of Cort's, was another matter entirely. Somber as an undertaker, rarely given to moments of humor or good nature, he was a man that seldom went out of his way to make friends. Essentially, he was a lone wolf, distrustful of other people, and skeptical that any such thing as brotherhood had ever existed among the human race. His nickname came from the slow, deliberate care with which he chalked his cue at the billiard table, and at that game there were few men his equal.

But he, too, had grander visions of the road ahead, and while Georgetown might be a little pond he saw no reason to settle for anything less than the biggest lily pad. After hustling a stake at the billiard tables, he had switched to poker as the shortest route to the wealth and status he craved. Anywhere on the frontier a master gambler ate high on the hog, and for a sodbuster who had left Ohio with holes in his shoes, that fatmeat sounded very inviting indeed.

Seated across a poker table, his icy manner and penetrating stare could give a fellow the shakes, and most men counted him a tough nut to crack. There was also talk that his hands might be quicker than the eye on occasion. But he was just naturally a man that people didn't warm to, and stories about him being a cardsharp were generally taken with a grain of salt.

Besides, those who had seen him outside town practicing with his sixgun didn't care to dispute the matter one way or another. They said he was fast as a snake, and while he was never known to have been in a gunfight, it just seemed like another good reason to let Chalk Wheeler tote his own load.

Their approach to Mattie clearly demonstrated the marked differences between these two men. Though they had both thought on the problem long and hard, their opening gambits were as dissimilar as chili peppers and hog jowls. Chalk shrewdly enlisted the aid of an intermediary. Cort just appeared.

Mattie had shooed all the girls out of the parlor in preparation for her gentleman caller. Earlier in the day a note had arrived from Louis Dupuy requesting a formal appointment for his good friend, and one of Georgetown's outstanding citizens, Chalk Wheeler. After being besieged by the camp's high rollers, Mattie was still a bit wary, but she figured that with Dupuy's recommendation it might just be worthwhile. Besides, she desperately needed someone to intimidate all those other clowns and Chalk Wheeler sounded like a name with real grit to it.

When he arrived, she was a little disappointed. While he was fierce-looking enough, formidable in fact, he certainly wasn't much to tickle a girl's fancy. Solemn as a judge was the thought that crossed her mind. But he was obviously the kind of man people respected. Or feared. Even if he couldn't string two sentences together without pausing to weigh his words. Just then, the doorbell rang.

Excusing herself, Mattie walked to the vestibule and opened the front door. In all his glory, there stood Cort Thomson. Candy in one hand, wild flowers in the other, and a grin as wide as the Rio Grande spread across his boyish face.

"Miz Silks, allow me to introduce myself. I am Cortez D. Thomson, late of the Confederacy, and only one jump out of Texas. And with your kind permission, ma'am, I have come seekin' the honor of callin' on you."

Amused, but nonetheless intrigued by his unusual line, Mattie opened the door wider and stepped aside. "Come in, Mr. Thomson. This seems to be my night for gentlemen callers."

Mattie's comment brought a puzzled look to Cort's face, which changed to outright disgust when he saw who was seated in the parlor. His temper was short-fused, and he had put too much thought into this little project to have it mucked up by the likes of Chalk Wheeler.

"Wheeler, what the hell are you doin' here?"

"Thomson, I might ask you the same thing," Chalk grated. "Since I was here first why don't you just take your play-pretties and get yourself lost."

"Not by a damnsight, I don't! And you're playin' with a cold deck if you think you're gonna rawhide me out the door."

"JACK!" Mattie's full-lunged shout brought both men up short, and they turned toward her in astonishment.

The hall door opened and a barrel-chested gorilla stepped into the parlor. At least that's what he looked like to Wheeler and Thomson. He was easily the biggest man they had ever seen in their lives and from the glint in his eye he might just be the meanest.

"Gentlemen, meet Handsome Jack Ready, my bouncer." Mattie smiled, gesturing toward the cold-eyed giant. "Jack, these boys were just leaving. And until they decide to behave like gentlemen, you're not to let them past the front door."

With that Mattie stepped from the parlor and walked off down the hall. Handsome Jack jerked a thumb as big as a two-by-four toward the door, then balanced himself lightly on the balls of his feet just in case. But the message was clear.

Sheepishly, the two gamblers gathered their belongings and beat a hasty retreat. Walking back up Main Street, they talked it over like gentlemen and decided it was a tossup as to which of them was the biggest asshole.

While tossing Chalk and Cort out on their ear hadn't shown it, Mattie was quite pleased with the way things had gone. They were like two gamecocks fighting over a particularly choice hen, and she wasn't in the least displeased with the turn of events. If she was any judge of character and she should be after ten years on the line—they would be back faster than ever. Though different as night and day, they were both proud, arrogant men, and she felt certain it wouldn't end here.

Thinking back, she had to shake her head at their boldness. Clearly, those two had laid back waiting for the town buckos to take their best shot. Once the rush was over, they figured to step in and sweep her off her feet. Actually, it couldn't have worked out better if she had planned it step by step. Now that the town's rankest high rollers were fighting over her, everyone else would stand clear. If she played her cards right, she might be able to stretch the fight out indefinitely. *Which meant she'd never have to crawl in bed with either of them!*

Chuckling, she recalled their slack-jawed expressions

when Jack stepped through the hall door. No doubt about it, Jack Ready was a bit unnerving when you first came face to face with him. And not because of his good looks, either. While someone back East had dubbed him Handsome Jack, she had always thought of it as more of a brutish magnetism. The ridged brow and square jaw were just a little too craggy for her tastes, like a piece of granite that had been flaked and chipped with a dull chisel. But she could see where a certain kind of woman would be taken with him. Come to think of it, there weren't a hell of a lot of girls in this very house who hadn't turned a trick for Jack when the mood struck him.

The thought persisted, and her mind turned backward in time, trying to recall if the women in Chicago had been starry-eyed about Jack. But the only thing she could really remember was the fight.

That was the year she wintered in Chicago, and it was there she had formed an alliance with Handsome Jack. The cowtowns closed down tighter than a virgin's buttercup once the trailing season ended, and only a fool would elect to endure the blizzards that swept down across the great plains. Over the years she had vacationed in Kansas City, St. Louis, Springfield, and once had even gone all the way to New York. But that particular winter, just prior to folding camp in Dodge City, she had decided on Chicago.

While she had always meant to look over the Windy City anyway, there were business reasons that also prompted her decision. Lou Blomger's closest crony was an old reprobate named Mike Donahue, who just happened to be the political boss of Chicago. Since Lou was embroiled in battling reformers in Springfield, they had decided that Mattie might be wise to establish another pipeline for girls. While whorehouses were a dime a dozen on the frontier, a parlor house had a reputation to maintain and it took connections to get the really pretty girls shipped West.

Donahue had solved the problem in less than a day, and that left Mattie free to enjoy the winter exploring Chicago. After being introduced to many of the local czar's associates,

Mattie was in constant demand by Chicago's gay blades. Soon her life became a whirl of theater, opera, horse races, and intimate dinners in the city's posh restaurants. Yet the most memorable evening of her entire stay had been the night she was escorted to her first prize fight.

But this was not a run-of-the-mill pugilistic exhibition. Chicago's current bare-knuckle champion was matched against three of the roughest thugs ever produced by the South Side stockyards. *Three?* Mattie couldn't believe her ears at first. Then her gentleman friend quickly explained that the champion, Handsome Jack Ready, was so lethal in the ring that challengers had become virtually nonexistent. The only way he could arrange a match was to increase the odds. On his last outing he had all but decapitated two bullyboys, and there seemed nothing left to do but try for three. Anticipating the bout with much glee, her escort allowed as how Ready might end up fighting a cage full of tigers before he ever got licked.

Handsome Jack Ready! Mattie was intrigued by the name, and after listening to her companion crow about the pug's ferocity she found herself wondering how he would have fared against Fitz. Poor Fitz, moldering alone and forgotten in Abilene's wind-swept boot hill. It was a thought that always brought tears to her eyes, and she turned her mind back to tonight's unusual match.

The fight was to be held in a spacious loft on the third floor of an old warehouse. When Mattie and her escort entered, they noticed rows of benches aligned around the room, forming a boxlike square in the center of the loft. Lighted by an overhead bank of lamps, the square looked to be about ten feet across, and had been covered with a thick carpet of sawdust.

Glancing around as the crowd claimed their seats, Mattie discovered she was the only woman in the room. Evidently such spectacles weren't for the faint-hearted. Suddenly a hush fell over the gallery, and she saw the spectators staring toward the opposite side of the loft.

Towering over his opponents, Handsome Jack Ready was

a yoke-armed brute of a man. Stripped to the waist, the corded muscles in his arms and chest rippled in the flickering light like the knotted flanks of a blooded stallion. Standing four inches over six feet, his burly frame packed not an ounce of suet and his gnarled fists looked like meaty rock-crushers. Sauntering to the far side of the ring, he cast an indifferent glance over the audience. Like a jaded gladiator hardened to his craft, he was unmoved by the odor of sweaty fear that hung over the crowd. Vaguely, he heard the referee informing the spectators that this would be a fight to the finish—no time limit, no rest periods, and no holds barred.

The corners of his mouth twisted in a tight smile as he wondered how long the three plug-uglies would last. Turning, he caught sight of Mattie at ringside and their eyes locked. Ready slowly looked her over, noting her delicate build, the golden sheen of her hair, and the tenacious set to her lovely face. Then it dawned on him that Mattie was making her own cool assessment, and he grinned audaciously. Somehow, he had a feeling this plucky little woman was a kindred spirit, one who could match him in will if not in brawn. Thrusting his hands through a tousled thatch of red hair, Jack decided to make it a fight she would be a long time forgetting.

The referee finished his spiel and hurriedly stepped to the side of the ring. From this point on, his only function would be to raise the hand of the winner. As he reached the outer edge of sawdust a tense sigh swept across the spectators, then stillness settled over the loft.

Jack Ready stood motionless under the hot lights, waiting. He had faced gangs many times in the past, and forcing them to show their hand at least added a little spice to the scrap.

The three ruffians knew his reputation well, and while they were cautious, they weren't afraid. Surprisingly, their opening move suggested a pre-arranged battle plan.

Circling, two of the men moved in on the flanks, while the third ambled slowly forward. Apparently, the leader of this grisly trio was the man who intended to tackle the champion head-on. Though shorter than Ready, the thug was flat-nosed and heavily scarred, clearly a man who had been weaned on rough-and-tumble brawls.

Before entering the ring, Handsome Jack had casually studied the stockyard toughs, concluding that the man with the pug nose was the most dangerous of the lot. Now, he purposely avoided eye contact with the leader, glancing instead at the men on his flanks. Shifting, he turned slightly, cocking his fist as if to lash out at the man circling from his right. Like wolves leaping in to hamstring their prey, the other two moved instantly from the rear.

Gauging their movements perfectly, Ready whirled and kicked the flat-nosed hooligan squarely in the kneecap. The man's leg buckled with a loud crack, and he began falling. The leader had to be immobilized first, and with that thought uppermost in his mind, Jack ignored the blows raining down on him from either side. Stepping in, he kicked the thug in the side of the head, and grunted with satisfaction as the man crumpled forward in the sawdust.

Slinging blood from a split eyebrow, Ready ducked beneath the attack and pivoted to his left. Then he struck, exploding a whoosh of air from one of the ruffian's lungs as he buried his fist in the man's stomach. But the third man was now pommeling him in the back of the head. Spinning, his elbow swung in a looping arc and bones crunched as it connected with the hoodlum's jaw. Knocked back on his heels, the man swayed unsteadily, his eyes blank, cocked askew. Laying his weight behind a searing left hook, the burly giant dumped him in the first row of spectators amidst a shower of screams and up-turned benches.

Crouching, Handsome Jack spun just as the remaining thug regained his wind and started forward. Looking about wildly, the man realized he was the only one left and began scuttling toward the edge of the ring. Incensed, the crowd surged forward and bodily threw him back into the arena. Floating in limbo between the outraged spectators and his hulking opponent, the man backpeddled furiously. But the crowd grew more menacing with each backward step, and after a moment he decided Ready's fists might be the wiser choice.

Halting, he shuffled forward and launched a whistling round-house right. The crowd roared as Jack snared the man's wrist in midair and bore down with a crushing grip. Struggling desperately, the man heaved and wrenched as a hush settled over the room. Jerking the rowdy upright as he would a thrashing doll, Ready shifted weight and drove a paralyzing blow flush between the man's eyes. Reeling backward like a gored ox, the last of the stockyard toughs toppled to the floor in a cloud of sawdust.

Chest heaving, blood dripping from the wide gash on his brow, Handsome Jack stood alone in the center of the ring. The mixture of sweat and blood coating his chest glistened in the reflection of the overhead lamps, and for a moment he stared curiously at the sprawled forms. Then pandemonium broke loose, and he slowly became aware of the crowd's roaring chant. Leaping into the ring, the rabid spectators mobbed him, straining to get closer as they shouted themselves hoarse.

Heedless of the chaos around him, Ready searched ringside with his eyes. Finally, his gaze settled on Mattie, who was engaged in animated conversation with her escort. Sensing his stare, she glanced around and their eyes again fused in a moment of silent appraisal. Smiling, her face softened, then she nodded in mute affirmation of his savage victory.

Later that night, as she lay in bed thinking of the fight, it occurred to Mattie that Handsome Jack's cold precision in the heat of battle was startlingly reminiscent of Fitz. Obviously, Ready was brighter than poor Fitz, probably even quite sharp as a matter of fact. And he was much better-looking, of course. Still, there were marked similarities between them, and the thought nagged at her so persistently that she found sleep impossible.

Then it dawned on her! *Why not hire Handsome Jack to replace Fitz?* But you didn't just hire a celebrity like Jack Ready. A man with all of Chicago at his feet would scoff at the notion of working in a whorehouse. Or would he? There was something in the way he had looked at her. Hungry, certainly, but something more. And a girl would be a fool not to take advantage of a man's rutting instincts. Of course, the pot would have to be sweetened over and above mere wages. But after four years of hiring stumblebums and drifters to protect the house, it might just be worth it. Still, it was something to sleep on.

Within the week, Mattie had made up her mind and through Mike Donahue arranged a meeting with Ready. Her offer was direct, and backed with indisputable logic. His job would be to police the house and help manage day-by-day operations. In return he would receive room and board, and ten percent of the net, which in a normal month amounted to something over one thousand dollars. He couldn't earn that much fighting every night of the week, and she knew it. She also knew he was going to accept even before he spoke, for the look of the hunter had entered his eye. And Mattie never doubted for a moment that she was the quarry.

But they had been partners over a year now, and he hadn't gotten her into bed yet.

Thinking about it, Mattie had to laugh. Jack had tried everything in the book to get in her pants, and then some. But while he hadn't made an inch of headway, he didn't seem in the least discouraged. By now it had become a game, with her sweet diddly as the prize, and it was almost as if he enjoyed the chase more than the kill. Still, she had more immediate problems to think about. Such as keeping the high mucketymucks uptown off her back. And if she had judged Thomson and Wheeler correctly, it shouldn't be too hard to keep the whole town on tenterhooks while she played them off one against the other.

Georgetown had lived up to Mattie's expectations with a vengeance. The high rollers avoided her doorstep in droves, and it had been over a month since any slick-haired strangers with juicy propositions had rung the doorbell. Not that they didn't appear regularly to play horse with the girls, for Mattie's was the only parlor house in town. And a real high roller had to be oiled to the gills before he would lower himself to patronize a dancehall crib. But everyone in the village was talking about the contest between Thomson and Wheeler for Mattie's favors, and so far no one seemed the least bit inclined to make it a three-way race. Among themselves, the Georgetown elite frankly admitted that they were more interested in the outcome between the two gamblers than they were in forking the pretty little madam. Of course, it was left unsaid that a fellow might get himself ventilated if he bought chips in what had now become a two-man game.

Mattie was as happy as a speckled pup with a bowl of cream. Her plan had worked with unerring success, and at times she felt like a puppeteer pulling the strings while her wooden dolls obediently performed a mating dance. It was all rather calculated, even a bit Machiavellian for her tastes, but a mining camp was no place for the squeamish. A woman had to look after herself, especially in her line of business, and until she found a man who suited her fancy, she would just have to go right on conning the entire town.

Not that she wasn't pleasantly intrigued by both of her anxious, if somewhat frustrated, beaus. Chalk and Cort had returned separately, just as she predicted. Hat in hand, mumbling apologies for his conduct, and each in his own way eager as a boar hog with a hard on. Sulky and aloof at first, she had allowed herself to be swayed by their awkward entreaties, and finally relented. But in exchange for her consent, she exacted a promise from both men that they would call on her only at appointed times, and never together. Privately, she had to laugh at the absurdity of the whole affair. Only in a mining camp, where women were as scarce as nits on a bald-headed preacher, would the madam of a sporting house find herself being courted like a dewy-eyed virgin at her first cotillion.

Still, she had to admit that both of these men were not without appeal. Whatever it is that stirs a woman's loins seemed vaguely responsive to each of them. But in different ways. Thinking about it, Mattie herself wasn't even quite sure what caused this curious effect.

Chalk was usually stiff as a board: reserved, preoccupied with his consuming ambition, and given only to brief moments of sardonic humor. But there was something fascinating about him in a deadly sort of way. Like sitting down for a social chat with an amiable rattlesnake. In a sense, it was the kind of fascination one derives from flirting with danger, knowing all the while that even if the devil jumps up and grabs you it was worth the risk. More than one woman had dreamt of being ravished by a hairy beast of some sort, and in Chalk's company the prospect seemed very real indeed. There was a predatory manner about him, as if he were carefully stalking a victim, and Mattie often wondered what it would be like for him to suddenly pounce and carry her off to bed. No kisses, or foreplay, just an aroused animal grunting and hunching until it was done. In a perverse, depraved way, it sounded sort of exciting.

Cort was another matter entirely. He was a madcap, reckless, devil-may-care hellion, whose lust for life was bounded only by an infinite curiosity. Without thought to the consequences, he was constantly testing and probing, driven by a mischievous obsession to find out just how far he could go without getting his fingers burned. He traded on the fact that people were drawn to him, making the most of his good looks, dashing smile, and a natural gift for the witty comeback. Men were no less susceptible to his charisma than the ladies, and he was as welcome in a saloon full of foul-mouthed miners as he was at a matronly church social. Just exactly why people were drawn to him was something no one in Georgetown had ever bothered to define. They only knew that he was happy-go-lucky, always laughing, and the softest touch in town when a man was down on his luck. Moreover, he was a winner, one of the chosen few who had been tapped by the gods to stumble over a bushel of goodies at every turn. And even a sucker who had been fleeced of his last double eagle just naturally couldn't help loving a winner.

But Mattie saw all this, and more, in Cort. The carefree, impish side of his nature was like a shiny reflection on a mountain brook. Beneath the surface lay rock and cold steel, a hard, unflinching resolve to win at any price. And behind the laugh in his slate-colored eyes dwelled the icy ruthlessness that made other men's lives forfeit should they somehow stand between Cort and what he wanted. But knowing the paradox existed, Mattie was still attracted to this wild, high-soaring Texan. Within him she sensed an abandon that crested above the trivial longings of other men, and in that solitary trait she saw a core of determination to match her own.

But while Mattie had Cort and Chalk figured out down to the last nubbin, they remained completely baffled by her seemingly fickle ways. Whatever tack a man took she somehow managed to throw him off-balance just at the last moment, sort of like trying to catch a butterfly in a strong wind. For a lady in the poontang business she seemed damnedly hard to bed, and they were both growing more frustrated with each passing day. Every woman in that house screwed like a mink, and so far they hadn't even gotten a smell. The thought infuriated them, and as is often the case when men are caught up in something that defies their best efforts, the two gamblers ceased to doubt themselves and began to doubt Mattie.

Not whether she would, or did, or even wanted to. She was too much woman to doubt that. But who she was doing it with was something else again. At first they suspected Handsome Jack, but somehow the theory just wouldn't hold water. Then, because they had ceased speaking entirely, they began to suspect one another. Chalk figured Mattie was exercising Cort's tallywhacker every other night, and Cort got a distinct vibration that Chalk was hosing Mattie on his off night. The more they chewed on it, the harder it was to swallow, and before long they were both walking around town as sour-tempered as a bear passing peach pits.

There was an added little matter that also raised their

hackles a notch higher. Every man in town shared their suspicions, and opinion was pretty evenly divided as to who was getting his wick dipped—Chalk or Cort. Who was doing what to whom became the most widely debated subject in Georgetown, and it just naturally didn't do much for either man's pride. Especially since they both figured it was the other fellow that was getting his pole greased. Something had to give, and being rasher by nature, it was Cort who finally brought things to a head.

Chalk had been playing poker all night in the Silver Palace, which was his usual haunt. While there were some who questioned his talents as a lover, there was hardly a soul on this night who doubted his skill with cards. His winning streak had been nothing short of phenomenal, and most of the cash in the game was stacked in a golden mound at his elbow. The other players doggedly hung on, convinced that his run had to break sometime. But their concern at the moment was that before the worm turned, he might just break them.

Then a gradual hush settled over the saloon, beginning at the front door and working its way back to the farthest corner. The uncommon silence broke Chalk's concentration, and he looked up to find Cort standing on the opposite side of the table. This in itself was no little thing, for the two men rarely frequented the other's hangout. As if by unspoken agreement, they each kept to their own hole, and so far as anyone knew they had never sat in the same poker game. Cort showing up unannounced in the Silver Palace had an ominous ring to it, and every eye in the room was centered squarely on Georgetown's two most prominent high rollers.

"Mind if I take a seat?" Cort's smile seemed strangely tight, but his voice betrayed absolutely nothing.

"Your money spends." Chalk casually came erect in his chair as Cort seated himself. "Table stakes. Check and raise. Draw or stud, dealer's choice."

"Seems to be your night." Cort nodded, indicating the pile of coins in front of Wheeler.

"I've had worse." Chalk's terse comment came as the man on his left began dealing stud.

"Well, maybe I'll change these fellers' luck." Cort smiled, glancing around at the other players. No one flicked an eyelash, but the meaning was clear. Changing their luck meant that he had to bust Chalk's winning streak.

The game went on with the talk limited to betting. But the stakes increased sharply as Cort and Chalk began butting heads over the larger pots. There was an undercurrent here that escaped none of the men at the table, and though they played to win, they were clearly engrossed in the contest that had nothing to do with cards.

The deal passed quickly from man to man as the game speeded up noticeably. There were no longer any jokes or bantering among the men, and each hand evoked nothing more than bets, raises, and the clink of coins. The hubbub in the saloon hadn't returned to normal either, and men around the room quietly sipped at their whiskey while they watched the game with mounting excitement.

Something was brewing, but nobody knew exactly what. Chalk and Cort were running neck and neck, each man winning from the other just about as often as he lost. Yet a curious thing was happening. Cort had held his own throughout the game. But he had lost every hand, and some unusually large pots, whenever Chalk dealt the cards. Everyone at the table had become aware of it, and none more so than Chalk. For a while he thought something fishy was going on, because there were a couple of times he could have sworn Cort had him beat. But maybe this was just his night to howl. There were some nights a man couldn't be beat, no matter what. And besides, he'd always wanted to cut that wise-assed Texan down a few notches anyway.

After something over an hour had passed the two gamblers were still about even. Cort was losing to Chalk, but he was winning from the other men. When it came Chalk's turn to deal, he called stud, deftly shuffled, and after the cut began flipping cards around the table. Cort's first up-card was an ace, and when he peeked at his hole card he found he had a pair back to back. He bet fifty dollars, noting that Chalk had a jack showing. The next card didn't change the look of the board much, and Chalk again called his bet. But on the fourth card, Cort caught another ace, and Chalk paired his jack. When Cort bet two hundred dollars the other players dropped out. Chalk studied the table for a moment, then raised three hundred. Cort again peeked at his hole card, like a man hoping it might have changed since he last looked. The third ace was still there, but he merely called the raise. Chalk dealt the last card, which did nothing for either man. Cort checked, and Chalk bet five hundred. The Texan pondered his opponent's hand for a moment, then called. Chalk turned his hole card, another jack, and smiled like a dog trailing a gut wagon.

"Three jacks," he announced. "What do you say aces?"

"Beats me." Cort folded his three aces and tapped the cards thoughtfully against the table as he gazed at the three jacks. It went against the grain to deliberately fold a winner. But he had been doing it all night whenever Chalk dealt, and it was too late to back off now. "Chalk, you're almighty lucky, for a fact. Unnatural, some folks might call it."

"Meaning?" Chalk's hands paused over the stack of coins in the center of the table, and his cold black eyes stabbed out at the Texan.

"Meaning the first time I saw that jack of diamonds it was on the bottom of the deck. The next time I saw it sorta puzzles me. Somehow or other, it turned up as your third jack."

"Whatever you're saying, make it plain, Thomson. I want to be sure everyone in this room hears it before I kill you."

"Why, Chalk, I'd say it's about as plain as a horse fart in a broom closet. Every time you've dealt tonight you beat me goin' away. Maybe these fellers aren't up on such things, but I learned all about dealin' seconds before I could spit. If you want it any plainer, I'm sayin' you're a goddamn tinhorn."

Chalk kicked his chair backward as he came erect, clawing at the sixgun holstered on his hip. But before the Colt cleared leather a .41 Derringer appeared from Cort's vest.

Still seated, he drilled Chalk dead-center through the brisket. The gambler grunted as the slug jolted him back a step,
but he wasn't done for yet. Gamely, he steadied himself and
jerked the sixgun clear. Cort coolly extended his arm and
shot him squarely between the eyes. Dead on his feet, Chalk
staggered backward, tripping over his own chair, and toppled to the floor with a splintering crash.

Standing, Cort calmly returned the Derringer to his
vest, and began pocketing the coins in the center of the
table. Glancing at the body on the floor, he shook his head
sadly. Then he looked around at the other players and
smiled crookedly. "Never could stand a man that cheats
in a friendly game. You gents ever feel like playin' some
honest poker, come see me over at the Lucky Tiger."

Walking away, he nodded pleasantly to men he knew,
smiled at the ladies, and set his hat at a jaunty angle as he
stepped through the door.

Twenty minutes later, with a fresh shirt and his hair
spruced back, Cort entered the parlor house. Leaning against
the doorjamb of Mattie's small office off the vestibule, he
grinned as she looked up in surprise.

"Chalk won't be able to make it tonight. He got himself
killed."

Mattie started, half-rising, then sank back in her chair.
"No need to ask who did it. I suppose that makes you top
dog now?"

"Maybe." Cort dropped his hat on her desk, and flashed
another grin. "Whichever way it is, I reckon it's about time
you and me came to an understandin'."

"Yes, I guess it is. You didn't have to kill him, you know.
I probably would have picked you anyway."

"Probably wasn't good enough. I had to make sure. Besides, you're too much woman for a snake like Wheeler. You
need a man you can count on in case anyone jams you up
between a rock and a hard place."

"Cort, I'm beginning to feel like a woman who just won
a three-ring circus in a raffle. It's going to be interesting."

Smiling wearily, she shook her head. "The bedroom is the third door on the left. You can move your things in tomorrow."

Mattie was momentarily distracted by the billowing curtains. The first currents of autumn were drifting down from the mountains, and there was a faint moan in the wind. Pausing, she filled her lungs with the fresh scent of the breeze, then sighed and returned to her calculations. She was determined to close the books on her first six months in Georgetown even if it took the rest of the night. After some hours poring over the columns of figures her head was fuzzy, and for the first time in years she was finding it difficult to concentrate on matters dealing with money.

Already it was apparent that she had cleared something over forty thousand dollars since coming to the mining camp. How much more really didn't seem worth bothering with at this point. What she had on deposit with the local bank added to this week's receipts still wasn't enough to build the elegant house she had in mind. And her discouragement was compounded by the thought that even if she had the money she certainly wouldn't erect such a house in a grungy mining camp. But if not in Georgetown, then where?

The new house had become an obsession, filling her mind night and day. She had visualized every room and stick of furniture down to the last detail, sometimes sitting in her rocker by the window for hours imagining how it would look when she was finally done. Money was no object, especially in daydreams, and she meant for it to be the most lavish parlor house in the West. Grander even than those she had heard about in San Francisco. But woolgathering was one thing, and the harsh realities of her finances were something else again. The house she had planned couldn't cost a penny less than fifty thousand. And she had to have at least another twenty-five in reserve for operating expenses and payoffs to local politicos, *wherever* she built this fanciest of all sporting houses. All of which meant another three, maybe even six, months in Georgetown. *Christ!*

Cort took great delight in teasing her about the dream house, which he gleefully referred to as Pussy Palace. The goddamn thing would cost so much to build, he once told her, that it would make for the most expensive piece of ass in the history of screwing. And that took in a lot of territory. Still, he let her know in little ways that he was impressed with her determination to be the best at what she did. Cort understood pride, and the importance of being first, and while he joshed her constantly there was never any doubt that he backed her all the way.

Mattie's life had taken on a whole new dimension since Cort began sharing her bed. There was something about the light-hearted Texan that made every day a tiny treasure all its own. Chipper and always smiling, he somehow managed to brighten even the dreariest of days, and the house was filled with laughter and good spirit from morning till night. But more than that, he treated her with the tenderness and selfless concern that she had always hoped to find in a man. Sometimes, he acted as if she were a fragile china doll, too delicate for anything except the gentlest of cuddling. But when they were alone, deep in the warmth of their feather bed, he turned her into a raging tigress, clawing and moaning with pure animal lust for the last ounce of his love. For the first time in her life she felt truly content as a woman, and she secretly thanked whatever gods there were for having sent Cort to her.

Now, if she could only get her business on the right track. *And somehow lay her hands on enough money to finance the new house.* Disgusted that the profits so far had fallen below her expectations, she wet a pencil on the tip of her tongue and returned to the ledgers. Somewhere, hidden in all those damnable figures, was a way to tighten up the operation. Grumbling to herself, she plunged once more into the scrawled columns with a vengeance.

"That's a bad sign when you start talking to yourself. Almost as bad as people who laugh at their own jokes."

There was something strangely familiar about the voice, and Mattie turned in her chair. Squinting, she saw a pudgy little man whose corpulent frame all but filled the doorway. Watchfully towering over him was Handsome Jack, who had no intention of leaving until he was sure Mattie knew the stranger. The dim light from her desk lamp obscured the man's features, but she had the curious feeling that she should know him. Shading her eyes, she peered more closely as a rumbling laugh erupted from his belly. Suddenly her doubt vanished.

"Lou Blomger. Oh, Lou!" Bounding from the chair, she flew across the room and threw her arms around his neck. "My God, what a start you gave me. But where did you come from? And what in Christ's name are you doing in Georgetown?"

"Slow down, towhead." His laugh filled the room. "Let me at least get a look at you before you start bombarding me with questions."

"I'm just so excited to see you. God, it's been almost two years." Stepping back, she saw a patient smile spread across Blomger's face. "All right, I'll calm down. But only if you talk fast and tell me everything about yourself."

Mattie asked Jack to bring drinks, and motioned Blomger toward a chair. Crossing the room he moved with the purposeful stride of one accustomed to maneuvering a frame of considerable bulk. Over the years he had acquired a rounded paunch, which bulged out in front of him like the prow of a river barge. In the light, Mattie also noted flecks of gray streaking his hair, and she was saddened by how much older he had become in such a short period of time. But the most amazing change was in his nose. It was a huge, bulbous thing, all red and mottled, giving him the appearance of an aging libertine who had sampled life's delicacies too freely.

"Mattie, I'm damned if you're not prettier than the last time I saw you," Blomger observed, settling himself in the chair. "From all appearances, I'd say living out here must agree with you."

"Lou, you haven't changed one bit. Still the same roly-poly charmer with a gift for gab. Now, quit greasing me and start explaining what you're doing in a godforsaken mining camp."

Jack returned just then with a whiskey bottle and two glasses. Glancing curiously at Blomger, he left the room without a word. Mattie smiled to herself, for she knew he wouldn't be far away. After pouring drinks, she waited while Blomger sipped at the liquor, obviously savoring its sharp taste.

"Good whiskey. Takes the chill out of a man's bones." Grinning, he watched her fidget with impatience. "Now, before you die of curiosity, I suppose I'd best tell you why I'm here. I've moved my operation to Denver, and within the month I'll make my opening play to take over the rackets there."

"*Denver!*" Mattie could hardly believe she was hearing right. "I thought Ed Case had Denver sewed up. And what happened to Springfield?"

"God, you just don't give a man a chance with all those questions. All right, I'll start at the beginning. The reformers closed Springfield down faster than an ice house in a blast furnace. So I sold all my holdings and caught the first train West. I figured there had to be someplace left where an honest thief could still make a living, so I spent six months scouting the towns out here and finally settled on Denver."

"Lou, you've already told me that. And I just got through saying that Ed Case is just another name for Jesus Christ in Denver."

"Not quite. In fact, I found Case to be a very agreeable sort. It's true he controls the politics in Denver, but his only interest in the rackets is the payoff. He doesn't care who runs things so long as the money's right. I made a deal to give him a bigger slice of the cake, and in exchange he's agreed to keep city hall and the police out of it when I make my play."

"Well, Lou, you're no piker, that's for sure." Mattie frowned, and thought for a moment as she sipped her drink. "You're playing for big stakes, and the people out here threw away the rule book a long time ago. They can get damned rough when someone tries to horn in on their game."

"Mattie, crooks are crooks the world over. And any trick they know I can double it in spades." He studied the amber liquid in his glass as if reflecting on more important things. "A wise man once said that those who can't remember the past are doomed to repeat it. Well, let me tell you something, Mattie. I'll never forget how those hidebound fanatics ran us out of Springfield. I spent a half year of my life hunting for the right town to make sure it'll never happen again. Denver is the hub of most of the mining camps out here, and one day it will be the richest city in the West. I intend to have a lock on a good part of it when that happens. And I'm not going to be too squeamish about cutting a few throats if that's what it takes to get it."

"But what about an organization? You can't just waltz in and announce you're the new kingpin. Those boys in Denver won't roll over and play dead that easy."

"Hah! By Christ, now you're getting down to the meat of it." His booming laugh again shook the room. "I'm bringing my whole crew out from Springfield, and you never met such a raunchy bunch in your life. Thimble-riggers, drifters, bunco artists, head-bashers. Mattie, we'll take over Denver so fast they'll think they've been struck by lightning."

Observing him as he spoke, Mattie slowly became aware that this wasn't the Lou Blomger she had once known. The jolly, pot-bellied good Samaritan who had long ago befriended a naive young girl no longer existed. The old Lou Blomger had been swallowed whole by greed and ambition, and the man that had emerged was as cold and ruthless as any she had met in a decade on the frontier. Her worry for his safety suddenly withered under heavier scrutiny. It was the gang in Denver that was in danger, not Lou Blomger. He meant what he said, and she believed him. Inside of a year, he would probably own half of Denver and be scheming to gimmycrack somebody else out of the other half.

Watching her, Blomger drained his glass, then dropped the bombshell. "Towhead, there's one part of the operation I haven't mentioned yet. And that's where you come in. Before long I'll be running every racket in Denver, and when the time comes I'll need someone to help me organize the houses and keep 'em on the straight and narrow. I want you to throw in with me and handle that part of the deal. I'll not only make you rich, but by this time next year you'll be queen bee of the sporting houses. And that's not bad for openers."

Mattie stared at him in bafflement. It was a fantastic scheme, and it could put her on easy street for the rest of her life. Or get her killed. But it was all happening too fast and there was something that bothered her. Something about Lou and the malevolent gleam in his eyes behind that fleshy mask. "Lou, I'm just not sure. I mean, you come sailing in out of nowhere and tell me you're going to set me up as some kind of mogul of the madams. It's all a little sudden. I'm not satisfied here, that's for damn sure. But the only thing I really had my mind set on was a fancy parlor house. You know, something elegant and refined, like back East."

"Christ, Mattie, you're not listening. I'm offering you that and more. A half-dozen parlor houses of your own and a percentage off the top from every two-bit crib and dollar whorehouse in Denver. You're talking about peanuts, and I'm offering you a shot at the real goodies."

Mattie gazed at him blankly, her mind in a quandary. There was something overripe about the whole deal. But if she couldn't trust Lou Blomger, then who could she trust? They went back a long way, and their friendship had been cast within the crucible of time and hard knocks. Somehow she couldn't believe that Blomger would hoodwink her, and she'd stake her life on the fact that he would never move on

Denver if he wasn't absolutely certain of taking over the rackets. In fact, if she joined him she would be doing just that: staking her life on his word. Well, like Cort was fond of saying, nobody ever got rich scratching his ass.

"Lou, you've got yourself a girl. You tell me when and where, and I'll be there with bells on."

CHAPTER SIX

———◆———

Gold was discovered on Cherry Creek in 1859. And the rush was on. Over the next three decades thousands of reasonably sane men hocked their souls and struck out for Colorado Territory. According to reports, nuggets as big as hens' eggs could be found strewn about the countryside, and all a man needed to get rich was a gunnysack and a strong back. Eastern journalists noted that gold was among the heaviest of metals, and advised those of a weak or sickly disposition to bring along horses to tote their precious loads back to civilization. Fortune awaited any man with the daring to cross the Great Plains, and time would prove that not even a wilderness crawling with Indians could deter those infected with gold fever. Thousands came, and a few got rich.

The unlucky ones fanned out across the western territories, convinced that it was only a matter of time and shifting fate before they too struck the mother lode. Some found gold, but most found lead or silver or copper. Bedraggled, footsore paupers became millionaires overnight, and from the bowels of the earth sprang Deadwood, Leadville, Tombstone, Virginia City, and a hundred more like them. When the rush showed no signs of slackening, Congress finally relented and began turning territories into states.

Colorado's turn came in 1876, almost twenty years after the hamlet of Denver was founded on the banks of Cherry Creek. What was once a sad collection of log huts spread and grew, reproducing itself a hundredfold, until finally a glittering metropolis had been created amidst the gold fields. By early 1880, Denver had become a cosmopolitan beehive, with theater, opera, plush hotels, six churches, four newspapers, three railroads, and an entire street devoted to nothing but whorehouses. The most noteworthy civic virtue was greed, and to an observant stranger it seemed that most of the city's thirty-five-thousand residents were devoted exclusively to separating the unwary from their pocketbooks. But as Lou Blomger had predicted, it was rapidly becoming the richest city in the West. And Mattie loved it.

Holladay Street was the center of Denver's wild and wicked tenderloin. Known locally as The Row, it was a lusty, brawling fleshpot, with a scattering of parlor houses and a veritable crush of dollar cribs. Something over a thousand brides of the multitude plied their trade in the red-light district, and the revenues generated by their license fees were the only thing that kept the city treasury afloat. Most of the hook shops along Holladay consisted of two tiny rooms: parlor in front, boudoir in back. Girls in short, spangled dresses and black-silk stockings stood in the doorways, soliciting customers with the ageless invitation, "Come on in, dearie." Some of the more enterprising went so far as to hang signs in the window.

MEN TAKEN IN AND DONE FOR

But most were simply a girl and a bed, available by the trick or by the hour, coin of the realm. And whether a man's tastes ran to white, black, or yellow, every crib on The Row reeked of stale sweat, rotgut whiskey, and cheap perfume.

Still, Holladay Street had something for everyone, rich

or poor. Though hook shops dominated the tenderloin, there was no scarcity of high-class bagnios, and the swankiest parlor house in town belonged to Denver's newest shady lady, Mattie Silks. Lou Blomger had kept his promise. Mattie was given a blank check, and instructed to build a house that would make everything else in town look like a two-bit clip joint. Blomger meant for Mattie to rule Holladay Street from the outset, and the surest way to pull it off was to erect a bordello unlike any Denver had ever seen.

Mattie had waited for this moment almost ten years, and she tackled the project like a Hun assaulting the Holy City. She knew exactly what she wanted, and with money no object she selected the choicest piece of real estate in the red-light district. The house was a three-story brownstone, with covered steps leading to the entrance, and a dank, cavernous basement. One block away was Larimer Street, where the city's high rollers pursued Lady Luck, and it was only a short ride to the posh restaurants and theaters uptown. Within a few steps of the front door was another diversion for clientele with a taste for the bizarre. Known throughout the city as Hop Alley, it was a narrow passageway running between Holladay and Larimer. Chinese fantan parlors vied with the faint, sweet odor of opium dens, and those addicted to the Orient's heady delights beat a steady path to this backstreet Lotus Land.

All things considered, the location couldn't have been better. The house was within easy walking distance of every vice known to man, and more than a few especially designed for the ladies. The floor plan of the building was well suited to a sporting house, and while the interior decor left much to be desired, the massive stone facade fronting Holladay Street gave it just the right note of stability and refinement. Mattie promptly purchased it for fourteen thousand dollars, and prepared to build her temple.

With Handsome Jack relaying the orders, she hired a swarm of carpenters and craftsmen, and as a first step gutted the entire building. Then she began creating, transforming the vision in her mind into reality; with painstaking detail, she explained to the workmen what she wanted and exactly how it must look when done. Work progressed on all three floors and the basement simultaneously. She had set a deadline of six weeks for opening night, and it was generally agreed among the crew that she had missed her calling as a construction foreman. Berating, cajoling, sometimes cursing pungently, she drove them night and day, and in the process flung money around with the abandon of a drunk sailor in a strange port. Five weeks, six days, and sixty-three thousand dollars later, Mattie Silks opened the most elegant whorehouse ever seen or heard tell of in the wilds of Colorado.

Everyone who was anyone in the tenderloin attended opening night at Holladay Street's newest parlor house. Mattie's alliance with Blomger was not yet common knowledge, and politicians, police, and high rollers alike were keen to get a look at the inside of this much discussed brothel. Rumors had been flying thick and fast about Mattie's wild spending spree, and the word was out that screwing in Denver was about to take on a whole new meaning. There was also considerable talk about her boarders, sort of a potpourri of pussydom, so it was said. Mattie's search for girls had been as exacting as her decorating demands, maybe even more so. In addition to the usual blondes, brunettes, and redheads, she was offering one high yellow, one real yellow, and the queen of spades.

But as it happened, the girls played second fiddle that night. Fifty years later, doddering old men couldn't remember whether the girl they had forked was black, white, or muckledydun. Yet with little or no prompting they could recall two things as if they were again standing in that foyer for the first time. Handsome Jack Ready poured into a white-tie monkey suit, and the goddamnedest, eye-boggling splendor they had ever seen.

Stepping through the door the first thing they saw was a long foyer. The walls and ceiling were done in brilliant, royal-blue silk panels, interlaced with ornate gold trim, and a massive crystal chandelier swayed overhead. Carved blackamoors formed a silent gauntlet along the walls, and underfoot the deep pile of an Oriental carpet cushioned each step. Beckoning the caller forward was a spacious Renaissance nude, hung appropriately just beside the parlor door.

The parlor itself was decorated with the lavish grandeur of a Byzantine palace. Silk damask draperies gently screened the arched window bays, and every entrance was guarded seductively by lewd marble voluptuaries, mounted atop dusky onyx pedestals. The walls of the room were covered in resplendent, blood-red velvet, and the ceiling was a richly burnished pattern of raised leaf, forming a backdrop for dozens of spun-gold cupids in poses that left nothing to the imagination. The floor was a wall-to-wall sea of crimson softness, tugging at the foot like furry quicksand, and delicate gold lamps lent intimacy and warmth to the room. In one corner was a bar with champagne and vintage wines, and in another a pearly-toothed black man pounded out the latest tunes on a sparkling white piano. Every stick of furniture in the parlor was imported French Rococo, and over the mantel hung the masterpiece, a nubile full-length nude that was at once brazen seductress and childlike innocence. All in all, it was a room that left the mind reeling, and in need of a good stiff drink.

Downstairs, in what had once been a musty basement, the decor turned very masculine. The room had been paneled in dark mahogany, and large, overstuffed divans lined the walls. For entertainment, there was a well-stocked bar, billiard and pool tables, and another piano player with a small dance floor for those who got the urge.

But the final touch in sensual gluttony was reserved for the eight small bedrooms on the second floor. Each was a minor miracle of provocative artistry. The decor in every room was done in bold, stimulating colors, and each bedstead was a massive wood carving of explicit erotic foreplay. French plate mirrors covered the ceilings for those who enjoyed the dual role of spectator and participant, and the downy beds were built wide and low, with a scattering of gigantic pillows that fairly screamed for some wicked, depraved experimentation.

The third floor was Mattie's private suite, consisting of bedroom, parlor, and bath. Tastefully decorated in comfy furniture, with a brightly burning fireplace, it was as unlike the rest of the house as Mattie could make it. Garish elegance was all right for business, but home was where all pretense and artifice were cast aside. And this cozy little suite was the first real privacy she had had in the last ten years.

Opening night was a ball-buster first class. Everyone got politely squiffed on imported wine, Handsome Jack only had to bounce two rowdies the whole night long, and not a man left the house with strength enough to pull his pecker out of a pail of lard.

As false dawn broke with a dusky glow, Mattie snuggled up in Cort's arms and relived each savory little moment of the long night. She had made it, at last. After ten grinding, sometimes miserable years she had made it to the top of the heap. And it was only the beginning. Denver was hers for the asking, and from here on she meant for it to get better and juicier every step of the way.

Lou Blomger slowly mounted the steps to Ed Case's office over the Progressive Club. Trailing him was his bodyguard, a ferret-faced little man who looked like he couldn't have weighed much more than a wet chip of wood. But size can be misleading. A little snake can kill just about as fast as a big one, and more often than not he's nastier-tempered. Blomger had seen the little man in action, and knew how deadly he was with the twin Colts snugged down tight in his shoulder holsters. Right now Blomger's main interest was in staying alive, and with this beady-eyed runt at his side, he felt very safe indeed.

Pausing to catch his breath on the second-floor landing, Blomger mopped perspiration from his face with a silk handkerchief. Being big and fat added many annoyances to a man's life. Perhaps the most irritating of the lot being that it gave other men more to shoot at. Still, the shooting had been sort of one-sided lately, and so far his team had scored all the points.

Without knocking, Blomger turned the doorknob and entered the office. Case was seated behind a desk studying a sheaf of official-looking documents, and he didn't even glance up. From the heavy tread on the steps, he had known it was Blomger before the door opened.

"Lou, someday you're going to walk through a door like that and find yourself staring down a gun barrel."

"That's what I got him for," Blomger replied, jerking a pudgy thumb toward the little man. "With Slats around people get real careful about guns. Some folks even get to wishing they didn't own one."

Case nodded as if the statement said it all. "Have a seat, Lou."

Blomger plopped down in a chair and heaved a wheezing sigh, like a cow with screw worms. Those damnable steps took it out of a man. Slats closed the door and leaned back against the wall, gazing at nothing, yet somehow conveying the impression that he saw everything.

Ed Case stared back at them, and began to realize that he was a man with a problem. Three months ago he had been as close to a czar as a dyed-in-the-wool Democrat can get. He owned four gambling dives around town, and at times it seemed like it might be easier to count the money with a scoop shovel. City hall was bursting at the seams with hacks he had handpicked personally, and from the mayor down there wasn't a politician in Denver that didn't sweat blood every time he got a summons to appear at the Progressive Club. The rackets operated quietly, if openly, without arousing any public outcry, and the little black bag showed up regularly on the first of each month. If ever a man had cause to thank providence for the good life, it was Ed Case. But that was three months ago.

Things had changed drastically since Lou Blomger came to town, and it didn't take a crystal ball to see that the dance had only begun. Denver had suddenly become a very violent place for certain people, and Case was too astute a man not to see even larger storm clouds forming on the horizon.

Essentially, Ed Case was a backwoods philosopher, a man who believed that logic and reason, mixed with a little sleight of hand, would prevail every time. He deplored violence, for it only disrupted the orderly nature of things, took a man's mind off making money. He saw life in the larger perspective, somewhat like that Darwin fellow, the Englishman who would cause such a row in a few years. Man was the eternal presumptuous ape, shallow, pompous, full of greed and harebrained ideas, and not a hell of a lot more worth mentioning. Case had further observed that mankind shared a congenital weakness with his hairy ancestors, an inability to grasp that over the long haul those who relied solely on strength and brute force eventually killed each other off. This flaw in man's character forged a link between the foolish, bumbling masses, and ultimately it was the purveyor of illusion who ended up with all the marbles. The one with the knack of making things appear not as they are, but as others want to see them.

But there was nothing superficial about Ed Case. This amused cynicism was concealed beneath a finely chiseled mask, and he rarely betrayed even a flicker of what went on inside his head. Staring at Blomger now, he regretted ever having made a deal with such a sweaty tub of lard. Some things cost more in dignity than they were worth in money, and he was quickly discovering that being aligned with Blomger was a very expensive proposition indeed. Still, a man had to be pragmatic about business deals, even with a fat scorpion like Blomger. And if he read the signs right, it was too late to shed the murdering bastard anyway.

"Lou, the reason I asked you to come by is that we've got a little problem." Case glanced at Slats, whose pale eyes still registered double nought. "Talk's going around that you're eliminating Boyle's gang at the rate of about one a day. And the powers that be are getting a bit edgy."

Until recently, Barney Boyle had been the underworld kingpin in Denver. But with Blomger's arrival, strange things began happening. Boyle's underlings started disappearing on a regular basis, without a trace. Whether they had been scared off or killed was open to question. But rumor had it that a new graveyard had been started somewhere outside town and was doing a landslide business.

Some people were reminded of the mountain men who used to sneak into an Indian camp at night and cut the throat of *every other* warrior. Generally those still alive developed a sudden urge to see faraway places, and the curious disappearance of his cohorts had had much the same effect on Barney Boyle. While he hadn't run as yet, he had taken to avoiding dark streets and was seldom seen without a small army of bodyguards.

Blomger branded such tactics underhanded and cowardly, professing complete ignorance of the whole affair. But when his henchmen started strongarming some of the sleazier dives for weekly payoffs, the handwriting suddenly came clear. The way to take over the rackets in any town was to gain a foothold at the lower echelons, and gradually undermine the big boss. Blomger saw nothing wrong with that, but his overall strategy was to speed the process along by eliminating his rival's lieutenants in a systematic manner. Of course, if the rival himself happened to drop his guard in an off moment then the whole matter could be settled with simple finality. And right now, it was Barney Boyle who found himself with his back to the wall.

Blomger eyed Case shrewdly for a moment, then chuckled. "Ed, the last time I stopped to count, the powers that be weren't anyone but you. You run this town like a ringmaster in a one-tent circus, so it must be you that's getting edgy."

Case blinked, and decided he would be wise not to underestimate this fat man. "Well, in a way you're right, Lou. I am a little concerned. When we made our deal, I really didn't give much thought as to how you would work the takeover. Foolishly perhaps, I just sort of assumed you would kill Boyle outright, or else run him out of town with a minimum of violence. But killing off his men, one by one, is frankly more than I bargained for." And, Case thought to himself, it shows a hell of a lot more calculation than I want to see in the man running the rackets. Barney Boyle is just a nice, thick-headed hooligan, but this tub of guts evidently knows how to use his brain.

"What you bargain for and what you get aren't always the same thing, Ed. Just between me and you I figured Barney could be eliminated quick, too. But the bastard has never got less than a half-dozen gunmen around him, and I'm not ready for an open war just yet."

"Now, let's not misunderstand one another, Lou. I don't want a bunch of men gunned down in the street. This isn't Tombstone, or Dodge City. We run a clean operation here. We give the people what they want, and everyone down the line gets his share of the grease. But we can't have anyone upsetting the applecart. So getting rid of Boyle has to be done neatly, and with a minimum of fuss."

Blomger shook his head ruefully, like a man trying to explain something to a backward child. "Ed, I must not be getting through to you. So far there hasn't been one shot fired. Not that anyone has heard, that is. There are no dead bodies on the street. No gangs ambushing each other all over town. No innocent citizens getting caught in the crossfire. Seems to me you've already got what you're sitting there asking for."

"You're twisting my words, and I don't like that." Ed Case was accustomed to being obeyed, without any backtalk, and his temper was fraying around the edges. Then Slats shifted position against the wall, casually crossing his arms, and Case's temper plummeted abruptly. He decided to try another tack.

"What I'm saying, Lou, is that this thing has to be done in such a way that the voters won't get disturbed. There's already talk about these strange disappearances, and nothing frightens people more than the thought of men being stalked like animals. We've got too much at stake here to louse it up by giving the do-gooders more fodder for their reform movement."

"Christ, man, you must think you're talking to an imbecile. The tenderloin swings the vote in this town, and if I don't already control it, I will inside a week. So what the hell are we doing wasting our time talking about reformers? They don't carry any more weight in Denver than a drop of batshit in a hailstorm."

Case had the look of a man who has stared into still water and seen reflected the shadow of things to come. This fat pig wasn't after the rackets; he was after Denver. And if a certain fellow named Ed Case wasn't careful, he'd find himself out on the street cadging for nickels. Or maybe just gone. Disappeared like the others. An icy claw took a hold on his spine, and his guts shivered.

"Yes, I guess you're right."

"Tell you what, Ed. You just leave the tenderloin to me, and I'll leave city hall to you. What could be fairer?" Blomger rose and walked ponderously toward the door. He would have to move fast now, before Case had time to swap sides again. The man was scared, and the quickest way to get yourself killed was to turn your back on someone who's afraid. "C'mon, Slats. Let's get back to work. Ed, you just leave everything to me. I'll see to it personally."

The door closed, and Ed Case was once again alone. *You pig-eyed sonovabitch! I'll just bet you'll see to it personally. The trouble is will I see you do it, or will I just get it in the back?* Suddenly, he had the feeling that he didn't want to be alone anymore, night or day.

Cortez D. Thomson was a lonely man. And slightly bitter, too. In Georgetown he had been the cock of the walk, the rankest high roller of them all. Men envied him, and the ladies swooned as he dashed across the finish line in his pink tights. There wasn't a poker game in town he couldn't bust if the mood struck him, and wherever he went people stood in line just to buy him a drink. Part of it was fear, for no one doubted that he was the fastest gun in town. Yet the people of Georgetown genuinely liked this brash Texan, with his flashing smile and cocksure manner. He was their showhorse, the arrogant, blue-blooded winner that each of them secretly longed to be, and they loved to brag to the pilgrims about their resident celebrity. But that was Georgetown, and this Denver. And Cort had fallen on hard times.

While Cort wouldn't admit it to himself, there was a hidden nook in his mind that held Mattie largely responsible for all his troubles. She was the one that wanted to leave Georgetown, even when he had insisted that Blomger wasn't a man to be trusted. Then there was the house. *That gaudy, tinseled, goddamn monstrosity of a house!* Mattie thought it was some kind of high-water mark in refinement and good taste, but for him it was like living inside a spangly Christmas tree. Only St. Nick wasn't about to come down that chimney!

Maybe he didn't resent the house so much as what it had done to Mattie. She just didn't seem to have time for him anymore. He could understand those first six weeks when she was all wrapped up in getting the house rebuilt and ready for opening night. But afterwards, he thought it would go back to normal, like it had been between them in Georgetown. Instead she was up to her neck scheming with Blomger, laying the groundwork to put a snaffle bit on every whorehouse in the tenderloin. She was at it morning, noon, and night. And the only time they saw each other was after the house closed, and then she always had some lame excuse. *Oh, Cort, I'm just too tired tonight.* Or too sleepy. Or some damned thing. It was enough to make a man want to puke.

Still, he had to admit he loved her, even if her fancy new ways did make a man's stomach churn like sour buttermilk. There were just certain things more important than a cruddy whorehouse or whipping the other madams into line, and damned if he sometimes didn't regret ever getting tangled up with an ambitious woman.

But the main source of Cort's bitterness was Denver itself. In one leap he had gone from a big frog in a little pond to a tad in a bottomless sea of high rollers. The gamblers in Denver considered anyone from the outlying mining camps a yokel, pure and simple, and Cort's reputation meant no more than a mouse fart in a stiff wind. Denver was loaded with gamblers, gunslingers, and bunco artists, and many were household names across the width and breadth of the frontier. Bat Masterson was manager of the Palace Variety, one of Ed Case's dives. Doc Holliday, now the most feared mankiller in the West, had snuffed out a gambler named Budd Ryan only last year. Soapy Smith and Troublesome Tom Cady, thimble-riggers supreme, were daily fleecing visitors out of their last shirt stud. Wherever he turned, Cort found himself confronted by men who were masters of the very skills that had won him a brief moment of fame in Georgetown.

Now Cort was the one riddled with envy, the outsider trying to make a name for himself and at times it seemed he was butting his head against solid granite. The high rollers weren't just uppity and clannish; they acted like he didn't even exist. Whenever he tried to join in they either ignored him or became highly patronizing, like a coachful of bankers talking to a farmer with one cow and boils on his ass. Then, just when he'd had all he could stomach, he discovered the California Gang.

Pariahs are a breed unto themselves, and wherever they roam they are drawn as if by some sixth sense to their fellow outcasts. In Denver, the watering hole for outsiders, lepers, and upstarts alike was Murphy's Exchange. Located on the corner of Larimer and Twentieth Street, only a block from Mattie's bordello, it was known locally as the Slaughterhouse. Here, death was a permanent resident, one of the boys almost. Men had been blown apart with guns, butchered with knives, and beat to death with everything from bare fists to a butter crock. Rarely did an evening pass without at least one brawl, for the men who frequented Murphy's Exchange met on a common ground of hate and envy. And it was here that Cort finally met his own kind.

The California Gang was an unsavory band of murderers, grifters, and common swindlers that had been run out of San Francisco. While they passed themselves off as gamblers, the gang had been too much even for the Barbary Coast, and they skipped out only one step ahead of a vigilante's noose. But in Denver it was every man for himself, devil take the hindmost, and though they weren't welcomed with open arms, the California Gang hadn't been sent packing. Not yet, anyway.

Cort had stumbled onto the Slaughterhouse only after being rebuffed in the classier joints, and it seemed he had found a home at last. Standing at the bar, he struck up a conversation with Cliff Sparks, one of the gang's lesser henchmen, and the two hit it off immediately. From there it was only a short step to being accepted by the others, and before long he found himself a regular member of the motley crew.

But if Cort found solace in the company of his new comrades, Mattie was livid. Even in the tenderloin the California Gang was considered scum, water rats scattered from their nest, and she was outraged that he would lower himself to their level. As Denver's foremost madam she had a certain standing to maintain, and word was already spreading that her man had aligned himself with the scurviest bunch to hit town in a decade. Still Mattie had no monopoly on stubbornness, and the matter had been simmering between them for some weeks when Cort made the error of coming home with the first rays of sunrise. Opening the door to their suite, he found Mattie seated before the fireplace, her face etched with a mixture of petulance and worry.

"Well, I see you've still got the home fires burning." His feeble attempt at humor was wide of the mark and he saw it the minute her crackling eyes leveled down on him.

"Just where the hell have you been?" she snapped.

"Why, just about where you think I've been," he growled back. "Out raping old ladies, and robbing little kids of their play-pretties. Where else?"

"Listen, Cort Thomson, don't you get on your high-horse with me! I've been sitting here all night worried sick, wondering if those wharf rats had cut your throat, or dumped you in Cherry Creek."

"Well, at least something managed to keep you awake. Here lately you've been so goddamn tired and sleepy I was afraid you'd come down with some kind of tropical disease." The words tumbled out even before he realized what he was saying. But it was almost a relief to have it out in the open at last.

"And what's that supposed to mean?"

"Just what it says. We're livin' in a house devoted to screwing, but the lord and master hasn't even got a sniff lately. Course, maybe instead of gettin' screwed I'm just plain gettin' fucked."

"Don't be crude." Mattie turned back to the fire, clearly shaken by the truth of what he said.

"Crude, my ass!" His voice rose, harsh and sardonic, filling the room. "I'm talkin' about you turnin' your back to me night after night, and you tell me to mind my manners. Bullshit."

"Cort, please try to understand." She still couldn't look at him, but her tone was imploring. "We've got a chance to be *somebody* in this town. Not just a gambler and a whorehouse madam, but people with power and the money to back it up. Maybe I haven't treated you right lately. But it's only because I've got so much on my mind, not because I don't want you. I do, really I do. And I'll make it up to you just as soon as things settle down."

"Mattie, you talk like somebody eatin' loco weed. Or maybe you just can't see what's going on around you." His voice had gotten louder, and now he started pacing up and down the room. "Money and power! That's a laugh. Everyone in town is talkin' about how you're in cahoots with Lou Blomger. And they're scared shitless he's gonna murder half of Denver before he gets what he wants. Do you really think they're gonna treat us like anything except what we are?"

He stopped pacing and stood over her, shouting. "Do you know what those sonsabitches call me behind my back? A pimp. Do you hear that, Mattie? *A pimp!* And you're sittin' here telling me we're gonna play footsie with the swells. Shit!"

"Cort, please don't take it like that." She stood and put her arms around his neck. Then she kissed him, and smoothed the hair back from his forehead. "It will only be a little longer. I promise. And even if those devils uptown don't accept us, we're going to run Denver. I promise you it. . . ."

A knock on the door interrupted her. Exchanging quizzical glances with Cort, she walked to the door and opened it. Handsome Jack Ready stepped halfway into the room, looking from her to Cort.

"I heard shouting. Thought maybe something was wrong."

"Everything's fine, Jack." Mattie smiled gratefully. "Just a little family argument."

"You sure you're okay?" When she nodded he turned to leave, then stopped and looked back at Cort. "Thomson, she may be your woman, but I'm telling you now, if you ever hurt her you won't walk away."

Mattie shoved Jack out the door and shut it before Cort could reply. His face was drained of color, and his voice shook with rage. "You better tell your pet baboon to stay clear of me. Next time I'll kill him."

Wearily she sank down into a chair, and stared at the fire. "Cort, I just couldn't take that. Jack's my friend, and he's only trying to protect me. Couldn't we just forget any of this happened and go back to—?"

The door slammed, and when she turned, Cort had gone. But somehow she just couldn't be bothered. She was too tired. And there were too many things to think about. *He'll be back. And then I'll make it up to him. Once we're running this town he'll look back and see that I was right.*

The most elegant house on Holladay Street was a place where trouble dwelled these days. The tension was caused not so much by what was said as what was left unsaid. Cort and Handsome Jack had ceased speaking entirely, which under the circumstances was probably the best thing for everyone concerned. But it was a shaky truce, and Mattie lived in constant fear that one of them would somehow miscue in a moment of anger. Both were short-fused, and while each had reason to respect the other's deadly skills, it wouldn't take much to ignite the situation.

Thinking about it, Mattie reluctantly admitted that Cort had become *one* of her thorniest problems. He spent less and less time in the house, and according to the grapevine he had become thicker than ever with the California Gang. What they were planning was a matter of open speculation throughout the tenderloin, but it was certain to be some tricky dodge that wouldn't stand a high wind. Cort had also taken to drinking quite heavily, and it showed in his moody disposition as well as a worn and haggard look around the eyes. Whenever she mentioned this, or showed any interest in his activities at the Slaughterhouse, all she got for her efforts was a cold stare. While she had intentionally become more responsive in bed lately, it hadn't helped much. There was a certain indifference in Cort's lovemaking, which would have been apparent to a wooden Indian. And this, along with his drinking and Handsome Jack and the California Gang, sometimes seemed more than she could bear.

But in some ways, Cort was only a prickly irritant in her crown of thorns these days. He was flesh and blood, and no matter how sulky or obstinate he might become, it was something she could deal with face to face. Her other troubles were less visible, like a spooky apparition that recurs night after night in a bad dream. And it was slowly tearing her apart for the simple reason that she couldn't make it go away.

Lou Blomger's campaign to take over the rackets had broken out in open violence at last. Within the last week three of Barney Boyle's henchmen had been shot down in cold blood, and left in the gutter as a grim warning. There was talk along The Row that the latest tally for Slats and Blomger's other mercenaries now stood at eleven dead, including one madam, who had stubbornly refused to switch allegiance from Boyle's organization. There was also a rumor, which Mattie found both frightening and slightly incomprehensible, that Ed Case had thrown his support behind Boyle at the last minute. But it was too late, much too late.

Blomger already controlled the greater part of the tenderloin and everyone in the rackets went hollow-eyed at the mere mention of his hired killers. Gang wars were all part of the game, something a person lived through by minding his own business. And from a practical standpoint, the saloonkeepers, madams, and gambling impresarios couldn't see that it mattered *who* collected the weekly tribute. The payoffs went right on whether the name was Boyle or Blomger, and the only important thing was to somehow survive the changeover.

But for Mattie it wasn't quite that simple. She wasn't just another madam with the vexing problem of deciding which gang had the upper hand. She was a key member of Blomger's juggernaut, and by now everyone in town knew it. Her job had been to organize the madams, to convince them that it was far more prudent to back a winner than to stick with a man who was slowly having his legs chopped out from under him. She took small satisfaction in the fact that it had gone amazingly well. The madams were old hands at this sort of thing, and when the tides shifted they knew how to avoid the undertow. Still, Mattie could see the contempt in their eyes and knew they were thinking that she had sold out quicker than a two-bit whore.

That stung, but it was only the beginning.

Some madams had hedged about making the switch, but they shrewdly kept their mouths shut and waited out the storm. Sallie Purple, a veteran of every tenderloin from New Orleans to San Francisco, chose to flaunt her opposition to Blomger's takeover. She went up and down The Row, telling the other madams to *hang on,* that it was only a matter of days until Boyle rendered that fat pig into a barrel of lard.

The next morning Sallie Purple was found in an alley, stuffed in a barrel with a pig's foot clenched between her rigid jaws. The message was clear. And the madams wasted no time in joining Blomger's camp.

Mattie was sickened, unable to elude the thought that Sallie Purple's death indirectly fell on her shoulders. Certainly Blomger had ordered the murder, and just thinking of it made her queasy. But over and above that, she was revolted with herself, riddled with guilt that she had unwittingly contributed to the woman's grisly end. Suddenly the ruthlessness and brutality just seemed too much, almost as if she had awakened one morning to find herself bird-dogging victims for a pack of wild animals. She resolved to make a clean break with Lou Blomger, and work out some way of paying back the money spent on the house.

But that was in the morning. Shortly after lunch she had a visitor.

When Blomger walked through the door of her office, she stiffened, unable to conceal her revulsion. Not for the man, oddly enough. But for what he was, or more accurately what he had become. The thought came over her that he looked like a swollen grub, a fat, slimy thing that had just crawled up out of the earth to devour the world. Something you wouldn't want to touch or run the risk of ever having it touch you. But it had touched her. Not so much her flesh as her life, and for the first time in memory she suddenly felt like a whore.

"You look like you've seen a ghost. You're not sick are you, Mattie?"

She stared at him for a moment, steeling herself to have done with it before he could twist her words, and drag her any deeper into the slime. "Yes, Lou, I'm sick. Sick of killings, and beatings, and seeing fear in people's eyes just because they know I'm one of Blomger's Gang. I want out, Lou. This minute. I'll pay you back for the house, but I want it ended here and now."

Blomger's jowly features went ashen, and he started to speak. Then he thought better of it, and took a chair, clamping down hard on his anger. After a moment he shook his head, smiling crookedly. "I'm afraid it's not that easy, Mattie. If you lie down with dogs, you get up with fleas. And if you've got an itch, you'll just have to figure out a way to scratch it for yourself."

"Don't talk in riddles, Lou. Say it straight out."

Blomger studied her, gauging his words carefully. "All right, if that's how you want it. I can't afford to have you check out of the game right now. You're a big name in Denver these days, and if you resign, so to speak, it might give certain people some dangerous ideas. Ed Case and his jackals are just waiting for an opening so they can jump in and cut my throat. You bought cards, Mattie, and I regret to say, you'll just have to see it through."

"That sounds vaguely like a threat." She looked at him steadily, trying to see beneath the fleshy mask. "Don't we go back a little far for that kind of thing?"

"Yeah, we do go back a long ways. And that makes me all the more disappointed in you. Or maybe you conveniently forgot that it was me who helped you all those years, and set you up in a house you'd never have built on your own."

"Oh, Lou, I haven't forgotten. How could I?" She looked away, unable to meet his stare. Some moments passed before she spoke again, her voice hollow, drained. "Lou, did you have to kill Sallie Purple?"

"That's the fall of the dice." His face was inscrutable, but there was a flicker of comprehension in his eyes. This didn't have anything to do with ten men being murdered or people being afraid of her. She was upset because that loud-mouthed old slut got rubbed out. It was as simple as that.

"Mattie, let me tell you something. When you reach for the sun, you're just bound to get a few blisters. We're playing in a table-stakes game, and the chips are human lives, yours and mine. You knew when we started that either Boyle would get us, or we'd get him. And don't try to deny it. If you were too dumb to realize it, I wouldn't have picked you as a partner. So don't start balking just because some old hag talked herself into an early grave. You are willing to bet your own life, so why get choked up just because someone else made the same bet and lost?"

Mattie shuddered, and closed her eyes, trying to erase a blurred image of Sallie Purple with a pig's foot crammed in her mouth. "Lou, it was just so cruel and . . . oh, hell, I just don't know anymore."

"Sure it was cruel, but I didn't make the rules. This world operates on one simple law, and it hasn't changed in a thousand years. The strong fight the strong for possession of the weak. And the little fellow gets the short end of the stick. If you can't buy that then you'd better resign yourself to a dreary life and a lonely grave. The only ones that eat high on the hog and go out with a roar are the ones that have the grit to stand up and claim the goodies."

"Lou, I know everything you've said is true. Do you remember what Bill used to say? 'Only runts suck hind tits.'" They both smiled, recalling Hickok's singular gift for the trenchant phrase. "It took me a long time to learn what he meant, but the cowtowns were a good teacher. And you're right about something else, too. More than anything else on this earth, I want to be somebody. Whether it's money or power or just plain gumption, I want whatever it is that makes people look up to you. And I'll do damn near anything to get it." Then she paused, suddenly aware of what her last statement implied. "But I can't be a party to any more killing, Lou. I just can't."

"Poor little towhead." He smiled with some of the old warmth. "Well, you just set your mind at rest. I'll have Barney Boyle in a sack within the next couple of days, and that ends it. Before the week is out, we'll own this town—lock, stock, and barrel."

"What about Ed Case? He's still the power uptown."

"I'm not sure Case would agree with that right about now. Since I control the tenderloin that means I control the vote. And in this case, the vote means Denver. Offhand, I'd say Case better bone up on taking orders. He's probably a little rusty, but he strikes me as a man who catches on pretty fast." Blomger's heavy features relaxed, and he smiled, as if recalling an amusing anecdote. *"Quid pro quo.* Ever hear that? Well, it's a Latin phrase lawyers like to throw around.

Roughly translated, it means if I scratch your back you'd better be damned sure to return the favor. Where Mr. Case is concerned, it means I'm going to grant him his life and in return he's going to be my Polly Parrot with the uptown crowd."

"You mean you're going to let people go on thinking he still runs the town?"

"Sure. Why not? Everybody thinks Ed Case is the salt of the earth. Maybe what I've got in mind won't be so hard to swallow if they hear it coming out of his mouth." Blomger's mind drifted off again, and this time his jowls lifted in a huge, fat grin. "The immortal bard once wrote, 'The gods are just, and of our pleasant vices make instruments to plague us.' Now Ed Case has one particular vice that he thinks of as a virtue. He believes that a smart reasonable man can always outwit a smart strong man. But he's about to find out that the gods don't always play according to the rules."

"Lou, sometimes you talk like you just ate a dictionary. What do gods and vices have to do with Ed Case?"

Blomger chuckled like a bloated wolf, and patted her knee. "Quite simply, Mattie, it means that I'm going to make him take another look at his hole card. And when he does, he'll discover that the devil has got him by the short hairs."

After Blomger had left, Mattie thought back over the conversation and decided he had been right on every count. Abruptly, she was struck by the futility of playing Miss Goody Two Shoes in a world built around the principle that the strong eat the weak. If the only choice was to eat or be eaten, then as horrible as it might seem, it was better not to end up on the platter. Still, it wasn't the same as kill or be killed, regardless of what Lou said. That was ridiculous, and she just wouldn't think of it in those terms.

Mattie was in a rage. Unable to sit still, she paced back and forth in the third-floor suite. She wanted to throw something, destroy everything about her, to hurt someone. But enraged as she was, she couldn't bring herself to hurl any of her treasured knickknacks in the apartment. And at the moment she wasn't quite sure just exactly *who* it was she wanted to hurt.

Cort was out tomcatting, that much she knew. Last night he had come dragging in with rouge smeared across the shoulder of his shirt. Not his coat, but his *shirt*, was Mattie's immediate reaction as she watched him undress. Which meant he had to have the jacket off, and some paint-smeared hussy cuddled up in his arms. Flirting with saloon girls was one thing but when a man takes his coat off, he's *already* somewhere that isn't far removed from a bed. All of this ran through her mind as he wordlessly crawled into bed and conked out before his head even hit the pillow. He was drunk, reeked of rotgut whiskey, and thoroughly pussy-whipped. Climbing the stairs only moments before, it had flashed through his numbed brain that a cold glass of water and another piece of ass might just kill him.

But Mattie wasn't exhausted or even tired for that matter. She was wide awake, seething with hurt and anger, and she had all night to plan her next move. He sadly underestimated her if he thought she would take such an affront like some mousey little dimwit. Cort was her man, and no two-bit tart was going to steal him away. Long before the first light of dawn she knew exactly what must be done.

Now she waited, and paced the floor. Her anger mounted with each passing moment, for even then the conniving bastard was probably out with some frowsy slut that would turn a trick for a nickel beer and a free lunch. As she paced, she also worried about what was going on downstairs. But the house would just have to get along without her tonight. She had already appointed one of the girls to supervise things, and even if the whole operation went to hell, she just couldn't be bothered. Tonight she had more important matters on her mind.

Then a knock sounded at the door. She ran across the room and threw it open. Handsome Jack Ready stepped into the small parlor and shut the door, his face set in a grim scowl.

"C'mon, Jack, spit it out," she demanded. "Where is he?"

"You were right. He's holed up in a grimy little hotel over on Blake Street."

"And? Quit trying to spare my feelings. Let's have the rest of it."

Handsome Jack ducked his head, avoiding her eyes. Around Mattie he was like a huge teddy bear, and he couldn't stand to see her hurt. "He's with Lillie Dab, that redhead they call Tidbit. They went to the Slaughterhouse for a couple of hours. Then they went over to this hotel. Didn't check in, just walked right on upstairs, so that must mean he keeps a room there regular."

"Lillie Dab. Christ, is that the best he can do?" She began pacing again, thinking furiously as she talked. "That henna-haired bitch is no more a redhead than I am. Her roots have probably forgot what color they were." Then she stopped abruptly and faced Ready. "All right, Jack, you're a man of the world. What should I do about it?"

"Mattie, he's a real stem-winder, and that's a fact. But if you want the truth, I don't think he got sense enough to wad a birdgun load. He's scatterbrained as a titmouse, and I can't see where anything you do is going to change him."

"Maybe so." Her eyes sparked, and her body seemed to vibrate with anger. "But you still haven't answered my question."

"Well, it's a cinch he's not worth the hole to bury him in, so there's nothing to gain by killing him. Not unless you want me to do it." Handsome Jack glanced at her hopefully, but Mattie shook her head. Then he smiled as an afterthought occurred to him. "Back where I come from they have an old saying. Don't get mad. Get even."

"By getting even, you mean tit for tat. And who do you suggest I jump in bed with? Or did you have yourself in mind?"

"You could do worse. Matter of fact, just offhand, I'd say you already have."

"Never quit trying, do you, Jack?" She smiled thinly, then her face clouded again. "But you're right about one thing. It's time I got even. Way past time."

Without another word, she walked to a desk against the far wall and began slamming drawers. After a moment she turned, grasping a small pearl-handled revolver. "Bill Hickok gave this to me back in the cowtowns. And he taught me how to hit what I aim at, too."

"I thought you said you didn't want Cort killed."

"Not Cort, maybe. But there's nothing to stop me from putting a few leaks in Lillie Dab. At least her blood's red even if her hair isn't."

"Killing someone isn't like slapping their wrists, you know. It's sort of permanent. Are you sure he's worth all that?"

"I don't know, Jack. I really don't know." She turned the thought over in her mind, then her face stiffened with resolve. "But he's mine, and no hot-assed little hooker is going to take him away from me. Let's go."

With that she walked from the room, and Handsome Jack lumbered after her. Ten minutes later they entered the lobby of the Alhambra Hotel, and in exchange for a twenty-dollar goldpiece the desk clerk gave them Cort's room number. Mattie led the way upstairs and stopped in front of the right door. From inside they could hear giggling, and the drone of a man's voice. Mattie pulled the little revolver from her purse and glanced at Jack.

"Kick it in."

Ready reared back on one leg and struck with his massive brogan. The door splintered with an abrasive screech and flew open, hanging cock-eyed from its hinges. Cort and Lillie Dab jerked erect in bed, naked as jaybirds. Then the stunned expressions on their faces froze in rigid disbelief as Mattie stalked through the door. In one glance they saw her, the gun, and Handsome Jack Ready.

Lillie screamed and leaped to her feet, bouncing unsteadily on the rickety bed. Her ponderous breasts swayed like bowls of chilled jelly as she hop-scotched back and forth, trying to decide which way to run. Then Mattie whipped the revolver level and fired. A round knob on the headboard disappeared in a cloud of splinters, and the room suddenly became very active. Cort grabbed Lillie's puckered buttocks in both hands and shoved her off the far side of the bed.

"Run, Tidbit! Run before she kills you!"

Tidbit ran all right, but it was in fits and starts, like a rabbit hunting for a hole that didn't exist. She dodged from one side of the room to other, frantically trying to avoid the gun barrel that tracked her every movement. On her first trip across, a mirror shattered to smithereens just as she passed by, and she bounded away with a shrill scream. But that brought her up short against the street-side wall, and as she turned to come back, a window behind her exploded in a shower of glass.

Mattie's cursing could be heard above the roar of the gun, not so much at the girl as at her own lousy marksmanship. Then Cort came hurtling off the bed, his eyes gleaming with fury. This crazy woman had to be stopped, even if he had to bust her head. Handsome Jack brushed Mattie aside like a leaf just as Cort's feet hit the floor. The burly pug stepped forward and unleashed a paralyzing blow to the naked stomach of Georgetown's pride and joy. Cort shuddered to a halt, like he had been impaled on a battering ram, and sunk slowly to his hands and knees. His gut heaved and his mouth opened in a retching groan. Then his face turned green and he spewed the better part of an evening's whiskey across the worn carpet.

Lillie Dab, fondly known as Tidbit, was nothing if not an opportunist. Though it was something of a bare-assed opportunity, she figured it was the only one she was likely to get. With Mattie on the floor, and Cort puking like a drunk mule, the coast was clear. Red hair streaming in her wake, she darted through the door, raced down the stairs, and headed for the street.

Cursing fluently now, Mattie scrambled to her feet and made a headlong dive for the shattered window. When Lillie appeared on the street below, she fired her last three shots, kicking up spurts of dust around the girl's heels. Lillie screamed louder with each shot and gained speed going

away, boiling down Blake Street like Lucifer himself was
fanning hot coals beneath her tender rump. Mattie stood
at the window clicking the empty gun until Tidbit's shiny
hindquarters disappeared into the night. Then she turned
back to the room, her anger replaced with sheer disgust.

Handsome Jack shook his head with an amused grunt.
"Did you say *Wild* Bill Hickok taught you to shoot?"

"So I'm a little out of practice. Don't get smart." Mattie
glanced at the revolver as if maybe it had a crooked barrel.
"Besides, I would have got her if you hadn't knocked me
down."

Just then Cort groaned and settled to the floor on his
belly. Glancing up at her, like a small boy soliciting pity,
he croaked, "My mouth tastes like I just ate breakfast with
a buzzard."

"That's one way of describing it, lover. But if you want
to know the brutal truth, you look like something you disagreed with just *ate you*." She watched him for a moment,
then looked back at Ready. "Jack, get him dressed, and
bring him on home. And along the way explain to him
that if he ever gets hot pants again, I'll shoot his tally-
whacker off. I wouldn't have any trouble hitting *that* for
damn sure."

Without a backward glance, she shoved the toy pistol in
her purse and stormed out the door. Handsome Jack took a
chair, and waited for Cortez D. Thomson, late of the Confederacy and one jump out of Texas, to get his tally-whacker
presentable for a late-evening stroll.

Suddenly it occurred to him that Mattie had been right
after all. Tidbit really wasn't a redhead.

The king is dead. Long live the king! While the ancient
maxim somehow seemed ill-suited to Lou Blomger, it was
nonetheless amusing, and jokingly made the rounds in the
tenderloin.

Barney Boyle had made only one mistake, his first and
his last. He visited his favorite whorehouse on the sly one
night, accompanied by only two bodyguards. Supposedly

his presence was a secret, but he presumed too much where the madam of the house was concerned. She wanted nothing more to do with a loser, and promptly sent a message to Blomger's headquarters. When Boyle and his underlings emerged some hours later, Slats was waiting with four of his mercenaries. The night came alive with the roar of shotguns, and Barney Boyle pitched to the ground with a quart of buckshot up his gizzard.

Blomger had won. The tenderloin was his, just as he had promised Mattie some months before. He was now overlord of the rackets, king of the underworld, and there were none left alive to dispute his claim. With Boyle out of the way, the fat man's word became law, his rule absolute, and few sovereigns wielded the degree of power he now held over Denver. Ed Case capitulated, humbling himself before the tenderloin's new monarch. As Blomger had predicted, they made an exchange. *Quid pro quo.* Case was allowed to go on living, and in return he became Blomger's mouthpiece with the uptown crowd and the politicos on Capitol Hill.

For Mattie, the subsequent declaration of peace came none too soon. She had learned something about herself in the brief, but explosive encounter with Lillie Dab. She was capable of killing, coldly and without mercy. While it was true that Blomger killed solely for power, there was only a hairline of difference in their motives. Dead was dead, regardless of the provocation, and only a hypocrite would take refuge behind the palliative of emotional rage.

Mattie had searched her soul after trying to wing Lillie, and she didn't like what she saw. Cort was all sugar and spice now, complimented in some perverse sort of way that she was willing to fight for him. But she saw the incident in a wholly different light. Clearly, she was not above killing if it involved something she wanted desperately enough. Just as Blomger had no compunction about resorting to murder if someone stood in the way of what he wanted. And before she could find out more about herself, she wanted to see the rackets' war over and done with.

But if Blomger's takeover of Denver came none too soon

for Mattie, it was timed perfectly for a tiny band of outlaws who had fled Arizona only the week before.

The first indication Mattie had of trouble brewing was when she heard that Doc Holliday had been arrested in the Interocean Club, another of Case's gambling dives. She knew that Doc was in town, and like most people in the rackets had kept up on what was happening in Tombstone over the last year. The newspapers frequently carried articles on Wyatt Earp, and his attempt to gain political control of Tombstone. Along with his brothers and Doc, he had backed the town into a corner, and even from a distance it was clear that something had to give. When news broke about the shootout at the OK Corral, Mattie had thought to herself that Wyatt's days in Arizona were numbered. The months that followed brought reports of more killings, and it came as no great surprise when she heard that Wyatt and his gang had fled the territory with murder warrants hanging over their heads. Now Doc was in jail, facing extradition, which was merely the law's roundabout way of saying he had a date with the hangman.

There were few secrets in the tenderloin, and almost before it happened Mattie knew that Bat Masterson had gotten a friend in Pueblo to lodge a bunco charge against Holliday. She had to admire Bat's loyalty, if not his reasoning. He hoped to block the extradition proceedings by placing Holliday under a Colorado warrant. But he was sadly mistaken if he thought the governor would refuse to extradite on a murder charge just because a man was accused of a petty bunco game.

Strangely, she hadn't been surprised when Bat showed up unannounced at the house one night. Somehow she had half-expected it, for if Doc was to be freed then political clout must be brought to bear from some quarter. She knew that Wyatt was bound to Doc in some curious manner that few people understood, and he obviously wouldn't leave any stone unturned to help his consumptive friend. And she just happened to be the stone whose turn had come.

Bat had just returned from Gunnison, where Earp was

hiding out, and the message he carried didn't mince any words. Wyatt felt that Mattie owed him a favor from the old days and wanted her to intercede on Doc's behalf. Everyone knew that she was Blomger's partner, and more significantly, that Blomger had a direct line into the state house.

Mattie agreed, but with some reluctance, pointing out that getting politicians to indebt themselves to one another was a ticklish business. While she couldn't promise anything, she would try, and that was the most Wyatt should expect. She told Bat to inform him that the wheels of political skulduggery ground slowly, and that he wasn't to do anything hasty without first consulting her.

When she broached the subject with Blomger he hadn't been too keen on getting involved. But Mattie put her foot down, insisting that old friends came at the head of the line. Besides, she observed, what better way to test the loyalty of Ed Case and his influence with the people on Capitol Hill? Blomger's mood changed abruptly. The situation did seem tailor-made to find out if Case had been broken to harness, sort of like hooking a gelding in the traces, for his first time out. The comparison made Blomger laugh so hard that his jowls turned beet-red, and he promised to give Case the bad news without delay.

There it sat for over a week, with no word one way or the other. She knew that Case was talking with the governor almost daily, but no decision had been reached as yet. Still, she wasn't too concerned. The tenderloin vote reached all the way into the state house, and even a governor couldn't ignore the realities of political clout.

Then, she received a cryptic message from Bat, stating that he and a *friend* would drop around that night after the house had closed. While it was risky for Wyatt to enter Denver, she recalled his head-strong ways well enough, and knew that nothing she could say would change his mind. She gave instructions for the house to be closed an hour early, and retired to her office. Shortly after midnight Handsome Jack escorted Earp to the door, then took Bat downstairs for a drink.

"Wyatt, it's good to see you. I often think about the old days in Dodge and Wichita." She lied gracefully, trying to hide her shock at the change in the man. He was thinner, worn and old before his time. But it was his eyes that told the story of what time had done to the young plainsman she remembered. They were pale and cold, like thin ice on a freshly frozen pond. The eyes of a killer.

"Mattie, you're better-lookin' than the last time I saw you." Wyatt also felt the strain, and his statement came out flat, uneasy. Almost seven years had passed, and while they had once shared the same bed, they somehow seemed like strangers. Taking a chair, he shifted so that he could see the door. "Appears you've done right well for yourself. Bat tells me you've got most of Denver wrapped around your little finger."

"Oh, you know Bat. He tells more windies than a barfly cadging drinks."

"Yeah, his stories aren't exactly reliable, and that's a fact. But I'd say this house sorta speaks for itself. Matter of fact, we even heard about you down in Tombstone. Word was that Mattie Silks was pullin' in tandem with the he-wolf around these parts."

"Lou Blomger?" Mattie smiled, and shook her head. "Somehow I can't picture Lou as a wolf of any sort. More like an elephant, if you want the truth." She observed Wyatt as a moment of silence grew. He didn't return her smile, and it was clear that he in no way meant this as a social call. He wanted something, but at the moment she wasn't quite sure what.

"Since you brought it up, the truth is what I'm after." The light reflected off his icy eyes, and she felt as if they were boring holes clean through her. "Bat sent word to Gunnison that your friends had agreed to get Doc out of jail. It's been over a week, and I still don't see nothin' happening."

"Wyatt, let's get a couple of things straight. My friends agreed to *try*. Doc's not exactly what you'd call an upstanding citizen, and the governor knows the lid will blow sky high if he refuses to extradite. Also, if you'll remember, I sent word for you not to get impatient. These things take time."

"Time's somethin' Doc don't have much of. Even if those bastards don't get him back to Tombstone and hang him, he's still lookin' down a short road. His lungs aren't much better than a sieve anymore."

"I'm sorry, Wyatt. I know he's been a good friend." But it wasn't Holliday she felt sorry for. It was Wyatt Earp. "Don't concern yourself too much, though. Lou Blomger is doing his best, and in Denver that means a lot."

"Maybe. Maybe not. I had a friend down in Tombstone that ran a newspaper. One of those fellows that thinks a lot." He paused to light a cigar, and his eyes mechanically checked the door before coming back to Mattie. "Anyway, he used to tell how folks once thought the earth was flat. Then some smooth talker convinced 'em it was round. But they finally wised up and figured out it was plain crooked. Now, your Mr. Blomger strikes me as being about as straight as a dog's hind leg. Doc Holliday don't mean any more to him than a load of horse dung. And he might just be talkin' out of both sides of his mouth."

"Meaning he might have agreed just to satisfy me, then sat back and waited for them to ship Doc south."

"It's been known to happen. Couple of times some sharpies even tried it on me. But it didn't work out exactly like they planned. I think the newspapers call it meetin' an untimely end."

Earp's words were casual, understated. But they carried an implicit warning, one that was meant to be only thinly veiled. Mattie saw now that the mark of evil was burned into his soul as with a hot iron. He had clothed himself in immunities that defied all accepted laws of God or man, and he knew only one response to those who crossed him in any fashion. Seeing him clearly for the first time, she thought it remarkable how similar he was to Lou Blomger. Thinner, maybe not so shrewd, but in his own way just as deadly.

"Wyatt, I don't know why you came here tonight, but let me give you some good advice. Don't brace Lou Blomger.

This isn't Tombstone, or Dodge, it's the big city. And the only game they play here is dirty pool."

"You're sayin' he'd sooner shoot me in the back than argue about it. What makes you think I wouldn't do it to him first?"

"Not a thing. Except you'd never get the chance. You're in his bailiwick now, and I'd lay odds he's had you covered since the minute you hit town."

"Could be. If the tables were turned, that's what I'd do." He studied her for a moment, and she could see in his eyes that he thought she had already informed Blomger of his presence. The silence deepened as he considered what she had said, then he stubbed his cigar in an ashtray and rose. "Tell you what, Mattie. You just give this Blomger a message for me. Tell him if he's real smart, Doc won't get sent back to Tombstone. Otherwise, he'd best have a ticket on the next train out, and hope it's not punched for the hereafter."

"Wyatt, I'm going to do you a big favor, just for old times' sake. I'm not going to tell Lou about that threat. If I did, Doc Holliday would swing for sure, and you'd never get out of Denver alive. Now I think that about settles our business. When you've got your troubles straightened out, come back and see me sometime. Maybe you'll be in a better mood."

Earp flushed at the abrupt dismissal, but before he could reply Handsome Jack Ready stepped through the door. Mattie suspected he had been waiting in the hall throughout the entire discussion.

"Mr. Earp, if you're ready to leave I'll call Bat. He's still practicing on the billiard table downstairs."

Earp looked from Handsome Jack back to Mattie, and a thin smile spread across his face. The kind of smile a seasoned campaigner reserves for one of his breed who has outwitted him at his own game. "Looks like I'm bettin' into a pat hand tonight. Forget what I said, Mattie. Just do your best for Doc and I'll owe you one."

"I will, Wyatt. Don't worry."

Mattie watched him go, a thin, stoop-shouldered man who had taken a shot at the big time and fallen short. Tombstone wouldn't be his last comedown, she felt sure. He was what people in the tenderloin called a born loser, a man who somehow always bit off more than he could chew. She was saddened for him, and yet in the same thought came a new sense of exhilaration. Where he had fallen short, she had measured up, and whatever it was that separated the high rollers from the chumps, she had it. Denver might not be New York or Chicago or even San Francisco, but it was more than most people ever had the nerve to tackle. And it was all hers.

CHAPTER SEVEN

Cort had suddenly become a man of means. Overnight he began sitting in on high-stakes poker games, and bucking the tiger at faro layouts around town. He was so flush that he even started buying Mattie expensive jewelry, which according to some was the mark of a real high roller. While speculation was rife as to *how* he had come by the money, there were few in the tenderloin who doubted its source. The California Gang was often out of town these days, and those who made a business of minding other people's affairs noted that Cort always went along.

What they didn't know was that Cortez D. Thomson had become an actor.

Cliff Sparks was the one that came up with the idea. *Since foot-racing was so popular in the mining camps, why not gaff the suckers with a well-rehearsed bunco game?* After all, Cort was as fast as greased lightning, so didn't it make sense to use his speed in setting up the rubes for a real haul? His cohorts were amazed at the simplicity of the idea. This was the one ingredient essential to any con game, and Sparks' scheme had it without question. Stirred well amongst a batch of miners with larceny in their hearts, it was all but foolproof.

Cort bought the idea hook, line, and sinker. Here was the chance he had been waiting for all these months. With a little luck it would put him right back at the top of the heap. *And Mattie wouldn't be so damnedly domineering once he was back in the chips!*

Over the next week the gang rehearsed with all the fervor of a Shakespearean troupe, and when the pitch seemed letter perfect, they took the show on the road. They hit Aspen first, and the miners fell over one another in their rush to bet. Then they toured Central City and Cripple Creek in quick succession, cleaning up like bandits. While the show played well, they kept adding refinements and by the fourth week they were ready for Leadville.

Saturday morning they started drifting into town singly and in pairs. Sunday was the day of rest in Leadville, and it was essential that the second phase of their scheme come off when every miner in camp was free to bet his entire poke. Their arrival took advantage of the fact that the mines worked around the clock, and was timed to coincide with the day shift coming off duty.

Disguised as miners, drummers, and common workmen, they mixed easily with the crowd, taking their assigned stations in various saloons along the street. Jim Jordan and Cort were the key men in the overall operation, and their target was the Bucket of Blood, Leadville's premier gambling dive. Jordan, who was masquerading as a whiskey drummer, wandered in first and began a hard-sell act with the bartender. Cort's role required him to wait fifteen minutes before making his entrance. He was dressed in tattered, baggy pants, a filthy shirt, and looked like he hadn't had a bath since the last time it rained. The costume made him appear a callow, underfed youth, and as he waited he kept repeating to himself the backbone statement of Cliff Sparks' instructions. *You got to make them believe you're a dumb kid that don't know his ass from a hole in the ground.*

At four-fifteen exactly, Cort walked into the Bucket of Blood. Stepping up to the bar, he ordered a beer and drank half of it in one gulp. Out of the corner of his eye he noted that Jordan had the head barkeep nailed, talking a mile a minute. Cort drained the glass in a long guzzle, and signaled the bartender.

Wiping his mouth on a dirty shirt sleeve, he strained an octave and slapped five double eagles down on the counter. "Bartender, I hear-tell you got a fast man in Leadville. Feller name of Gilbert, or somethin' like that."

The bartender eyed the coins for a moment, then nodded. "If you're talking about foot-racing, then you must mean Wally Gilbert."

"Well, where 'bouts do I find this Wally Gilbert. I wanna race him."

"You?" The bartender gave him an astonished look, then yelled down the bar. "Hey boys, did you hear that? This kid wants to race Wally Gilbert!"

There was a general stir of laughter as the men looked him over, shaking their heads in disbelief. Cort managed an embarrassed expression, then sucked up his stomach and slapped the double eagles. "That there's my last hunnert dollars, and I need two hunnert to get back to my girl in Georgia. I'm willin' to bet it all I can outrun this Gilbert feller."

The miners' interest picked up. This kid was serious, and even if it wouldn't be much of a race it'd be funnier than hell. Someone sent for Gilbert, and shortly he strolled through the batwing doors. Thin, hawk-faced, arrogant, he was an exact duplicate of Cort in his Georgetown days. Racing for such a trifling amount wasn't worth the effort, he declared, but since the boys wanted a little fun he'd be willing to oblige. The course was set, the bartender held the stakes and everybody retired outside to watch the kid eat dust.

Ten minutes later the miners trooped back inside, slapping each other on the shoulders and laughing to beat hell. The kid was game all right, but he never even came close. *And those clodhoppers he's wearin'! Kickin' up a cloud of dust every time he planted his foot.* The whole room roared with laughter, remembering the kid slogging along in Gilbert's wake. It had been something to see all right.

Then Gilbert came in, his arm around the kid's shoulders. Tears streamed down Cort's face, and snot dripped from his nose as he sniffed and snuffled. The crowd suddenly got very quiet, amazed that even a green kid like this would let himself break down in front of grown men. They edged closer, straining to catch every word as he laid his head on the bar and made pathetic little gasping sounds.

"Oh, now I'm never gonna see my girl. And her waitin' for me to come back with my pockets stuffed with gold so we could get married." He buried his head in his arms and Gilbert patted his back gently, looking like a man who had just robbed a piggy bank. Cort's moaning became louder, and finally Gilbert couldn't stand it any longer.

"By God, boys, I've never been one to take advantage of a kid. I'm gonna give him his money back, and I say we ought to take up a collection so's he can get on home to that girl."

There was a general murmur of approval from the crowd, and for a moment Cort thought he had overplayed the scene. No one had ever offered to return the money before, and he was at a bit of a loss. Then Jordan stepped into the breach, displaying the agility of a born bunco artist.

"No, by Christ, you're not!" Jordan's angry shout stilled the saloon, and the crowd turned to look at him. "I'm just a whiskey drummer, and maybe it's none of my business, but I say that kid deserves another chance. He didn't come in here askin' for charity. He came in like a man, and Gilbert's right when he says you boys took advantage of him. Why, just look at him!"

The miners turned for another look at the kid, feeling slightly ashamed of themselves now. Cort sniffed and snuffled some more, wondering just what the hell Jordan would pull next. He didn't have long to wait. Jordan walked over and clasped him on the shoulder, clucking sympathetically.

"This kid did his damnedest, and I'll say it again. He deserves to be treated like a man." Suddenly the expression on Jordan's face changed, and he began to feel Cort's arms, then his leg muscles. *"Why, this kid's a born athlete!* No wonder he lost, wearing those clodhoppers and overalls. Give him running shoes, and three paces' head start, and I'd say he stands a good chance to win."

"Mister, you're about to make a jackass out of yourself." One of the miners smiled skeptically, nodding at Cort. "Maybe we didn't treat him just exactly square, but that kid ain't no racer."

Cort's pulse quickened, and he bit down hard to stifle a chuckle. They were back on script.

"Is that so?" Jordan's tone seemed offended, like a man whose judgment in good horseflesh had just been questioned. "With something hot in his belly, and a good night's rest, I say this kid'll run right up Gilbert's back. Kid, how long since you had a square meal?"

"Mister, I ain't swallowed nothin' but spit since yesterday supper." Cort hawked and cleared his throat, trying his damnedest to look hungry.

"Well, keep your dauber up, kid. All's not lost yet." Jordan gave him a patronizing pat on the back, then turned on the miners. "See, what'd I tell you? You think this kid's not a racer, huh? Well, I tell you what I think. I'm gonna stake the kid to a hundred dollars so he can race Gilbert tomorrow, and get his money back like a man. And to show you what a jackass I really am, I got another hundred that says he'll leave Gilbert going away." Jordan jerked out a roll of bills and shoved it in the skeptical miner's face. "Now, big mouth, what'd you say to that? Put up or shut up!"

"Drummerman, it'd take a heap more'n you to teach this child to suck eggs." The miner whipped out his poke and began counting coins.

"Is that so? Well, a dog don't lie down just one way, you know. Since you're so all-fired sure of yourself, I got another hundred where this come from."

"Mister, so far as I can see, that kid's only got two gaits.

Slow and slower." This came from a second miner as the crowd gathered closer around Jordan. "You wouldn't just like to cover another hundred, would you?"

"You bet your dusty butt you're covered." Jordan wet his thumb and quickly counted the roll of bills. "Boys, I'm gonna send you back to the well. I've only got a little over a thousand on me, and it's mostly company money, but I'll bet all or any part that this kid makes monkeys out of the lot of you."

The miners crowded forward, and two fights broke out as they battled to cover Jordan's roll. Word quickly spread along the street of the impending race, and men began streaming into the Bucket of Blood to get a look at the kid. Most stared at him doubtfully, wondering aloud how a green kid like that could ever hope to shade Wally Gilbert. But there was a handful who believed they saw something the others had missed. Maybe the kid is sort of weakly looking, they observed, but hell, that's what makes horseraces. They seemed willing to back their judgment with money, and the miners were delighted that somebody besides that jug-eared drummer was willing to bet against the Leadville Flash. *Christ, bettin' on Wally was just like pickin' money up off the street!*

But Wally seemed to have a little trouble getting everything in gear the next morning. Maybe it was the change in the kid that put him off stride. With borrowed racing shoes and snug-fitting longjohns in place of tights, he still looked sort of comical. But he somehow just didn't look like the baggy-pants kid that had plowed up the street with his clodhoppers the day before. He was lean and muscular, and he wasn't dripping tears and snot like a little piss-Willie anymore. In fact, he looked downright confident. And when the starter's pistol went off, he ran just about the way he looked.

The Leadville Flash ate dust all the way down the street, and when they crossed the finish line he was almost tempted to keep right on running. While the kid had only beaten him by a yard or so, he knew without even looking back that the miners weren't exactly happy with their local champion. But then, they weren't too thrilled with the kid, either.

When Jordan went to the Bucket of Blood to collect his money the crowd looked like a flock of scalded owls. They weren't good losers to start with, and being whipsawed by a drummer and a snot-nosed kid was a little more than their dignity could handle.

After stuffing the money in his sample case, Jordan walked to the door and gave the miners a mock salute. "Life's short and full of blisters, boys. So cheer up. Tomorrow's another day."

But for the California Gang, there was no tomorrow. There was only today. Their traveling road show had played to *standing room only* in four straight mining camps, and in a little over a month they had cleared forty-six thousand dollars.

Things were looking up for Mattie, too. The rackets' war was now nothing but a bad memory, and peace once more reigned in the tenderloin. As Blomger had promised that night in Georgetown, her station in life had risen considerably since coming to Denver. While the uptown swells weren't inviting her to their social gatherings, she somehow couldn't be bothered anymore. She had money and power, in a sense the power behind the throne. And in a marketplace where the power broker ruled supreme, this was the most highly prized commodity among the men who bartered in Denver's backroom intrigues.

She saw now that Cort had been right when he said they would never be accepted by the uptown crowd. They were what they were, and maybe in the overall scheme of things they weren't meant to rise above their own kind. Not that it mattered any longer. The idea of being accepted by Denver's social elite now seemed somehow childish and absurd. Allied with Blomger, she had the power to do whatever she wanted, short of burning down city hall in broad daylight. And that was a hell of a lot more than could be said for the bankers and politicians who supposedly controlled Denver.

They took their orders from Ed Case, who in turn did the bidding of Lou Blomger, and if any of the boys uptown were unhappy with this little arrangement, no one heard them say it out loud. They did as they were told, somehow managing to foster the illusion that they still ran the city. But when they really wanted someone to plead their case before the tenderloin's new czar they had learned that the one to cultivate was the little lady behind the seat of power. And for Mattie, that's what it was all about.

Power meant money, and the more money she had the more powerful she became. Mattie didn't fully understand all the ramifications of power, but she sensed that it was self-perpetuating and she also knew how to use it with skill. People who wanted favors done, especially those who asked her to intercede on their behalf with Blomger, had not been ungenerous. Whether it was a madam plagued by greedy pimps, or a banker who wanted to organize a land grab, they knew the going rate. Curiously, it was always more than she would have asked had they simply let her set the price for services tendered. But it was all part of the game, and she had learned soon enough that people who want a favor always estimate its value at more than expected.

But, of course, this was almost like found money. What with her normal take from the house, and a cut of the payoffs from every bordello and crib in the tenderloin, Mattie was raking it in faster than she could spend it. Still, she had observed that people of wealth rarely allow their money to remain idle, and in her own way she had put it back on the street. Over the months she had bought two more houses on Holladay Street and, after a complete refurbishing, leased them to other madams. The arrangement called for an annual lease payment plus a stiff percentage of the gross, and it merely added to the flow of dollars that sometimes threatened to swamp her bookkeeping system. Fortunately, Jack had a head on his shoulders, as well as a strong back, and he had grudgingly assumed the role of treasurer.

Mattie had to laugh every time she thought of him slaving over those columns of figures. Somehow it didn't fit his image of himself, and while he did it better than she could have, he was still out of sorts after a session with the books. But handsome is as handsome does, and Jack Ready was seldom without a smile despite their running battle of wits.

Seated in her office one night, these thoughts were uppermost in Mattie's mind as she waited for Jack to walk through the door. He was as dependable as the parlor clock. Each night, toward the mid-evening lull, he would appear with scalding mugs of coffee, and she found herself looking forward to these moments of bantering discussion. There was something reassuring about Jack, as if he wouldn't give way for man or beast once he was headed in a certain direction. More and more, she realized how she had grown to depend on him, just as she had Fitz in what now seemed another lifetime.

Still, there was a monumental difference in the relationship. Where Fitz had been content as a faithful watchdog, Jack wanted more and he made no secret of the fact. He had designs on her body, if not her soul, and he wasn't above letting her know it in his own shy way. She frequently caught him watching her with a covetous glint in his eye, and while their discussions were completely aboveboard, there was always a suggestive overtone to his words. At times Mattie felt slightly guilty because she was unable to return the feeling or offer him even a scrap of encouragement. But then Handsome Jack Ready hardly needed encouragement. As one of the girls had observed in a moment of anger, when it came to bare-faced impudence, he had the balls of a brass monkey.

Occasionally, she couldn't help but chuckle when she saw Jack making the rounds of the girls' bedrooms. Whatever his feeling for her, he was still a man, and under the circumstances she wouldn't have expected any less. But he still led a pretty plush life. Warm bed, full belly, a nice slice of the profits. And his own little harem to diddle with anytime he got to feeling feisty.

All things considered, she wasn't in the least displeased

with their relationship. In a way, it was sort of exciting, like a harmless flirtation liberally spiced with intrigue. Still, she often wondered what it would be like if she didn't have the girls to work their trick on Jack's pressure valve.

"Is that a private game, or can anybody play?"

Mattie blinked and saw Jack standing in the doorway with two steaming mugs. "Come on in, Jack. Guess I was lost in my thoughts. Actually, if you want to know the truth, I was thinking about you."

"That's good enough for openers." He set the mugs down, and glanced at her sideways. "Anything you can repeat, or is it just one of those *secret* little thoughts?"

"Wouldn't that be the day!" She grinned, enjoying jousting with him.

"Don't knock it if you haven't tried it." He watched her over his coffee mug for a moment, and when she didn't respond he decided to change the subject. "Looks like it'll be another busy night."

"Long, busy, and profitable," Mattie noted. "You can always tell when the mines are doing good business. Just come down to Holladay Street and see how crowded the houses are."

"Yeah, it changes your whole outlook on things when you've got a piece of the action. Just look at me. Stopped living the fast life and started thinking about the real goodies. Like profits. Sad thing when you get right down to it. But I guess that's what comes of being a partner."

"Jack, you're a cynical man. Just a slave to money." Mattie's eyes mocked him, then she chuckled. "But you can forget about being a partner. Your ten percent still leaves me with all the votes."

"I'm not sure I want my good name sullied by such a heathen business, anyway." Smiling, he studied her as she sipped at the scalding coffee. Then the light moment passed, and his mind turned to more serious matters. "How's Cort doing these days?"

"I almost wish you hadn't asked." The brightness faded from her eyes and her face grew very somber. "Any day now

I expect to hear he's been strung up or shot. God, it's like a sickness with him. He just doesn't know when to quit."

"Yeah, word's around that him and that Slaughterhouse bunch are pushing their luck. Way I hear it, the next mining camp they go to just might be their last."

"That's what I keep telling him, and he just laughs and goes off like he had a magic charm of some kind. Last week they had to fight their way out of Blackhawk. The camps are on to their game, Jack, no doubt about it. But I think he's in too deep with those cutthroats to back out."

Jack shook his head and pondered a moment. So far as he was concerned the bastard would probably get just what he deserved. But that didn't help Mattie. "Couldn't Blomger get Cort out of the gang if you asked him to take a hand?"

"Sure he could," Mattie agreed lamely, as if the thought had crossed her mind more than once. "But that would just destroy Cort completely. He thinks he's out there proving to me what a big man he is. And I can't seem to get it across that he doesn't have to prove anything to me."

"Maybe it's not you. Maybe it's something he has to prove to himself."

"Like what? Look at all these diamonds." She flashed the rings on her fingers. "He gave me every one of those. Now, will it prove anything for me to end up with a fistful of rocks and him dead?"

"Not to you especially. But it might to him. You've struck it awful big here in Denver, Mattie. And the man sleeping with you might just have to prove to himself that he's in the same class."

"Oh, Christ! Male vanity again. Sometimes I get so sick of it I could just throw up. Won't you men ever learn that a woman just wants a man, not a bundle of nerve and injured pride?"

"Now that's one problem I don't have." Jack's broad features split in a grin. "I've got all I can do just to service those love-hungry soiled doves of yours."

"Love hungry?" Mattie laughed in spite of her troubles. "Jack, you'd better not let the girls hear you say that. They'll

claw your eyes out. And as for servicing them, I'd say it's just about fair payment for the amount of food you eat."

"Goddamn, you wouldn't want a fellow to get puny, would you? I've got to keep my strength up if I'm going to earn my ten percent."

"All I can say is, it's a good thing you've only got a piece of the action. If that's what you do for ten percent, I'll lay odds you'd kill yourself before you ever worked up to full partner."

Jack's eyes leveled on her, and beneath the amused twinkle was an outright challenge. "Check around. You might be surprised."

Mattie just smiled, and let him strut out the door with the last word. Jack Ready might think he was *the* grizzly bear of all ladies' men, but he had a long way to go before he caught the prize hen napping. Still, it was fun to watch him try, and she had to admit that life somehow wouldn't be the same if he ever grew weary of the game.

Denver was rapidly becoming known as a protected city. Lou Blomger had put out the word, and the underworld had no doubt that his edict would be backed to the hilt. *Crimes of violence would no longer be tolerated within the city limits.* Robbers, muggers, and penny ante extortionists were warned that their lives were forfeit if they dared to pull a job in Denver. Even yeggmen and grifters fell under the ban, for Blomger was determined that any caper involving potential violence would become a thing of the past in his domain.

What they did outside the city limits was their business. They could rob, kill and hijack, torture, maim and murder, and Blomger wouldn't bat an eye. But those reckless enough to practice the deadly arts in Denver proper would be dealt a swift, brutal lesson in obeying the law. Not the everyday, garden variety law, but Blomger's law. The kind that demanded an eye for an eye, absolute, final, without appeal or clemency—or even a second chance. And as the underworld had reason to recall, Slats and his mercenaries were chillingly skilled at performing neat, workmanlike executions.

There was no sense of civic duty behind Blomger's edict. On the contrary, he felt small obligation to anyone except himself. He was simply a pragmatic businessman, like a banker who forecloses on a widow or a merchant who cunningly undercuts his competition. Only in Blomger's case, the rackets were his business, and he meant to insure that they operated without undue publicity or any further acts of violence. The public felt it was entitled to certain harmless diversions in life, such as gambling and prostitution. Years of experience had taught him that the citizenry was blindly apathetic to almost any form of vice, so long as it was conducted quietly and out of sight. But violent crimes were not only highly visible, they were also extremely frightening. The man in the street wanted to know that he could get a little nookie when he felt like it, or drop a few dollars at the faro tables in the evening. Yet he also wanted assurance that he wouldn't be mugged on the way home to the wife and kiddies. And nothing could ignite a reform movement faster than a rash of robberies or murdered holdup victims.

Whores and crooked gaming dens, even bunco games and thimble-riggers, were all right, condoned as a matter of fact by the sweaty masses. But they drew the line at spilling any of their own blood or being forcibly separated from their wallets. And it was here that Lou Blomger also drew the line, declaring that any man who stepped over it would be judged an outlaw even among his own kind.

Peace settled over Denver like a warm, furry blanket. The public viewed the tenderloin as a playground for naughty adults, the rackets operated with blissful tranquility, and John Q. felt safe on the streets for the first time in two decades. Gunslingers, highwaymen, and thieves were welcome for as long as they cared to sample the delights of Denver's heady atmosphere. But only if they minded their manners, and weren't tempted to molest the local residents.

Otherwise they were found floating face down in Cherry Creek.

Just as the fat man had suspected, politicians and police alike hailed him as a civic benefactor, and jumped on the Blomger bandwagon. Crime was a thing of the past, according to city hall, and when municipal elections rolled around the political hacks naturally took full credit for making the streets of their fair city safe at last. Since the police didn't have anything to do but arrest drunks and collect payoffs, they were equally delighted. They got the glory for cleaning up the town and hadn't once fired a gun or scraped a knuckle in the process. After that the slightest request from Blomger got a faster response than a direct order from the mayor himself.

The foundation of Blomger's power, of course, remained in the fact that he controlled the rackets. The decision of who got paid off, and how much, was his alone. And the hardheads who wouldn't cooperate just didn't get greased. Yet there was more to it than mere payoffs. The tenderloin cast the swing vote in any election, and without Blomger's support a politician couldn't even reach office, let alone board the gravy train of corruption and bribes. Slowly, the tentacles of his power reached outward and upward, insidiously gaining a stranglehold on greedy officials at every level of government.

When the votes had been counted after the most recent city and county elections the results came as no surprise to the political hierarchy. Lou Blomger had bought himself a mayor, an entire police department, and a district attorney whose sole aim in life was to leave office a rich man. The county prosecutor was essential to his plans for expanding the rackets, and on the morning following the elections he was in a rare mood. Seated around the breakfast table, in his suite at the Windsor Hotel, Blomger gloated as his brother and the ever-present Slats listened attentively.

"Damned if I don't wish I could have seen Ed Case's face when he heard the news. Holy Mother of Christ! He must have broke out in a cold sweat. All these years he's been running Denver and he never once had a district attorney on the payroll. It just bears out what I've always said. Brains aren't enough. You've got to have guts, and you've got to have imagination. Right, Sam?"

Sam Blomger bore absolutely no resemblance to his brother. Most people found it difficult to believe that they were even related, much less sprung from the same womb. Though a year older than Lou, Sam lacked the cunning and organizational genius of his younger brother. Since they were kids Lou had been the leader and Sam the tag-along, the one who listened and obeyed simply because it made more sense that way. By virtue of their blood relationship, Sam had held key positions in Lou's underworld empire since the early days in Springfield. But his contributions were hardly of an executive nature. Where Lou was a man of perception and stealth, Sam was a strong-armed bully, only one step above a common thug. Still, they made a good team since each offset the other's weaknesses. Lou was cold and calculating, but physically a defenseless tub of lard. Sam was dimwitted, obtuse as a pound of lead, but a man of huge stature, fiery temper, and an absolute passion for beating the bejesus out of anyone who disagreed with his kid brother.

Now he dully searched Lou's face and tried to come up with a snappy answer. "That's right, Lou. You got to have guts. Guts and brains. That'll do it every time."

Lou exchanged glances with Slats, and stuffed an entire pancake into his cavernous mouth. After munching a couple of times, he swallowed, and a twisted smile spread over his thick lips. "Well, whatever it takes, it worked out just like I said. We own the law in this town, and tomorrow we're going to take over every policy shop in Denver. Before long we'll have to hire wagons just to haul the loot to the bank." Buttering another pancake, he looked back at Slats. "You got the boys all set?"

"They're ready." The little man's cold eyes brightened with thoughts of the morning to come. "We'll have men

standin' at the door of every shop when they open. By noon
we'll be runnin' the show."

"Slats, you're a joy to behold. I always did like to see a
man take enjoyment from his work." He sloshed syrup over
the pancake, and speared another slice of ham. "But remember, no killing. Bust a few heads and kick some ass, but *no
killing*."

The gunman's weasel face twitched with resentment,
like a snake that had just had its fangs pulled. But he only
nodded and went back to eating.

"Lou, I sure hope you got this thing all figured out." Sam
shook his head with the perplexed frown of a small boy trying to fathom the riddle of the multiplication tables. "Just
don't seem to me that them policy fellers are gonna give it
up without a fight."

Policy was the poor man's gambling game in Denver,
one of the earliest imports from the ghettos of the eastern
cities. While it was designed for those who couldn't afford
the gaming dives, it was popular with rich and poor alike,
and nearly everyone in town played at least one number a
day. There were twelve shops spread around the city, with
ownership divided among six men who had come west
seeking gold, and in a very real sense had found it. Some
years back they had formed the Denver Policy Association,
and to date this united front had discouraged anyone
from poaching on their highly lucrative operation. Each
day the winning numbers were taken from the Colorado
State Lottery, and paid odds ranging from five to one up
through sixty to one. But the chances of hitting with any
regularity were remote, and though many played, there were
few who won. And Lou Blomger meant to have a piece of
any game where the suckers actually stood in line to fling
their money away.

"Don't trouble yourself, Sam. They'll see it our way."
Blomger's voice was almost jovial. "By tomorrow night
we'll have the policy association in our hip pocket. They
know we've got the law backing our play, and even if we

didn't I don't think they're too anxious to lock horns with Slats. Wouldn't you say that about sums it up, Slats?"

"Boss, I sorta hate to say it, but I reckon that's how she lays." The little man's words reflected his disappointment in the peaceful ways men sometimes chose. "They haven't got no more fight than a billygoat with his gonads whacked off."

Blomger stared at Slats for a moment, curious that he never ceased to be fascinated by the man's pale, milky eyes. He had heard that snakes mesmerized their prey with just such a look, and he often wondered if the same thing happened to Slat's victims. *The little bastard would probably kiss my hand if I told him to kill a couple of men tomorrow just for good measure.* But that was a thing of the past. Denver was a peaceful town now, and he meant to keep it that way. Unless, of course, some meathead got big ideas and started trouble. Even then it wouldn't be any problem. He could just send Slats over and let him look at them for a while.

Mattie would always remember it as the night Matsu was killed. Around town it became known as the night of the Chinese riots. But this was wholly misleading since the inhabitants of Hop Alley were the victims rather than the aggressors. Most ran for their lives or tried to hide as the mob raged through Chinatown. Yet there were some who faced the howling rabble with dignity, determined not to disgrace themselves even in the face of death. Chin Lin Sou and his wife, Matsu, were among those who chose not to run.

Like many towns across the West, the festering hostility toward the Chinese had grown with each passing year in Denver. The Orientals were hated for a variety of reasons in the mining camps, most of which were groundless yet accepted without question. They were foreigners. Their skin was the wrong color. They worshiped idols instead of the one God, and clung to customs that were both offensive and unfathomable to the white man. But as it is with most of man's hate and petty intolerance, the real cause was founded along more mundane lines. The truth of the matter was, the Chinks just worked too damned cheap.

The railroads had employed whole boatloads of Chinese coolies as track was laid across the West, and the prejudice had its beginnings right there. The coolies gladly worked for a fraction of the wages demanded by whites, and nothing sours a man more than to have his livelihood jerked from beneath him by a foreigner. Especially a *slant-eyed foreigner*. But the real trouble began when the railroads completed their westward expansion and unleashed a yellow horde on the mining camps.

The Chinese approached the boomtowns with a completely different outlook. Their work on the railroads had been a device of the moment, a means of gaining entry to America and earning a little money. But now they wanted to settle down among their white neighbors and make a home for themselves in this vast land. There were riches enough for all, and their concept of democracy was that any man, regardless of race, creed, or color, had the right to try his luck. But they were in for a rude shock.

Chin Lin Sou had been among the first to arrive in the mining camps, and many felt that without him Denver would never have had a Hop Alley. He had saved his money and opened a small store dealing in Chinese silks, jade, lichee nuts, herb tea, pickled bamboo shoots, and other Oriental mysteries. Soon he took a wife, Matsu, and as more Chinese settled in the area he became known as a man of wisdom and incorruptible honesty. Even the whites held him in high esteem, and before long he had been given the honorary rank of mayor of Chinatown.

Along the back streets and alleyways of the tenderloin, there were now some two thousand Chinese residents. Many of them ran shops, such as that of Chin Lin Sou. Others operated gambling parlors, introducing Denver to fantan, pigow, and Chinese lottery, an Oriental variation of the policy game. And some set up opium dens, where for four bits a man could buy a night of escape from whatever devils inhabited his own personal hell.

But the small community could support only so many
shops, gambling parlors, and opium dens. This meant that
upward of a thousand Chinese had to find work outside the
Hop Alley district. And that spelled trouble, for as with the
railroad, they were still willing to work cheap.

The situation came to a head only a week after the elections which had consolidated Lou Blomger's control of
Denver. The Yellow Peril, as it was termed by candidates of
both parties, had been a heated issue during the election
campaign. But no one knew exactly what to do about it. The
politicians were long on talk and short on solutions. That
left it up to the voters, and the only thing they knew for certain was that the goddamn Chinks were taking bread right
out of their mouths. Everyone agreed, Republicans as ve-
hemently as Democrats, that something had to be done. Yet
there didn't seem to be any legal way of stopping the
Orientals from working dirt cheap.

Then, on the first Saturday night after the elections, the
seed of hate burst into a raging fury which spread through
the tenderloin like an inferno. Later, no one could remember
clearly how it had started. They recalled a few men outside
the Cricket Hall Saloon loudly debating what should be done
about the Yellow Peril. Then there were a hundred men, and
suddenly a thousand, and another thousand, and Curtis Street
filled with an ugly, chanting mob. Before anyone quite realized how it happened, the cry went up. *Run the slant-eyes
out of town! Kill the yellow sonsabitches!*

The mob roared its approval and split into bands, rampag-
ing through Chinatown with their bloodlust aroused. They
battered in the doors of shops, homes, gaming parlors, and
opium dens alike, dragging the occupants into the street.
Those who could not escape, or find a safe hiding place, were
beaten to the ground and stomped senseless. Some were
shot, and a few hung, but most of those killed were simply
surrounded and kicked to death by the crazed mob.

Mattie had heard the distant roar and stepped to the door,
thinking it must be another political rally of some sort. The
fools had been parading around town for the last month, and

though the election was over she assumed they hadn't gotten it out of their systems as yet. Handsome Jack joined her on the front steps, and as they watched, the mob turned the corner a few blocks away and surged down Holladay Street. They observed silently for a few moments as the angry rumble of the crowd got louder and louder.

"Jack, there's something about this that doesn't smell right. What do you make of it?"

Ready shook his head with a baffled frown. "Damned if I know, but I'll tell you one thing. Those men are up to no good. I've seen my share of mobs, and that bunch is out for somebody's blood."

Just then Cort came pounding around the corner of Twentieth Street and raced toward them. Glancing back he saw that the mob was only fifty yards behind him, and broke into a headlong sprint. As he drew closer they saw that his hair was disheveled and one sleeve of his coat had been ripped from the shoulder. He slid to a halt before them, sucking air into his lungs in great gulps.

"Get back in the house." His chest heaved, and the words came out in a choked rush. "They're killin' the Chinamen, and it's not safe for anybody outdoors."

Suddenly a terrifying roar went up from the mob, and they glanced around just as several men ran an elderly Chinese to earth. Mattie shuddered as they crowded around like a pack of animals, stomping and kicking until the old man lay still. Then someone produced a rope, flipping it around his neck, and within moments the body was dangling from a lamppost. The hanging whipped the mob into a frenzy, and they headed once more toward Hop Alley.

Mattie fought against the shock of what she had seen. Her stomach churned, and she felt sure she was going to be sick. Then it suddenly dawned on her that the mob's target was Hop Alley. *Chin Lin and Matsu!* Their shop was on Hop Alley, and they were the closest friends Mattie had among the Chinese. They had befriended her during the time she was renovating the house, bringing little gifts of welcome and inviting her to lunch in their living quarters behind the shop. While they wouldn't dare to enter a brothel, they accepted her as a person, extending their friendship freely, and she had been a guest in their home countless times. Now this mob of animals was out to kill them!

"Cort!" She grabbed his coat, jerking him around. "Chin Lin and Matsu. You've got to save them. Do you understand? You've got to!"

Without a word Cort turned and ran toward Hop Alley. Handsome Jack jumped from the steps and pounded after him. Together they turned the corner and raced down the narrow passageway with the mob hot on their heels. Coming to a halt before the shop, they spun to face the onrushing crowd. Cort jerked a pistol from his hip pocket and prepared to make a stand. For once, he was even glad to have Handsome Jack beside him. While Ready never carried a gun, his mere presence was a threat in itself.

"That's far enough!" Cort shouted as the mob approached. "The first man that tries to go in this shop is gonna get ventilated."

Jammed shoulder to shoulder, the crowd ground to a halt and stared at him indecisively for a moment. Then one of the leaders shook his fist at Cort. "Thomson, you're lookin' to get strung up, too. We're here for the mayor of Chinatown, and we don't mind takin' you along with him, if that's how you want it."

"Boys, I'm afraid I just can't oblige you." Cort flashed a wide grin, waving the gun casually toward the shop. "Why, if I let you have Chin, who the hell's gonna do my laundry?"

Many of the men laughed despite the nature of their errand and for a moment Cort thought he had them hooked. Then a fresh roar went up from the mob as the shop door opened and the Chinese couple stepped outside.

Chin Lin and Matsu were scared, but they still retained their dignity. The shopkeeper bowed to Cort and Handsome Jack, then smiled weakly. "You good men. We thank Missy Silks for send you. But you must not die for us. We go now with men."

Chin Lin started forward, but Cort grabbed his arm and

jerked him back. Just then a shot rang out and Matsu gasped, clutching her breast as she sagged to the ground. Cort always thought the shot was meant for him and Chin Lin was equally convinced that he was the one marked for death. But they never found out.

Handsome Jack Ready hurtled through the air and grabbed the mob leader before he could cock his pistol for a second shot. He clutched the man's gun arm with one hand and grasped him around the throat with the other. Before anyone could move, Ready jerked the man aloft, took two swift strides across the alley, and slammed him against the brick wall of a building. The man's head burst like a ripe melon, and when Ready released him he slumped forward, dead before he hit the ground.

Cort jerked his other Colt and leaped to the center of the alley as the mob surged toward Handsome Jack. *"All right, you cocksuckers! The first man that makes a move gets drilled!"*

The men froze in their tracks, their eyes fastened on the two Colts. Then Handsome Jack stepped forward beside Cort, and the crowd suddenly decided they no longer liked the odds. Slowly they began edging backward, forcing the men behind them to give ground. After a few moments of cursing and shoving the alleyway was once again clear.

Cort and Jack waited until the last man had scuttled around the corner, then turned back to the shop. Chin Lin knelt on the ground with Matsu cradled in his arms, rocking her back and forth like a baby as he stroked her raven hair. The two men looked at each other, both dreading to tell Mattie. Cort reholstered his pistols, and stood dead still, as if wrestling with some bothersome thought. Abruptly, he stuck out his hand. Handsome Jack stared at it for a moment, considering. Then he grasped it and they solemnly shook hands. Leaving Chin Lin to care for Matsu, they turned and walked slowly back toward the house.

"Use this soap and scrub your sins away! Cleanliness is next to godliness, and I see men before me who are in need

*of both. Step right up, gentlemen! Let me interest you in a
soap as pure and white as the snow on those distant mountains."*

A small crowd began to form on the corner as something
in the man's melodious voice caught their attention. There
was a hint of the Bible-thumping revivalist in his resonant
spiel, but that meant nothing. Preachers were a dime a
dozen. What stopped them was less definable. The merest
suggestion of something for nothing, the one lure few men
could resist.

"Step closer, gentlemen. Let me tell you of my mission
in life. The great God Jehovah meant for his children to
be clean, and I have come forth in this wilderness of
backsliders and miscreants to give you the word. Soap,
my friends! *Soap!* Therein lies salvation for saint and
sinner alike. Concocted in my own laboratory, the fruit of
ancient formulas evolved in the holy land. And as I look out
before me I see people who have never needed anything as
desperately in their lives as the purifying, soul-cleansing
qualities of my soap.

"Why, just look around at your neighbor. Go on, take a
careful look at his hands and face. I defy you to tell me that
man isn't in dire need of soap and water. And his ears!
Look in his ears! Great heavens to Betsy, you could drop
a kernel of corn in there today and have roasting ears before morning."

The crowd laughed, hooked now on his rapid-fire deliv-
ery. Their numbers had grown, spilling off the boardwalk
onto the street. Then the man dramatically held two bars
of ivory-tinted soap aloft for all to see. The laughter died,
and the tempo of his evangelistic cadences picked up,
munching words like an animal eating its young.

"Soap, brothers! Salvation for your skin and your soul
in a single bar of the finest soap known to God or man. Now,
who will be the first to step up and give me twenty-five
cents . . . a lowly two bits . . . for a chance at salvation. Oh,
yes, I know what you're thinking. Why should you pay two
bits here when you can buy common, everyday soap for a

nickel at the mercantile? But ask yourself this. Will that pot ash and lye sold by those greedy merchants do anything more than scour the hide off your weary bones? *Will it save your soul?*"

The men in the crowd glanced around at one another with skeptical smiles, and a murmur swept back over their ranks. Now they knew his game. He was just another pitchman trying to con them into buying nickel soap for a quarter. No one made a move to step forward, and there was a restless stir among the crowd as they started to drift away. They had seen the show and now it was time to be about their business. Then the spieler's booming cry brought them up short, rooted in their tracks.

"Cleanliness is next to godliness, brothers. But I also offer paradise on earth for the man who has no objection to combining *profit* with salvation." Suddenly a hundred-dollar bill appeared in his hand, and he slowly waved it around the circle of faces as they edged closer. "Crisp greenbacks for those who would cleanse their souls of the devil and turn a profit at the same time. Did I not tell you my mission in life is to get people to use soap? And if I have to, I'm willing to *pay you* to do it! Step up, my friends. Watch closely."

There was much pushing and shoving now as the crowd jostled for a better look at the hundred-dollar bill. Before the spieler stood a sample case on a tripod loaded with bars of unwrapped soap. Swiftly his dexterous fingers twisted the bill around an ivory cube, then wrapped it in a square of blue paper, tossing it carelessly back into the sample case. Almost faster than the eye could follow his nimble hands began wrapping one bar after another, enclosing ten- and twenty-dollar bills in each package. Then a groan went up from the crowd as he stopped including money, and began wrapping plain cubes of soap.

"Don't despair, my friends. Already before you is a veritable fortune. Over five hundred dollars tucked snugly among my little pile. Now, you wouldn't buy my soap at twenty-five cents so I'm going to offer you another shot at salvation. Only this time you have a chance of winning one of those greenbacks with the big numbers. Make your choice. Cleanse your hide and your soul, and turn a profit, too! I'll sell you any bar in that tray at the ridiculous price of only five dollars.

"Brothers, you're all sports, I can see that at a glance. And for the paltry sum of five dollars you might well earn that century greenback. You all saw me wrap the bills, and the quickness of your eye determines the amount of profit you'll make. Now, who will be the first to buy my soap?"

"Mister, you're pretty quick, but by grannies you didn't catch me nappin'." A coatless man in a filthy shirt and raggedy trousers stepped from the crowd. He slapped five dollars in the spieler's hand and paused for a moment as he studied the tray of soap. Then his grimy hand rummaged through the pile, and a sly smile crept over his face as he selected a bar. Eagerly he unwrapped the package and triumphantly held aloft a crisp twenty-dollar bill. "Hallelujah! I told you, mister. You just wasn't fast enough. Looka there, boys. A twenty! By golly, I'm just gonna trade that back in on four more chances. I'll get that hundred, or my name ain't Will Frickens."

"Sorry, old-timer." The spieler warded him off, refusing to accept the twenty. "Only one bar of soap to a customer. Can't let you get greedy when these other boys haven't had their chance. Now, gents, who's going to be next at taking a stab at that century greenback? It's still there, just waiting for a man with a keen eye, and a little faith in the Almighty."

The crowd swarmed over him, thrusting gold pieces and five-dollar bills in his hand as they fought to snatch a bar of soap. But the tray held far more soap than there were men and when the last of them had made his selection there were still twenty odd packages left in the sample case. Two of the men shouted jubilantly as they jerked ten-dollar bills from their packages, but the rest of the crowd glumly turned the blue wrappers inside out and found they had won nothing more than a nickel bar of soap.

Folding his sample case, the spieler stuck it under his arm and looked about at the solemn faces. "Don't regret your decision, friends. The great God Jehovah meant for each of you to win. And you have! Take that bar of soap to the nearest tub of water and lather up your own salvation. Cleanse your immortal souls. And make sure you wash behind your ears, too!"

With that Jefferson Randolph Smith walked away from the train station and headed toward the center of town. It had been a good morning. If his count was right, he had made close to three hundred dollars in less than a half hour. He still got a thrill out of gaffing the rubes. The damn fools just never believed that a man's hands could move fast enough to palm the money as he was wrapping the soap. Let a couple of them win just to make everything look on the up and up, and from there on it was downhill all the way. He thought back over the pitch, savoring every moment of it with gusto. These days he had less and less chance to keep his hand in at fleecing the suckers. There were just too many details and problems facing him, leaving no time for the things he really enjoyed. As he walked on toward town he was struck by the thought that bossing a gang was really just a large, sharp pain in the ass.

Soapy Smith, as he was better known throughout the underworld, was a man with a king-size headache. The headache was currently enthroned at the Windsor Hotel, and its name was Lou Blomger.

Soapy had come to Denver long before anyone ever heard of Lou Blomger. Starting out as a street corner hustler with his soap game, he had slowly put together a gang of thimble-riggers and grifters second to none. With the patience of Job, he had taught them the nuances of the shell game, three-card monte, and bunco steering. Within a year he had opened the Tivoli Club, where suckers were shorn of their last dollar in record time, and his fortune seemed made. The only real competition he had was the California Gang, and so long as they didn't poach on his hunting grounds, he was willing to live and let live. There were times, as a matter of fact, when he felt like a man who had the world by the short hairs.

Until Lou Blomger came to town.

Just thinking about it made him livid. Blomger demanded a quarter of his gross haul, and there wasn't a damn thing he could do about it. If he didn't fork over every week, he knew that the police and the courts would put him out of business in short order. Blomger controlled the law in Denver, and anyone who refused to kick back just didn't operate. The ten percent he used to pay to Barney Boyle had been bad enough, but this fat slob was the greediest bastard he had ever seen. And if he was any judge of men and circumstances, it wouldn't end there.

Walking into the Tivoli Club, he spotted Troublesome Tom Cady at the bar belting down a shot of rye.

"Little early in the morning, even for you," Smith commented.

"Soapy, we got real troubles." Cady knocked down another slug, and reached for the bottle.

"That's news?" Smith remarked acidly.

"No, I mean *real* trouble. Word's out that the California Gang is rigging something big. And they're gonna pull it off here in town."

"In Denver? You must be talking through your hat, Tom. They know I don't allow any bunco deals unless it's cleared through me first."

"Yeah? Well, maybe they're not convinced you meant business." Cady gave him an owlish frown. "I'm tellin' you, Soapy, they're out to pull off a big one. I got the word from a barkeep over at the Slaughterhouse, and he ought to know what he's talkin' about."

Soapy Smith chewed that over for a moment, glaring at himself in the mirror behind the bar. "Those sonsabitches are gettin' too big for their britches. That's what it really comes down to. They've been out in the backwoods hustling rubes, and now they think they're ready to jump *our* claim." Then he was struck by a sudden insight. "Goddamn, Tom. You know what just came to me? The real trouble is that skinny little pimp, Cort Thomson. His woman is Blomger's partner, and the California bunch figures that with the fat man running the town we won't have the guts to call their bluff."

"Do we?" Cady inquired balefully.

"You better get your head out of that bottle, and come up for air. There's more than one way to skin a cat, and I've got a feeling we might just put Thomson and his gang out of circulation for good." The germ of an idea had formed in his mind, but there were still a few bothersome details that hadn't quite jelled. "Course, we'll have to think of some way not to ruffle Blomger's fur. Otherwise, he might sic that beady-eyed little runt on us, and I'm not anxious to get backshot in the dark."

Troublesome Tom Cady looked very troubled indeed. He poured a shot glass right to the brim and tossed it down in one gulp. This deal was getting hairier by the minute, and the mere thought of Slats waiting somewhere in the dark was enough to give a man the shakes. Reaching for the bottle again, his thoughts settled on the notion that a smart man would get off his butt and start hunting for a safer line of work.

Mattie and Handsome Jack were seated on the first row of benches in city court. Behind them the room was filled to capacity, with late arrivals crowded along the walls in the back. Mattie recognized many faces from the tenderloin among the spectators, and she knew that swarms of people had been turned away because the courtroom was already overpacked. This promised to be a good show, and everyone in Denver was awaiting the outcome with open curiosity. *Mattie Silks's man had been arrested, charged with operating a bunco game involving almost two hundred thousand dollars.* At least that was the charge according to the morning newspaper, and those who had attended the race yesterday had no doubt as to its validity.

Still, the gamblers along Larimer Street were laying odds of five to two that Cort Thomson would never serve a day for his part in the shoddy conspiracy. After all, Thomson was the roommate of the woman who sat at the right hand of Boss Blomger, and anyone standing downwind only had to sniff to catch the distinct aroma of a fix.

Looking back, Mattie knew that her suspicions had been right from the very beginning. When Cort had announced that he was turning promoter, she sensed there was something overripe about the whole deal. But Cort had sworn that everything was on the up and up, convincing her that it was a chance for him to go legitimate and make a name for himself as a sports promoter. He had been so enthused and eager to make a good showing that she finally shunted her fears aside. Some promoter! Now she cursed herself for ignoring those first intuitive doubts, instead of digging deeper and exposing the scheme before he got in over his head.

Cort had found himself a racer somewhere, and to hear him tell it they were going to make a million dollars touring the mining camps. But first he wanted to stage an extravaganza at the Denver Fair Grounds to build a name for his protege. While no one had ever heard of the man, Cort sang his praises up and down the tenderloin, declaring that within six months Bill Simmons would be the Rocky Mountain champion. When questioned closely, Cort neatly skirted the fact that he personally was washed up as a racer. The mining camps had had their fill of his shenanigans, and his days for toeing the mark were long gone. But if he could build Simmons's reputation with one big race then the miners would welcome the chance to avenge themselves on his pupil. At least this was the story he told around the tenderloin, and as anyone could plainly see, he really was high on Bill Simmons's chances of making a clean sweep of the outlying camps.

But the high rollers around town weren't convinced. The more they studied Simmons, the less imposing he became. He just didn't look like a racer, lacking the lithe form and springy step associated with the breed. Besides, it was common knowledge among the sporting set that in their secret-training sessions Thomson had left Simmons going away in every heat. When the newspapers announced that Simmons had been matched against Tim Campbell, Denver's current champion, everyone in town had visions of making a real killing. But first they had to find someone willing to bet on Simmons. With the hope that there were enough suckers who couldn't resist a long-shot, the gamblers shrewdly offered Simmons at nine to one.

While the price was right there still wasn't much action during the week before the race. Cort had bet three thousand dollars and Mattie loyally ventured another two thousand dollars, but that was to be expected. Then on the morning of the match Simmons money began to surface in a flurry of betting. Before the high rollers could get their heads together they had covered over twenty thousand dollars at nine to one. Suddenly there was a very fishy smell about Cort Thomson and his protege, and the sporting fraternity had the first indication that they had been gaffed right where it hurt most.

The second jolt came when Simmons left Denver's pride and joy in a cloud of dust as he roared across the finish line. Maybe Simmons didn't look like a racer, but when those stubby legs began churning it appeared Campbell had been matched against a cannonball on wheels.

Then, before the shock wave even had time to settle, word began circulating through the crowd that the winner was racing under false colors. *His name wasn't Bill Simmons. He was Wood Kittleman, The Hugo Trade Wind, famed throughout the California gold fields as the fastest thing on two legs. Thomson had imported him under a false name and rigged the whole thing to make it look like he had discovered a new racing sensation.* There was an immediate outcry for Thomson's blood, and only with considerable head-thumping were the police able to save him from being lynched. Within hours, Cort and the entire California Gang had been arrested, and charged with conspiracy to defraud the public.

Thinking about it, Mattie had to admit it took the cake

for sheer nerve. And it had almost worked. If Cort had pulled it off in Denver he could have gone on tour with an unknown who just happened to be Wood Kittleman, and cleaned out every mining camp in the Rockies. His first mistake was in allowing the California Gang to use him as a shill. The second was in being dumb enough to think he could pull a bunco job in Soapy Smith's backyard. Word was already spreading that it was Soapy and his gang who had blown the whistle. How they had found out about Kittleman, or when, no one was quite sure. But it was now plain that Soapy had waited until after the race to expose the caper, figuring that the police would have no choice but to arrest Cort and his confederates. Whatever her feelings for Soapy Smith, she had to give him credit. He had played his hole card with cunning and skill, and it worked out just as he had planned.

Suddenly a door opened at the far end of the courtroom and the bailiff ordered everyone to rise. Judge Thomas Hobart walked quickly to the bench and took his seat. Moments later another door opened and three deputies herded the California Gang before the bench. Cort looked hollow-eyed and grubby, but otherwise he appeared not to have suffered any ill-effects from a night in jail. Watching him, Mattie wondered if he even suspected that Judge Hobart already had his orders.

The prosecutor rose and read the charges in a bored monotone, and the gang's lawyer responded with a quick plea of "Not Guilty" for his clients. Judge Hobart clucked like an old hen, looking down the line at the defendants as if they were a passel of naughty schoolboys. With the first words out of his mouth everyone in the courtroom knew that the matter was cut and dried.

"Gentlemen, you have behaved abominably. There are few things worse than trying to defraud your fellow townspeople. However, I am taking into consideration that this is the first time any of you have appeared in a Denver court. Also, let us not lose sight of the fact that every man is innocent until proven guilty. Therefore, I offer you a choice. Those who wish to plead guilty may do so, and will be fined five hundred dollars. Otherwise bail is set at five thousand dollars and the case will go before a jury later in the month."

The spectators groaned with disappointment. They had come to see a show and all they got for their trouble was a sleazy little charade. The defendants quickly changed their plea, visably relieved that they wouldn't have to face a jury of angry racing buffs. The courtroom emptied as they lined up to pay their fines, and it was some minutes before Cort joined Mattie and Handsome Jack outside the railing.

"Let's go home, Cort." Mattie's voice would have chilled a hot rock. "I not only don't want to be seen with your *friends,* I don't even want to talk in front of them."

Turning, she marched from the courtroom with Handsome Jack at her heels. Cort cast a crestfallen glance at his cronies, then followed along like a scolded pup. The carriage ride home was the most strained ten minutes of Cort's life. Mattie refused to look at him, staring out the window in frosty silence. When the carriage drew up before the house, she alighted and stormed inside, heading straight for the third-floor suite.

Moments later he entered the parlor to find her cold-eyed and waiting, seated on a chair with her hands folded primly in her lap. He knew that Mattie had a temper, but this was a side of her he had never seen. Cold, withdrawn, glaring at him with all the compassion of a riled cobra.

"Sit down, Cort. We've got a few things to get straightened out."

"Mattie, I'm sorry. I know I mucked things up and . . ." Before he could go farther, a sharp motion of her hand cut him off.

"Cort, I want you to be quiet for a minute and listen to what I've got to say." There was an edge to her voice that would brook no argument, and he wearily slumped into a chair. "The fact that you made an ass out of yourself and caused me to lose two thousand dollars isn't even worth talking about. And yet that's all that's really bothering you, because you can't see any further than the end of your nose."

"Well, then, suppose you just tell me what the hell is so important. I didn't murder anybody, you know. And that's a damn sight more than you can say for some of your friends."

"You'd better be glad I do have friends in the right places. If it had been up to Lou Blomger, he would have let you and that bunch of wharf rats rot in jail. I had to pledge my soul to get him to put in the fix."

"So? What's the big deal?" He squirmed in his chair, not sure how much more he could take. "So we owe Blomger another piece of our soul. What's new about that?"

"Not your *soul,* lover." Mattie's eyes thawed for the first time, and a note of concern crept into her voice. "Because I'm Lou's partner this deal made him look like a fool, too. There's even a rumor that he masterminded the whole thing. What I'm trying to say, Cort, is that you're a luxury he can't afford. No matter what you mean to me, he just won't allow his name to be linked with outright fraud." She paused and studied her hands, unable to look at him. "Lou told me to tell you that the next time you do something like this, you've signed your own death warrant."

Cort suddenly grew very still. "In other words, I'd have to get Slats before he got me."

"That wouldn't do any good. Lou's got a dozen just like him." Then her gaze swung up, beseeching him to listen, to understand. "Can't you see that it's not just Lou? If you keep on working with the California Gang you'll get killed sooner or later, no matter who does it. I couldn't take that, Cort. I just couldn't. I need you, and I want you alive and well, so we can enjoy what we've got. I'm asking you, *begging you,* to give it up before it's too late."

Cort remained silent for a moment, considering what she had said. Then his jaw set in a tight, rigid smile. "All right, I tell you what I'll do. You quit Blomger and I'll quit the California bunch. That way we both break clean and start fresh."

Mattie stared at him, comprehending the rightness of what he said, yet unable to struggle against the forces within herself. "I can't, Cort. Please don't force me to make that choice. I need you. You know I do. If I didn't love you so much, then why would I go to all this trouble? But I need the things Lou gives me, too. I can't explain it. I just know that I have to be *somebody*. Otherwise, I'm nothing."

"What you're saying is that you're hooked on power. Just like Blomger. You've gotten a taste of it, and now you can't get your jollies off unless you've got this life-and-death hold over a bunch of squirming little turds. Isn't that it?"

She couldn't look at him, and her voice was almost a whisper. "I only know that I have to be something more than a whorehouse madam. I can't just settle for that."

"And I can't settle for being a *pimp*," he retorted. "So where does that leave us?"

Tears welled up in her eyes, and her voice quavered. "Right back where we started, I guess."

Cort's throat tightened, as if someone were working his guts over with a steel file. Then he moved across the room and lifted her from the chair. "Let's go to bed. Whatever else happens we've still got that. And if we're gonna suffer we might as well enjoy it."

Mattie clung to him like a small child suddenly confronted by a darkened room. She had a sense of being sucked under by a hell of her own making, yet there seemed no way to fight or pull back. After tonight she knew that there would never be any compromise between them. Cort was being consumed by his own furies, just as she was, and they were as powerless together as they were separately. They were both driven by compulsions that had names, but defied domination in any form. And wherever the road led they had no choice but to follow.

Then she awoke to Cort's gentle caress, and for the moment it no longer seemed important where they were going, or what path they would take in getting there. All that mattered was that they do it together.

BOOK THREE

—◆—

STRANGE BEDFELLOWS
ONE AND ALL

CHAPTER EIGHT

———◦∭∮∭◦———

The matched black geldings stepped along at a lively pace. They seemed to know where they were going, and the driver had little to do except hold them to a respectable gait. Mattie and Cort sat back in the plush velvet seats, enjoying the warming rays of the sun and the curious stares as the coach trundled through South Denver toward Overland Park. Life had been good to Mattie these last few years, and as she gazed out at the modest dwellings lining the street she was reminded that for a lowly farm girl she had done very well indeed.

She now owned four houses along Holladay Street, and while none of them rivaled her own palatial establishment, they each made a steady contribution to her growing wealth. Yet as profitable as the houses were, she wasn't about to put all her eggs in one basket. Businessmen and politicians who frequented her house often talked of their investments, and she had learned that the first law for amassing a fortune was to always hedge your bet.

She had once overheard a discussion in the basement game room in which some of Denver's more prominent speculators were debating the merits of various investments.

One wise old owl, who was noted for his financial wizardry, as well as downright greed, had made a statement Mattie never forgot. *Buy land, gentlemen. It's the one thing God isn't making any more of.* She was struck by the simple truth underlying his observation. Denver was growing by leaps and bounds, having doubled in population in only five years, and there seemed no end in sight. One day every square foot of land in the city would be worth its weight in gold. And the time to buy was when men's minds were preoccupied with mining stocks and the tonnage of ore that could be gouged from the earth. What worked for others could easily be made to work for her, and she promptly hired herself a shrewd lawyer. Acting as a front, he set about acquiring commercial and residential real estate throughout the city. Whenever he touted her onto a particularly attractive mining stock she reminded him that long after the mines had petered out the land would still be there. And she ordered him to buy more. The lawyer had followed her instructions to the letter, and over the last few years her land holdings had come to include two warehouses, four stores, a small office building, three residential homes, and a tract of acreage just outside of town. And five whorehouses, of course.

Yet when all was said and done, the accumulation of wealth was really a very boring business. The counting of assets, balances, and deeds could only hold a person's attention so long. Somewhere along the line it tended to get very tedious. A girl needed a hobby, something that was fun and exciting—a wild, deliciously expensive pastime that had nothing to do with musty records and dry balance sheets. Much to Mattie's delight, a group of wealthy sportsmen had provided a diversion that exceeded her wildest dreams. It was exciting, barrels of fun, and so damnedly expensive that only the very rich could afford to play. They called it Overland Park, and during the racing season it was home to the finest sulky horses west of the Mississippi.

Once infected by the racing bug, Mattie went at it like a whirling dervish. She imported Frank Nott, one of the

East's outstanding trainers, handed him a blank check, and sent him off to buy a stable of blooded racers. When Nott returned she found herself the envy of every horseman in Denver. He had bought two stallions, Jim Blaine and Topgallant, and a stable of eight lesser contenders. And he had spent less than forty thousand dollars, a bargain by any yardstick for a girl who needed a respite from her legitimate enterprises, as well as the demands of her active involvement in the rackets.

But of all her possessions—horses, whorehouses, and real estate alike—Mattie was proudest of her English Kensington Coach. It was the most visible symbol of her wealth and influence, and never failed to create a sensation when she rode through the streets of Denver.

The coach had cost her a small fortune, and tales of its startling appearance spread throughout every mining camp in the Rockies. She had designed it herself, and if she had purposely chosen to flaunt her standing in Denver's power structure, she couldn't have selected a more appropriate means.

The exterior was a resplendent spectrum of stark colors, arrayed in such a manner as to leave the viewer goggle-eyed with wonder. The surface of the massive coach fairly glistened with an immaculate white finish that had been waxed and hand-rubbed until it somehow looked pure and undefiled. Sweeping upward from the frame, circumscribing a heavy arc around the cab, was an ornate pattern of raised leaf, which shimmered with burnished hues of spun gold. The wheels were even more stunning than the cab itself, as if one had suddenly encountered four rolling sunbursts. Sparkling brass trim decorated the bright yellow wheels, and galvanized blue spokes radiated outward from the hub to form a lurid, dazzling glow. Upon first sighting it the overall effect was a bit staggering. But with closer inspection it became apparent that the coach was a minor masterpiece in bold, harmonious colors.

While some found it gaudy and offensive to the eye, none walked away from viewing it without feeling slightly

overwhelmed. Which was exactly what Mattie had in mind.
The uptown swells might stick their noses in the air, but
they damn sure couldn't ignore that coach.

Like her fortunes, Mattie's mode of dress had also
changed with passing time. But while her wealth was in-
creasing daily, her tastes remained unconventional, if not
downright eccentric. She had seen a reproduction of Ru-
bens's painting of Marie de Medici, and from it received
an inspiration that left her dressmaker mildly aghast. The
costume consisted of a cloak with a long train, worn over a
tight bodice with a broad, flaring turned-up collar. Accom-
panying the bodice was a skirt of tiered lace flounces, white
gloves, and a huge lace parasol. Mattie had also become fascinated with the lovely actress, Lily Langtry, and promptly
adopted her hairdo. Along with the Medici gowns she now
wore her hair piled atop her head in a swirling maze of
blonde curls. And in a hidden pocket, specially designed at
the side of the skirt, she constantly carried the pearl-handled
pistol that was her one keepsake from another life.

Since Cort's narrow brush with the law, and the resul-
tant threat from Blomger, she had never been without the
small pistol. Cort and the California Gang had run on hard
times after the bungled race at the fair grounds, and merely
showing their faces in a mining camp was good for a night
in jail. They had turned to gambling as a livelihood, and
quickly developed a reputation as the rankest tinhorns in
town. The high rollers wouldn't be caught dead in a game
with them, and for the most part they relied on streetcorner
hustlers to steer the pilgrims into their lair. Cort had taken
up steady drinking as a solace, consuming immense quan-
tities of whiskey in a given day. Before long his appearance
began to change, reflecting his inner dissolution as a man.
While he still dressed in sporty fashion, he had put on considerable weight and his features bore the pallid, fleshy look
of a confirmed wastrel. Filled with self-loathing for what
he had become, he no longer shied away from accepting
Mattie's money, and throughout the tenderloin he was now
known as The Gigolo. Yet there were none who used the

term to his face, for he was a morose, embittered man, and as fast with a gun as ever.

But whatever Cort had become, he was still Mattie's man and she meant to see that he got a fair shake if push came to shove. So she carried the little pistol now wherever she went. Should anyone come looking for Cort, be it Slats or some other gunman, she was ready. She owed him that much, for he had ruined himself trying to match her rise to prominence. And when the day came, she meant to pay the debt.

Still, such grim thoughts were far from her mind on this bright summer day, for the racing season was in full swing. This afternoon Topgallant would meet the stiffest competition he had yet faced, and she was caught up in anticipation of the event. As the coach came to a halt outside the paddock area, Frank Nott left a groom to finish harnessing the stallion and came to greet her.

"Afternoon, Miss Silks. Mr. Thomson," he said, touching the brim of his cap. "Looks like we've got a fine day for a race."

"Oh, I hope so, Frank." Mattie fairly bubbled with excitement. "Now, give me the lowdown on Carbonate. Do you think he's as good as they say?"

Nott removed his cap and scratched his head thoughtfully. "Well, that's hard to say, ma'am. He's a big gray stud, and he looked mighty good in workouts. Course horses are like pugilists; sometimes they leave all their fight in the gym. I allow as how he'll make a good showing, but if I was a betting man, I'd be tempted to put it on Topgallant."

"That's good enough for me." Matie unsnapped her purse and brought out a thick wad of bills. "Cort, run over to Phil Archobald's book and put six thousand on Topgallant. Five thousand for us, and a thousand for Frank."

"Why thank you, ma'am," Nott grinned. "That's right generous of you."

Cort accepted the money, but made no move to leave. "Mattie, don't you think that's going a little overboard? Hell, this Carbonate's only been at the track a week, and they might've been holdin' him back in workouts."

Mattie smiled, yet her eyes were firm and hard. "Lover, I used to bet more than that on you when you were racing half-drunk. Now don't argue. Just run along and get the bet down like a good boy."

Cort climbed from the coach and walked off, looking like a man in need of a good stiff drink. Mattie shook her head ruefully, then turned back to Nott.

"Frank, there are some men that just never grow up. It's like you have to keep tying their shoelaces so they won't trip and break their neck."

"I know just what you mean, Miss Silks." The trainer nodded his head wisely, but in the back of his mind he wondered just what the hell this high-toned floozy was talking about.

Mattie's gaze wandered across the paddock to where Topgallant was being harnessed to the sulky. *What the hell! Easy come, easy go. If the big bastard loses it won't put a kink in my tail. Besides, a girl's got to have a little fun once in a while. And it is my money!*

Frank Nott noted the absent look in her eyes, and rightly concluded that she was absorbed in some thought that no longer concerned him. Tipping his cap, he turned and walked toward the stallion. On the spur of the moment, he tossed out a silent little prayer that he hadn't lost his touch for picking a winner. That extra thousand wouldn't be hard to take at all.

Oscar Wilde was coming to town! The apostle of aestheticism was touring the West and had been booked to lecture at the Tabor Grand Opera House. Ireland's most distinguished poet-playwright-author was pictured by the *Tribune* as a long-haired gnome in velvet coat, knee breeches, and silk stockings, gazing fondly at a lily. And all of Denver was agog.

But for very dissimilar reasons.

For the *nouveau riche* on Capitol Hill, this was an honor

of the highest magnitude. The appearance of such a world-renowned celebrity meant that Denver had at last been recognized as the mountain stronghold of culture and sophistication. Even the newspapers were caught up in the excitement, proudly dubbing the city The Athens of the Rockies. Accordingly, the lorgnette set hastened to bone up on the Irishman's writings. But for all their recently acquired culture, they found aestheticism rough sledding.

The not-so-rich of the tenderloin were of an entirely different opinion. They couldn't even pronounce aestheticism much less understand it, and anyone who stood around in knee breeches ogling a flower seemed a bit strange, to say the least. Rumor had it that Oscar also rode sidesaddle, which put a whole new light on the matter. In the tenderloin where men were men, and women were glad of it, the denizens of Denver's underworld hastily concluded that the poet's visit was just a lot of claptrap designed to titillate the uptown swells. So far as they were concerned, culture was like horseshit. Anybody could step in it.

But if most of those in the tenderloin scoffed at the idea of a grown man contemplating the beauty of a lily, there were some who saw Oscar Wilde's arrival as a rare opportunity. The mayor had planned a rally at the train station to meet the Irishman, and afterward the dignitaries were to parade through town in open carriages. The streets were sure to be jammed with throngs of curious onlookers, and upon arriving at the opera house the official party was certain to be met by a crowd of Denver's uppercrust. That meant masses of people loaded to the tills with jewelry, fine watches, and fat bulging wallets. And nowhere does a pickpocket work better than in an excited, jostling crowd. A rare opportunity indeed!

Soapy Smith planned well, and his crew was out in force when Ireland's poet laureate preened and postured his way from the train station to the opera house. The night seemed filled with gentle nudges and nimble fingers, and long before Oscar mounted the stage in his velvet knickers the crowd had been plucked clean. While it had nothing to do with philosophy, the Soap Gang was not without appreciation. And in their own way, they found aesthetics to be a very rewarding pursuit.

Shortly before noon the next day, Buffalo Bill Cody burst through the door of the Holladay Street parlor house. Brushing past Handsome Jack, he stormed into Mattie's office.

"Mattie, you've got to help me!" Without a word of greeting he launched into a vitriolic harangue. "The police in this town are the most incompetent, mule-headed, lard-assed bunch of bastards I've ever run across. Those sonsabitches told me there wasn't a goddamn thing they could do about a man being robbed right on the streets of Denver. Said half the town had been cleared out last night, and that they just didn't have time to be out chasing pickpockets. Told me to get a private detective. Goddamn, can you believe that? A private detective!"

"Whoa! Slow down, Bill." Mattie was more than a little startled to have Cody suddenly appear out of nowhere. While she knew of the fame he had garnered with his wild west show, she hadn't seen him in over a decade. "Jesus, give a girl a chance to catch her breath. At least say hello, or tell me what you're doing in Denver."

"Ah, hell, I'm sorry, Mattie. It's just that I'm so goddamn mad." He pulled her from the chair, kissed her soundly, then sat her down again. Formalities done with, he went back to ranting. "The governor invited me down to see that curly headed Irishman run his long tongue, and somewhere along the line I got my pockets picked. The money don't matter so much, but the bastards got a watch given to me by the Grand Duke Alexis. He's Russian, you know. Fine feller, even if he is a foreigner. Anyway, it's got a gold buffalo head mounted on the case, and it's just the prettiest damn watch you've ever seen. I've had it for years, wouldn't take anything for it. And those miserable dogcatchers that call themselves police say there's not a damn thing they can do about it."

Mattie restrained a smile. She had heard that Bill had grown rather pompous and overbearing with fame, but she hadn't suspected to what extent. The white buckskin jacket and ten-gallon hat made him look like a dude among real westerners, and in a way she felt sorry for him. Around Denver they called him "See me Bill," because he was such a showoff and given to telling big windies about his days as a scout. Still, he was an old friend.

"Well, Bill, if the police can't do anything, what makes you think I can help?"

Cody's eyes narrowed slyly as his head jerked around. "Mattie, c'mon. This is Bill you're talkin' to. Everybody in town knows you're thick as fleas with Boss Blomger. Christ, if he can't get that watch back, nobody can."

"Bill, I hate to tell you this, but Lou Blomger wouldn't lift a finger to turn up some tinhorn pickpocket. Besides, I've got my own reasons for not wanting to ask any favors of him just at the moment." She studied his downcast look for a moment, then relented. "Tell you what, I'll send a couple of my boys out to ask around. Maybe we can get a lead on it."

Cody thanked her effusively, declaring he would never forget the favor. After briefly rehashing the old days at Fort Hays, he hurried out, promising to stay in touch. Mattie knew he wouldn't. Old friends who had gained some measure of respectability seldom called on her except when they needed something. And Cody was no different. Just more so.

Mattie called Cort and Handsome Jack in, and asked if they would mind casing the tenderloin to see if there was any sign of the watch. Neither of them was overly enthused by the idea. Cody was considered an oddity in the under-world, like Oscar Wilde or an albino whore, and they weren't anxious to have their names linked with his. But he was a friend of Mattie's, and that counted for something. Also, they took perverse amusement from the fact that the *big buffalo hunter* needed help to track down his own watch.

Cort had a pretty good idea where they would find the watch. Since he still owed Soapy Smith for squealing to the police, the project began to take on more appeal the longer

he thought about it. And besides, it might just convince
Mattie that he was still a man. The way she had been treat-
ing him these days, he might as well start gazing at lilies.

Ten minutes later, Cort and Handsome Jack walked
through the doors of the Tivoli Club. Soapy and Tom Cady
were seated at a table eating breakfast, and various members of the gang were lounged around the barroom. Cort
pulled out a chair and sat down, while Jack remained standing. Soapy stopped eating long enough to give them both a
corrosive look, then went back to his ham and eggs.

"Soapy, a friend of Mattie's has got a little problem.
Someone lifted his watch." Cort paused, but the gang leader
didn't even glance up. "Probably just an honest mistake,
seein' as how everyone knows Bill Cody is an old pal of
Mattie's. We thought you might be able to help us out."

"You're just a sack of surprises, Thomson." Smith
snorted, grinning like a short-fanged wolf. "What makes
you think I know anything about Cody's watch?"

"Soapy, don't give me any of your shit. Your cannons
work this town like they had a license. And we both know
there's not a purse snatcher in Denver that isn't on your
payroll."

"Go fuck yourself."

There was an instance of silence as Cort considered the
odds. "You figure you've got us outnumbered. But don't
count on walkin' away, Soapy. Before you can drop that fork
I'll dust you on both sides."

Everything in Smith's face moved at once, like a water
spider that manages to stay on the surface by never being
still enough to sink. The muscles in his jaw clenched, his
mouth tightened, and his eyes flicked around the room sizing up the advantage. The gang braced themselves for a
shootout as a deathly stillness crept over the room. Then
Smith shook his head, calling them off.

"Thomson, you ain't worth the powder it'd take to blow
you off a johnny pot. The only thing saving you is that I
can't afford a killin' in my own club." His expression was
astringent, vindictive, a silent promise that the matter

wouldn't end here. "Now get your ass out of here. And take that gorilla with you."

Handsome Jack struck the edge of the table with his knees, dumping the plate of ham and eggs in Smith's lap. "Mister, you'd better watch your mouth or I'm gonna be forced to stunt your growth."

Cort chuckled as Smith got busy wiping egg yolk and grease off his shirt front. Tom Cady looked like he had a bone in his throat, and his eyes darted bleakly between the three men.

"Soapy, since we're so downright frank, lemme leave you with a parting thought." Cort glanced around, enjoying himself now. "I've seen a lot of sonsabitches in my time, but you're double distilled, and that's a fact. Now pony up that watch before I get nervous and forget you've got me surrounded."

Smith glared at him for a moment, then nodded to a man standing at the bar. Ducking his head, the man hurried through a door leading to the back room and came back shortly with the watch. Not a word had been spoken as he crossed the room and returned. When he laid the watch on the table, Cort stuck it in his vest pocket, then shoved his chair back.

"Soapy, you've been a real sport. If you ever want tickets to Cody's wild west show just lemme know." He grinned sardonically, like a kid that had just won all the marbles. "You'd probably like it. They don't shoot nothin' but blanks, either."

With that Cort and Handsome Jack strolled out of the Tivoli Club and nonchalantly made their way back down Larimer Street.

Soapy Smith stared at the door for a full minute after they had gone. His face was the color of cherry juice, and only a fool would have missed the murderous rage that seared his guts. No one dared speak, and the moment lengthened into an eerie, chilled silence. Then abruptly he jerked erect and kicked the fallen plate across the saloon, where it shattered against the far wall. Turning, he stalked from the room, ashamed to look his own men straight in the eye.

Slats admitted Mattie to the suite in the Windsor and showed her to a seat in the parlor. Once a week, generally on a Monday afternoon, she delivered the take from whorehouses and cribs to Blomger personally. Her share was twenty percent of the haul, and for this she was expected to collect the payoffs, keep the madams in line, and see to it that Holladay Street operated without undue publicity. Handsome Jack and a small contingent of collectors actually handled the details, and there was rarely any trouble. The Row had prospered greatly under Mattie's supervision as a matter of fact, and the madams seldom made a fuss about the payoffs. Though substantial, the kickbacks insured that the houses were protected from the police, the district attorney, and even the United States' prosecutor, who had recently been added to Blomger's payroll.

Those madams who did harbor resentment kept it to themselves. In the tenderloin it didn't pay to become too vocal concerning Boss Blomger.

While Handsome Jack normally accompanied her to the suite, Mattie had asked him to wait in the lobby on this particular Monday. There was a matter she wanted to discuss privately with Blomger, and whatever the outcome, she preferred that it remain just between them. Though she had rehashed it in her mind a hundred times, she was still trying to decide on the best approach when Blomger entered from an adjoining bedroom.

"Mattie, nice to see you. And prompt as usual. That's a trait I've always admired. Especially where money is concerned." Blomger had grown even fatter with time and an enormous appetite for fine cuisine. Instead of walking he now waddled, as if a huge mound of butter had been jammed atop two fireplugs. Watching him settle into a chair, it occurred to Mattie that in a blubber contest he could beat a bull walrus hands down.

"Here's last week's collections." She withdrew a thick

stack of bills from her purse and handed it to him. "By my count it's $8,900 on the nose. My cut came to twenty-two hundred and change."

Blomger casually tossed the money to Slats, who turned and walked into an adjacent room that served as an office. "Mattie, your count is always good with me. If I can't trust you, then who can I trust? Incidentally, speaking of on the nose, I understand that horse of yours is whipping the bejesus out of everything on four legs. Topgallant? Is that right?"

"Yes, Topgallant. You ought to come out to the park and watch him run sometime." She glanced around the suite and shook her head. "Staying cooped up in this hotel isn't good for you, Lou. You need fresh air and some exercise. A ride out to Overland Park might be just what the doctor ordered."

"Oh, I know you're right, Mattie. But I've just got too damn many irons in the fire." He paused to light a long, black cigar, and smiled at her through a cloud of smoke. "Believe it or not, I've organized a new little venture."

"Lou, you're impossible. If you don't watch out you're going to end up like King Midas."

Blomger's rumbling laugh shook every ounce of his bloated frame. "Just turn into a blob of gold. Is that it? Well, hell, that wouldn't be so bad when you stop and think about it." He puffed contentedly on the cigar for a moment. "Actually, the fact of the matter is, I just have an aversion to sitting idle while everyone allows a big-money caper to lie fallow."

"Care to run that past once more? I got the gist of it, but you lost me on a word or two."

"Well, it's like this. There's a million dollars to be made in this town with the right bunco game. But no one's got the touch to pull it off. Oh, Soapy Smith and his thugs promote a few deals, but they're strictly small potatoes. I'm talking about tapping the big marks, the ones that can afford to lose twenty thousand if the gaff is sunk deep enough. Christ, Mattie, there are men wandering into Denver every day that could even come up with a hundred thousand if the bait was laid just right."

"That's a little out of my league, Lou. With the exception of yourself, I can't think of anyone in town slick enough to handle a game that big."

"Exactly my point. That's why I've imported Adolph Duff. Back East he's known as Kid Duffy, and let me tell you, he has engineered some deals that would make your head swim. Getting him was a stroke of genius on my part, and I don't mind bragging about it. He's just the man we need to trim some of these pilgrims that come out here thinking they're going to snooker the country boys."

Blomger's eyes brightened, and he came up on the edge of his chair as he began describing how the new bunco game would work. Phony stock exchanges would be set up around town, staffed with men playing the roles of employees as well as customers. The next step was to find the suckers, but that would prove to be the simplest part. Hotel clerks and bellboys were always good tipsters, and the gang would also have scouts watching the newsstands for prosperous-looking men who bought out-of-town newspapers. The important thing was to make sure that only tourists and visitors were gaffed. Fleecing Denver residents was hitting too close to home, and there was no need to rock the boat when the Brown Palace and other hotels were jammed with pigeons of every description.

Once the mark was spotted he would then be approached by a steerer. The steerer's purpose was to establish contact, and quickly gain the sucker's confidence in some manner. Usually a dropped wallet in the hotel lobby was sufficient bait. The stranger would find it crammed with many juicy items—fake newspaper clippings describing a stockmarket manipulator who had just made a killing, letters of credit from various banks in the East, a bond for one hundred thousand dollars guaranteeing faithful performance of the man mentioned in the newspaper articles. If the right mark had been selected he would contact the desk clerk and insist that he be allowed to return the wallet personally. Such men invariably had larceny in their hearts, and as victims of their own greed, they were by far the easiest pigeons to trim.

When the wallet was returned, the mark would *naturally* refuse a reward. Such things were beneath his dignity, but as the conversation progressed he never failed to make some casual remark about mining stocks. This was the steerer's opening wedge. After modestly downgrading his own success, he would reluctantly allow the sucker to talk him into suggesting a stock. The steerer would then introduce him to his *personal* broker, and the game was off and running.

While the mark was allowed to play on margin at first, the day soon came when he was required to establish credit. Since his gains had been so enormous he had no objection to covering a large share of his purchases with cash. Unfortunately, the market took a capricious nosedive within hours, and he was left holding worthless paper. Wiped out, he and the steerer took turns crying on one another's shoulder, lamenting the unpredictable nature of God and mining stocks. Generally, most marks would catch the first eastbound train at that point, and crawl home to lick their wounds. Those who became suspicious found the police thoroughly uncooperative, if not downright insulting. Even when they somehow induced the law to accompany them, the mark could only sputter and fume upon discovering that his favorite stock exchange had gone out of business overnight.

Adolph Duff's brilliance lay in the fact that he could juggle three stock exchanges and a half-dozen suckers at the same time without missing a stroke. With Blomger's protection, he had only to assemble the machinery, gaff the marks, and pump out a ton of money regularly.

And Lou Blomger couldn't have been happier if he had just fathered a two-headed freak worth millions in circus royalties.

Pausing in his discourse, he puffed on the cigar and observed Mattie like a bullfrog who had just swallowed every fly in sight. "Well, what do you think?"

Mattie was just the least bit awed. "I don't know what to think, Lou. Except that I hope it doesn't turn on you. More than one man has been eaten alive by his own monster, you know."

"Yeah, I suppose so. But none of them was named Blomger. And they didn't have a town tied up in six different kinds of knots the way I've got Denver."

Mattie couldn't dispute that. She was about to ask a question when she suddenly remembered her purpose in being there. "Lou, I need your help. You just mentioned what a tight grip you've got on this town, and I want you to use it to take a weight off my shoulders."

"Anything you want, towhead. Within reason, of course. Maybe you don't know it, but if I've got a weak spot, it's you."

"I hope so, Lou. I surely hope so." Mattie faltered for a moment, then sucked up her nerve and plunged on. "Cort's in trouble again. He and Soapy Smith have a feud brewing and it's liable to bust open any moment. Now, I know you warned him not to make waves. But it's not his fault, Lou. Honestly, it's not. I caused it through sheer stupidity, and it's not really important why. The important thing is that Cort and Soapy are gunning for each other."

"*Christ!*" Blomger angrily flung his cigar in the fireplace and glared up at the ceiling. "As if I didn't have enough problems running this town, I've got to worry about two chowderheads starting a war. Now I suppose you want me to have Soapy call off his dogs. Or perhaps you just want me to have Slats kill him so Cort will be nice and safe."

"No, Lou, that's not what I want. If Cort's ever going to be a man again, he's got to handle this for himself. I just want to know that you won't send Slats looking for him if it does come to shooting. I want you to promise that Cort can settle it in his own way without having to look over his shoulder. He needs it, Lou. And so do I."

"Mattie, that man of yours is soft in the head, do you know that?" Blomger waved his hand in disgust. "All right, you've got my word I won't interfere. Maybe if they kill each other off it'll be better for everyone concerned."

"Thanks, Lou. I'll make it up to you somehow. And I promise, this is the last time he'll make any trouble."

Blomger saw her to the door, his whole day spoiled by the simpleton antics of men who fought out of hate rather than for gain. In the hall, Mattie found that her hands were shaking and her stomach felt queasy. She had maneuvered Cort out from under the threat of Slats's gun, and now all she had to worry about was Soapy. Somehow, it didn't seem like much of a bargain.

The carriages began arriving shortly before dusk. Rattling across the wooden bridge spanning the South Platte, the drivers brought their teams to a halt in front of the Olympic Gardens. Each coach was packed to the gunnels with excited, noisy revelers who had clearly gotten a head start on the party. Leaping to the ground, the men helped their ladies alight, then arm in arm strolled through the pavilion doors. Laughing uproariously, they greeted each familiar face like long-lost cousins, hugging, kissing, clasping hands with mad abandon. Everyone who was anyone in the tenderloin would be there tonight, for Mattie Silks was throwing a whingding to end all whingdings. And this was their night to howl!

Just that afternoon one of the tenderloin's own had given the Capitol Hill swells their comeuppance at last. Mattie Silks had won the coveted gold cup in the Colorado Derby, and the high muckety-mucks of Denver society were fit to be tied. They always held a gala ball at the Denver Athletic Club on the night of the derby, but this year there would be much wailing and gnashing of teeth among the uptown crowd. The fact that the snobs had never invited anyone from the tenderloin to their annual bash had even lost its sting. Mattie Silks had thrown it back in their faces by refusing to invite any of the bluebloods to her own celebration. Instead she had hired the Olympic Gardens for the entire night and thrown the doors open to the tenderloin's high rollers and hoi polloi alike.

The Olympic pavilion was located on the west bank of the Platte, and tonight's celebration was to be a no-holds-barred orgy of fun and games. The river marked the city's western boundary, and *whatever* they did on this side of the Platte, they would be responsible only to themselves. Mattie had ordered up a supper party with tubs of chilled champagne, a variety show, and dancing till dawn. But that was only the beginning. Anything could happen here tonight. And probably would.

Their caterwauling set the wolves and coyotes in the Gardens' small zoo to howling, and as coach after coach continued to disgorge a mob of drunks it was often difficult to distinguish the cries of man from beast. The calm night was shattered as the crowd swelled into the hundreds, and even in the bright starlight hardly an eye in a coach-load could focus clearly on the towering Rockies a few miles to the west. Storming into the pavilion, they began popping champagne corks with frenzied laughter, oblivious of the fact that the guest of honor hadn't yet arrived. George Bartholomew, proprieter of the Olympic, instructed the orchestra to start playing immediately, suddenly overcome with second thoughts about renting his club to this horde of madmen. Not to mention their brazen, volatile ladies.

Then Mattie waltzed through the front door, with Cort on one arm and the derby gold cup clutched tightly in the other. A roar went up from the crowd and as they swarmed over her, Cort and Handsome Jack tried to clear a path to the dais. There a row of tables had been set up for the tenderloin's more notable characters, and as Mattie mounted the platform she was greeted by Madam Featherlegs, Johnny Behind The Deuce, Tinhorn Bill Crooks, Monte Verde, Cooney The Fox, and a host of others. Mattie's eyes glistened with tears as she threaded her way to the seat of honor. These were her people, and they had turned out one and all to pay homage to the Queen of the Tenderloin. Grabbing a magnum of champagne she emptied it into the gold cup and held it aloft for all to see. Then she loosed a leather-lunged shout that stilled the hall.

"See this! Feast your eyes on this cup, my unholy friends. Today my gorgeous Topgallant made those uptown swells get down on their knees and eat horse biscuits. He whipped the best they had to offer, and left them sucking hind tit. Well, I want to propose a toast. No! Two toasts! First, a toast to the granddaddy of all sulky racers. Topgallant!" Lifting the cup she took a mighty swallow of champagne, and everyone in the room followed suit. "Now, I want to propose a toast to the people who made this town what it is today. A toast to every grifter, cardsharp, thimble-rigger and whore in the tenderloin. *You're my kind of people, and I love you!*"

All hell broke loose. Men and women doused one another in champagne, the orchestra shook the rafters with a peppery tune, and the pavilion went mad with the screeching, squealing shouts of *Mattie's people* kicking over the traces for the long night ahead. Waiters began carting in great trays of roast pig, venison steaks, and slabs of barbecued ribs. Madam Featherlegs leaped from the dais, threw her skirts over her head, and went into a crazy, high-stepping dance with Cockeyed Jack Dancy. The crowd roared their approval, pounding out the beat with empty champagne bottles, and fell on the food like the hounds of hell let loose in God's own larder.

Mattie swigged champagne from the golden cup and looked on with regal pleasure. Tonight she was going to get squiffed to the gills, stoned out of her tree. She had ridden Topgallant to the very top of the heap, and tonight's party would be one that neither the tenderloin nor the Capitol Hill snobs would ever forget. She was Mattie Silks, queen of all she surveyed, and there wasn't a man, woman, or child within a hundred miles who would doubt it after tonight.

Watching, her, Cort was mildly surprised. Mattie was crocked. Her eyes had gone glassy and an insipid smile was plastered across her face. He had never seen her drunk in all their years together, but the idea somehow amused him. She had started on champagne immediately after the derby, and hadn't come up for air since. Now she was loaded to the eyeballs, and so far as Cort was concerned she could burn Olympic Gardens to the ground if she wanted to. She had earned it.

Suddenly a tall, good-looking brunette loomed up out of the crowd, listing slightly to port as she weaved toward the dais. Cort almost choked on his last swallow of champagne as he saw her heading straight for him. *Katie Fulton! Jesus Goddamn! Not here. Not now. Please, Katie, don't do it!* His silent exhortation had absolutely no effect on the brunette. She kept right on coming.

"Cort, you handsome old sugartit of a man." Katie wobbled to a halt in front of the dais. "Get your butt out from behind that table and come on down here and dance with me."

Cort glanced at Mattie and saw her eyes go smoky. He had been diddling Katie for some months now, but he was almost certain that Mattie had never suspected. Until now. She looked from Katie back to him, and the expression on his face told the tale. Even stewed on champagne she knew a guilty lover when she saw one, and right about then she started remembering all those nights he *said* he was hung in a poker game. Maybe he hadn't learned his lesson with Lillie Dab. *By God, maybe it was time for a real lesson!*

Mattie's eyes scorched the brunette from head to toe. "Katie Fulton, if you've got the brains of a pissant, you'll hike your skinny ass back across that bridge and stay the hell away from my man."

"Your man!" Katie cackled, somewhat like a hen that had just laid an eight-pound egg. She glared about the dais, weaving unsteadily, clearly drunk as a lord. "Don't make me laugh. That's not your man, Mattie. That's *our man!*"

"That does it." Mattie scrambled erect, overturning her golden goblet. "Somebody give that bitch a gun. Give her a gun, goddamnit! I'm gonna teach every sonovabitch in the tenderloin that nobody messes with my man."

Cort grabbed her arms, certain she would jerk her little

pistol at any moment. "Mattie, c'mon now. Katie doesn't mean any harm. It's just a joke."

"Joke, my ass! You two-timin' sonovabitch!" She whirled on the crowd, still now and watching breathlessly. "Somebody give her a gun, or by Christ, I'll shoot her where she stands."

"She's right. I've always wanted a crack at that stuckup bitch." Katie wobbled around the dance floor, trying to spot somebody that was armed. "Gimme a gun. Gimme a gun, goddamnit! We'll have it out right now."

Handsome Jack suddenly appeared behind Mattie, and exchanged worried glances with Cort. "You're gonna have to do something fast, Cort. Otherwise she'll start blasting away and kill a half-dozen people trying to hit Katie."

"We could take that popgun away from her."

But Mattie wasn't that drunk. She jerked the pearl-handled pistol and waved it in their general direction. "By God, I'd like to see you try. I'd just like to see you try it, lover boy."

Cort looked at the little gun and decided he didn't want to try. At that range she might just hit him. Disgusted with the whole affair, he turned back to Ready. "Jack, what do you say we take them outside and let them fight a real old-fashioned duel."

Handsome Jack grinned, intrigued by the idea. "You mean back to back and thirty paces A real duel."

Cort nodded, smiling like a cat in a cream pitcher. "Sure, why not? Hell, they're so drunk they couldn't hit a bull in the ass. How about it?"

"Well, I damn sure don't want to try taking that gun away from her." Handsome Jack glanced around to see Mattie eyeing them suspiciously. "I don't suppose it can hurt anything. Besides she's gonna start shooting pretty quick if we don't do something, anyway."

Cort called for silence and made the announcement to the crowd. This would be a square fight following all the rules of the *Code Duello. And may the best woman win!* That got a laugh from everyone but Mattie and Katie. They just glared at one another like two alleycats fighting over the neighborhood Tom. Cort appointed himself Mattie's second, and Sam Thatcher, a gambler, volunteered to act for Katie. The entire assemblage then trooped out to a grove of cottonwoods along the banks of the Platte. Someone had loaned Katie a little hideout pistol by this time, and the crowd backed off to give the girls plenty of room.

Handsome Jack had been designated to act as referee, and without wasting any time he got Mattie and Katie back to back. The cool night air might sober them up, and he wanted to have this done with before they got their eyes uncrossed. Cort and Sam Thatcher stepped off fifteen paces each, then stood back to one side. Handsome Jack began counting and the girls staggered off in opposite directions, intent on reaching the distance marked by their seconds before the count stopped. When they were in position Handsome Jack hastily backpeddled toward the crowd, shouting the command to fire when ready.

Both girls whirled instantly and popped off a shot. The roar of the guns reverberated throughout the grove, and the night was splintered by a shrill cry of pain.

Cort dropped to the ground like a poled ox, writhing in the dust as he clutched at the back of his neck. Mattie and Katie stared at one another in bafflement, unable to comprehend how *Cort* had been shot.

Then Mattie dropped her gun and threw herself down beside Cort. By that time Handsome Jack had inspected the fallen man, and announced to the crowd that it was only a flesh wound. Upon hearing that Mattie's hackles went up again and she jumped to her feet, glaring at Katie who was now sobbing uncontrollably.

"Tell that squalling bitch to shut up. This two-timing bastard only got what he deserved. But I'm going to put an end to all this right now. As of this moment, I am formally announcing the marriage to be of Cort Thomson and me, Mattie Silks. Just as soon as he gets the kink out of his neck, we'll tie the knot. And by God, if any of you girls get ideas after we're married I'll make damn sure I don't miss next time."

Mattie was excited, nervous, and just the least bit apprehensive. *Nervous as a whore in church!* The old saying flitted through her mind and made her chuckle even if she didn't feel particularly festive. And that's what bothered her. She should feel happy, blissful, even elated that the big day had finally arrived. Every girl should feel joyful on her wedding day. But she didn't.

Living with a man was one thing. Being married to him was something else again. And the distinction had become very real to her with each minute that ticked past. So long as she wasn't legally spliced to a man she retained the power to write him off, kick him out, have done with him whenever she chose. But once the words had been said a monumental change occurred in the relationship. She was then bound to him by law, answerable for the good or bad that manifested itself in their lives. *Responsible for his conduct in a way that had never been before.* That was it! The thing that bothered her. Like a tiny fishbone stuck in her throat, she couldn't swallow the fact that after today she would be held accountable for Cort's whimsical behavior.

God alone knew what the man was capable of. She sure as hell didn't, not even after sleeping with him all these years. One moment he would willingly give his life for you, and an hour later he could be sacked out with some two-bit slut that would spread her legs for a bulldog if the price was right. About some things he was as brave as any man she had ever known. Like the way he had killed Chalk Wheeler back in Georgetown or faced down Soapy Smith right in his own dive. Oddly, he had no hesitation at all about wagering his own life against that of another man. Almost as if he had no qualms about the outcome, one way or the other.

But was that really what separated the men from the boys? Was the willingness to face another quick gun the true test of a man? Or was there a greater courage? The kind that made a man face himself, look inside his own soul, and somehow learn to live with what he saw revealed. Certainly Cort had been unable to do that. She knew it as surely as she knew her own name. He longed for the life of a high roller, to be admired, envied even as a man of cunning and infallibility. Yet there were some men who just didn't have the strength of character to withstand the crunch of a table-stakes game. Not when the ultimate bet was their manhood. Oh, they would gladly bet their lives, but never their manhood. Especially if the man was driven by a compulsion to outdistance the very woman who shared his bed. And knew in the darkest pit of his soul that he didn't have what it takes.

Cort knew, but he couldn't live with it. He had to keep on scheming and maneuvering, taking one desperate chance after another to prove to himself that he hadn't lost his balls. Sure, he had promised to reform, to behave himself once they were married. In the two weeks since Katie Fulton's wayward slug had creased the back of his neck he had become a changed man. On the surface at least. He had stopped drinking so heavily, been more attentive and loving than Mattie could ever recall. Curiously, without any prompting, he had even limited his dealings with the California Gang to a couple of nights a week. And that was no small accomplishment in itself.

Still, Mattie's sixth sense warned her that it wouldn't last. Call it hunch, or intuition, or just plain skepticism, but it had never failed her in the past. She might love Cort, yet she wasn't blind to his faults. He was as unpredictable as the fall of the dice, and in some ways living with him had much in common with shooting craps. He meant well, and she never for a moment doubted his sincerity. But his promise had about as much value as a fistful of Confederate scrip.

Suddenly it occurred to her that she was just borrowing trouble. There was nothing to be gained by worrying needlessly about something she couldn't change anyway. In a few minutes they would be married, and like the book said, for better or worse they would just have to work it out for themselves. Besides, she couldn't call it off now, no matter how apprehensive she felt. Not after Lou Blomger had co-erced a preacher into performing a wedding ceremony in a whorehouse.

Thinking about it, she had to smile. A man of God in a house of sin. Big deal. She wasn't sure that it mattered much who said the words. While she had been baptized a Lutheran back on the farm, she wasn't exactly what people would call a practicing Christian. Truth to tell, she wasn't certain that she even believed in God. Not the kind that preachers talked about anyway. And Cort was just an outright heathen. Indians had more religion in the dirt under their fingernails than he had in his whole soul. Facing it squarely, he had about as much chance of redemption as a snowball in hell. Which was right where he would end up when the clock ran out anyhow. And if she didn't precede him, she wouldn't be far behind.

There was a knock on the door and she called for Hand-some Jack to come in. She knew it was him without asking. She was to walk down the aisle on his arm, and according to the clock on the wall, it was just about that time. Handsome Jack opened the door and stepped into the parlor, attired in the same white tie and tails he had worn the night of the grand opening. That had been a long time ago, but looking at him, Mattie couldn't see that he had aged a day. Still the same brutish good looks and jaunty smile as the night she found him at that prize fight in Chicago. *God how time passed.* They had come a long way together, and at this mo-ment, more than any other, she realized again that Jack Ready was the one steadfast friend she had in the entire world. She loved Cort, maybe even adored him. But they would never be friends.

Handsome Jack just stood there gazing at her, unable to speak for a moment. Her gown was of white silk, with a high lace collar and a sheer tulle veil. Her cheeks were flushed, eyes shiny bright, her hair never more golden and lustrous than it was at that very moment. And Jack Ready thought her the most beautiful woman he had ever seen in his life.

"Mattie, you don't leave a man with much breath, and that's a fact."

"Thank you, Jack." She stepped closer and kissed him on the cheek. "I'm glad I've got you with me. To tell you the truth, my legs feel a little weak."

"Well, just brace up and hang on tight. Except for the mayor and the chief of police there's nobody down there you're not on speaking terms with."

"The mayor?" Mattie stared at him incredulously. "Jack, are you sure?"

"Sure I'm sure. Lou Blomger came dragging them in by the scruff of the neck about ten minutes ago. Course they look like they're gonna wet their pants any minute. Probably scared to death some reporter will get wind they came to a wedding on The Row."

"That sounds just like Lou. He's probably beside himself watching them squirm." Mattie smiled, picturing Blomger's delight at their discomfort. Then she glanced up at Jack. "Is everything ready downstairs?"

"Just waiting on the bride." Handsome Jack gave her a searching look. "Are you dead certain you want to go through with this? You've still got time to back out."

"I'm sure, Jack. I know you don't think he's the man for me, but I love him and I'm willing to take the chance." Then her eyes sparkled mischievously. "Besides, you big lug, you're just trying to make me wait around until there's no one left but you."

"Like I say, don't knock it if you haven't tried it." Jack drew her to him, and gave her a crushing hug. Then he put her arm through his and led her from the parlor.

Descending the stairs, Mattie saw that the crowd was backed up into the vestibule. These were her people, the tenderloin's elite, and they had turned out in their best finery to see Holladay Street's reigning madam take the vows. Cort was making an honest woman of her at last, something that rarely happened in the kingdom of whores, and they wouldn't have missed it for the world.

The parlor was jammed shoulder to shoulder with a

throng of well-wishers, and as the rinky-dink piano broke
into the wedding march, Mattie caught a glimpse of Blomger
grinning like a bloated chessy cat. Gowned in pale yellow
silk, the bridesmaids, *her beautiful little soiled doves*, fell
in behind as Handsome Jack led her down the aisle separating the guests.

Then she saw Cort, smiling nervously, yet with obvious
pride, as he watched her advance across the room. He and
Cliff Sparks, who was acting as best man, stood at the side
of the mantel, which had been decorated with a wagonload
of wild mountain flowers. Next she saw the preacher, a tall,
cadaverous man in a black frock coat, who looked as if he
were going to swoon and pitch over on his face at any moment. The man of God in the house of infidels. Maybe she
could get one of the girls to teach him all about tallywhack-
ers and buttercups after the ceremony was over. What a
sermon he could preach on hell and brimstone after that!

Then she was standing beside Cort and he took her hand.
He drew her close and she felt his strength flowing out to
her. She wouldn't worry anymore. He was her man, and
everything would be all right.

Sunday nights were usually pretty tame in the Slaughterhouse. Unlike the mining camps, Denver took after the eastern cities, where the day of rest meant just that. Though the
tenderloin dives remained open, trade was generally slack,
and at the moment there were less than a dozen men in the
saloon. Things were so quiet that Johnny Murphy had given
his bartender the night off and was doing the honors himself.

Cort had wandered in shortly after supper. After lazing
around the house all day he had grown restless, and decided
to have a couple of drinks with the boys. Mattie had even
agreed, commenting that he was as grumpy as a sore-tailed
bear, and that a little fresh air might improve his mood.
Once that would have brought a rise from Cort, but these
days he was a happy man, if not wholly content. While they
had been married less than a month, he had already noted

a marked change in Mattie's attitude. She no longer seemed so domineering or bossy, and somehow she had become vastly more feminine since they were spliced. It was a curious thing, and he hadn't quite gotten used to it yet. Nor did he fully understand it, for it was almost as if Mattie was slyly pushing him to take charge. Like she was willing to take orders, and was only running the show until he got the feel of things. She now discussed business matters with him as a matter of course, openly seeking his advice, where before he was rarely made privy to any of her affairs. Oddly enough, Handsome Jack had even come around asking his opinion on a couple of deals, and that was revealing in itself.

Cort suspected that they were working in cahoots with one another, trying to build his confidence so that he could eventually take over management of Mattie's legitimate enterprises. And he had to admit that she was swamped from morning till night overseeing her little empire. He had been stunned when she revealed the extent of her real-estate holdings. She was an extremely wealthy woman, and at first he was somewhat miffed that she had been so secretive in the past. Still, it was her money and she could jolly well do with it as she pleased. He appreciated her subtle efforts to get him involved in her business affairs, but it just wasn't his cup of tea. Stepping in and taking over after she had already accumulated the fortune still smacked of a gigolo, and any man with gumption ought to have more respect for himself than that. He wanted to make it on his own, without help from anyone, especially a woman. And if he couldn't then he'd just damn well go under in a shitstorm of his own making.

Cort had been surprised to find the Slaughterhouse so empty. Even for Sunday night, it was unusually quiet. Cliff Sparks had been nursing a drink at the bar, evidently the only member of the California bunch out on the prowl tonight. He hadn't seen hide nor hair of the rest of the gang, and assumed they were off playing house with their women. Cliff was the gay blade of the crowd, seldom harnessing himself to any one woman, and he had actually seemed a little lonesome. Since Cort had gotten married they hadn't spent much time together, and Cliff was genuinely delighted that he wouldn't have to spend the night drinking alone. Sharing a bottle, they began reminiscing about the good old days when they were knee-deep in clover and trimming the mining camps like Mexican bandits. The stories got louder and more hilarious as they recalled the many ridiculous predicaments they had faced together, and before they realized it the hour had grown quite late.

Suddenly the door burst open and Jim Jordan stormed into the saloon. He was holding a bloody rag to his head and appeared a little unsteady on his feet. Astonished, they could only gape as he marched to the bar, poured whiskey over the rag, and clamped it back on his head. They could see a long gash running from his hairline back into the scalp, and he cursed pungently as the alcohol bit into the wound.

Cort finally recovered his wits. "Jim, what in Christ's name did you tangle with?"

"I didn't tangle with nothin'. I never even got in a blow." Glaring at them through bloodshot eyes, he winced as the whiskey really took hold. "That greasy little bastard, Tom Cady, cracked me over the head with a cane."

"Well, I'll be dipped in shit," said Sparks, clearly amazed.

"Cliff, that's just about how I feel right now," Jordan remarked. "I was over at the Missouri Club when the squint-eyed mouse fart comes in and starts blowin' off about how the Soap Gang put the skids to us. He knew I was standin' there, but he had one of Soapy's gunslingers along and thought I wouldn't say nothin'. Well, I had just enough to drink that he got my hackles up and I allowed as how any dog that had been faced down in his own den didn't have much room to howl. Then, before I had time to blink, the squatty sonovabitch whacked me over the head with that cane he always carries. The next thing I know, I wake up out in the street."

"Well, what happened then?" Cort urged him on. "Did you just walk away?"

"Hell, no, I didn't walk away!" Jordan gave him an owlish frown. "I had the dirty little cocksucker arrested."

"Arrested!" Cort and Cliff Sparks echoed the word like trained parrots. In the Denver underworld there was tacit agreement that disputing parties never resorted to the law to settle a personal score. Only scum finked to the police, and such a thing was beneath the dignity of a real man.

"Damn right! Arrested!" Jordan's tone was hotly defensive. "What'd you expect me to do? Try an' outdraw Soapy's hired gun? Maybe a night in the can'll teach that sneaky little shit not to be so free with his cane."

"You're just kiddin' yourself, Jim," observed Sparks. "Tom Cady could lie his way out of a locked safe. Do you really think a judge is gonna fine him for whappin' you upside the head?"

"You're both barkin' up the wrong tree." Something in Cort's voice brought them up short. "Instead of Cady you'd better start worrying about Soapy Smith. Listen, that cold-blooded bastard pisses ice water, and he'll have a price on your head before morning. He can't afford to let anyone get away with havin' one of his men arrested. If he did, he'd be washed up in this town."

Jordan's pinched face had an oxlike expression. He had just heard his own death warrant read, yet he was too hard-headed to believe it could happen to him. Swabbing absently at the blood, a stubborn cast settled over his eyes.

"Cort's right," Sparks said. "You've got to get out of town tonight. Otherwise you'll end up backshot in some alley."

"Like hell I will!" Jordan retorted. "Maybe I'm not so fast with a gun, but I'll be goddamned if I'm gonna run with my tail between my legs."

"That's right, Jordan. You ain't runnin' anywhere."

The three men whirled to find themselves confronted by Soapy Smith, Tom Cady, and two hardcases who bore the unmistakable stamp of gunslingers. Smith had walked through the door just as Jordan made his last statement, and he already had his gun out and cocked.

"I figured you might try to blow town tonight, so I hustled on over and bailed Tom out of jail. Now we can just get this deal settled between ourselves, without any help from the law."

Cort edged away from the bar, playing for time. "Soapy, you've got a lot of nerve yellin' about police. I seem to recall you blew the whistle on us once when we rigged that race at the fair grounds."

"Thomson, you'd be smart just to stand still," Smith growled. "I didn't come here lookin' for you, but if you wanna take a hand I'd be real pleased to deal you in."

"I don't know what you've got in mind, but you'd better think it over." Cort saw out of the corner of his eye that Sparks had also moved away from the bar. The gang now had to concentrate on three targets instead of one. He could feel the Colts in specially waxed holsters in his hip pockets, and he suddenly felt alive, and very cocky. "I warned you once before not to tangle with me, Soapy. You've got a better chance of standin' on your head and pissing straight up than you do of shading me with a gun."

"Unless you want Mattie to end up a grass widow, you'd better pull in your horns." Smith moved his head slightly and the two gunhands eased to opposite sides of the room. "We only want Jordan. You and Sparks mind your manners and you won't get hurt. All right, Tom, get it done."

Tom Cady twisted the head of his cane and withdrew a thin, wicked-looking sword. "Jordan, you shouldn't have sicced the law on me. I'm gonna cut you up some just to teach you a lesson. But if you try and fight back you'll walk out of here packin' your innards in a bucket."

Cady advanced on Jordan, flicking the sword before him. His face was twisted in an evil smirk, like a hungry cat, toying with a cornered mouse. With nowhere left to turn, Jordan elected to fight. He clawed at the pistol inside his coat as Cady lunged. But as his revolver came clear Smith's gun exploded and he dropped to the floor.

Cort jerked his right-hand Colt and drilled the gang leader through the shoulder. Before he could fire again one of the gunslingers placed a slug squarely between his ribs, and he felt himself stumbling backward. But as he fell he snapped off another shot and grunted with satisfaction as he saw Soapy Smith clutch his thigh and topple forward.

Cliff Sparks was trading shots with the other gunman, and both men abruptly ceased firing in the same moment. They stared at one another with something akin to disbelief for an instant, then each man wavered and fell, dead before they hit the floor.

Momentarily distracted by all the shooting, Cady made the mistake of assuming his quarry was dead. As he turned toward the door, Jordan raised up on an elbow and shot him in the back of the head. Cady's brains exploded in a pink mist across the room, and he pitched face down beside the bar.

Just at that moment, the first gunslinger cocked his gun to finish Cort off, who was struggling to hoist himself erect. Then Johnny Murphy finally decided to join the fight. Whipping a sawed-off shotgun from beneath the bar he triggered both barrels in a blinding roar of light. Jolted by the double load of buckshot, the gunman hurtled into the wall, then slid to the floor like a bloody rag.

The room suddenly went very still. Johnny Murphy was the only man left standing, and dense clouds of gun-smoke obscured the fallen. The tomblike silence seemed deafening, yet the quick and the dead were past caring. Their night at the Slaughterhouse was done.

CHAPTER NINE

The aftermath of the gunfight at the Slaughterhouse had not been pleasant. Five men had been killed in the space of ten seconds, and a spasm of outrage swept over Denver. Perhaps the shock wouldn't have been so great had Soapy Smith and Cort Thomson also perished. But somehow they lived, cursing one another even as they were carried from the saloon. And in the opinion of the townspeople, justice would have better been served had there been no survivors.

Dinner newspapers gave the bloodbath page-one coverage, indignantly likening it to the barbaric antics of mining camps such as Leadville and Tombstone. Sizzling editorials roasted public officials and underworld leaders alike, declaring there was no room in a civilized community for wholesale murder. Then the preachers began, screaming themselves hoarse as they pounded their pulpits and denounced the wanton bloodshed as a sign from the Almighty. Then the governor felt the repercussions, and politicians huddled in guarded conferences as a hue and cry swelled throughout the city. Like an angry surf tearing at a rotted wharf, public reaction mounted against Denver's entrenched corruption, and for the first time in years a hush settled over the tenderloin.

But Mattie paid scant attention to the furor around her. Cort had one foot in the grave, and her every waking moment was spent at his bedside. The slug he caught in the gunfight had perforated his left lung, and despite the doctors' best efforts he contracted pneumonia on the following day. The next week had been touch and go as he hovered between life and death. Sinking one day, rallying the next only to sink again, he floated in a limbo where many men enter but few return.

Then the tide began to turn, slowly at first but with marked improvement each day. The chalky pallor covering his features started to fade, and color once more appeared in his cheeks. His wheezing, labored breathing gradually slackened, and the fever that had raged within him disappeared altogether. Miraculously, or so it seemed to Mattie, he awoke one morning with a clear mind, and grinned weakly at her tears of joy. But if he was lucid, he was far from chipper, and the ordeal had yet to run its course. His once muscular frame had been ravaged by the double onslaught of a lead slug and pneumonia. While he had never been a beefy man, tending to the lean side, he was now as thin as a rail, and sapped of the great vitality that had always been his trademark. Yet he was alive and on the mend, which came as a shock to those who had seen him carried from the Slaughterhouse drenched in his own blood.

The doctor observed that a lesser man would have succumbed within days of being shot. Still, some men had a fierce will to live, defying all the odds in their determined struggle to survive. Shaking his head, the doctor readily admitted that Cort's recovery owed more to his tenacious grip on life than it did to medicine. But there was a long period of recuperation ahead, and he cautioned Mattie that Cort must have adequate rest and plenty of nourishing food before he tried to resume a normal life. He even went so far as to suggest that it might be wise to send Cort to one of the many health resorts that had sprung up throughout Colorado.

But for the moment Mattie meant to keep a watchful eye on her patient. There would be plenty of time to consider such things as health resorts once he was back on his feet. Handsome Jack could run the house while she tended to Cort, and as for Lou Blomger, the tenderloin, and everyone else, they could go straight to hell until he was well again.

And the way things were going, that might be exactly where the tenderloin and Denver's underworld boss were headed. The newspapers hadn't slackened their tirade one iota in the last two weeks, calling for nothing less than total reform. According to their lurid prose, the city government was founded on a quagmire of corruption and greed. The only solution was to kick the rascals out and begin anew. Elections were less than a year away, and the newspapers joined in urging their readers to organize a popular movement that would drive the scoundrels from office. In the meantime, the editors called on the state house to begin an investigation of the graft and corruption that permeated every level of city hall and the county courthouse. The governor saw the handwriting on the wall, as well as the printed page, and he immediately appointed a commission to determine the complicity of public officials in underworld activities.

Politicians throughout the city sensed that their very future in public life was in jeopardy. Granted the shootout at Murphy's Exchange was regrettable, they told one another, but left to their own devices the voters would have forgotten it inside a month. The newspapers were magnifying an insignificant gunfight between a bunch of hoodlums in order to whip the public into a frenzy. And for what? Because the editors were zealots of good government, advocates of law and order, safety in the streets? Not on your tintype! They were looking to build circulation, steal one another's readership, and all this righteous indignation was just a smokescreen. But whatever the newspapers' motives, the politicians couldn't evade one simple fact. They were caught

between the frying pan and the fire. They couldn't denounce
Blomger, and they couldn't support him, not with their very
survival at stake. They were damned if they did and damned
if they didn't. Like a man standing neck-deep in shit, they
couldn't decide to duck or take it in the face when the next
shovel load came their way.

Mattie was seemingly oblivious to the storm of contro-
versy. She fussed over Cort like a mother hen with one
chick, and coolly ignored Blomger's repeated summons to
the Windsor suite. Handsome Jack could handle the payoffs
without any help from her, and until Cort regained his health
the fat man would just have to wait. But while she could shut
herself off from the turmoil that raged outside, she couldn't
elude the more imminent problem of what to do with her
husband.

Cort was finished in Denver. The gunfight was the
clincher in destroying whatever chance he might have had
of breaking with the California Gang and restoring his
once-solid reputation. Though he would never be indicted,
since he had fired only in self-defense, the onus of those
bloody ten seconds had marked him for life. Soapy Smith
was recovering from his wounds, and few doubted that he
would exact retribution when the time seemed ripe. And if
he didn't there was every likelihood that Blomger would,
as it was generally accepted that but for Cort's interference
there would never have been a gunfight. Or the heavier
threat that now hung over the tenderloin.

The underworld had its own code and the first tenet was
that only a fool backed an underdog. Cort was a pariah, a
man without welcome among his own kind, and there was
no place left for him in Denver. Should he remain he would
be doomed to the life of a tinhorn, a pennyante hustler only
one step above rolling drunks. Assuming someone didn't
kill him first, which according to the oddsmakers was even
money.

But what to do with him? Mattie had racked her brain,
but the whole affair seemed to defy solution. She couldn't
keep him locked up in the house, yet she knew he wasn't

safe on the streets. He was growing steadily stronger each day, and had already informed her that wild horses couldn't drag him to a health sanitarium. Then, as his convalescence stretched into a month, an idea slowly took shape in her mind. The longer she pondered it, the more practical it seemed, and considering the circumstances it appeared to be her only out. Now if she could only convince Cort.

With her arguments well rehearsed, she decided to brace him on a bright, sunny day in late March. Winter was gradually releasing its grip on the city, and with spring just around the corner it seemed a good time for a man to begin a new life. She found him sitting up in bed with a deck of cards, smiling as if he hadn't a care in the world as he practiced dealing seconds.

"Look at that," he laughed, deftly squeezing an ace from the deck. "Another week and my hands will be as quick as ever."

"Very good, lover." Mattie nodded appreciatively, watching his nimble fingers caress the cards. "But I've got something in mind for us that's going to take a lot more skill than that."

Something in her voice aroused his curiosity, and he stopped dealing. "Yeah, what's that?"

"I seem to recall your mentioning once that your family had a plantation down in Texas." Mattie played her opening gambit in an offhand manner, taking a seat on the edge of the bed.

"Well, not a plantation really." Cort grinned like a small boy owning up to a big windy. "Actually, it's more like a half farm and half ranch. Too bad I had to skip the country or I would've come into the chips."

Mattie studied his face for a moment, as if grappling with a difficult decision. When she spoke, her tone was hesitant, uncertain. "Now, Cort, I want you to level with me. Do you really know your rump from base fiddle about ranching?"

"Why, that's the goddamnedest insult I ever heard!" He reared back in mock indignation. "Mrs. Thomson, you are lookin' at a man who can sniff a bull fart in a wind storm.

Listen, if there's anything I don't know about ranchin' they just flat haven't discovered it yet."

"Oh, I've heard you brag before," she countered, eying him dubiously. "What I'm asking is if you know enough about ranching for me to sink a wad of money in a cattle spread?"

"Why, hell yes. I've forgot more about steers than most folks ever knew. But what's all this talk about a ranch? I thought you'd got enough of the country life when you were a girl."

"I don't mean to live there, silly. I'm talking about an investment. My lawyer says that cattlemen are making money hand over fist, and since I've always got a surplus of cash he suggested we look into it." She paused, apparently mulling it over further. "Of course, if we had a ranch it might solve some other things, too."

"Like what?"

"Well, for one thing, I've never cared much for keeping my sulky horses cooped up in stalls all winter. They ought to have a place where they could run and get some exercise. Every spring they're fat as butterballs and it takes a month to get them in shape. Then, too, we've got to think about you. The doctor said you need fresh air and lots of it if you don't want to come down with consumption. Sitting around smoky gambling dives certainly isn't going to do that shot-up lung any good."

"Whoa, hoss!" Cort threw up his hands as if to ward her off. "Just count me out. I'm not ready for a rockin' chair on some half-assed ranch."

"Who said anything about half-assed? I'm talking about a big operation. My lawyer says that's where the real money is." Mattie glanced absently out the window, chewing her lip as if puzzled by something. "Cort, is there such a thing as a cow plantation?"

"Cow plantation!" He howled. "Christ on a crutch, I wish the folks back in Texas could hear that. Damned if it don't beat anything I ever heard. A cow plantation!" The idea thoroughly amused him, but as ridiculous as it sounded

there was also something vastly appealing about it. Not every man was the master of a plantation, cow or otherwise. After a moment he stopped laughing, and peered at her owlishly. "Mattie, just how serious are you about buyin' a ranch?"

"Oh, very serious, honey. I'm thinking of sending my lawyer out to look for one before spring."

"Now just hold on a goddamned minute. That lawyer might know something about city real estate, but he don't know ass from elbow about cows. Why, he could cost *us* a fortune without even tryin'." The longer he thought on it the more the idea intrigued him. A cow plantation. "Tell you what. I'll find you a ranch and get it runnin' like it should. I'm not promisin' I'll stay there, you understand. Maybe a few months, but no more. Just till the kinks are smoothed out." Fingering the deck of cards, he began shuffling them distractedly. "You know, the doc might have something at that. A little fresh air would probably get me right back in the pink."

"Oh, Cort, you're the sweetest man I know." She cuddled up next to him and gave him a big kiss. "To tell you the truth, I was scared to death that lawyer would buy something that'd really put *us* in a bind. But with you handling it, I won't have to worry." She snuggled closer and put her head on his shoulder. "Now why don't you show me how you made that ace pop up out of the deck."

Times had changed. Ed Case knocked on the door of the Windsor suite, and never was he more conscious of the ebb and flow in men's lives. Only a few years past, Lou Blomger had been the one knocking on doors. Then it had been the fat man who was at Case's beck and call. But the shifting tides sometimes deal men harsh blows, and Ed Case was now a man who dwelled much on what had been. Today there was a different ruler in Denver, and when his summons went forth the vassals responded with alacrity. One of them was standing at that very moment before Boss Blomger's door.

Still, there was the smell of rebellion in the air, and as Ed Case waited to be admitted to the inner sanctum, he took pleasure from the thought that this slippery tub of guts might yet be hauled from his throne.

Then the door opened and Slats greeted him with a stony expression. The little man's icy eyes never failed to send a shiver down Case's spine, and as he entered the suite he felt like death itself was walking only a few paces behind. Blomger was in the midst of polishing off a gargantuan lunch, and more than ever he looked like a hog being fattened for the slaughter. *Now, there was a thought that really appealed to Case.*

Blomger waved him to a chair, noisily sucking the marrow from a ham hock. Then he burped into a napkin and dabbed the grease from his mouth. "You took your own sweet time getting here. I sent for you over an hour ago."

"I had things to do," Case said, trying to suppress the resentment that shot through him like hot sparks.

"Mister, when I send for you there's only one thing you've *got* to do. And that's trot it on over here without delay."

Blomger dug at his teeth with a toothpick, and eyed Case as if he were sizing him up for the cooking pot.

"Now, the reason I called you over here is to get a report on what the boys in city hall are talking about these days. Try not to waste words. Give it to me as succinctly as your limited vocabulary will allow."

Case hated this man. Hated his whalelike blubber, his imperious attitude, and most of all his deliberate use of four-dollar words. "I can sum it up in two words. They're scared."

"No shit." Slats chuckled, like a ferret crunching the head of a mouse, and it suddenly occurred to Case that it was the first time he had ever heard the man laugh.

"I know they're scared, Case," the fat man replied heatedly. "They've been running scared since the day they were weaned. What I expect from you is an evaluation of *how* scared, and what they're likely to do if this reform movement develops any momentum."

"Your guess is as good as mine. It's sort of like throwing cow dung against a barn wall. Whatever sticks you can count on. Whatever doesn't you just write it off."

"Jesus Christ! Don't give me any of your homey riddles." Blomger's face purpled with mounting irritation. "I want facts, not parables. Have any of them been courting the governor? Which ones are playing footsie with the newspaper editors? What are they saying behind closed doors when they think no one is listening? Those are the things I need to know. Facts."

"The answer to the first two questions is yes. A few of them have put out feelers to the governor, and generally they're the same ones that are sucking up to the newspapers. Behind closed doors they're wondering what you're going to do to protect them when the reform movement gets into full swing. So far as they're concerned it's not a matter of *if* the reformers will organize, but only when. The signs are too clear to doubt it any longer."

"That much I know. But I never thought I'd see it happen in Denver." Blomger's expression seemed numb, like an obese dog unable to outrun its own fart. Then his eyes glistened with anger, and he was himself again. "So they're going to organize. Let 'em, and good riddance. We'll give 'em a lesson about democracy in action they'll never forget."

"I don't know what you've got in mind, but I'll tell you one thing." Case felt Slats's eyes boring into the back of his head, and it occurred to him that he was a damn fool to speak out. "This town won't hold still for any more violence. One more killing and they'll ride us out of town on a rail."

"Case, you and your political pals amaze me. One gunfight and you act like a bunch of old ladies with your tits caught in the wringer. So long as I control the tenderloin, I control Denver. And you'd do well not to forget it."

"Maybe. But you're talking about a swing vote when the two parties are butting heads. If the newspapers and the reformers can get everybody behind a coalition ticket then the tenderloin won't swing anything but itself. By the neck."

"It'll never happen. Even if we have to rig the election."

Blomger grinned like a fat spider with its web ready and waiting. "Now you trot back and give your cronies the word. It's very simple, and they won't have any trouble remembering it. Anyone that breaks ranks, or tries to double-cross me, is going to take a one-way trip down the South Platte. And they won't be back."

Blomger dismissed him with a wave of the hand, and Case headed toward the door. Sometimes he felt like a gutless piss-willie when he allowed this lard ass to treat him as if he were a dog. Worse even. At least a dog got a kind word and a pat on the head once in a while. Well, hell, even at that, it beat a one-way trip down the Platte. Stepping through the door, he passed close to Slats and got a whiff of the little man's breath.

It smelled like dead flowers, only stronger. Somehow that seemed very fitting.

Ab Kellogg and Johnny Cole reined their horses to a halt at the hitching rack in front of Pigfoot Grant's saloon. They were bone-tired, filthy, and in dire need of a good stiff drink. The men had been riding for three days, coming from the north where they had spent the winter trapping wolves. As they dismounted a swarm of flies buzzed around, looking interested. Clad in greasy buckskins, they were covered with a six-months' accumulation of grime and sweat, and even for wolfers they smelled a little ripe. Behind them trailed two pack horses loaded with pelts, but the flies seemed more fascinated with the men than the wolf hides.

Slapping dust from their clothes, Kellogg and Cole entered the saloon, followed closely by the gathering cloud of flies. Pigfoot Grant stood behind the bar talking to a city dude. Sighting them, he whooped and came forward, displaying a mouthful of gold teeth that made his grin as square as dice. Grant also had a cock eye, which skewed around with a will of its own, and at times the flashing teeth and wandering eye could make a man forget his supper.

"Ab! Johnny! Switch me if I hadn't about give you up for dead." Grant pumped their hands, casing them with his one good eye. "Now that I get a look at you I ain't so sure but what you might be at that. Boys, you must've spent the winter swimmin' upstream in shit creek."

"Listen, you old chuck of bearbait, we didn't come in here to get insulted." Kellogg laughed and pounded the bar. "Set up some of that rotgut of yours, and let a man rinse his innards."

"Comin' up, boys. And if you drink me dry I got another batch brewin' out back." Grant placed two bottles of white lightning on the bar, and nodded proudly when the men shuddered as they tossed down the first drink. Local talk had it that his cock eye was the result of drinking his own liquor, but most folks in Wray still preferred it to those puny eastern brands.

"Whooeee! That is sure-'nuff drinkin' whiskey!" Cole took another jolting slug, then turned his nose skyward and howled like a wolf. "Man, I'm gonna get drunker'n a blind dog in a meat shop. I'm gonna drink till my toes curl up, and my tongue grows hair, and I ain't gonna quit till I'm stone cold dead."

"That's the ticket! Lap it up, Johnny." Kellogg slapped him on the back, and a puff of dust scattered the flies that had settled on their buckskins. "Livin' or dead, I'll tie you on your horse and take you along."

"Whatta you mean, take him along?" Grant asked. "You boys just got here. What's your rush?"

"Pigfoot, we got a load of wolf skins outside there." Kellogg gestured toward the door with his bottle. "We got to get on over to Yuma and cash 'em in. Until we sell them pelts we're flatter'n a busted flush."

Yuma was the county seat, some thirty miles west of Wray, and the closest place where bounty money could be collected on wolves. While Wray was situated only a few miles from the junction of the Colorado, Nebraska, and Kansas state lines, it was still a shorter ride to Yuma than any of the towns across the border.

"Besides, you ain't got no cathouses here." Kellogg took another drink and sloshed it around in his mouth like

soda-water. "Pigfoot, I been layin' out in that cabin all winter with a hard on like a big sweet toothache. I've plumb
wore out Mother Thumb and her four daughters, and tonight I'm gonna have me a real woman. Now Johnny here
is gonna drink himself blind. But I'm gonna waltz myself
over to Rosie Kelly's ridin' academy and pick out a fillie
that'll buck all night. And boys, lemme tell you somethin'.
With the load I'm carryin' she's gonna come up rearin'
when I ram it between her shafts."

"Well, hell, Ab, you got plenty of time to get to Yuma
before dark. Besides, we got a lot of jaw-bonin' to catch up
on. And looka here, you haven't even tried my new batch
of pigs' feet yet." Pigfoot Grant had but two claims to fame,
his whiskey and the pigs' feet he pickled himself. Since the
people of Wray couldn't quite handle calling him Rotgut,
they just naturally decided to dub him Pigfoot.

"Now you're talkin'." Kellogg rammed his hand in the
jar of pigs' feet. "Next to poontang and whiskey, I been
thinkin' about them hogs' knuckles of yours. Toward the
end there we sorta run shy of grub and we been eatin' shit
that would've colicked a bitch wolf."

Cole began munching hungrily also, talking between
mouthfuls. "Ummm, that is good eatin'. Pigfoot, you ain't
got no idea what it's like to be starved so bad you got the
hungries even sleepin'. I done cinched my belt to the last
notch, and my gut's still tighter'n a bull's ass in fly season."

"Well, boys, that's all behind you now. Once you cash
them wolf hides in you'll be rollin' in green, and you can
just lay around and fatten up like a couple of old boar hogs."

"Naw, hell, we can't." Kellogg disgustedly tossed a piece
of gristle on the floor. "It was a bad winter, Pigfoot. Colder'n
a sonovabitch. Why, would you believe we seen days that'd
freeze spit on a stove? And we didn't get enough pelts to
see us through the summer, much less stake us for next
year."

"I'm sorry to hear that, Ab." Pigfoot shook his head sympathetically. "Maybe you boys ought to find yourselves
another line of work."

"Christ, I don't know what the world's comin' to anymore." Cole knocked down another slug of white lightning, holding his breath till it hit bottom. "All the buffalo is gone, and now wolves is gettin' scarce as snake tits. There just don't seem no way for a huntin' man to make a decent livin' no more. Maybe we oughta take up bank robbin'. Hell, you couldn't get no hungrier at the end of a rope than I been this last winter."

"Gentlemen, I don't mean to butt in, but I might just have a proposition you'd be interested in." The city dude pushed away from the bar and walked toward them. He wore a pearl-gray Stetson, a black undertaker's suit, and a vest embroidered with Texas bluebonnets. But the thing they noticed was that he wasn't packing a gun. In this neck of the woods that seemed the least bit peculiar, if not downright stupid.

"Why sure, mister, come on up and meet the boys," Pigfoot said. "This here's Ab Kellogg and Johnny Cole. Two of the best hunters you'll ever run across."

The three men exchanged handshakes, and the wolfers were surprised at the firmness of the stranger's grip. While he looked sort of lean and puny, there was evidently more to him than met the eye.

"Glad to make your acquaintance, gents. I'm Cort Thomson of Denver. Couldn't help overhearin' your conversation, and it sounds like you've had a run of bad luck. Been there myself a time or two, so I know how you feel. But if you know this part of the country we might just be able to strike a deal that'd put you back on your feet."

"Well, me and Johnny is good listeners." Kellogg was sizing the stranger up, wondering if his wallet matched his wardrobe. With wolves getting scarce, maybe it was time they started hunting bigger game. "What'cha got in mind?"

Cort noted the look, and calculated he had judged these men right on the button. For twenty dollars and a bottle of whiskey, they'd cut the nuts off a mission priest. "I'm out here lookin' for land. Intend to set up a ranch and run some cattle. Haven't had much luck between here and Denver

though. I must've looked at a million acres and anything
that's not already homesteaded just isn't worth havin'. That's
why you fellows interested me. What with huntin' this country you must know it pretty well."

"Mister, if we ain't seen it then it ain't out there," Cole
bragged. "Do I understand you're lookin' for someone to
scout you up a piece of rangeland?"

"Somethin' like that. Only what I'm lookin' for isn't
gonna be easy to find."

"Well, let's try'er on for size. See how she fits," Kellogg
remarked. "Like Johnny says, if what you're after is out
there we know how to put you on it."

"Sounds fair enough. What I'm after is a big chunk of
land that's off away from anyone else. It's got to have good
graze, good water, and not be more'n two days drive from
the railroad." Cort paused and looked around at the three
men, choosing his next words carefully. "And it's got to be
within short trailin' distance of Kansas and Nebraska."

Kellogg and Cole glanced at each other, then at Pigfoot.
While none of the men so much as batted an eye, an under-
standing of some sort passed between them. Not wanting to
offend the dude, Pigfoot tried to make his question casual.
"Not much land along the border that ain't already taken.
'Bout how far would you consider to be close enough?"

"Anything under a day's drive."

"Or a night, maybe?" Cole blurted the words out before
he had time to catch himself.

"Or a night." Cord nodded, flashing his grin. They understood one another.

"Well now, that's sorta illuminatin', ain't it?" Kellogg
observed. "Mister, I got an idea we might be able to do business after all. But before we get all bogged down why don't
we do a little jawbonin' about money. You see, me and
Johnny, we got this thing about eatin' regular."

"Don't blame you a bit," Cort said. "Suppose we just say
you're both on the payroll at a hundred a month. Assumin',
of course, that you come up with the right piece of land."

The men just stared at him. The figure he quoted was

three times the going rate for a cowhand, and if there had been any doubt before, it now vanished. Kellogg was the first to recover. "Mr. Thomson, we know just the spot you're lookin' for. There's a block of land that sorta sits catywampus between Arch Armstrong and Lew Ashton. They're big ranchers north of here. It's got a fair-size lake that stays fresh the year round, and I'd say it ain't no more'n two miles from Nebraska, and maybe ten or twelve from Kansas. Whatta you think of that?"

"If it's so good, why hasn't somebody bought it?"

Pigfoot snorted. "Nobody around here's got the money 'cept Ashton and Armstrong. And they figure why buy it when they can graze it free. The people that owned it got froze out in the blizzard of '87, and the county's been holdin' it for taxes ever since." The skewed eye rattled crazily in its socket as he glanced slyly at Cort. "Might cost a feller upwards of ten thousand to get the title squared away. But I know the man to talk to over in Yuma."

"Pigfoot, I can see we're gonna have to put you on the payroll. You've got too much talent to let it go to waste." Grinning, Cort looked back at the wolfers. "Boys, when can we get a look at this spread?"

"Hell, no time like the present," Kellogg commented. "We can leave first thing in the mornin'."

"Now don't that beat all," Pigfoot chuckled. "What about them big plans to get your pole greased tonight?"

"Shit, Pigfoot, you heard the man. I'm on the payroll. Anyway, after waitin' six months I reckon it'll stay hard a little longer."

"Pigfoot, how much is a bottle of that rotgut?" Cort's question took the saloonkeeper unawares.

"Why, uh, I usually get about three dollars. For a whole bottle, I mean."

Cort dropped a ten on the counter and hefted a bottle in his left hand. "Gents, I always like to let folks know the rules when they take a seat in my game. So I'm gonna let you see my hole card, just in case you get to figurin' you've hooked yourself a pilgrim."

With that, he tossed the bottle toward the ceiling over
his left shoulder. Crouching, he spun and a Colt appeared
from his hip pocket in a blurred motion. The sixgun roared
and the bottle exploded before it was halfway to the floor.
Cort reholstered the pistol, and turned back to the slack-
jawed threesome.

"Any questions?"

The wolfers stared at him in dumb amazement. Pigfoot's mouth opened in a golden smile, and his cock eye
skittered heavenward. "Just one. You sure you ain't Billy
the Kid?"

The men all started laughing at the same moment. *Hell,
any fool knew that Billy the Kid was long dead and buried.*
The wolfers slapped one another on the shoulder, the flies
swirled up in an angry swarm of protest, and Pigfoot Grant
poured everyone a shot of white lightning. Hoisting their
glasses, they drank to their unholy union, and to eastern
Colorado's newest cattle baron.

Mattie stared at the wire, thoroughly puzzled. WE ARE
NOW IN THE COW PLANTATION BUSINESS. BREAK
OUT YOUR CHAPS AND SADDLE UP. WILL
RETURN IN A FEW DAYS. She knew that Cort had a
fondness for jokes, but this was carrying things a bit too far.
The least he could have done was give her a few details, like
how much money he had spent and where the ranch was
located. The telegram was datelined Wray, Colorado, which
told her little or nothing. Looking at some old maps her attorney had secured, she finally found a tiny dot represent-
ing Wray, situated smack-dab on the borders of Kansas and
Nebraska. Now why in God's name would Cort buy a ranch
a hundred and fifty miles east of Denver? Especially when
they had agreed that he would look for land to the south,
toward Colorado Springs or Pueblo. It just didn't make
sense. And the longer she pondered it, the more irritated
she became.

Her mood wasn't too pleasant these days anyway. After
packing Cort off she had gone to see Blomger, and that was

enough to depress anyone. The toad, as she now called him privately, had pitched a raving fit about Cort's part in the Slaughterhouse gunfight. When she reminded him of his promise to let Cort and Soapy settle the matter in their own way, his jowls had fairly quivered with rage. They hadn't settled anything, he shouted, they were both still alive. The only thing they had done was to get five other men killed, and provide the reformers with an excuse to start babbling *Onward Christian Soldiers*. After she explained that Cort was about to become a rancher, Blomger seemed somewhat mollified. But he warned her that if her husband ever again caused trouble in Denver he'd be cold meat inside of twenty-four hours. Mattie lost her temper then, demanding to know if Blomger had given the same message to Soapy Smith. The fat man told her to mind her own business, that Soapy brought money into the organization, whereas Cort was nothing but a small-time parasite. And the argument had ended on that note. Even Mattie couldn't push Blomger past a certain point.

But the threat weighed heavily on her mind. She couldn't keep Cort from coming into Denver occasionally, and she wasn't even sure that she could persuade him to take up ranching permanently. Now, on top of everything else, there was this cryptic telegram. Sent from the middle of nowhere, with absolutely no explanation, and she was left to stew until Cort returned. Sometimes she thought the girls had the right idea. *Screw all men. Never give them an even break or they'll shit on you every time.* While she knew she could never share that twisted outlook, she had better reason than most to view men with a jaundiced eye. So far the ones in her life had been nothing but first-class bastards.

"From the look on your face, someone is getting roasted over the coals."

Mattie looked up to find Handsome Jack standing in the doorway of her office. "Come on in, Jack. I was just trying to figure out who gives me the most problems. Lou Blomger or Cort."

"Why, what's Cort done now?" Mattie handed him the

wire and he read it over twice before dropping it on the desk. "Well, he did what you told him to. What's wrong with that?"

"That's just the point. He didn't do what we agreed." She tapped the telegram with her forefinger. "Wray, Colorado. Ever hear of it?"

Handsome Jack considered for a moment, repeating the name to himself. "No, can't say as I have."

"Neither have I. But that's where my loving husband bought a ranch." She shuffled the map around on the desk, and stabbed at the pinpoint. "Here. Right in the middle of those godforsaken plains."

"Well, that looks like a good place for a ranch to me. I mean, if you're going to grow cattle you need grass, and there's sure as hell enough of it out there."

"Oh, there's plenty of grass out there all right. And Cort probably bought a good spread. But it just happens to be in the opposite direction from what we agreed on."

"What's wrong with that? You know, you can't just look at a map and say *that's* where I'm going to buy a ranch. Maybe there's no land available in that area, or could be it's not even the right kind of land for cows."

"C'mon. There are lots of ranches around Colorado Springs. And we agreed to buy land down south because it's warmer and the climate would be better for his shot-up lung." Mattie studied the map solemnly, trying to make the pieces fit. "No, there's something more to this."

"Mattie, sometimes I think you like to worry. So the man bought land over to the east instead of in the south. Hell, maybe he just didn't find what he was looking for down there."

"Jack, you're missing the point entirely. Cort's only been gone a little over a week. He hasn't had time to look for land in both places. Obviously, he went from here almost directly to this place called Wray. Which means he intended to settle out there from the beginning, and never said the first word to me about it."

Handsome Jack thought that over for a moment, but it didn't seem to make sense one way or the other. "Well, you know Cort. Maybe he just got a wild hair up his ass and decided he wasn't gonna let you dictate where he bought a ranch."

"Dictate?" Mattie gave him a withering look. "Christ almighty, Jack, I didn't dictate. I conned him into the whole thing. He went out of here like a little boy with a new toy."

"Then maybe you're not as good at bunco as you thought. Handsome Jack gave her a teasing smile, amused by her fiery little tantrum. "Appears to me you're more mad at yourself than you are at Cort. Don't get your dander up just because your con job didn't work."

"Oh, listen to the big smooth talker, would you? Well, don't you believe it. I helped write the book on conning men." Then she noticed his humorous expression and smiled. "But you're right about one thing. It didn't work out just the way I planned."

"Sure, that's the way to look at it. What the hell do you care where he bought a ranch? Wherever it is, it's to hell and gone from Denver. And according to what you said, that's really the only thing that counts."

"Yes, I know. But there's just something that doesn't smell right about the way he handled this." She pondered the matter a few moments, unable to put a name to her sense of misgiving. Then a small ray of light peeped through. Not an answer, merely a clue. "Jack, I think you hit it a moment ago when you said something about Cort not finding what he was looking for around Colorado Springs. Perhaps he didn't go down there because he knew all the time he wouldn't find what he wanted to the south. Maybe he figured all along that what he was looking for was over to the east, around this place called Wray."

"Yeah, that makes sense. But what's he looking for?"

"I don't know, but I wish I hadn't given him twenty thousand to buy it with."

"I'll say one thing, Mattie. When you back a fellow, you sure enough back him to the hilt." Handsome Jack had a fleeting vision of a thousand double eagles, and more than ever he wished this blonde little hellcat belonged to him.

"Well, he said in that wire he'd be back soon, so I guess you can just ask him straight out what he's got in mind."

"That's something else that bothers me. Why is he coming back here so soon? We agreed that he was to find a ranch and get it operating before he came back to Denver. Let a month or two pass so that things would simmer down around town."

"One thing I learned about Cort a long time ago: you've got to accept him on his own terms. He's about as predictable as a roulette wheel, and you've got to figure he won't always do what's expected. Maybe he just wants one more look at the bright lights before he starts herding cows, or whatever it is you do to 'em."

Mattie shook her head pessimistically, clearly worried. "Jack, it doesn't make a damn what he wants. I'm trying to keep him from getting killed. And every minute he spends in Denver could very easily be his last."

"Then why don't you just tell him?" Handsome Jack urged. "Sit him down and explain the facts of life."

"I can't. You know better than that. If he suspected I dreamed up this ranch scheme just to protect him, he'd never leave town. He's too proud. I could beg and scream till I was blue in the face, and he'd stay just to prove that he's not afraid to face another gunfight."

"Yeah, it's a problem all right." Handsome Jack frowned, and chewed it over. "What about Blomger? Can't you get him to put a leash on Soapy?"

Mattie laughed sardonically, her eyes spitting fire. "The toad? No, I'm afraid not. As usual, he's thinking only about himself. He talked about Soapy like the bastard lays golden eggs. Said Cort was just a leech that didn't contribute anything to the organization. Jack, he told me outright that if Cort gets in one more scrape the only way he'll leave Denver is feet first."

"Which is just another way of saying that Cort is caught in the middle. Even if he got into it with Soapy and came out alive, he'd still have to face Slats. And that's not anything to sneeze at. I'm not even sure I'd want to go up against that frosty-eyed little runt."

"Jack, sometimes it seems like there's no end to it. The killing and hate, and now the newspapers on our backs. Why can't people just live and let live? You no more than make something of your life and somebody pops up and wants to take it away from you."

"Well, that's really not so strange when you stop and think about it. I'm not exactly a philosopher, but you don't have to be educated to figure out that man is a greedy son-ovabitch. He always wants what the other fellow's got, even if he doesn't need it. Or if it's something he doesn't particularly want for himself, then he kicks up enough dust so the other fellow can't have it either. As a race we're not especially anything to be proud of."

"You surprise me. Underneath all that charm you're nothing but a dyed-in-the-wool cynic." She smiled wanly, but her heart really wasn't in it. Her mind kept coming back to Soapy and Slats, and that damn telegram. After a moment the smile faded, and she took her friend's massive paw between her own dainty hands. "Would you do something for me?"

"Anything you say." Handsome Jack's voice seemed hollow, like a man talking inside a barrel. In all the years they had been together, this was the first time he had ever held her hand.

"Would you look after Cort? Somehow try to keep him from getting himself killed while he's in town?"

Handsome Jack just nodded, staring at her intently. Then the moment passed, and she slowly withdrew her hands. They both seemed unsettled by the brief intimacy, and he quickly changed the subject. If the weekly collections were going to be on time, Jack Ready declared, then he'd best get at it. And he did, leaving her alone with her thoughts.

Cort sailed through the front door with Pigfoot Grant in tow. Greeting Handsome Jack effusively, he presented the burly giant with a bottle of Pigfoot's special blend of pop-skull. Ready looked like a man who had been presented with a live bomb, and he gingerly placed the bottle on a hallside table. Cort appeared to be a changed man, laughing, cracking jokes, expansively relating the highlights of his trip. Clearly he and Pigfoot had polished off a liberal sampling of white lightning on the train. Still, Handsome Jack was struck with the thought that whatever had happened in Wray it had some-how restored Cort's old cockiness and devilish wit.

Just then Mattie stepped from her office, alerted by all the commotion in the vestibule. Cort raced down the hall, lifting her high in the air, yowling like a banshee. Then he smothered her in a long embrace, oblivious to the stares of Handsome Jack and Pigfoot. Slightly taken aback, Mattie was still composing herself when Cort turned and signaled to his companion.

"Honey, I want you to meet Pigfoot Grant. He's just an old country boy, not much to look at, but he's ace-high where it counts."

"Ma'am, I'm pleasured to make your acquaintance." Pig-foot doffed his battered hat, somewhat thunderstruck by Mattie's beauty. "Cort told me you was a looker, but he shore didn't do you justice."

"Why, thank you, Mr. Grant. I'm always happy to meet any friend of Cort's." Mattie was growing more bewildered by the moment. This man was a hayseed if ever she had seen one, and what's worse, he smelled like a goat herder. "Are you from Wray?"

"Oh, yes, ma'am. Settled there back in '67." Pigfoot's chest swelled up and he preened like a molting rooster. "Don't mind sayin' I own the biggest saloon and general store in town."

"How nice. Jack, why don't you take Mr. Grant down-stairs and fix him a drink. Cort and I have some things to discuss, and afterwards we'll join you."

Pigfoot thought that a dandy idea, and gladly followed Handsome Jack toward the stairs to the game room. Mattie turned on her heel and marched into the office. Cort had a sudden feeling that the prodigal's return wasn't going to rate a fatted calf. As he came into the office Mattie whirled on him, bristling with anger.

"Cort, I want some answers, and I'm not in any mood for your hijinks. Now, first off, who is that old reprobate and what's he doing here?"

Cort grinned and eased himself into a chair. "Mattie, lower your sights. Pigfoot's a good-enough sort, even if he is a little rank. He helped me sew up the deal for the ranch, and I promised him a trip to the big city in return. That's all there is to it."

"Not quite all, by a damnsight!" She found his casual tone abrasive, and her temper began to rise. "Suppose you tell me how we ended up with a ranch in some pigsty called Wray when we agreed you'd find a place outside Colorado Springs?"

"Christ, there's not any good land down south of here. Don't you think I would've bought some if there were?"

"Lover, you're skirting the truth, and I don't like that." Her eyes had grown wary, slightly hurt. "You haven't been anywhere near Colorado Springs. You didn't have time to go there and then get out to Wray before you sent me that wire."

"Is that all that's botherin' you?" Cort's poker face never once flickered. *Damn that quick little mind of hers anyway!* He was thinking fast now. "Hell, I got to talkin' to some cattlemen down at the train station the day I left. They told me the best grazin' land was in that country out around Wray. If we're gonna run horses and cattle we'll damn sure need good graze, so it just didn't make any sense to waste time down south. Besides, what'd you care where the place is so long as it's a good spread?"

"I don't really." Mattie had to admit that this part of it wasn't what concerned her. "It just galls me that you'd change our plans all around, and take off on your own without even telling me."

"Mattie, I'm a big boy, remember. I don't need anyone to hold my hand. And besides, I seem to recall your sayin'

you'd trust my judgment when it came to buyin' a ranch."
Cort grinned engagingly. He had her boxed in now, and he
knew it. "Quit acting like an old fussbudget, and gimme
another kiss."

She smiled, unable to resist his boyish charm, wanting to
believe. Accepting his hand, she sank down on his lap, resting her head on his shoulder. He kissed her slowly, yet hungrily, running his hand across her breast. She moaned and
wiggled closer in his arms. When they came up for air, she
nestled against his chest, sliding her hand inside his coat.

"Sweetie, if you keep that up, Mr. Pigfoot is going to
have to spend the rest of the day by himself."

Cort chuckled huskily. "Maybe we'd better wait till tonight. I can't ignore an old friend like Pigfoot, 'specially
when he pulled the strings to get us the ranch."

Mattie sat up, her curiosity again whetted about the land
deal. "Cort, tell me about the ranch. I mean, where is it?
How much did it cost? You know, all the details."

"Well, it's about two days' ride due north of Wray.
Mattie, it's the prettiest place you've ever seen. The graze
is mostly bluestem, nearly two thousand acres all told, and
a damn fine lake. Used to be an old buffalo wallow, but
over the years it's turned into a big lake, something over
twenty acres. Lots of room for your horses and a herd of
maybe three, four hundred steers. And over on one side of
the lake there's a little rise with some cottonwoods that's
just perfect for the house."

His enthusiasm was infectious, and Mattie started to get
excited. "Oh, Cort, it sounds marvelous. When can I see it?
How soon can you get a house built?"

"Slow down, speedy. Things like this take a while." He
laughed and gave her another kiss. "I've already hired a
couple of men and bought a hundred head of good breeding
stock. And I've ordered the lumber for the house. Should be
there by the time I get back. But we're gonna have to order
the furniture here and have it shipped to Wray. That's one
reason I decided to come into Denver."

"One reason? What's the second?" Mattie sensed what was coming.

"Well, I hate to say it, but this is costin' a little more than we expected." Cort glanced at her, picking his words carefully. "The ranch ran about twelve thousand dollars what with one thing and another. Then there were the cows and the lumber. That was another six thousand. And I hired these two men. Of course, we need the furniture, and I really ought to buy some feeder steers for fall shipment. So it looks like we're gonna need some more pesos just to get this thing movin'."

While he actually spent less than fifteen thousand, Cort had no qualms about lying. The money really didn't matter all that much, but he just couldn't resist the chance to promote someone. Even Mattie.

She watched him a moment, somehow uneasy about his arithmetic. But, what the hell, it was only money. And if it kept him out of Denver then it was well spent. "Okay, lover. What's it going to cost? Break it to me gentle."

He rubbed his jaw, as if weighing all factors. "Well, including getting your horses shipped out there after racing season, I'd say we ought to be able to bring it in for another ten thousand."

Mattie sighed and got to her feet. Walking to the desk she pulled out a ledger and wrote a check. Handing it to him, she suddenly remembered something.

"Incidently, where's the deed for the land? I'll put it in the safe here."

Cort dug a folded paper out of his coat pocket, and gave it to her without comment. Mattie opened it, reading slowly down the page. Then her eyes widened, and she carefully read over a certain section again. When she looked up, she wasn't smiling.

"This is made out in your name. Wouldn't it have been smarter to have it registered in both our names?"

"Hell, Mattie, I'm your husband, aren't I? Whatever's mine is yours accordin' to the law. Besides, if anything happens to me you're the only one could inherit it, so what's the difference?"

Mattie still couldn't get over how much he was like a little boy. This was his play-pretty, and he wanted it in his name. Well, why not? "You're right, lover. No difference at all. Now, why don't you run along and show Mr. Pigfoot the bright lights. And don't get drunk! I want you back here in good shape to finish what you started a few minutes ago."

Cort kissed her lightly, slying pinching her nipple. When she swatted at him playfully, he ducked out the door and yelled for Pigfoot. Moments afterward, they stormed out the front door, laughing and carrying on like two jayhawkers come to see the tall cotton.

Later, looking back, Mattie regretted having given him the check before he was ready to leave town. Cort and Pigfoot promptly went on a binge that left half the dives in the tenderloin reeling in their wake. While Handsome Jack shadowed Cort's every step, just as he had promised Mattie, his presence in no way hampered their wild spree. The celebration lasted three days, and by Handsome Jack's reckoning cost at least a couple of thousand. But the clincher came on the fourth day and somehow it seemed a fitting climax to Cort Thomson's departure from Denver.

Early that morning Cort passed the word around that his good friend Pigfoot had died of some strange malady during the night. The body could be viewed at Biddle's Undertaking Parlor, followed by the services at the graveside. While Cort had few cronies these days, a small crowd nonetheless gathered at the funeral home. There they found Pigfoot Grant laid out in a fine rosewood coffin, his pallid features set in a cold smile, as if he had gone under enjoying the last moment of his trip to the big city. After an appropriate time the coffin and floral wreaths were loaded into a hearse, and the somber company set out for the graveyard.

Once at the gravesite, a minister read a brief prayer from the good book, then the coffin was slowly lowered into a freshly dug hole. Suddenly a woman screamed, and the small band of mourners drew back in horror as the lid of the coffin creaked open. Like the risen dead, Pigfoot Grant leaped from the grave, brandishing a quart of whiskey and brushing talcum powder from his face.

"Whoeee!" he howled. "Boys, I wanna tell you, if you ain't never been there, it gets plumb stuffy in one of them boxes."

The spectators gave ground as if Lucifer himself had suddenly materialized before their eyes, and most appeared as ashen-faced as the recent corpse. Though racked with fits of laughter Cort managed to roll a keg of whiskey from behind a bush, and informed the shaken funeral cortege that Pigfoot Grant's wake would now commence in earnest.

For Mattie, it had been a harrowing four days. After putting Cort on the train the next morning, she went home and collapsed with a good stiff belt of anisette.

Mattie found it odd that both Slats and Sam Blomger were to attend the meeting. Something out of the ordinary was going to take place, she sensed it in her bones, and her nerves were strung taut as catgut. The very fact that Blomger had summoned her on Saturday, rather than waiting for her normal Monday visit, meant that something strange was afoot. When she and Handsome Jack entered the suite, she knew immediately that the rules of the game had changed. But to what purpose?

Blomger made it a practice never to have anyone but Slats at his business conferences, and Sam's presence instantly put her on guard. The older brother was a dimwitted hooligan, whose only value lay in intimidating those who opposed Lou. The mere fact that he was standing here posed the threat of an even greater danger, for he was apt to repeat anything he overheard when in his cups. All of this flashed through her mind as she greeted Blomger, and she knew for a certainty that the toad had some grungy scheme up his sleeve. Sam was present to forestall any interference on the part of Handsome Jack, of that she had no doubt. Knowing this, and suspecting much more, she waited for Blomger to speak.

"Mattie, I'm glad you came right over." Blomger smiled, but his eyes were flat, deadly serious. "We've got a problem, and it seems to be one of those things that won't go away simply by ignoring it. Specifically, I'm referring to this burgeoning reform movement. The newspapers show no signs of relenting, and as I'm sure you are aware, they're even beginning to bandy about the names of certain prominent businessmen for the office of mayor."

"Yes, I've been reading about it," Mattie replied. "But it's hard to believe people would seriously consider any of those stuffed shirts for mayor."

"Oh, don't deceive yourself. Don't forget, I went through a reform battle in Springfield." Blomger paused for a polite belch, as if the thought had unsettled his stomach. "You'd be amazed at the raving lunatics people will put into office once they get hooked on reform. They start pounding drums and marching around in torchlight parades, and in the process somehow take leave of their senses."

"Speaking of that, I seem to recall your once telling me that you had decided on Denver because reformers would never have a chance here." Throwing it back in his face brought a moment of immense gratification. She seldom had a chance to prick that blubbery hide. "What happened to change that?"

"An asshole named Cort Thomson, who didn't know enough to mind his own business." Blomger drew a deep, wheezing breath, clamping down hard on the sudden flare of temper her question had sparked. "Now let's not go into matters that are already settled. I understand Cort has left the city, and we no longer need concern ourselves with his penchant for making headlines. However, we are still faced with the reform movement that his recklessness set in motion. And the one lesson I learned from the Springfield incident is simply stated. To survive we must strike first and in a manner of speaking dismember their movement. Violence alone isn't enough, although it can be applied judiciously. Instead, we must somehow chop the legs out from under these righteous fanatics before they have a chance to get organized."

"Well, Lou, I'm just a little bit puzzled by all this. I've heard you say countless times that the tenderloin vote controls Denver, and if that's the case, then why are you in such a dither about a few reformers?"

"I'm afraid you're somewhat mistaken on that score, my dear. While I find it a distasteful admission, Ed Case pointed out a very salient fact to me not long ago. The tenderloin casts the swing vote. That's a distinction which bears thought. Should the newspapers come up with a candidate acceptable to both Democrats and Republicans then the name of the game changes drastically. What I'm saying is that the possibility of a coalition exists. And should both parties solidly back the same candidate then the tenderloin vote becomes meaningless. Do I make myself clear?"

Mattie remained silent for a moment, suddenly gripped by a startling revelation. *Lou Blomger was scared!* While he appeared calm on the surface, beneath all that lard he was riddled with fear. "I see what you mean, but the situation just doesn't seem all that desperate to me. If we go under then almost every politician in Denver will sink with us. Are you saying they're just going to stand around and let that happen? That they're not going to lift a finger to organize a counter-movement?"

Blomger shrugged disdainfully, like a man shorn of illusions concerning his own breed. "Mattie, the greatest truth of our time is that politicians make strange bedfellows. The immortal bard once commented, 'Were kisses all the joys in bed one woman would another wed.' While his observation related to another subject entirely, it's not without relevance in our present situation. The political hacks we elected jumped into bed with us because they saw a chance to screw the public and make themselves rich. But there are joys that can be even more seductive given the right circumstances. Namely, survival. And let me hasten to assure you, the politicians of this town wouldn't hesitate a moment to double-cross us if they had the slightest inkling we were weakening."

"So what do we do, put the fear of God in the big boys by rubbing out a few of their underlings?" Mattie's tone bore the faintest trace of sarcasm, and Blomger blinked, wondering if he had heard right.

"As a matter of fact, I've already attended to that. Ed Case is passing the word that anyone who tries to cross over won't even make it to the other side."

"What makes you think Case can be trusted? He certainly has no reason to love you, and if he's loyal it's only because he's afraid you'll kill him."

"A good point. I can see you're beginning to grasp the essential problem that confronts us. And that's exactly why I've decided to cast a little bread upon the waters, so to speak." Blomger paused, priming her as he let the suspense build for a moment. "We're about to undertake a campaign known by the unsavory distinction of corrupting the innocent."

Mattie glanced around at the other men, shaking her head. "Lou, I don't know about the boys here, but you just lost me."

Blomger smiled like a hog in a cabbage patch, enjoying himself. "Do you recall that Jesus once fed the masses with a loaf of bread and some fish? Well, there's a great lesson to be learned from that, Mattie. If you teach a man *how* to fish you feed him for the rest of his life. But if you simply *give* him the fish then he is dependent on you for his very existence. Being lazy and slightly larcenous at heart, most people are content with the handout rather than being bothered with catching their own. What I have in mind is giving these reformers a taste of the sweet life. Unless I miss my guess their righteous shouting will come to an abrupt halt when they're invited to share in the honeypot. And I intend to start with the newspaper editors."

"You're going to offer them a share of the spoils, is that it?" She thought it over for a moment, visibly impressed with Blomger's underhanded cunning. It was a shrewd move, and with the newspapers on their side the reformers would peter out in no time flat. "What if the editors turn you down? There might be more honest men around than you think."

"Oh, I have something else in mind in that event. But that's neither here nor there. Right now we have to concern ourselves with building up a war chest. Bribing the innocent is always more expensive than bribing the corrupt, and we're going to need a substantial increase in revenues. That's why I called you over here today. As of this week, I want payoffs from all the houses and cribs jumped to fifty percent."

"Fifty percent!" Mattie stared at him as if he were mad. This was the crunch, what she had feared the moment she walked in the door. "Lou, they just won't hold still for it. Twenty-five percent was bad enough, but the madams will revolt over this. Christ, they'd join hands with the reformers before they'd cough up half their take."

"That's where you come in," the fat man rasped. "You've had easy pickings for a long time, and now I'm calling the debt. Jack and his boys are to collect fifty percent, and not a nickel less. And if they have to bust a few of those old hags upside the head to get the message across, then that's exactly what I expect them to do."

"Lou, I just can't do it! I know these madams, and they'll bow their necks at anything like this. Fifty percent isn't a payoff, it's robbery. You'd have to start the killing all over again to make it work, and I refuse to be a party to that."

"Goddamnit, Mattie, you don't seem to understand. You don't have any choice. I'm ordering you to do it." Blomger's jowls turned beet-red and he glared at her angrily. Then his gaze shifted to Handsome Jack, who was standing behind Mattie's chair. "Jack, you heard me, and I don't want any argument. Fifty percent from every whorehouse in the tenderloin, and if you have to get rough to do it, then trot out the muscle."

Handsome Jack locked eyes with the fat man, and he didn't give an inch. "Blomger, I take orders from Mattie and no one else. If you want somebody to rough up women then you'd better send your own hooligans over to The Row."

Slats came away from the wall, where he had been leaning near the mantel, fixing Ready with an icy stare. Mattie saw him tense and knew that the little killer was only waiting for Blomger to nod his head. While Slats's attention was diverted by Jack, Mattie ran her hand in the purse lying on her lap. Then Sam Blomger snorted contemptuously, and lumbered toward Ready.

"Sonny, you shouldn't of spoke to my brother like that. When he says frog, you squat. Just so's you'll know next time, I reckon I'm gonna have to teach you a few manners."

Sam Blomger wasn't as tall as Ready, but broader in girth, weighing close to three hundred pounds. He had never been whipped in a rough-and-tumble fight, and he evidenced not the least doubt that he was about to clean Jack Ready's plow. Still, Handsome Jack wasn't the tamest man in captivity himself, and when the chips were down he never believed in giving the other fellow an even break.

As Blomger passed Mattie's chair, Handsome Jack feinted with his left. Blomger ducked, but the expected blow never came. Instead, Handsome Jack stepped in and drove his right fist up to the wrist in Blomger's paunchy groin. Air burst from Sam Blomger like a steamboat whistle, and his face went chalk-white as he grabbed between his legs. Twisting slightly to his left, Handsome Jack reared back and kicked him squarely in the face. Blomger's nose and mouth flattened in a pulpy blotch, and he toppled to the floor with a crash that shook the room. He was out cold, twitching and wheezing like a beached whale.

Then Slats crouched, his hand streaking toward the shoulder holster underneath his jacket.

"Touch it and you're dead!" Mattie's hoarse cry brought everything in the room to a dead stop.

While everyone else was watching the fight she had eased the little pistol from her purse, and now had it trained on Slats. The little man had heard that she couldn't hit the broad side of a barn, but at that range he didn't feel inclined to test the rumor. He relaxed, dropping his hands to his sides.

Lou Blomger arose, motioning Slats to back off. "Mattie, you shouldn't have crossed me. You've made a big mistake."

Mattie came out of her chair, backing to beside Handsome Jack. "You're the one that's making a mistake, Lou. I told you once you were creating a monster here in Denver that might turn on you. If you try to make the houses and the dives come up with half their take you'll pull this town down around your ears. As of right now, Lou, I resign. I'm out of the rackets. You don't bother me and I won't bother you. That's a promise. I'll run my house, and you can do whatever you damn well please with the tenderloin. But if you try to get rough with me or my people, I'll bring Cort back and hire a pack of gunslingers that'll make Slats look like a Maypole fairy. I've always been as good as my word, Lou, and you know I'll do it. So don't push me."

Mattie and Handsome Jack backed toward the door, closing it softly behind them. Lou Blomger glared around the silent room, speechless with rage, looking for something to smash. Then he strode forward and kicked his fallen brother squarely in the balls.

BOOK FOUR

COLD DECKS
AND BUSTED FLUSHES

CHAPTER TEN

Harvey G. Tannen was a man governed by habit. The patterns of his life were as rigid and unwavering as the grid lines on a surveyor's map. From the moment he stepped out of bed in the morning till far into the night, his thoughts were devoted to a sole passion, *The Denver Tribune*. Shorter than most men, and thin as a reed, Tannen rarely indulged in the temptations that others found so appealing. He ate sparingly, never fooled around on his wife, and considered gambling the most foolhardy of man's childish proclivities. It wasn't that he had any moral stand against gambling. He was simply appalled that people thoughtlessly ignored the odds against winning, especially in the tenderloin where the dives gave even Lady Luck a nose bleed. Besides, it wouldn't look right for a Sunday School teacher to be seen in a gambling den.

Like most of Denver's early settlers, Tannen had come to town with not much more than the clothing on his back. But he was an ambitious man, in his own modest way, and he foresaw the day when Denver would become a thriving metropolis. While he had been an itinerant printer most of his life, he harbored a secret longing to be a newspaperman.

After tapping a small vein of gold, he invested in a press and fulfilled his lifelong dream. *The Tribune* was a conservative paper, reflecting the outlook of its owner, and over the years it had prospered greatly. From a one-man shop it had grown to a large organization, dominating the other papers in both circulation and influence. And Harvey G. Tannen, diminutive, prudent, deceptively shrewd, became a man to be reckoned with in the capital city.

Tannen was something of a bloodhound where the mood of the populace was concerned, and after three decades there were those who believed him to be absolutely clairvoyant. When Cort Thomson and Soapy Smith shot it out in the Slaughterhouse, Tannen had sensed the public was ready for a change. Actually, he had seen it coming for almost a year, but coolly sat back and bided his time. What he needed was an incident worthy of igniting the public conscience, and five dead men had provided more than enough kindling. When *The Tribune* bannered the gunfight, calling for an end to underworld rule, the other newspapers were only a step behind. Within a week, everyone in Denver was talking about corruption and graft, and before the month was out a reform movement had been organized and was gaining converts rapidly. Now, with election time drawing near, the reformers were solidly entrenched and there was every likelihood that the crooks would be turned out of office at last. All that remained was to find candidates acceptable to both parties, and with a coalition ticket Denver's turbulent tenderloin would become a thing of the past.

Harvey Tannen had mixed feelings about sounding the tenderloin's death knell. While it was wicked and rife with violence, there was something curiously alive and engaging about an institution devoted exclusively to man's baser instincts. Once it was gone life wouldn't be quite the same. Saner perhaps, certainly more law-abiding and democratic, but never again as exciting. Still, he was philosophical about his role in the tenderloin's demise. As a student of history, he recognized that civilization has a way of encroaching on man's gamier pursuits, notably gambling and prostitution.

It had to come sometime, even in Denver, and once the public decided on reform there was no power this side of perdition that could stay their will.

Just tonight, he had written essentially these same words in his editorial for the morning edition. Then, on the stroke of ten, as the paper was being put to bed, he walked from *The Tribune* offices. This was a deeply ingrained habit, one he had seldom deviated from over the years. He would be home within the quarter hour, in bed by eleven, and up again at dawn. Assuming, of course, that his wife didn't disrupt his sleep. Josephine Tannen was the all-time Rocky Mountain champion of snorers, building to a crescendo along about midnight that wasn't unlike a swarm of farmers sawing gourds. At times he had considered separate bedrooms, but the idea somehow never jelled. Every man had his cross to bear and his just happened to be a mountain of flesh who could awaken the dead with her grating snorts.

Walking along the street, Tannen found himself hoping that this would be one of Josephine's off nights. He was tired, and he could do with a good night's rest. Suddenly a huge form appeared from an alleyway, blocking his path, and Tannen came face to face with Sam Blomger.

"Don't get edgy, Mr. Tannen," Sam grunted. "I don't mean you no harm. My brother sent me to fetch you."

"Fetch me?" Tannen glanced around the darkened street, profoundly aware that they were all alone. "For what purpose?"

"I don't ask questions, Mr. Tannen. I just take orders." Sam peered at him like a near-sighted gorilla. "Why don't you be a good fella and do the same?"

"That sounds vaguely like a threat. Are you abducting me?" In the dim light, Tannen could see that Sam's face looked like a piece of raw liver and idly wondered who had worked him over. He also saw that Sam didn't understand the question. "What I mean to say is, are you forcing me to go with you?"

"Now don't get your hackles up. My brother only wants to talk. That ain't gonna hurt you, is it?"

Tannen hastily concluded that talking with Lou Blomger might hurt a lot less than resisting this dimwit. Besides, his curiosity had been aroused. The first rule he instilled in cub reporters was that a man never knew where he might run across a scoop. And a conversation with Boss Blomger could easily merit the front page.

"Lead on, Sam. I'm yours to command."

Sam blinked, not at all sure that the little snit hadn't insulted him, but he said nothing. Lou had made a point of saying that he didn't want the newspaperman roughed up, only delivered. Turning, Sam crossed the street and struck out toward the hotel, with Tannen trotting along at his heels.

Ten minutes later they entered the Windsor lobby and Tannen found that he never ceased to be amazed by life's lesser absurdities. Glancing toward the desk clerk, the publisher noted something that had long since slipped his memory. The hotel had installed its safe in the wall behind the desk, ten feet above the floor. This had been done to foil robbers in the early days and the safe could be reached only by means of a special ladder. Somehow this struck him as ludicrous, since a permanent guest in the hotel just happened to be the town's biggest thief. In fact, that might make a good lead for the story he intended to write about this unexpected night beat. Or maybe he should comment on the incongruity of an underworld boss residing in a hotel where Denver's most illustrious citizen maintained a suite. Crossing the lobby, which was paneled with diamond-dust mirrors and roofed with stained glass, he was reminded again that Horace Tabor, the Midas of the mining world, was the Windsor's chief claim to fame. But if Tabor was the hotel's most illustrious guest, then how did the owners look upon their most infamous lodger?

Tannen was still speculating on these juicy tidbits when Slats admitted them to the suite. But one look at Slats was enough to reorient his thoughts. Abruptly, he realized he was about to face a man who had ruthlessly ordered the death of at least twelve known victims. This really wasn't any matter to be taken lightly and for the first time he felt a tingle of fear down around the base of his spine.

Blomger came forward to greet him, but without extending his hand. He wasn't about to lose face by having Tannen refuse the handshake. "Very good of you to come, Mr. Tannen. I've hoped that we might have a chat for some time now."

Tannen took the chair indicated by Blomger before speaking. "I'm not exactly here of my own volition, Mr. Blomger. But I assumed you had something worth saying, so I didn't debate the issue with your brother."

"I can appreciate that. Sam's not the most tactful of men even on his best days." Blomger glanced at his brother, who quickly retreated into the office. "May I offer you a brandy, Mr. Tannen, or possibly a sherry?"

"Mr. Blomger, let's get one thing straight." The little publisher's voice was firm even though his guts felt like jelly. "I didn't come up here to drink with you or to make social chitchat. I came because your brother left me no choice. Also, I have to admit I'm curious. Now, suppose you just tell me what's on your mind."

Blomber's piggish eyes narrowed at Tannen's tone. This wasn't going anything like he had expected. But the only thing to do was plow ahead, and to hell with the amenities. "Very well, Mr. Tannen. I'll give it to you straight, without any frills or embellishments. I find myself being outflanked by Denver's newspapers. I'm afraid you and your associates paint a rather sordid picture of my activities. While I have no qualms concerning the upcoming election, I would prefer that the press stop inciting the rabble, so to speak. In effect, what I'm looking for is an arrangement whereby the candidates I select will receive favorable mention in certain publications from time to time."

Tannen stared at him for a moment, hardly able to credit his own hearing. "Do I understand that you are actually trying to bribe me?"

"Please, Mr. Tannen. You do me an injustice. I'd hardly resort to anything so gross as a bribe. What I'm offering you is a partnership. A chance to share the wealth in a manner of speaking."

The publisher smiled wryly, shaking his head. "Sorry, no sale. I haven't got much, but at least I know that whatever gets printed in *The Tribune* is the truth."

Blomger's face swelled with anger. "I judged you to be a smarter man than that, Tannen. It disturbs me when I don't get what I want, and that often makes it unpleasant for the other people involved."

Tannen paled, suddenly aware that Slats was watching him from beneath hooded eyes. But he was a staunch little man, not easily intimidated. "Blomger, if you're threatening me, come right out and say it. However, I'll tell you right now, threats won't work any better than a bribe. You can scare me, but you can't make me crawl."

"Men sometimes regret hasty decisions. You ought to think it over." Blomger studied him for a moment, then resumed in a flat, malignant tone. "Maybe you don't care about yourself, but you have a family to consider. Two children, I believe."

"You must really be desperate to threaten a man's children." Tannen was no longer frightened. Just mad, and thoroughly sickened by this obese globule of flesh that called himself a man. "Blomger, you couldn't have gotten where you are by being stupid. If you start killing newspaper editors and their families, you'll have the vigilantes measuring you for a rope inside of twenty-four hours. Also, keep in mind, your candidates are already shaky and at the first sign of violence they'll run like scalded dogs."

"You sound very confident for a man who might not make it home tonight."

"You won't harm me. You're not sure you've lost yet, and as long as there's a chance to win you can't afford even one mistake." Tannen glanced at Slats, then back to Blomger. "May I leave now?"

Blomger dismissed him with a contemptuous wave, sinking deeper in his chair. Tannen walked stiffly to the door, and the fat man's beady eyes followed him every step of the way. Jesus, when little farts like that get starch in their backbone there's something out of kilter. But what, goddamnit? What?

Tannen knew, and as he closed the door he was already planning an editorial that would explain it to Boss Blomger. It would be about dinosaurs, saber-toothed tigers, and other whalelike anachronisms.

Work on the ranch house was all but completed. Carpenters imported by Cort had knocked together a rambling one-story structure situated in the grove of cottonwoods overlooking the lake. The house consisted of a spacious living room dominated by a huge stone fireplace, dining room, office, two bedrooms, and kitchen. At the last minute, Cort had added a bathroom, with an immense porcelain tub and a king-sized johnny pot. The ranch hands could use an outhouse, but the head of this fledgling outfit had no intention of sacrificing his luxuries. Besides, he had hired an old pot walloper known as Dirty-Face Murphy to handle the cooking chores and look after the house—which included emptying the king-sized johnny pot.

Workmen had also erected a bunkhouse with an adjoining kitchen, and a sprawling stable for Mattie's race horses. Much like the master of the house and the hired hands, the cow ponies would be kept in a separate corral, off away from the blooded stock. Cort had bought a remuda of twenty range-savvy horses, and a hundred feeder steers that were already cutting a swath through the lush spring grasses. Ab Kellogg had been appointed ramrod, and in addition to Johnny Cole had hired two former cronies to round out the crew. While none of them knew a great deal about cattle, they weren't burdened by an overactive conscience, which dovetailed neatly with the plan Cort had been formulating for some weeks.

Cort had every intention of becoming a cattle baron. Standing on the knoll, looking out over his little domain, he felt like a man reborn. Denver, and its contemptuous high rollers, were now behind him. The days of being a kept man were gone, done with, and never would he return to that life. He was determined to make his own fortune, become a leader, a man of stature and prominence. No longer would he be dependent on Mattie for handouts or toe the line simply because she controlled the purse strings. While he loved her, he also blamed her for the battering his self-esteem had taken in Denver. She had been a crutch. Handy, willing to support him, always anxious to make him more reliant on her unstinting generosity. Or so he saw it, at any rate. Here, he would become his own man again, and come hell or high water, he meant to pick up all the marbles this time. Then, once he was flush, he'd return to Denver and show those high-toned bastards what a real, live cattle baron looked like.

But if he meant to become wealthy, he also had his own ideas as to how such a thing could be most readily accomplished. Only suckers worked. Cort's adult life had been spent in an underworld atmosphere where legitimate enterprise was regarded with open scorn. For longer than he could remember, his way of life had been peopled by two very distinct classes . . . those that took and those that got taken. Far too much water had passed under the bridge for him to change now, and he couldn't bring himself to consider an operation that would yield a square livelihood. Dealing from the top of the deck had become foreign to his nature, and he found it inconceivable that he should turn a hand to honest toil. He would become a cattle baron, all right, but even in this range racket there were shortcuts a smooth operator could take. All it took was balls, and Cort had recently reclaimed his with a vengeance.

The prairie grasslands of Colorado, Nebraska, and Kansas were literally teeming with thousands of cattle. Great herds of longhorns had been trailed north after the close of the Indian wars, and most of the ranchers in the area were transplanted Texans. But this didn't deter Cort in the slightest. While they were fellow Texans, they still walked erect and anything that stood on its hind legs was a prime sucker. Regardless of its origin.

Some years back, blooded shorthorn stock had been introduced among the herds, and the cattle now bore only passing resemblance to the rangy mavericks from Texas. Steers were shorter, blockier, and often reached weights that brought hefty prices from eastern cattle contractors. While a man could turn a handsome profit buying feeder steers and fattening them, there were other ways to play the same game. Riskier perhaps, but far more profitable. And profits were much on Cort's mind these days. Especially the kind that involved other men's cattle.

By the time the ranch buildings had been finished, Cort was ready to move. He had a legitimate front, the northern plains were swarming with fat steers, and he saw nothing to be gained by delay. The evening after the carpenters and workmen had departed for Wray, he called a meeting in the main house. The hands trooped in and took seats around the living room. Ab Kellogg, Johnny Cole, Lute McGivern, and Eddie Watson. A gamier-looking crew he had never seen, thought Cort, but each was a skilled hunter. And for what he had in mind, stealth was what would separate the men from the boys.

"Gents, I reckon it's about time we had a little talk," Cort began. "Things have shaped up pretty good around here, and I wanted you to know I'm real pleased with the way you're handling the stock. Course, I know that with only a couple hundred head and a bunch of horses you're not too busy, so I thought we might as well hash out the next step in this operation."

Cort paused and lighted a cigar, scanning their faces through the blue haze of smoke. "Now I think all of you had a pretty good idea of what I've got in mind when you signed on. Just in case you're not too clear, though, suppose we hear from anybody who hasn't figured out why I'm payin' double wages."

The men glanced at one another out of the corners of their eyes, then got busy rolling cigarettes. They wouldn't touch that with a ten-foot pole. Finally, Ab Kellogg chuckled lightly and flashed a mouthful of brownish teeth. "Why, hell, boss, we just naturally ain't the kinda fellers that asks questions. We figured you had your reasons and sooner or later we'd hear about it."

Cort didn't return the smile. "Ab, you might be a good wolf hunter, but you're a hell of a poor liar. I'd lay odds you boys have kept the bunkhouse hoppin' with talk about what I'm gonna want for that double pay."

"Well, sure, there has been some talk," Kellogg admitted. "We're all as curious as the next feller when we run up on an easy touch. But we're full-growed, and I don't reckon any of us is slick behind the ears."

"Glad to hear you say it. There for a minute I was beginnin' to think you boys weren't too bright." Cort smiled now, and the men relaxed, knowing that they were going to get the lowdown at last. "What I aim on doing is to buy a hundred head of feeder stock the first of every month. But we're gonna drive a herd of three hundred to different railheads at the end of each month. Now if you boys paid attention in school you know that means we've got to come up with an extra two hundred head every month. Which means you're gonna be puttin' in lots of night work."

Kellogg darted a glance at Cole, then studied his hands for a moment. "Boss, we ain't got nothin' against rustlin' cattle, but your loop's a little bigger'n we expected. You only got a couple thousand acres on this spread, you know. Where the hell you figure on hidin' all them cows?"

"I don't figure on hidin' them at all, Ab." Cort grinned, and pulled a folded paper from his jacket pocket. "This is my registered brand. Signed, sealed, and delivered. Pass it around. You'll find it interestin'."

The men huddled around the document, puzzled by Cort's air of confidence. While most of them couldn't read, they could make out the broad strokes of the HXX brand registered to one Cortez D. Thomson. After a moment they looked up, more dumbfounded than ever.

Cort shook his head, smiling dryly. "It's really very simple, gents." Removing pencil and paper from another pocket, he began sketching. "Now, right across our eastern boundary line is Lew Ashton's place, and his brand looks like this: 4X. Then over on the west we've got Arch Armstrong and his brand is made somethin' like this: Hʌʌ. What do you think will happen if we take my brand and lay it down over either of these? Let's see."

Cort slowly dotted in characters with his pencil. First 4X, then Hʌʌ. Holding the paper out so the men could see his handiwork, he next connected the dots, resulting in identical markings of HXX and HXX. Which by a remarkable coincidence happened to be the brand registered to eastern Colorado's newest cattle baron:

"Well, I'll be goddamned," Kellogg muttered in awe. "You figured all that out and made your brand up on purpose so it'd lay down over Ashton's and Armstrong's."

"Go to the head of the class, Ab," Cort swelled with pride, clearly delighted with himself. "We're gonna rustle their steers, get 'em branded by the next mornin', and nobody'll ever know the difference. Course, I'll want you boys to make a few raids over into Kansas and Nebraska. But we can get most of what we need right here at home."

"Speakin' of gettin'," Kellogg said. "Just what do we get out of this besides wages?"

"Good question. On top of wages you'll each get a three percent share. In dollars that'll mean another two, maybe even three hundred a month." Cort smiled to himself. *What you knuckleheads'll never figure out is that my share will come to over a hundred thousand in less than a year.*

This was a real windfall to men who rarely cleared a hundred dollars a year. Everyone nodded and grinned except Lute McGivern, who was frowning like a screech owl. "Mr. Thomson, I don't know as how I'm too keen on this deal. I figured we'd be doin' all our night work across the border. Hell, Armstrong and Ashton will be half-froze to swing us from a tree when they start missin' that many steers."

"Let's don't get bent out of shape," Kellogg said hurriedly. "If the boss was smart enough to work out this deal, he's smart enough to keep us above water."

Cort raked them with an icy glare. "Anybody that figured this was a Sunday School picnic shouldn't have signed
on. The only way out now is feet first, and if you think I'm
funnin', just try me. While we're at it, I'll tell you somethin'
else. There'll be no more drinkin' in town. Some of you
boys can talk a man's molars right out of his jawbone when
you've got a snootful, and that could get us all strung up.
As of right now, I'll supply the liquor and any drinkin' that
gets done is gonna take place over in that bunkhouse. Any
argument?"

The men looked everywhere but at Cort, and got busy
rolling more smokes. Like he said, the only way out was in
a box, so why sweat it? Besides, how many wolfers had a
shot at that much money and free whiskey to boot?

Mattie was going through the morning mail when she ran
across Wray's small weekly, *The Rattler.* Cort wasn't much
of a letter writer, and she had subscribed to the newspaper
just to keep herself up to date on what was happening in
his neck of the woods. She hadn't seen him for close to two
months, and had received only one scrawled excuse for a
letter. Still, she wasn't worried. Where Cort was concerned,
no news was the best kind. When anything bad happened,
she always heard about it fast enough and she was quite
content with the calm that had settled over the house with
his departure.

The rest of the mail was either bills or letters for the girls.
She set these aside for the moment, unfolding *The Rattler.*
Just then, Handsome Jack appeared in the doorway of her
office, his mouth twisted in a sardonic smile.

"Mattie, you're not going to believe this, but about half
the Denver Chamber of Commerce is waiting in the vestibule to see you."

She couldn't have been more surprised if Jack had announced the Queen of Sheba. The pillars of Denver society
just didn't visit Holladay Street whorehouses. Not in broad
daylight, anyway. There was something fishy about this, and

she could smell it all the way from the vestibule. "Did they say what they want?"

Handsome Jack shook his head with an expression of detached amusement. "Nope. Just said it was urgent, and that they had to see Miss Silks right away."

Mattie tried to sort it out in her mind. *What the hell kind of business would such men have with a madam? Could this be some trick of Blomger's? Have the house condemned, or maybe raise taxes sky-high? No, Jack had said they were from the chamber of commerce, not city hall.* But no matter how she turned it, their presence still didn't make sense.

"Show 'em in, Jack. But hang around. I don't know what they want, but I might just need a witness."

Presently, Handsome Jack returned with three men, and Mattie got her second shock. She knew who they were even though she had never met them personally. John Shaffer, the lawyer; Benjamin Leonard, owner of Leonard's Emporium; Gus Purdy, head of Purdy's Freight & Storage. While the men would never have suspected it, they had been her business partners, in a very real sense, for a number of years. This deal was getting more interesting by the minute.

She sat through the formalities as each man introduced himself, then motioned toward the couch and single chair. "Have a seat, gentlemen. I understand you have something urgent on your minds."

The men exchanged glances and finally John Shaffer came up on the edge of the couch. "Miss Silks, I don't quite know how to put this, but the chamber of commerce is faced with a dilemma that only you can solve. No doubt you have read of the fact that we are attempting to persuade one of the nation's foremost financiers of Denver's future potential. Naturally, I am referring to Mr. Syrus Laird, who I believe has visited your house almost every night this week."

"Not almost, Mr. Shaffer!" Mattie retorted. "He's been here *every* night, and I'd take it as a personal favor if you would ship him back wherever he came from. Just to be frank about it, he's a pain in the ass."

The three men stared at her curiously for a moment, not quite sure if she intended a pun. But the whites of her eyes lacked humor, and they decided she hadn't spoken in jest. The lawyer cleared his throat before responding. "Yes, I daresay there are some who would term that an apt description of Mr. Laird. However, Denver needs industry and commerce to grow, and Syrus Laird just happens to be a man who could supply both. But I regret to say, he is a capricious man. A man given to strange whims, to put it charitably."

"From what my girls tell me, perverted might be a better word. But I still don't see what all this has to do with me."

Gus Purdy suddenly came alive. "Miss Silks, you know how it is. The chamber brings these big moguls into town and wines 'em and dines 'em, and if they want a little extra fun, why we just have to provide it. We had one of the boys bring him to your house because it's noted as the best in town. Then nothing would do but what he had to come back every night, and now the old devil has really made the cheese binding."

Mattie just waited, not really sure she wanted to hear what was coming next. The men looked at the floor and one another, and the moment lengthened into strained silence. Finally Benjy Leonard couldn't stand the suspense any longer.

"Miss Silks, what these gentlemen are trying to say is that Mr. Laird was less impressed with your house than he was with you personally."

"No kidding? You act like that was news to me, Mr. Leonard." Mattie's temper was rising swiftly. "Let me tell you something. That old lecher propositioned me every night he was in here, and he's damned lucky I didn't have him thrown out on his ear. I don't need that kind of nonsense."

Leonard looked awkwardly at the other two men, but they weren't about to help him out. "I'm afraid it's rather expensive nonsense, Miss Silks. Syrus Laird is willing to invest a sizable amount of money in Denver, but only on one condition. He insists that you accompany him on a tour of California."

Mattie stared at him incredulously. *These holier-than-thou snobs were out pimping for old dingle-bulls. They had found their mark and they meant to gaff him no matter what. It was just a con game, only on a higher level.* The whole affair suddenly struck her as absurd, and really not worth the energy it required to get angry.

"Sorry, boys. I can't oblige you. I've been a madam since I was nineteen, but I've *never* been a whore. And Syrus Laird just doesn't seem like the place to start. Besides, my husband would fill him full of holes if I went traipsing off to California. Then you'd really be up a creek."

Gus Purdy's face turned florid, and he began gesturing wildly. "But you don't seem to understand, Miss Silks. If you don't do what Laird wants, Denver is going to lose over a million dollars in investment capital. This city has been good to you, young lady, and I'd think you would want to repay the debt."

"Also, consider this fact," Shaffer interjected smoothly. "Laird has his own private railroad car and I'm sure he would be extremely generous over the course of the trip."

"No sale, gentlemen. The whole deal just leaves me cold."

"There is another point to consider." Benjy Leonard had a sly smile plastered across his face, like a chicken hawk that has just zeroed in on a plump hen. "We're not without influence in Denver, and we understand you are no longer aligned with Boss Blomger. We could save you a great deal of trouble in the days to come. On the other hand, if you don't cooperate, we could make things very difficult for you. Perhaps you should take some time and think it over."

Mattie's cheeks flushed, and her jawline went rigid. *These bastards are trying to blackmail me!* "You boys picked the wrong day and the wrong woman. Now, just so you won't feel like your time has been wasted, I'm going to give you a lesson in high finance. Mr. Leonard, you lease a very nice building uptown. I believe your comment was that it's the *perfect* location for an emporium. And Mr. Purdy, you lease two warehouses in South Denver that I understand are essential to the growth of your business. Well, boys, I hate to tell you this, but I own all those buildings. Even though my lawyer collects the rent, I'm your real landlord. Sort of makes your stomach curdle, doesn't it?"

Purdy and Leonard looked like two old rams that had just been shorn naked. Before they could regain their composure, Mattie axed them again. "The lesson is really quite simple. Don't go around acting like big-deal *financiers* until you've got your own little nest in order. If you want it any plainer, I'll spell it out. You bother me again and I'll put you both out of business. Do we understand one another?"

"What about me, Miss Silks?" John Shaffer broke in crisply. "Do you also own the building where I have my offices?"

"No, but I might just buy it if you don't watch your smart mouth. That's not a bluff, Mr. Shaffer, so you're welcome to call the bet if you don't believe me."

"I'm afraid not, dear lady. I believe you have made your point. Gentlemen, shall we be on our way?"

The other two rose in a daze and followed Shaffer from the office. Handsome Jack grinned at Mattie over his shoulder, then escorted the men along the hallway.

Mattie didn't know whether to be angry or amused. The whole thing was so ridiculous, yet those three had actually tried to blackmail her. Still, it was just another pinprick in the illusion of righteousness that the swells built up around themselves. *Ethics only apply when the other guy is doing it to you! That was their motto.*

Mulling it over, she decided she was neither angry nor amused, just disgusted. She would pretend it never happened, and simply raise their rent a thousand dollars next year. *Hit 'em in the pocketbooks, right where they live!* Somehow that had the ring of justice to it.

Unfolding the Wray *Rattler*, Mattie caught her breath. A

stark headline seemed to leap up off the page, and for a moment she felt faint.

TWO KNIGHTS ARRESTED

Pigfoot Grant and Rancher Thomson Corralled Riddle Saloon and Terrify Train Passengers

SAD AFFAIR

Sad indeed! Mattie no longer felt faint. She came up out of her chair mad as a hornet, and yelled for Handsome Jack.

The crew had been slightly flabbergasted when Mattie arrived at the ranch. Pigfoot Grant had told them she was a beauty, but the old reprobate was a born liar, so they figured it was just another of his big windies. Once they got a look at her in the flesh they realized that Pigfoot had told the truth for a change, and they stammered like schoolboys when Cort introduced them to Mrs. Thomson. While they knew she ran a sporting house in Denver, they weren't in the least fazed by that, and it was generally agreed that the boss was a mighty lucky fellow.

But their envy shortly received a setback when the argument started. Even from the bunkhouse they could hear the screaming and shouting. The lady, as the crew now referred to Mattie, sounded like a sow grizzly with a sore paw. She had ridden the train from Denver, then hired a livery man and buggy for the two-day ride from Wray. She was tired, caked with dust, and, above all, downright mad.

Cort managed to hold his own in the infighting, but from the bunkhouse it was clear that he was taking a real shellacking. Tangling with the lady, the men observed, must be sort of like crawling in a gunnysack with a wildcat. Before you knew what hit you the fight was all over, and other than being cut to ribbons, all you got for your trouble was a handful of fur. And right then, it sounded like the boss was getting sliced up seven ways from Sunday. Even Dirty-Face

Murphy got to thinking they were going to kill one another, and came on down to the bunkhouse so he wouldn't have to witness the bloodshed.

Still, the men couldn't exactly say they sided with the boss. After all, it was him that broke his own rule about no drinking in town and they figured he pretty well deserved whatever he got. Course, Pigfoot was a bad influence on man or beast, and they allowed as how Cort probably wasn't entirely at fault. But then, he wasn't exactly a babe in the woods, so a person couldn't rightly say he was innocent, either. The fact remained that they had gotten crocked on Pigfoot's white lightning and shot up Wray's only other saloon just for the hell of it. Which wouldn't have been so bad if they had stopped there. Lots of people shot up saloons in this part of the country. But then they dragged a drummer from the local mercantile and force-fed him a quart of rotgut. Even that wasn't so outlandish, since drummers weren't exactly known as teetotalers. Wray's constable sort of got his dander up, though, when they chased the drummer to the train depot, dusting his heels with their six-guns. The final straw came when they started peppering the locomotive bell with lead.

The constable thought that was going a little too far and he locked them up to sleep it off. The next day they had been fined twenty-five dollars and costs in city court, which wasn't anywhere near as bad as their stomachs felt. Pigfoot's pop-skull had been known to draw blisters on a rawhide boot, and what it could do to a man's innards was pure misery.

Now the lady had shown up unexpectedly, and from the sound of things the master of the house was coming out on the short end of the stick. Then a funny thing happened. Along about dusk the battle came to an abrupt halt and an eerie quiet settled over the main house. The crew waited awhile, just to see if the boss and his Mrs. were getting their second wind. But it seemed sort of strange that no lamps had been lighted. Finally, their curiosity got the better of them and the men elected Dirty-Face to check things out.

The cook snuck up the knoll and crept indoors, certain he was going to find at least one cadaver. Shortly, he came hot-footing it back to the bunkhouse, fit to be tied. The boss and his lady, Dirty-Face declared, had shifted the action to the bedroom. And if they were set on killing one another, they were sure going about it in a jim-dandy way. The crew reversed their field again, deciding that the boss was the luckiest son of a bitch that ever drew a breath. With that they hauled out the free rotgut and got busy trying to take their minds off of what was happening up on the hill.

When Mattie and Cort stepped from the house next morning they looked like a couple of lovebirds, and the boys were more impressed than ever with the boss. While they knew he was many things, they had never suspected that he was also a ladies' man. Whatever he had done in that bedroom had wrought a powerful change in Mrs. Thomson, which considering the way she had stormed the fort the day before was no small accomplishment.

Mattie seemed delighted with everything about the ranch. She thought the house was just perfect, and felt it would be even more homey after she added a few feminine frills here and there. But the thing that really amazed her was how much Cort had been able to do in such a short period of time. This was a real working ranch, not anything like the backwoods' lark she had expected Cort to sling together. And from the little bit she had seen so far it seemed entirely likely he would turn it into a profitable venture.

Cort promptly took her on the grand tour. First he showed her the stables where her race horses would be quartered once the season closed, and she was pleasantly surprised by the clean, spacious stalls. Then they rode out and had a look at a herd of steers grazing on a distant swale of blue-stem. Mattie was shocked when Cort explained the difference between steers and cows. Somehow she had thought of all cattle as cows, and it saddened her to find that these poor creatures had to sacrifice their manhood just so people could have tender steaks. But they were sleek and fat, and didn't seem any worse for it, so maybe they were better off.

From her experience, there were too many bulls in this world anyway.

Along toward mid-morning they rode back into the compound and left their horses at the stable. Walking toward the house, they noticed two riders coming in from the west. Mattie felt Cort stiffen as the horsemen circled the lake and she saw that his features had turned to chilled stone. He moved forward as the riders approached, motioning for her to stay back. The men brought their horses to a halt, but made no move to dismount.

"Mornin', folks." Arch Armstrong greeted them, tipping his hat in Mattie's direction. "Thomson, if I'd known your missus was visitin' I'd have brought along a quart of my old lady's preserves."

Cort's expression didn't change. "Armstrong, say what you've got to say, and be on about your business. I've told you before, I don't want you on my range."

"Thomson, you're a hard man to get on the good side of, for a fact." Armstrong removed his hat and wiped the sweatband. "I got to thinkin' we just got off on the wrong foot somehow, and figured I'd have another try at talkin' reason."

"You can talk till you're blue in the face and it won't change anything. You're not welcome on my place today, tomorrow, or any other day."

Armstrong's leathery features grew a little tighter, and his smile faded. "Have it your own way. I'm only tryin' to be friendly. But that doesn't change the fact that I'm missin' over a hundred head of steers in the last month. Business is business, and you've got no call not to let me scout around and see if they wandered over on your range."

"Like it or lump it, that's the way it is," Cort growled. "If we find any of your stock we'll haze 'em back across the line, so quit pesterin' me."

"You know, we could come on over and just take a look for ourselves," Armstrong said pointedly. "I'm only askin' permission 'cause it's the neighborly thing to do."

Cort nodded, his eyes gone steely. "Yeah, you could. But

the first sonovabitch I catch on my range that don't belong there is gonna end up cold meat."

The rider beside Armstrong brought out a pint of whiskey and drained the last slug in a long gurgle. Wiping his mouth, he looked Cort over, like a gamecock sizing up an adversary. "Mister, you oughta try bein' more polite. Folks might get the impression you think your shit don't stink."

Cort returned the man's gaze, noting the cut-down holster, the soft hands, and pallid face. Clearly a man whose occupation had nothing to do with punching cows. Then he looked back at the rancher. "Armstrong, you must really be lookin' for trouble when you start bringin' in hired guns."

"I'm not lookin' for nothin' but my cattle. So far I'm out over five thousand dollars, and one way or another it's gonna stop. This here's Del Cox, and he works for the Cattlemen's Association. Specializes in *strayed* cattle, in a manner of speakin'."

The gunslinger shifted the bottle to his left hand. "Just so you won't think Mr. Armstrong is pullin' your leg, I'll leave you a little something to think about." He tossed the bottle high in the air, and clawed at the pistol on his hip.

But before Cox could clear leather, Cort's hand flashed to his pocket holster. The Colt roared and the bottle shattered into a thousand pieces. Cort cocked the gun again, casually centering it on the pop-eyed gunslinger.

"Mister, where I come from, we eat piss-willies like you for breakfast." Then he glanced at Armstrong. "As for you, the next time you come around here hintin' I'm a rustler, I'm gonna nail your hide to the wall. Now make tracks and don't look back."

The two men reined their horses about and spurred off in the direction they had come. They were in a hurry to put distance between themselves and that Colt, and they never once glanced back. Cort chuckled, thoroughly pleased with his morning's work. Then he turned to find Mattie eying him speculatively.

"Lover, you and I have some things to talk over."

"Mattie, don't start in on me again, I'm warnin' you.

That old sorehead just doesn't know how to run his own range, and it don't have a goddamned thing to do with me."

She gave him a cool look and walked off toward the house. Cort kicked at the dusty earth in exasperation, then trailed along behind.

That night the boys in the bunkhouse were treated to the second installment in Cort Thomson's private fireworks' factory. The crew got gloriously drunk, and made side bets on how long it would take the boss to get her bedded this time. The lady might be a stunner, they agreed, but being fiddle-footed and fancy free sure beat the hell out of getting your ears pinned back every night.

"Raise five hundred."
   "Call."
   "I'm out."
   "See the raise."
   "I fold."
Senator Edward Walmott spread his cards on the table. Three queens. The two men who had called the raise pitched their cards in the center of the table. Walmott scooped in the pot, sorting the greenbacks into stacks according to denomination. Not the best pot of the night, but nothing to sneeze at. Probably three thousand, give or take. Walmott was quite pleased with himself. By rough calculation he was already five thousand ahead, and the night was still young. Then he cursed himself, forcibly ejecting such thoughts from his head. Any gambler worth his salt knew it was bad luck to count your winnings before the game ended.

Samuel Baur, President of the Denver National Bank, collected the cards and began shuffling. The low overhead lamp reflected dully off the green-felt table and the large piles of cash arranged before each man. On Baur's left sat Titus Rich, recognized as the real-estate king of the capital city. Next came George Baldwin, one of Denver's millionaire mining speculators. Then Senator Walmott. And finally, Judge Lawrence Stack, head of the state democratic machine, but wealthy enough to feel right at home in such august company.

Horace Tabor had just left for a dinner engagement, which saddened the other players. Tabor played poker like a greenhorn, often dropping immense sums, and his contributions would be sorely missed. Still, his departure hadn't noticeably affected the action. The remaining players were among the wealthiest and most powerful men in the state of Colorado. Their influence spread to every nook and cranny of government, politics, and big business. While some were Republican and others Democrat, they never let politics interfere with the really important things in life. Like the game of poker. Each Friday evening they met in a private room above Clifton Bell's uptown club, and engaged in a lusty cutthroat game that would have provoked a gunfight every hour on the hour in the tenderloin. Table stakes, check and raise, two-hundred-dollar ante, stud or five-card draw.

Baur swiftly dealt the first two cards of stud and nodded to Judge Stack. "Ace bets."

The judge bet three hundred and as it came around the table Senator Walmott raised two hundred. Walmott was noted as an incorrigible bluffer, but the trouble was that he only bluffed about half the time. The other half he had the goods, and a man could lose his ass trying to figure out bluff from the real article. Right now Walmott only had a king showing, and he had raised an ace. The other men just called.

The third card paired Judge Stack's ace and Walmott and Baldwin saw his bet of five hundred. Baur and Rich folded. But on the next card Walmott caught another king, and, when Stack checked, the senator bet a cool thousand. Stack studied Walmott's face for a moment, but it was somewhat like contemplating a finely chiseled piece of granite. Finally the judge gave it up, and plunged ahead on gut instinct.

"Raise two thousand."

Baldwin folded without comment. Walmott blinked and

glanced again at the judge's aces, then just called. On the last card the senator caught a nine and Stack pulled a trey, apparently doing nothing for either man's hand.

"Thousand," the judge said, tossing a wad of bills on the table.

Walmott hesitated only a moment. "Raise two thousand."

Stack came right back. "Call, and up another two."

"And once more. Only this time let's make it five thousand," The senator quickly riffled a pile of greenbacks onto the table.

The judge scrutinized Walmott's hand again. It could be three kings, but somehow he just didn't believe it. "Call."

Walmott flipped his hole card. "Kings and tens beat aces every time, Judge."

"That's right, Senator. Except when aces are accompanied by a little pair of treys." Stack turned his hole card to reveal a trey, matching the one he had pulled on his very last card. Still, the judge was sweating freely. Walmott hadn't been bluffing! He'd had two pair wired, and if it hadn't been for that last trey, he thought, old Larry Stack would have been up shit creek without a paddle.

Walmott just nodded phlegmatically, and tossed his cards in. *Win a few, lose a few. Hell, that's what made the game interesting!* But that was still one fine pot. Of course, there were other things to be considered. Such as the fact that he now had the judge set up for the kill next time he caught a real bluffing hand.

Titus Rich shuffled, and after the cut began dealing draw. As the cards zipped around the table, Walmott's thoughts shifted to a matter that had been weighing heavily on his mind for some weeks. Now seemed like a good time to broach it, for the tides waited on no man and elections were fast approaching. The men gathered around this table were the movers and the shakers in the community, and if they couldn't pull it off then Denver stood every chance of going to hell in a handbasket.

"Gentlemen, while we're playing, I suggest we discuss a matter of vital importance to both Denver and the state of

Colorado." The others glanced up from their cards, somewhat surprised by his grave tone. The senator was the voice of the people in Washington, and whether Democrat or Republican, not a man present could afford to treat his words lightly. "I refer specifically to the forthcoming elections and the fact that the future of our state's capital city remains in jeopardy."

There was a murmur of agreement from the men around the table. Then Judge Stack spoke up for the loyal opposition. "Senator, no one would dispute that we're faced with a damnable mess. You're talking about reform and certainly Denver is long past due. But talking about it and making it a reality are two different things. Like it or not, we're still saddled with Boss Blomger."

"I'll open for three hundred," George Baldwin said.

The men came back to the game long enough to call the bet. But as Rich started dealing the draw cards Walmott returned to the political issue. "Judge, you have a point, I grant you. But Blomger is only a threat as long as we allow ourselves to remain divided. I have given this matter serious consideration in the last few weeks, and I've come to the conclusion that until we rid ourselves of Blomger and men like him this city will never be anything more than a waystation for the West Coast. Commerce and investment capital simply cannot be enticed into a town that allows itself to remain in the stranglehold of the underworld. Perhaps it will never happen again in our lifetime, gentlemen, but for once . . . *for this one election* . . . we must form a coalition."

Their reaction was like he had said a dirty word at a church social. Silence. The men concentrated on the cards, betting, raising, until finally Samuel Baur took the hand with three sevens. Baldwin gathered the cards, shuffled, and began dealing stud.

Only then did Judge Stack frame a reply. "Senator, that all sounds very grand and everyone is in favor of axing Blomger. But there are two monumental problems that have no apparent solution. First, the rank and file of both political parties are violently opposed to coalition, as you well know. And Moses himself couldn't bring them together. Second, even if we did manage to ditch Blomger somehow, he would promptly air all our dirty linen in public. And when I say *our dirty linen*, Senator, I refer to both Republicans and Democrats. Which means that any number of our associates would rapidly find themselves facing a grand jury."

The judge was so engrossed in his speech that he was surprised to find himself with two jacks showing. Delighted, he bet five hundred. Baur folded and everyone else called. Clearly there were some potent hands building, and this might just be the best pot of the night.

Walmott peeked at his hole card and noted that he had two nines, then he looked back at the democratic chieftain. "Judge, you make a good argument, I can't deny that. But there is a way around both problems. And I believe I've found it." The play ground to a halt as the men observed him with renewed interest. "Instead of attempting to organize a coalition ticket encompassing all candidates, suppose both parties were to form a very simple pact. For openers, we both agree not to accept the help of Boss Blomger, whether in terms of money or tenderloin votes. Next, we hold a normal, no-holds-barred election for all offices at both the county and city levels. With the exception of *one* office. I refer specifically to the post of district attorney. There we choose a coalition candidate who is above reproach and both parties back him to the hilt."

The men were stunned by the simplicity of the plan. It had everything, assuming the two parties could be whipped into line on one crucial candidate. Baldwin came awake long enough to remind the judge it was his bet. Stack hadn't helped his jacks, but Walmott had the pleasant sensation of sitting on three nines. The judge again bet five hundred.

As the bet came around the table, the senator concluded his pitch. "Gentlemen, the plan I propose will probably put Boss Blomger behind bars and, more importantly, it will return politics to the hands of those best suited to govern. Needless to say, it will also forestall the possibility of *our* dirty linen being aired in public. Judge, we're at the point of sink or swim, so I'll ask you straight out. Are you willing to commit your people to such a pact?"

The judge pondered for a moment, then chuckled. "What the hell, I guess we could work with you Republicans on one election. Senator, you've got a deal. But only on district attorney, mind you. Everything else is up for grabs."

"Done!" Walmott announced, and reached across the table to shake Stack's hand. Then he glanced back at the cards. "Now that that's out of the way, Judge, I'll just raise you two thousand."

"Senator, you're trying to run one over me. I'll see and up you three thousand."

The other men hurriedly dropped out, and Walmott smiled engagingly. "Judge, it's true I've been known to bluff. But it'll cost you five big ones to find out." He calculated that if Stack called the pot would be worth almost twenty-five thousand.

"Find out! Christ, I just wish I could raise again." Stack dumped a fistful of bills on the table and exposed his bottom card. "Read'em and weep, Senator. Jacks and fives."

"Sorry, Judge." The senator slowly turned his hole card. "Three nines."

"Well, I'll be a sonovabitch! He had'em again," Stack moaned. "Ed, for a Republican you play damned crafty poker."

"Larry, it's in the nature of things, but don't lose any sleep over it. I showed you a hole card tonight that will make us all rich. Democrat or Republican."

The deal passed to Senator Walmott and he deftly shuffled the cards. This had all the earmarks of being his night to howl. He had just won a hell of a pot, and it didn't have a damn thing to do with poker.

"Ante up for five-card draw, gentlemen. The only thing wild is the dealer."

Mattie's visit to the ranch had been brief. The situation in Denver was building to a thunderhead, and at best, she

could spare only a week away from Holladay Street. While
Handsome Jack was capable of handling most problems,
there was simply too much at stake, and she wanted to be
on her home turf should any new threat arise. Yet she was
torn by an equal need to remain with Cort. Though he
wouldn't admit it, she knew he was up to his neck in some
harebrained scheme, and without her restraining hand
he might easily go off the deep end. Still, she couldn't put
him on a leash like a lap dog, and she also couldn't ignore
the precarious circumstances in Denver. Finally, after Cort
swore there was nothing for her to fear, Mattie departed despite a nagging reluctance. He was an accomplished liar,
as she had good reason to know, and even upon boarding
the train she couldn't shake a deep sense of foreboding.

But if Mattie had been hesitant to leave, Cort was over-
joyed to see her go. Her fiery tirades at the ranch had hu-
miliated him in front of the men and for the first time in
his life he had been tempted to strike a woman. While the
crew never let on, he knew what they were saying behind
his back and more than once he had felt the urge to give her
a good, sound beating. Yet he found himself gripped by the
same impotent rage that had become the curse of his life
with Mattie. When it came to a showdown he somehow
seemed powerless, unable to resist her will, overcome with
the futility of even trying. Maybe she had the Indian sign
on him or perhaps he was just too damned chivalrous. He
liked to think it was the latter, but at the core of it, he really
didn't know what the hell kind of hold she had over him.
He only knew that when she was around he was the master
of nothing, not even himself. And he was goddamned relieved to shove her pert little ass on that train and ship her
back to Denver. With her gone, he was accountable to no
one but himself. Now he could get back to building his empire and the business of being a man.

Thoughts of casting a long shadow were much on Cort's
mind these days. The rustling operation was running
smoothly, despite much bellyaching from Armstrong and
Ashton, and he felt a need to branch out. A man of his

talents needed to stretch himself, to grasp for the brass ring, and aside from money, rustling just didn't satisfy the furies that gnawed on his vitals. Casting about for some new devilment, he fell headlong over politics. And Cort was suddenly smitten with visions of becoming the he-wolf of Yuma County.

The town of Yuma had been the county seat for close to two decades, but the citizens of Wray never cared much for the arrangement. Shortly after Cort's arrival on the scene, Pigfoot Grant had organized a band of insurgents and forced a referendum on a new county seat. Such struggles were common at the time, for people had awakened to the fact that wealth just naturally flows to the town that controls the county. Pride was involved to some small degree, yet the root of the issue was nothing but old-fashioned greed, pure and simple. But there were some whose motives stemmed from an even earthier source.

While Pigfoot Grant had nothing against bettering himself or his hometown, he was a born troublemaker at heart and just couldn't resist a good fight. Some men find solace in God, others take refuge in liquor, and occasionally one comes along that gets his jollies from chaining two dogs to the same bone. That was Pigfoot. The sport was what counted, a push here, a shove there, until finally he had everyone lined up in opposite camps shouting for blood. Normally a knock-down, drag-out brawl on Saturday night kept Pigfoot's curious appetite for violence in check. But with Cort's appearance, his horizons had somehow expanded sharply. For years he had talked of wresting the county seat away from Yuma, yet as far back as anyone could remember it had remained just that, mere talk. Such an undertaking required a cool head and if things got hairy, it might just call for a fast gun. Pigfoot figured he had the head for it, but Wray wasn't exactly overrun with gunslingers. Then Cort came to town and stuffed in his hip pockets were the missing links.

When Pigfoot broached the idea, Cort jumped for it like he had been goosed with a roman candle. With the county

seat in Wray they could get a stranglehold on the law and
even rustling might come to look like small potatoes. There
was no limit to the schemes they could promote once they
held the whiphand. Cort had seen Blomger pull it off in
Denver and anything that lard-gut could do he could
double in spades.

Pigfoot was as good as his word. Being a likable old
cuss, people just couldn't say no and over the next few
months he seemed to be everywhere at once. He organized
the movement, forced the county into a referendum vote,
and brought it down to the wire just as they had planned.
Armstrong and Ashton opposed the movement from the
start, being naturally skeptical of anything promoted by
Pigfoot Grant and his Johnny-come-lately friend. Their
losses from rustling had already grown to enormous sums,
and while they weren't sure about Pigfoot they felt certain
that Cort was the guiding force behind the night riders.
They just hadn't been able to prove it.

But Pigfoot hadn't gone to all that trouble just to let a
few hardnose ranchers spoil his fun. When the big day
finally rolled around, he voted every gravestone, stray
dog, and saddlebum within a day's ride of the town limits.
Everyone else got all the rotgut they could drink simply for
showing up and casting their vote, and the stampede just
about put Pigfoot out of business. All things considered,
hardly anyone was surprised by the final tally. When the
ballots had been counted Wray became the new seat of
Yuma County.

The citizens of Yuma itself took the whole thing sort of
hard. Sore losers, Pigfoot called them, when they refused
to hand over the county records for transfer to Wray. But
Pigfoot was a great believer in the law, especially when it
suited his purpose, and he promptly obtained a court injunc-
tion ordering them to surrender the records. Still, possession is nine points of the law and someone had to go get
those records. Considering the temper of Yuma's townspeople there was a sudden dearth of volunteers for the job.
Voting was one thing, but getting your ass shot off for a

bunch of musty documents was carrying local patriotism just a mite too far.

Rising to the occasion, Pigfoot had Sheriff Jake Fairhurst swear in Cort and his crew, along with himself, as deputies. Personally, Pigfoot was delighted with the way things had worked out. Invading Yuma with the sanction of the courts and a sheriff at your side was the frosting on the cake. This was going to be a real humdinger, just the way he'd planned it. And with Cort along he had every confidence that the fur would fly thick and fast before they returned to Wray.

Bright and early next morning, they pulled into Yuma and backed a wagon up to the courthouse steps. Cort and Sheriff Fairhurst stood guard while Pigfoot supervised Ab and the boys in loading the records. Working quickly, they systematically emptied each office, and within an hour had the better part of Yuma County's files crammed in the wagon. It might take a month or so to get the papers sorted and straightened out again, but somebody else could worry about that. Their main concern was to fill that wagon as fast as possible and get the hell back on the road to Wray. The building was absolutely deserted, like a graveyard at the side of an abandoned church, and the stillness had them spooked. While Pigfoot tried to keep their daubers up with a line of chatter, they each had a pretty fair idea what would be waiting about the time they hit the outskirts of town.

But the good citizens of Yuma didn't figure to give them that much of a head start. Like Pigfoot had said, they were sore losers and they meant to impress on their visitors that stealing a county seat was a costly proposition. For the last half hour Cort and the sheriff had been watching knots of men gather in front of the bank at the southwest corner of the square, but that wasn't what bothered them. The crowd was merely a diversionary tactic. What did bother them was the road leading from the square over on the opposite corner, the one they had to take out of town. Along one side of the road was a row of trees and on the other side was a ditch.

Which was no great cause for alarm, except that behind the trees and in the ditch were somewhere around twenty men armed with rifles. Since it was too early for hunting rabbits, they clearly had bigger game in mind. And it wasn't the kind a man brought home to hang in the smokehouse.

When the last of the records had been loaded, the men scrambled into the wagon. Wedging themselves between the bundles, they made ready to run the gauntlet, which in jest might have been termed a farewell committee. But none of Wray's gladiators was feeling particularly festive right about then, and their conversation was limited to muttered curses for letting themselves get jackassed into this deal. Squatted behind the driver's seat, Pigfoot took the reins and Cort crouched beside him, both Colts out and cocked. Pigfoot popped the lines and the startled team leaped away from the courthouse. Then he cracked their rumps a good one, and the horses broke out in a full gallop.

Roaring across the square, they swerved onto the road and barreled eastward. Precisely on cue both sides of the lane came alive with the sharp crack of Winchesters. And the dull boom of shotguns. *Those goddamn bastards were using buckshot!* Curiously, none of the bushwhackers tried to down a horse, almost as if they didn't want the wagon to stop till it reached St. Louis. But if that were the case they fully meant for it to be loaded with nothing but dead men. The wagon was enveloped in a storm of lead, raked from stem to stern, as if an angry swarm of hornets had climbed aboard and refused to go away.

Cort was firing as fast as he could thumb the hammers back, laying down a deadly barrage among the row of trees. But even as he fired the thought flittered through his mind that this was just plain damn foolishness. *Facing a lone man with a gun was one thing, but this was a goddamned war!* Slugs thudded and thumped all around him, and they were hit. Then as fast as it began, it was over. The horses were running clear and easy, and Yuma was rapidly fading into the distance. Slumping against the sideboard, he felt something warm and sticky running down his leg, and was surprised to see a widening blotch of crimson on his thigh. *What the hell? It's not the first time. And probably not the last!* Binding up the wound, he chuckled real privatelike, just to himself, suddenly very glad to be alive.

Behind they left one dead man and four wounded, and everyone in the wagon had taken at least one slug. But they were still kicking and no one would dispute it now. Wray was the county seat at last!

Pigfoot threw back his head and bayed like a hound under a full moon. "Whoooeeee! We done it, boys! We done it! Pulled it off slicker'n greased owl shit!"

CHAPTER ELEVEN

⊶⊷

Mattie still couldn't believe it. Even when she read the head-line in the morning paper it somehow didn't seem real.

BLOMGER MACHINE DEFEATED

There it was in black and white, but some inner part of her refused to acknowledge that Lou Blomger had been brought to earth at last. Considerably more than a decade had passed since that night he talked her into leaving Georgetown and over the years she had come to look on him as something apart from mere mortals. Not a god, certainly. More on the order of the devil incarnate or Ivan the Terrible. But none-theless omnipotent, wrathful, immune to the frail codes that governed lesser men.

When Handsome Jack had returned to the house late last night even he seemed mildly stunned. The polls had been closed for hours by that time, and early reports indicated that not one of Blomger's candidates would be elected. Then an eerie quiet had descended over the tenderloin as word spread throughout the district. Madams locked their doors and saloons filled with the numbed conversation of men who couldn't comprehend what was happening. This wasn't a simple rackets' war, with winner take all and business as usual. If Boss Blomger couldn't protect the tenderloin anymore, then who would? The Democrats? The Republicans? Were they going to send a man around with the little black bag every week? *Or just what the hell did they have in mind?*

When Mattie had sensed the stillness along The Row she knew it was true, just as the calm at a wake brings home the reality of death. But true or not, Blomger must still have an ace up his sleeve. He just couldn't be defeated that easily. It was impossible. He would demand a recount or send Slats out to gun down the winning candidates. Or something. She didn't know exactly what, but she just couldn't believe that Lou Blomger had gone under without a roar.

There were many things Mattie wouldn't have believed had she known. The weeks prior to election day had been a time of wheeling and dealing among Denver's politicos. The old rules no longer applied, especially the one that said all public officials must humbly genuflect before Boss Blomger. The lid was off and it was a wide-open race, with no man tethered to the tenderloin vote as in years past. Both parties had decreed that Blomger was to be ignored, in terms of money, votes, and threats. This was strictly between Democrats and Republicans and anyone caught sucking up to the underworld would be dumped on his ear. Candidates were encouraged to woo the reformers in their search for ballots, for in this election it was the do-gooders who would cast the swing vote. Denver was again going to be ruled by politicians and vested interests, the ones best qualified to govern. Naturally, the will of the people would be heard. But as in any democracy, the leaders would have the last word.

The one exception to this political free-for-all was Paul Vandever. Practicing lawyer, upright Christian, a man of impeccable morals, Mr. Vandever had been tapped as Denver's next district attorney. While he was a bit stuffy for a ward heeler's tastes, Vandever was acceptable to the reform element and both parties climbed on his bandwagon with all the fervor of old-time religion. Not everyone was privy to the details of the pact between Senator Walmott and Judge Stack, but it was hardly a secret that Paul Vandever had been given *carte blanche* to clean up Denver. With the exception of some shyster Boss Blomger threw into the breach as an Independent, Vandever was the only man running for district attorney. And the amazing thing to all concerned was that he came out as a Populist candidate, the first in the city's history.

But if the politicians were amazed by this curious turn of events, Lou Blomger was almost catatonic with shock. The one thing he had never figured on was Democrats and Republicans working together. Somehow it seemed like dirty pool. In one stroke, they had eliminated the power of the tenderloin vote and at the same time chopped his legs right out from under him. He felt like a man staring at a mother lode that had just petered out. The bloc of votes he controlled was now valueless, without meaning in a game that had been rigged with fresh dice and new stick-men. Still, in the political arena, just as in war, there were some rules that never changed. Not so subtle, perhaps, but gambits that had never failed in the past. Like bribery and intimidation.

And right about then, the fat man got the rudest awakening of all. Candidates of every stripe and persuasion just laughed when his emissaries went forth to show them the light. They not only backed off from an audience in the Windsor suite, they flatly refused to deal with him in any manner. Their reasoning was quite simple. If they were even suspected of any shenanigans with Boss Blomger their party would drop them faster than a hot rock in a heat wave. Once bounced they became candidates for nothing but oblivion, and even a cord of political deadwood wasn't about to save the fat man's hide. They might be scared, but they hadn't taken leave of their senses. He couldn't bribe them and killing them would serve no useful purpose, least of all his own.

Thank you very much, they said, but no thanks. And off they loped, jockeying furiously for the inside track in the new order of things.

Paul Vandever was an even greater disappointment. He wasn't just uncooperative, he was absolutely unapproachable. Guarded around the clock by a small battalion of deputies, he was like a man ringed by a moat of fire. Maybe he couldn't get out, but it was damned certain no one else could get in. Blomger even penned a formal letter, enclosing a draft for fifty thousand dollars as a campaign contribution. No strings attached. It was returned in a small envelope, shredded into even smaller pieces. Disgusted, the fat man announced his own lawyer as a candidate for district attorney, knowing all the while that he had no more chance than an icicle in a blast furnace.

The world had suddenly spun on its axis, gone topsy-turvy in a frenzied outpouring of integrity and forthrightness. While the politicians were bad enough, there was also something afoot in the tenderloin. He couldn't put a name to it, yet there was a mood that only a blind man could have overlooked. And these were his people, the thimble-riggers, grifters, and whores he had protected for almost sixteen years. It all surpassed belief, but there it was, staring straight down his gullet.

Still, there were some things that even Boss Blomger didn't know about, little things that might have dispelled a few of the enigmas being heaped over the fat man these days. Like a clandestine meeting deep in the night between Denver's next district attorney and former political czar Ed Case.

But by then it was too late. Election day came and by nightfall the tumult and shouting of the uptown crowd told the story. Boss Blomger and his underworld juggernaut were a thing of the past, ancient history, buried in an avalanche of ballots that expressed the collective will of the people. Little white slips of paper that spelled kiss my ass in Gothic bold.

Now, as Mattie sat staring at the morning paper, she was

still a bit unnerved by the thought of Lou Blomger being dethroned. Yet her concern wasn't for the fat man. Scorpions like him always lived to fight another day. She was thinking of herself, her girls, and the days that lay ahead. Seated in the upstairs parlor, absorbed in the dancing flames of the fireplace, she idly wondered where they would all be a year from now. Or tomorrow. Then her musings were interrupted by a knock, and Handsome Jack stuck his head through the doorway.

"Brought you some fresh coffee." Striding across the room he set the tray on a table, and gave her a scrutinizing look. "You intend to stay up here and brood all day, or are you going to come down and open the house?"

Mattie just stared him for a moment before answering. "Oh, we'll open for business, Jack. Can't let those uptown swells think they've got us buffaloed. Besides, I doubt that even the Crucifixion stopped people from getting a little lovin', so I imagine we'll have callers as usual tonight."

"Wouldn't surprise me a bit." Handsome Jack took a seat and nodded at the newspaper. "After sleeping on it, what do you think about Blomger getting his ashes hauled?"

"Hard times, that's what I see. Hard times and troubled days down the road. The reformers would like nothing better than to put the tenderloin to the torch."

"Then you don't think Blomger will be able to make any kind of deal with city hall?"

She smiled wryly, and tapped the newspaper with her finger. "Did you read how the balloting went? Lou's candidates didn't get ten percent of the vote. And I'll wager even the politicians were surprised by the drubbing he took. They've heard the word and our friend Blomger might just find himself stuffed and mounted in a museum somewhere."

Handsome Jack lifted the corners of his mouth in a sly grin. "That wouldn't make you lose any sleep, near as I recall that last meeting with him."

"Oh, Lou is just like the rest of us, Jack. He'll get what he deserves. Only I suspect there's not enough oil in Denver to boil him in."

"Well, he had a good run, there's no denying that. Unless I miss my guess he's got enough salted away to carry him long and far with plenty of comfort."

"God, I'd think so!" Mattie agreed. "He damned sure knocked down enough from us over the years. But I stopped worrying about Lou a long time ago."

The big man eyed her closely. "Meaning it's time we started worrying about ourselves?"

"Way past time! I've got a hunch we're sitting on a powder keg. And if those reformers have anything to say about it people are going to start dropping matches all over the place."

Handsome Jack shrugged, clearly unable to share her concern. "Sounds to me like someone cutting their nose off to spite their face. Christ only knows how much money Blomger has taken out of the tenderloin, and if I was a smart politician I'd sort of figure it was my turn on the gravy train. Besides, if they close down the dives and cathouses they'll have to raise taxes. Which means those same reformers will have to come up with a potful of gold every year just to keep this town afloat. They might be good Christians, but I've got an idea they don't hate sin that much."

"Jack, when it comes to cynics, you're king of the hill," Mattie chuckled, but her eyes remained troubled. "Maybe you're right. I certainly hope so. I've come a long way, and I'm tired of fighting. But you want to know something? I wouldn't retire if Mr. Holy Ghost himself served the paper."

Then it was Handsome Jack's turn to grin, and he got busy pouring coffee while Mattie went into the bedroom to dress. Business as usual, he thought—rain, shine, sleet, or snow. And today only, a special for reformers. Half and half for half price. Damn, that'd convert anybody!

Cort's features were set in a grim scowl as he rode into Wray. This time he hadn't come to town for fun and games, as anyone could tell by the look on his face. He was like an old bull with screw worms, which meant that anything could happen, depending on who got in his way. But at the moment he was looking for only one man. John Gilly.

Gilly published the local newspaper, and in last week's edition he had written a vitriolic article about the spreading menace of rustlers. While highly sympathetic toward the larger ranchers, such as Ashton and Armstrong, he had been something less than charitable where the smaller outfits were concerned. It was commonly accepted that little ranchers preyed on the big ones, he declared, yet there was a limit to how much people would stand. Branding a maverick calf or a few stray steers that legally belonged to someone else was all part of the game. Even killing another man's cow for fresh beef could be overlooked on occasion. But outright rustling of entire herds couldn't be tolerated. Ranchers in all three bordering states were losing cattle at an alarming rate, and, according to informed sources, they intended to do something about it. If the law couldn't bring these rustlers to justice, announced the editor, then the bigger spreads were determined to take matters into their own hands. They had wrested this land from the Indians, tamed it, fought off blizzards and drought, brought civilization westward. Ridding the countryside of a few mangy rustlers shouldn't be any problem at all, the article concluded.

Gilly's comments normally wouldn't have bothered Cort. Such tripe might give some people the shakes, but he didn't count himself among the faint-hearts. Slam-bang against this article, however, was another that did set Cort's blood to boiling. It was devoted exclusively to Wray's hellion in residence, one Cortez D. Thomson. After elaborating on some of Cort's gamier escapades, such as shooting up saloons, bullying townspeople, and provoking two near gunfights, the article got down to brass tacks. Very casually, Gilly dredged up Cort's months-old run-in with Arch Armstrong and the range detective, Del Cox. Armstrong's missing cattle were given prominent mention and a snide reference was made about Cort's refusal to let anyone inspect his herds. Cort had blinked when he read that. Clearly it was no coincidence that the editor had run this article shoulder to shoulder with the one about rustlers. The implication was as plain as the bumps on a horny toad, and only a fool could have missed the point.

Then Gilly went too far. Commenting on Cort's part in the Yuma courthouse raid, he observed that the abrasive rancher seemed to be uncommonly thick with certain county officials these days, notably the sheriff. As if wondering out loud, the article then posed the question of Cort's political ambitions. Any man who controlled the law from behind the scenes was a man to be reckoned with, particularly if he meant to use it for his own ends. Not that there was any hard evidence to that effect, but there was much speculation among those concerned with such matters.

Gilly's finish was a real corker. Labeling Mattie The Shady Lady from Denver, he noted that she had been a cohort of the infamous Boss Blomger. Such people had the insidious habit of buying their way into the good graces of public officials, and then flaunting it at their leisure. *Could it be that Mr. Thomson intends to establish a similar sanctuary in Wray?*

Cort had seen the paper only last night, when it was delivered along with a load of supplies to the ranch. But one quick reading had been enough to light his fuse. After saddling a horse he thundered off toward Wray, mercilessly flogging the animal through the night.

Now he reined the lathered horse to a halt before the small building that housed the *Rattler*. Once a fine-looking chestnut, the animal was spent, standing spraddle-legged as it sucked in great gasps of air. But Cort made no move to dismount.

"GILLY!" His angry shout filled the street.

Some moments passed before John Gilly opened the door and stepped outside. Along the street people paused, staring curiously in their direction.

"What can I do for you, Mr. Thomson?" Gilly inquired mildly.

"You can start sayin' your prayers, scissor-bill. Your mouth's too big, and I mean to shut it." Cort looped the reins around the pommel, freeing his hands. "I'm gonna let you have first shot, Mr. Editor, so make it count."

Gilly very carefully spread his coat open. "As you can see, Mr. Thomson, I'm not armed. I make it a practice never to carry a gun."

"The way you write that's smart thinkin'. But it won't wash this time." Cort motioned toward the newspaper office. "I reckon you've got a gun in there somewhere, so just trot back inside and dig it out."

"Sorry, I also make it a practice never to fight duels. Printer's ink and gunpowder somehow fail to complement one another."

"Gilly, you better listen to me good. I've ridden all night, and I didn't do it just to hear you jawbone fancy words. I'm fixin' to kill you, and if you've got any sense you'll get yourself a goddamn gun."

"Thomson, I really don't think you'll shoot me. You might have the sheriff on your payroll, but he couldn't ignore outright murder." Gilly nodded up the street toward the gaping crowd. "Not with that many witnesses."

Cort's right arm moved in a blurred motion and a Colt appeared in his hand. The gun roared and the pane of glass in the door behind Gilly shattered in a silvery explosion. The editor just stood there, calmly returning Cort's murderous glare. The Colt bucked again and splinters flew off the doorjamb at Gilly's shoulder. Still he didn't move.

"Get a gun, you yellow sonovabitch," Cort snarled. "Defend yourself."

Gilly could feel sweat running down his leg or maybe he had wet his pants. He was so scared he really couldn't tell which. But he just shook his head, refusing the taunt.

Cort's face went black with rage. Slowly he raised the gun, sighting deliberately. Then the Colt belched flame and Gilly's right earlobe disappeared in a crimson spray.

"Get a gun, you crazy bastard!" Cort's scream was hysterical, almost manic.

The editor didn't move. Or couldn't. He just shook his head, tears streaming down his face.

The Colt came level again, and when it roared the thumb on Gilly's right hand flew off at the joint, falling lifelessly in the dust at his feet. A bright fountain of blood spurted from the stub, splattering his pants' leg and boots.

Gilly's eyes glazed with shock and he froze in his tracks. His blank gaze never once left Cort's face, like some dumb animal stolidly awaiting the death blow. Unable to move, incapable of speech. Then his knees buckled and he fainted. Swaying, he folded limply to the ground as if his backbone had suddenly been snatched clear, leaving nothing but a pitiful mound of flesh and rumpled clothes.

Cort stared at the editor for a moment, his eyes glinting with maddened bafflement. *What kind of a man was this that would let himself get shot to pieces rather than fight?* All of a sudden his gut heaved and he felt like he was going to puke. Savagely he reined the horse about and spurred up the street toward Pigfoot's saloon. The crowd scattered before him, for he still clutched the pistol. But as he passed they began running toward the fallen editor and calls went up for the doctor. Cort skidded to a halt before the saloon and tumbled from the saddle, leaving the horse to fend for itself as he stomped inside.

Twenty minutes later, Fred Noonan, the town constable, eased through the saloon door. Cort stood at the bar, drinking straight from the bottle, clearly working himself up to a mean drunk. Pigfoot just watched, his face scrunched up like an inquisitive old bird, saying nothing.

Noonan was quite plainly scared shitless. He was a big, hulking man built like a blacksmith, but he was no gunfighter. He had been hired to keep drunks off the street and chase stray dogs, not go up against madmen with blood in their eye. Slow-witted, much like an amiable bear, he was something of a joke around town. He wore big, floppy mule-ear boots, and his feet looked to be near the size of nail kegs. His movements were clumsy, almost disjointed, and he was about as light on his feet as an elephant. Easing along the bar in Cort's direction, he smiled sheepishly, as if he expected someone to kick him in the ass at any moment.

"Mr. Thomson, I'm plumb sorry to have to do this, but it's just my job, you know. Believe me, there ain't nothin' personal in it."

Cort's head swiveled around, and he gave the big man a cool, saturnine look. "Noonan, what the fuck do you want?"

"It ain't me, Mr. Thomson. You got to understand that." The constable swallowed, like his gorge was stuffed with gravel. "It's them folks up at the newspaper. They swore out a complaint against you."

Cort's laugh was shrill, gibbery, the spooky laugh of a loon in darkened woods. "And what do you figure on doin' about it?"

"Well, it ain't like I had no choice, don't you see what I mean? I got to ask for your guns."

Cort faced him then, his eyes gone icy blue like stained glass. "You're gonna lock me up, is that it?"

"Yes sir, that's the way she's got to be." Noonan moved another step closer. "Now if you'd just hand me them guns I'd be much obliged."

Then the big man halted as Cort came up with a Colt and centered it on his belly. "Noonan, how'd you like me to shoot your pud off?"

The constable didn't exactly know what a pud was, but he had a pretty good idea he didn't want his shot off. "Mr. Thomson, I ain't lookin' to get shot. I'm just a family man tryin' to earn a livin'."

"Well, now, Fred, you should've thought about your family before you came bustin' in here like John Law." Cort eyed him coldly for a moment. "Tell you what, I'll let you out of here alive, but only if you go out like I say."

Noonan was visibly shaken, unable to take his eyes off the big round hole in the end of Cort's pistol. "Yes sir. Anything you say, Mr. Thomson. That's the way she'll be."

"Fred, there's folks in this town that say you haven't got sense enough to pour piss out of a boot. But I'd say you're a pretty smart fella." Cort glanced around at Pigfoot. "Fred? Fred? Pigfoot, I'm damned if that don't sound like a dog's name. You ever have a dog named Fred?"

Pigfoot looked ashen-faced and he just smiled tightly, shaking his head. He had seen that wild look before, mostly when men were spooked clean out of their skulls. And friend or no friend, he didn't want any part of this game.

Cort's eyes got brighter and his mouth twisted in a peculiar grin. "Well, by God, we've got one now. And he's a whopper. Fred, get down on your hands and knees. Who the hell ever heard of a dog standin' on his hind legs?"

Slowly it dawned on the big man what was expected of him, and with his eye still on the gun he sank to his hands and knees. Cort's grin got wider and he waved the pistol toward the door. "Now, Fred, all you've got to do to get out of here alive is take off runnin' like a dog and bark your ass off till you're clean across the street. Except when you get to the middle of the street I want you to stop and lift your leg like a dog takin' a piss. Got that? Right in the middle of the street. And remember, I'll be watchin' you all the way. You ready? That's a good dog, Fred. Now scat!"

Cort fired the Colt into the ceiling and Noonan took off in a crablike run toward the door.

"Arf! Arf! Arf!" he yelped pitifully.

"Louder, goddamnit," Cort bellowed, loosing another shot. "You're supposed to be a *big* dog."

"Woof! Woof! Woof!" Noonan switched to a deep-throated bark as he scuttled through the door and down the steps.

Cort stepped quickly to the door and waited for the constable to reach the center of the street. When Noonan stopped and lifted his leg, Cort casually planted a shot in the dust directly beneath his crotch. The big man leaped to his feet and took off running like the hounds of hell were snapping at his heels.

Cort reeled back into the saloon, collapsing over the bar in fits of crazed laughter. "Goddamn, Pigfoot, you should've seen the sonovabitch run." Then his laughter became even more hysterical. "Get it? It's a joke. Son of a *bitch!*"

Pigfoot got it all right, but he didn't like it. And he wasn't

laughing. Shooting up some half-assed newspaper editor
was one thing. Messing with the law was another ball of
wax altogether. People didn't like to see their lawmen made
fools of, especially when somebody scared one so bad he
was willing to crawl like a dog. It made folks jittery when
the law couldn't toe the line, and sometimes that didn't leave
them nowhere else to turn except to themselves.

All of a sudden, Pigfoot Grant decided his alliance with
Mr. Cortez Thomson had just been dissolved—and none too
soon.

Kid Duffy would recall in later years that he had been skeptical of the mark from the very outset. After a lifetime devoted to separating the gullible from their bankrolls he had
developed a sixth sense when it came to suckers. And there
was just something that didn't smell right about this jasper.
Not that he didn't have the money—he was loaded and it
looked like a sure-fire cinch for a touch of at least twenty-
five thousand. Still, the amount of money in itself wasn't
suspicious. Lots of well-heeled dudes came through Denver looking for a sharp deal and a fast profit. No, it wasn't
the money. It was something less tangible, something he
couldn't put his finger on. Perhaps the mark had seemed too
anxious or too easy to convince. Or maybe the larceny in
his soul had been a mite too obvious. Whatever it was, Kid
Duffy had a premonition about this one, a gut reaction that
he later wished he had heeded.

The Kid had gone to Blomger with his uncertainty. The
standing rule, at any rate, was that the boss had to approve
all deals over ten thousand before money actually changed
hands. Blomger had his own sources of information, and he
was very wary of gaffing anyone with influential friends.
But that had been one of the fat man's off days. The elections were only a week away, and he was preoccupied with
matters of greater consequence. Besides, he had announced,
they needed the money more than ever before. Twenty-five
thousand would buy a great many votes, and the way things
were shaping up it seemed likely they would need all the

support they could get. Overriding the Kid's misgivings, he ordered that the sucker be trimmed. The faster, the better. Adolph Duff, alias Kid Duffy, did as he was told, turning in a stellar performance. The mark was gaffed, bled dry, and cued offstage in record time. And the whole affair was forgotten the moment it ended, just an insignificant charade in the hall of mirrors that Kid Duffy manipulated so adroitly.

But the insignificance of that minor little drama shortly returned to haunt them. Less than a fortnight after the newly elected district attorney had taken the oath of office, a curious group of men began gathering in a subterranean chamber beneath the state-capital building. They came singly and in pairs, only after it had grown full dark, slipping unnoticed through a rear entrance. Two burly state rangers guarded the door, and once a man entered he wasn't allowed to leave. Not even for the call of nature. Anyone with a nervous bladder would just have to tie a string around it, and hope that this strange meeting ended before the dam burst.

Few of the men knew why they were there and as the crowd grew they became even more puzzled. Slowly the room filled with state rangers, officers from the district attorney's staff, and a scattering of civilians. This latter group threw everyone into a real quandary, including themselves. For while they were influential members of the community, they had absolutely nothing to do with law enforcement. By ten that evening the crowd had swelled to more than fifty men, and each of them had a different theory as to the reason for their presence.

Then the door opened one last time and Paul Vandever strode to the front of the room, accompanied by the state adjutant general, Colonel Phillip Hamrick. Vandever raised his hand for silence and a hush settled over the assembled men.

"Gentlemen, I apologize for the lateness of the hour, but I assure you it's for a worthy purpose. No doubt you are curious as to the exact nature of that purpose, however, I would first like to thank you for maintaining the secrecy that our meeting demanded. Now, as you all know, I have recently been installed as district attorney, and you may recall that my central campaign promise was to the effect that Denver would be divested of its more unsavory element. Tonight we begin chasing the rats from their holes!"

A murmur of excitement swept over the crowd and they began jabbering in subdued voices. Then Vandever held aloft a stack of official-looking documents, and the hubbub melted once again into dead silence.

"These are indictments, gentlemen, handed down not an hour ago by a specially empaneled grand jury. These scraps of paper are so vital to the future of our city that even the grand jury has been cloistered here in the capital building for the remainder of the night. They represent warrants for the arrest of Boss Blomger and sixty-two of his henchmen. Before sunrise I intend to see that every one of them is behind bars. And with the evidence we have accumulated, I feel reasonably safe in predicting that each of these men will spend a number of years in the state penitentiary."

There was a moment of stunned silence, then the men all began chattering at once. The enormity of Vandever's plan was stupefying. And they were going to be part of it! The night that would end the underworld's domination of Denver politics.

But their excitement might not have been so great had they known what the warrants contained. Blomger and his men had been indicted on a simple bunco charge. Grand larceny, of course, but nothing more. Not one man, not even the Kingpin himself, would stand trial for nearly two decades of corrupting public officials. Such indictments had been considered, but only briefly, and by the most naive man in Denver politics.

On his own initiative, Paul Vandever had arranged a secret meeting with Ed Case some weeks before the elections. Without mincing words, Vandever promised Case immunity from prosecution if he would turn state's evidence on the graft and corruption that permeated every level of

Denver officialdom. Case knew a sinking ship when he saw one, and he leaped at the chance to save his own skin. He had been the liaison man between Blomger and the politicians, and his testimony in open court could scuttle half the officeholders in the city. While he would come out of it a ruined man, branded a turncoat and traitor, he would be free. And under Blomger's thumb that was a luxury he hadn't enjoyed for many years. But it was never to be.

When Senator Walmott and Judge Stack got wind of the deal they sat Vandever down and gave him a brief discourse on the facts of life. The first law of political survival, they counseled, was that one never upset the applecart of fellow public servants. Such things had a way of coming full circle, ultimately forcing the do-gooder himself out of office. And once on the outside looking in, he found that retribution came in massive doses. At the very least his career, be it law or otherwise, would wither on the vine. More likely, he would be dubbed a social leper and find his life plagued with a curious chain of personal misfortunes. Exposing corruption was somewhat of a Pandora's box, they explained. When opened, it had the damnedest way of tainting the entire party, perhaps even both parties. And the man responsible could look forward to a very lonely, and meager, existence. No, it was far better, they advised, to remove the source of corruption, the underworld bosses. Let the political fraternity handle its own problems in its own way. Otherwise a man might destroy public confidence in the system, not to mention himself.

While Vandever might have been naive, he wasn't without common sense. Principle must sometimes be tempered with pragmatism. Compromise, he told himself, was the bedrock of man's enduring struggle to rise above narrow-mindedness and shallow precepts. Even the Christian martyrs had eventually seen the futility of feeding themselves to the lions, and a reformer would do well to heed the example. Besides, he had grown rather fond of the role of political crusader, and a bit of flexibility might lead to even greater things. Like governor, or maybe even senator.

With the agility of an old pro, Vandever had rationalized the entire affair to his own satisfaction and once again consigned Ed Case to a back burner. Instead of the corrupted, he would topple the corruptors. Hadn't the good Lord lived by a similar code? Certainly, he had. And the way to bring Lou Blomger down was to trap him in a swindle. Which is exactly what he had done, employing a private detective from Kansas City and twenty-five thousand dollars from a political slush fund as bait.

Now he raised his hand again, stilling the excited talk among the men of his strike force. "Gentlemen, I congratulate you on being selected to participate in the first of many raids that will destroy the tenderloin. You will notice that there are no city lawmen among your ranks, for obvious reasons. This is to be a well-coordinated and highly secretive operation. The civilians present have been chosen because they are trustworthy, and quite frankly, because we needed good men to augment our force. You will be deputized and armed, and assigned to the raiding parties. We will strike at four in the morning and by dawn I fully expect that the underworld will be a thing of the past in Denver. Now, before Colonel Hamrick takes over to designate the raiding teams, I have but one thing to say. The men we seek this night are armed and they are dangerous. Should they resist, I authorize you to use maximum force. And the people of this fair city will bless you, just as they would if you shot down a mad dog. Thank you, and God watch over each one of you in this hazardous undertaking."

Colonel Hamrick, once in the vanguard of Sherman's march to the sea, knew all about the conduct of raids. Reading from a roster, he quickly assigned strike leaders and an equal number of men to each team. Then he briefed the teams one by one, using maps of their individual targets, and suggesting the best means of bottling up their quarry. Every team would strike at four on the nose, returning their prisoners to the capital-building basement, then scatter to hit their secondary targets. As Vandever had said, it was a well-organized, carefully calculated maneuver.

Later, after the raiders had departed, Vandever and Hamrick paced the room, nervously sipping hot, black coffee. They were confident that nothing would go awry, but there could always be a slip-up. Or, for all they knew, Boss Blomger could even have a spy planted on their own staffs. The man was diabolically clever, and nothing was certain till they saw him behind bars. Then, shortly after five, their worries vanished in a single instant. The door opened and officers started herding one batch of prisoners after another into the dank chamber. A few appeared battered and bruised, but nothing that would hinder a speedy trial. And in the second motley group to be shoved through the door was the object of Vandever's extraordinary manhunt. The boss himself, Lou Blomger.

Sighting the district attorney, Blomger strode forward arrogantly. "Vandever, what the hell do you mean rousting a man out of bed in the middle of the night?"

"Well, Mr. Blomger, we meet at last." Vandever casually studied the fat man, relishing the moment. "To answer your question, I believe a warrant for your arrest quite adequately justifies our actions tonight."

"A bunco charge? You must be out of your mind." Blomger's piggish eyes swept over the district attorney contemptuously. "I'll be on the street before you sit down to breakfast."

"Perhaps. But if I were a betting man, Mr. Blomger, I'd wager otherwise. You see we have quite a strong case against you. And to paraphrase the Good Book, I suspect that before the cock crows thrice more than one Judas will appear among your confederates."

Blomger laughed, but it was a superficial effort, like a medicine-show quack faced with an unruly crowd. "Vandever, I'm fond of quotes myself. So I'll make it an even exchange. To paraphrase one of my saltier ancestors, barnyards aren't the only thing full of shit."

Blomger turned and crossed the room to rejoin the prisoners. He'd had the last word, but winning a verbal skirmish was far removed from winning the war. The courtroom would tell the tale, and suddenly he felt very cold and clammy, drenched in perspiration. *Before the cock crows thrice. What an asinine thing to say.* But without Slats to back his play, what was left to stop a Judas from spilling his guts? He shuddered, remembering how Slats had withered under the hail of gunfire. But that was Slats. Anybody broke down your door, you opened up on them, even if they were wearing badges. *Well, the squinty-eyed little bastard had finally paid for his keep. And who knows, maybe going under his way screws the house after all.*

Handsome Jack took one last look up Holladay Street, then mounted the steps to the house and opened the door. Locking it behind him, he moved swiftly through the vestibule and entered the parlor. Mattie had her back to him, talking with two men who stood with their arms around a couple of the girls. Glancing about, he saw only two other girls, which meant there were four upstairs turning a trick. After what had happened last night he was surprised to see any callers at all in the house. But there was no explaining some men. They had to have it come hell or high water, and it occurred to him that tonight they might see a little bit of both.

Then Mattie turned, laughing at something one of the men had said, and Handsome Jack caught her eye. He jerked his head toward the hall, indicating her office. She nodded, then looked back at the johns with a frozen smile. He stepped into the hall and moved down the passageway, knowing she would excuse herself shortly.

Moments later she entered the office, anxiously searching his face for some sign. His sober eyes said it all, and she sank wearily into a chair.

"You don't have to tell me. It's tonight."

Handsome Jack took the chair next to her, leaning forward, elbows on his knees. "The grapevine has it that they'll start raiding tonight, but no one knows exactly when. The boys over on Larimer are laying odds it'll never happen, and I'm damned if I can believe it myself."

Mattie smiled ruefully. "You can believe it all right, Jack. I told you once before that when those Bible thumpers get a burr in their pants there's no stopping them. They're going to cast out the harlot and smite the heathen even if they have to destroy Denver doing it."

"Yeah, I guess you were right all the time." He shook his head with a perplexed frown. "It just doesn't make sense. Without the tenderloin this town's nothing. Christ, they'll have to tax everything and everybody inside the city limits just to keep Denver running."

"Probably. But you have to keep in mind that these people are blind to reality, Jack. They're hypocrites, and so far as they're concerned, there's only one path. The straight and narrow." She laughed bitterly. "Hell, I was raised up among them. My father was the biggest hypocrite that ever walked the face of the earth, and I know just exactly how they think. They sneak drinks down in their basement, and screw the maid out in the woodshed, and let everybody go right on thinking they're the holiest thing in long pants."

"But it's just damn foolishness! How are you gonna stop men from gambling or getting a little on the side? It just can't be done."

"Of course it can't. The gambling dives and whorehouses will just go underground. But don't you see, that's what they're after. They figure what you can't see can't hurt you. So they'll crawl back in their self-righteous shells and tell God what a good job they've done."

"Yeah, I see. But it beats me how anybody could be so damned nearsighted they can't even see the facts of life." Handsome Jack stared at the floor, thoroughly mystified by the whole affair.

"Jack, you have to live among them before you can really understand 'em. They're so all-fired set on getting into heaven that it's not enough that *they* walk the straight and narrow. Everybody else has to walk it with them. And if that means denying a man the right to choose his own form of damnation then the constitution just has to bend to fit their interpretation of the Good Book."

They lapsed into silence for a few moments, each absorbed in their own thoughts. Then Mattie sighed heavily and looked at him. "What did you find out about Blomger?"

"Not a hell of a lot. Word's out that Kid Duffy has been put off in a cell all by himself, so everyone figures he's going to sing a blue streak to save his own skin. But you know how things like that are. Nobody'll have the straight goods till the day they come into court."

"Well, whatever happens, Lou Blomger's the luckiest man I know. When I think of all the things he's done, and they've got him up on a bunco charge. It's almost laughable."

"Nobody's laughing in the tenderloin tonight. They're sweating blood." Handsome Jack straightened up, suddenly reminded of their own predicament. "Assuming they are going to raid tonight, don't you think we ought to do something? Like get the johns out of the house just for a starter."

Mattie sunk deeper into her chair, and her voice was terribly dispirited. "Yes, I suppose so, but I won't have it said anybody got short-changed in Mattie Silks's house. Tell the girls I said not to rush. Every man in the place is to get his money's worth. Maybe we're going out, but we'll do it with class."

Handsome Jack nodded solemnly and left the room. Entering the parlor, he briefly explained the situation to the girls, then sent two of them to warn everyone in the upstairs bedrooms. Once more he checked outside, but Holladay Street seemed as deserted as a graveyard, and just about as lively. Returning inside, he decided not to lock the door. The bastards would only kick it in. Just then two johns came hurrying down the stairs, dressing on the run, and rushed past him. A pall of silence had settled over the house. Even the piano player was gone, probably ducked out the back door. Handsome Jack smiled reassuringly to the girls huddled together in the parlor, then walked back down the hallway. There was nothing more to be done. Except wait.

As he neared the office, he heard small whimpering

sounds, almost like an animal makes when it is desperately
hurt. Easing through the doorway he saw Mattie curled up
in her chair, sobbing softly. For a moment he was too shaken
to move. He had seen her cry many times when she was mad
or throwing a temper tantrum. But not like this. Disconso-
late and forlorn, as if she were a little girl whose heart had
been broken for the first time.

Moving across the room, he knelt beside the chair, taking her small hands in his. His throat swelled around a moist
lump, and he cursed himself for being unable to shoulder
the burdens that made her so wretched. Then she slid into
his arms, burying her head against his chest, shuddering
convulsively as she tried to staunch the flow of tears.

"C'mon, now, don't cry," he consoled her. "Everything's
going to be all right. Hell, we've faced tougher things than
this. You're not gonna let a bunch of tight-assed reformers
get you down, are you?"

Snuffling, she pressed closer, as if his big arms could
somehow shut out the world. "Oh, Jack, it's not just the reformers and having the house closed down. It's everything
piling on all at once. Everything we've worked to build all
these years, and it's gone. Just wiped away. And Cort." She
moaned, racked with gasping sobs as her fingernails dug
into his coat. "Oh God, Jack, he's gone crazy. I just got last
week's paper this morning and it says he shot the editor
down in cold blood and chased the constable out of town.
They're saying he's like a rabid animal, and even the law is
afraid to go after him. I don't know what to do, Jack. Where
does it end? How many times can I save him from himself?"

"You can't, Mattie. You never could." Handsome Jack
stroked her hair, holding her tightly. "He's like one of those
heroes in the dime novels. He's got to go out with guns blaz-
ing and his boots on. Don't you see, it never mattered to
Cort what he was. It only mattered what people thought
he was. And he'd ride bareback through hell just so people
would never forget he was the rankest thing ever to come
down the pike."

"But, Jack, I've got to have him. Can't you understand?

I've got to!" Her voice had gone shrill, like the plaintive wail of a cougar mourning her young. "Whatever he is, I made him that way. And if I don't save him, nobody will."

Before Handsome Jack could respond, the door filled with uniformed men. They had come soundlessly down the hall, almost embarrassed to intrude at such a moment. Then one of them stepped forward, ducking his head as she tried to pull herself together. "Ma'am, I'm sorry to bust in like this. But you understand, we're just followin' orders. I'm afraid I'm gonna have to place you and Mr. Ready under arrest."

"That will be enough apology, Lieutenant." A wiry man in a dark suit pushed past the policeman. "Come, Miss Silks, it's time to pay the piper."

"Who are you?" She slipped from Jack's arms to face him.

"My name is Paul Vandever. The new district attorney, in case you hadn't heard." He stuck his thumbs in the pockets of his vest, posturing slightly. "I felt it only fitting that I assist in the arrest of Denver's most infamous harlot."

"You sanctimonious sonovabitch!" Her scream rocked Vandever back on this heels. Handsome Jack grabbed her, but she struggled against his grip. "I've never been a whore in my life! Do you understand? I'm a madam! And I know the law, too. This is a city arrest and the county has no authority here. Now get your ass out of my house, you goddamn publicity hound. Get out! Or I'll claw your eyes out and give the newspapers a real story."

Vandever wilted before her attack, and retreated through the door. The policemen exchanged amused glances and the lieutenant covered his mouth to hide a grin. Then the moment passed, and the officer's face turned somber. "I expect we better get along, ma'am. I've got a paddywagon pulled up out front, and your girls are probably loaded by now."

"A paddywagon," Mattie groaned. "Jesus, what a comedown. Will it be all right if I send a message to my lawyer?"

The lieutenant agreed and she sent Handsome Jack to find the maid. Presently, he returned with a tiny black woman whose eyes were round with horror at the sight of so many police.

"Everything's all right, Jannie. These men aren't after you." Mattie was calm now, once more in command of herself and the situation. "Now listen very closely, Jannie. Do exactly as I tell you. Go to Mr. Caruthers, my lawyer. You know where he lives. Tell him to come get us out of jail."

Jannie bobbed her head up and down, repeating the message to herself, and fairly flew out of the room. Mattie turned and gave the policemen a devastating smile. "Lieutenant, we surrender. Let's go have a look at that Black Maria of yours."

Leading the way through the house, she strolled regally down the steps and climbed aboard the paddywagon. Handsome Jack squeezed through the door, the policemen mounted, and the horses took off at a lively clip up Holladay Street. The Row was swarming with uniforms, and it promised to be a long night before the last *fille de joie* made the trip uptown.

Some hours later, Mattie and her brood returned to the house in a rented carriage. For a real-estate lawyer, Caruthers had done his job admirably and they were scheduled to appear in court two weeks hence. In the meantime, the houses had been ordered closed and shuttered, and Holladay Street placed under an around-the-clock patrol by the police department. Entering the house, Handsome Jack noticed a telegram that had been slipped under the door in their absence. The wire was addressed to Mattie, and when she opened it her face went ashen.

Cort Arrested. Stop. Come At Once. Stop. Things Look Bad.

Pigfoot Grant

Mattie and Handsome Jack went directly from the train station to Pigfoot's saloon. She was tempted to head for the jail straightaway, but the train ride from Denver had given her plenty of time to think. Presumably, Cort had been arrested for gunning down the newspaper editor. Pigfoot's cryptic telegram left a few gaps on that score, so it could be something else entirely. Cort had apparently ridden roughshod over the whole community, and knowing him, she assumed the law had ample reason to lock him up. But whatever he was charged with, she wanted to know the details before she went barging into the jailhouse.

The train had reached Wray right about suppertime, and when they entered the saloon it was all but deserted. Pigfoot was behind the bar and his only customers, two men playing pinochle, were seated at a table against the wall. The men looked up as she came through the door, their card game forgotten. Women in Wray wouldn't be caught dead in Pigfoot's joint and a stunner like Mattie just made it all the more unusual. Besides, the town was sort of short on pretty girls, and that alone was reason enough to gawk. Heedless of their stares, Mattie walked toward the bar and Pigfoot came forward to greet her.

"Miz Thomson, I'm glad you got here so fast," he said. "Never put much store in them telegraph folks before, but I reckon they must know their business."

"I got your wire late last night and we caught the first train out this morning." Mattie inclined her head toward Handsome Jack. "You remember my partner, Jack Ready."

"Sure thing." Pigfoot nodded at the big man, but didn't offer to shake. He recalled the last time, and his hand had been sore for a week afterward. "Just between us, I'd say you was real smart in bringin' him along. Howsome ever, I'm a little surprised to see you. I thought sure you'd hot-foot it over to the jail the minute you got in."

"I thought about it, but then I decided we'd better find out what the deal is before we go waltzing in there." She hesitated, almost afraid to ask the question. "What have they got him for, Pigfoot?"

He glanced at the two men along the wall, who were straining to catch snatches of the conversation. "Let's take one of them back tables. I don't reckon what I've got to say is the kinda thing that needs spreadin' around."

Pigfoot came out from behind the bar, and Mattie and Handsome Jack followed him to the back of the room. They took chairs around a scarred table and the saloonkeeper leaned forward, lowering his voice.

"Now, they got him charged with tryin' to commit murder. I forget all the legal hocus-pocus, but that's what it means. It's nothin' but damn foolishness, 'cause anyone that has seen Cort use them Colts knows he could've killed that newspaper feller anytime he'd wanted. That don't water it down none, though. Folks around here ain't just fed up with Cort, they're scared as a pig sittin' on a meatgrinder. And they mean to put him away for a long stretch."

Mattie was visibly relieved. The taut lines in her face relaxed and she seemed more composed. "It's not as bad as I thought. That editor all but slandered Cort in one of the papers I read and a good lawyer could make a jury see that Cort had cause to go after him They might even let him off, since he actually didn't kill the man."

"Ma'am, I hate to be the one to say it, but Cort ain't got no more chance than a snowball in hell." Pigfoot shot a glance at Handsome Jack, then his eyes came back to her. "First off, there's only one lawyer in this town and he wouldn't touch this case if you handed him a blank check and tied a lightnin' rod around his head. If he did, he'd like as not get tarred and feathered before he ever made it to the courtroom."

"Well, that's no problem. There are plenty of good lawyers in Denver. I'll just hire one and bring him out on the next train."

"Sure you could. But that won't change things none. The jury'll be made up of folks from around here, and I'm tryin' to tell you they mean to see him locked up for the rest of his natural-born life, if they can figure out a way to do it." Pigfoot's voice trailed off and for a moment he just stared at the tabletop. "You didn't see what he done, Miz Thomson. Short of killin' a man, it was near about as cold a thing as a feller could think up. And it just flat put the fear of God in folks. Like I say, he's headed for the state pen and no two ways about it."

Handsome Jack broke in before Mattie could reply. "Mister, I sort of got the idea you were Cort's friend. But damned if you don't sound like a man that's already thrown in the towel and started looking for another meal ticket."

Pigfoot paled, but he didn't back off. "Well, sir, when you come right down to it, I didn't exactly have no choice. Lemme tell you somethin'! Cort had the sheriff on his payroll; everybody in town knew it. But folks got so riled up he even had to get off the fence. Walked right in here and stuck a gun in Cort's back like he didn't know him from Adam's goat. Then marched him off to the hoosegow faster'n you could say scat." The saloonkeeper's eyes wavered for an instant, then he looked back at Mattie. "Ma'am, I'm gettin' up in years, and a feller's got to look out for himself. I figured I owed it to Cort to send you that wire, but I can't take a chance on gettin' tied to what him and his boys have been doin'. And like as not, some jasper'll make sure it gets brought up at the trial."

Mattie frowned, puzzled by this last observation. "What are you talking about? I thought you said he was just charged with the shooting."

"God almighty!" Pigfoot blurted, staring at her open-mouthed. "You mean you didn't know?"

Mattie's baffled expression was answer enough. Weighing Handsome Jack's cold look against what had to be said, he decided to go all the way. "Miz Thomson, Cort and that pack of gut-eaters he hired has been rustlin' cattle like there weren't never gonna be a judgment day. Everyone in the county knew it, but Cort wouldn't stand for anybody comin' near his place, and they'd never been able to prove it. Quick as Cort was arrested, I sent my swamper hightailin' it out there to tell them boys to destroy all the evidence. But he came back and said them no-account scutters just saddled up and got the hell and gone before he'd even got his mouth open. You can bet your last nickel Cort's neighbors is gonna be nosin' around that ranch like bear hounds on fresh track."

For a moment Handsome Jack thought Mattie was going to keel over. Her face blanched, and she couldn't seem to get her breath. He took her arm, steadying her, and somehow she pulled herself together. But when she looked at him her eyes were bright with terror. "Oh, God, Jack, he must be mad. We've got to do something before it gets any worse. It's like a nightmare that just keeps growing and growing."

"Ma'am, I know I don't have no room to butt in, but lemme give you a little advice." Pigfoot's gut tightened as Handsome Jack's gaze swung around, boring holes clean through him. "He's your man, and what I'm sayin' ain't gonna be easy to swallow, but it's your best chance. Get on over to the jail and talk him into pleadin' guilty to the shootin' first thing in the mornin'. That'll satisfy most folks, 'cause they'll know he's headed for prison. And it'll get him out of town, which ain't anything to be taken lightly. Then you could sell the ranch and make amends with his neighbors, and in a few years he'll come out of it a clean man."

"And it'll also get you off the hook, won't it, old man?" Handsome Jack's deep growl was charged with contempt.

Mattie touched his arm, holding him back. "No, Jack, he's right. The important thing is to get Cort out of this town just as fast as it can be arranged. Then, once I let the other ranchers know we'll make restitution, it'll all blow over. Maybe he'll have to spend five or ten years in prison, but at this point I'm beginning to think it's the only thing that will straighten him out."

She pushed the chair back and rose, observing Pigfoot's downcast look. "I thank you for sending the wire. You've done what you could and I appreciate it. And I don't blame you for wanting to stay clear of Cort's troubles. Sometimes I get the same feeling myself. Let's go, Jack." Turning, she walked from the saloon, with Handsome Jack hard on her heels.

Ten minutes later they walked into the jail, which was located only a short distance from the newly erected courthouse. Sheriff Jake Fairhurst came out of his chair and stepped around the desk, eying them curiously. City dudes didn't get to Wray much, and while he wasn't certain, he had a pretty good idea who they were.

"Evenin', folks. What can I do for you?"

"Sheriff, I am Mrs. Cort Thomson." She tried to smile graciously, knowing it wouldn't come off too well under the circumstances. "I would appreciate being allowed to see my husband."

Fairhurst just nodded, mulling it over for a moment. "Well, I guess it wouldn't hurt nothin'. Cort's taken all this pretty hard, and seein' you might cheer him up a mite. Course, I'll have to search you. That's the rule. My deputy don't come on till ten, and what with bein' here alone I can't rightly take any chances. Nothin' personal, you understand."

Mattie opened her purse and surrendered her toy pistol without a word. The sheriff looked a little surprised, but then he remembered what business she was in and smiled like an old chessy cat. After frisking Handsome Jack he took a ring of keys off the wall and unlocked the cellblock door. Stepping back, he motioned for them to pass through.

"You can't miss him, ma'am. He's the only boarder we got tonight. Second cell on the left. Sorry I can't let you in with him, but we got a rule about that, too."

Mattie and Handsome Jack stepped through the door and moved along a short corridor with three cells on each side. When they stopped in front of the middle cell, Cort was stretched out on a rickety bunk, staring off into space. Then his eyes came back into focus and he glanced at her with an odd expression as if she were a spook that had somehow materialized out of a moonbeam. Suddenly it dawned on him that she was real, and he leaped from the bunk, slamming full-tilt against the bars.

"Goddamn, Mattie, is it you? Is it really you?" He reached through the bars, touching her arms, then her face, as if to reassure himself that she wasn't some sort of apparition. His face split in the huge grin she remembered so well, and his eyes grew moist. "Jesus Christ, I've never been so glad to see anyone in my life."

For a moment, Mattie couldn't say anything. This wasn't the cocky high roller she had met in Georgetown so long ago, that laughing, devil-may-care Texan who had swept her off her feet. Thinking back, she could only stare and wonder where that man had gone.

"Hello, Cort. We only got word last night or we would have been here sooner."

"Hell, honey, don't give it a thought." He jerked his thumb back at the small cell. "This joint is first rate. Good food, soft bed, lots of time to sleep. Just my speed. Besides, you're here and that's all that counts. Now we can start workin' on some way to get my walkin' papers ironed out."

"Stop it, Cort! Just stop it." Mattie pulled away from his hands, willing herself not to cry. "You've played the fool so long you don't know what's real anymore. We've been to see Pigfoot, and I know the whole story—what you did to that newspaperman, the rustling—all of it."

"That back-stabbin' sonovabitch!" Cort snarled. "What'd he tell you? Nothin' but a pack of lies, if I know him."

"Not lies, Cort. The truth. And in case you don't know it, he's the only friend you've got in this entire town. He's just scared, that's all. Scared to death you're going to get him sent to prison, too."

"Listen, Mattie, they haven't got nothin' on me. That yellow bastard that runs the newspaper wrote things about me that nobody'd stand for. Not if he's a man, anyway. I called him out, but he wouldn't fight. So I shot him up a little bit. But I didn't kill him. Now you tell me, how can anybody prove I had intent to murder? Hell, it just won't hold water."

"That's what it's all about, isn't it? *Nobody would stand for it if he was a man."* Mattie's voice was harsh, cutting. "You had to keep on proving to everyone what a big man you are, until finally you went off the deep end. Cort, what you did to him wasn't the work of a man. Not unless you're crazy. I read those papers, everything he wrote, and it's all true. Every last word."

"Now you're against me, too! I always knew you were. And we've finally got it out in the open." Cort's face mottled and his knuckles turned white where he gripped the bars. "But those days are over, by Christ. I don't take orders from anybody, you understand? Not you or anybody else ever again. I've got a ranch and a potful of money, and I can do anything I goddamn please. Anything!"

Mattie blinked, fighting against the tears that threatened to spill over. "You poor, pathetic fool. You haven't got a thing in this world, don't you realize that? Nothing. Your ranch hands have deserted you. This whole town is out after your scalp. You're going to prison, Cort. Does that get through to you? Prison! And this time there's not a solitary thing I can do to save you. Do you understand? You finally went so far that not even my money can buy you out."

"Lies! All lies. My boys wouldn't run out on me. And you're barkin' up the wrong tree if you think I'm going to prison." But in his heart he knew it was true and an icy sliver of fear probed at his guts. Shooting a man was no big deal. Lots of men got shot. Rustling was something else again, though. The one unpardonable sin in cattle country. And if his men had left the ranch unguarded, he was in mortal danger.

Wearily, Mattie turned away, shaking her head. "Tell him, Jack."

Handsome Jack had remained in the background, trying not to intrude. Now he moved to the front of Cort's cell and let him have it right between the eyes. "Cort, you're going up for a long stretch. Ten years, maybe even more. With no one watching over that ranch the only out you've got is to put this town behind you. That means you're going to plead guilty to the shooting and let the state get you the hell out of here. There's no other way, so don't make it any harder on Mattie than it already is. Stop thinking about yourself for a change and see what this is doing to her."

A crafty gleam came into Cort's eyes and his hand reached out clawlike to grasp Jack's coat. "Listen, Jack, it doesn't have to be like that. There's another way, and you could pull it off. Easy as apple pie." His voice dropped to a near whisper, and he drew Jack closer. "There's no one out there now but old Fairhurst, and he'd be a pushover for you. You could wait beside the door and let Mattie call him in here. Then you coldcock him, get the keys out of the office, and we're home free. Hell, all I need is a horse and I can be in Kansas before anybody in this town has time to wipe his ass."

Handsome Jack peeled Cort's hands loose from his lapel, and glanced at Mattie. She just stared at Cort, tears streaming down her face. Turning back, he found Cort watching him anxiously. "Thomson, I took you to be a sonovabitch the first time I laid eyes on you. You always were and you always will be. You'd let Mattie break you out of jail and then you'd head for parts unknown. She'd be the one that goes to prison, and you'd be clear, and that's all you care about." Handsome Jack's gaze went steely and his fists clenched in tight knots. "Man, I wouldn't piss on you if your guts were on fire."

"You rotten cocksucker!" Cort screamed. "You're not foolin' anybody. You want her for yourself. You've always wanted her! What do you think I am, some kind of dummy? I've known it from the very beginning. I could see it written all over you. And now you're gonna railroad my ass into prison just so you can have her. Hell, maybe she's even in on it with you. Well, take her, you hairy fuckin' gorilla. Be my guest. Merry Christmas! And don't let the door hit you in the ass on your way out!"

Handsome Jack started toward Mattie then froze as the sound of angry voices erupted in the front office. Apparently some sort of scuffle was going on, but abruptly everything grew very quiet. Ominously so. Then the door opened, and Sheriff Fairhurst was shoved into the cellblock, bleeding from a cut over his right eye. Behind him came a group of at least ten men, dressed in range clothes, with bandannas pulled up over their faces. The leader carried a sawed-off shotgun and he nudged Fairhurst in the back, forcing him toward Cort's cell.

"Get it open, Jake, and be quick about it." Glancing at Mattie and Handsome Jack, he came to a halt as the sheriff stumbled forward with the keys. "You two just stand easy and you won't get hurt."

"Oh, no. God, no!" Mattie gasped as it dawned on her what was happening. "Jack, they're after Cort."

Handsome Jack instinctively started forward and the shotgun swung around on line with his belt buckle. The leader cocked both hammers with a flick of his thumb. "Mister, if you take another step I'm gonna let go with this scattergun, and I judge the lady would take a good part of the load. Lady, you think it over, too. If you don't want him dead, you'd better call him off."

Mattie caught Handsome Jack's arm and pulled him back, certain he would be cut in half if he moved another inch. Watching from his cell Cort suddenly broke out in a shrill, gibbering laugh. "See, what'd I tell you? The whore and her pet gorilla! Hell, I knew it all the time."

"Get that door open, Jake," the leader snapped. "We've wasted enough time."

Fairhurst spun around, ignoring the shotgun. "Del Cox, that mask won't do you any good. I know who you are and I know who you're working for, so don't think you won't be called to account for this. By God, we've got law in this county and vigilantes can be arrested just like anybody else."

"Jake, if you're real smart you won't remember nothin' when this is done with. You had your chance to catch the rustlers, but you was too busy gettin' rich. Hey, which one of you boys has them brandin' irons?" One of the men stepped forward and thrust two running irons in the sheriff's face. One bore the mark X. The other was shaped ʌʌ. "Jake we found these hidden in Thomson's stable, and if you ever get your ass up in the air about this deal tonight, we're gonna start askin' folks why *you* never found 'em. Savvy? Now open that goddamn door, pronto!"

Fairhurst did as he was told, clearly shaken by the man's threat. The door opened and the men swarmed over Cort, dragging him from the cell. As they hustled him along the corridor he looked back over his shoulder, his face twisted in a wide grin. "Mattie, I'll meet you in hell. And when you come bring a big jug. I got an idea it's gonna be thirsty work."

Then they were gone, moving swiftly through the office and out the front door.

The masked leader pushed Fairhurst into the cell, then motioned with the shotgun, herding Mattie and Handsome Jack in behind him. Locking the door, he tossed the keys to the far end of the corridor, then turned and trotted from the jailhouse.

Less than a quarter hour later the vigilantes stood grouped around Cort atop a railroad trestle south of town. The Texan had a heavy noose around his neck, with the knot snugged up tight under his left ear. The tail end of the rope had been cinched to the timbers underfoot, and looked to be about three feet shy of reaching the stream below.

The leader checked the noose once more, then moved behind Cort. "Thomson, if you got anything to say, I guess now's the time."

Cort grinned, remembering the gunfights, the men he'd conned, the women he'd screwed, and above all the little fire-eater he had never tamed. Hell, it had been a great life, and he wouldn't trade a minute of it to see a Chinaman mount a ring-tailed baboon.

"Boys, I've only got two things to say. Firstly, I think you're about the sorest bunch of losers I ever run across. And lastly, I don't mind steppin' off so much, but I sure ain't lookin' forward to that sudden stop."

The leader shoved him from behind and Cort made a brief try at walking on thin air.

Mattie sat alone in the dark. The flames in the fireplace cast a cider-colored glow over the small parlor, covering the walls with soft, fleeting shadows. Her eyes were like glazed alabaster, flat and unseeing in the reflected light. She stared into the flames and saw nothing, yet revealed in her mind's eye was the image of all that was and had been, and would never be again.

For nearly a month she had shut herself off from the world, searching for answers that proved as elusive and spectral as the shadows on the wall. Her thoughts were like a spun web, a fused kaleidoscope of the past, and her mind was suspended in the hollow emptiness of dead years and unexpired emotions. She sought absolution, an exorcising of the furies that ate away at her heart, and within the darkness of her torment she groped blindly for the truth of a time now gone.

So much had changed since she brought Cort home for the last time. Not just within herself, but more significantly in the world around her. Or maybe it had been changing all the time, passing her by even as she clung to a way of life no longer in accord with the scheme of things. Perhaps Cort's death had awakened her at last to the realization that nothing remains constant, neither in nature nor in the fragile sand castles that man builds around his brief assault on the universe.

Somehow, when Cort was lowered into his grave at Fairmount Cemetery, she had sensed that a part of herself was being buried as well. While he had been headstrong and reckless, she had loved him fully, in a way few women are privileged to know in a single lifetime. Whatever he had done, despite his crazed accusations in those final moments, they had shared that love to the very end. *Mattie, I'll meet you in hell!* He had meant it, for they had often talked of where they would meet when old scratch finally called the roll. Even in the face of death he wanted her to know that he was still her man, and she would carry to her own grave the knowledge that whatever he had become was in large measure her fault. The strong dominated the weak, and there she had failed him. For he deserved more than a mere six feet of earth, with his name on a stone. And the debt was one she would repay when they next met again.

But while her grief was strong, Mattie didn't particularly mourn Cort's passing. Death was every man's companion, especially those who thumbed their nose at life, and Cort had never been one to whine just because his string ran out. Weak he may have been, but he played the cards as they were dealt and she wouldn't mourn a man who had defied the odds with such mirthful abandon. Still, she hadn't yet come to grips with the fact that she had failed him when he needed her most. She grieved his senseless death, and was haunted by her search for some justification of what she had made of their lives. But she wouldn't mourn him.

Wherever he was, she knew he'd be whooping and hollering, and scaring the bejesus out of those around him. And it just didn't seem natural to mourn the wild, lighthearted Cort she chose to remember.

Yet in those troubled days that followed Cort's death, there were many things that preyed on Mattie's mind. Like a lost soul in limbo, she felt imprisoned in some frozen pocket of time. The years had passed too swiftly in her struggle to reach the top of the heap. Somewhere along the line, she had lost all awareness of man's impermanence in his race with the relentless advancement of time. It was as if she had closed her eyes for only a tiny moment and upon opening them found that the order of all about her had changed. While she wasn't looking the world had pushed on ahead, altering things in such a way that those of her breed had become misfits in their own lifetime. The frontier she had known and loved in some strange way was gone, moribund, trampled beneath the onrushing demands of a new century. Civilization had crept up on her, encroaching, bit by bit, on a way of life that she thought would go on forever. Those who had led the way west, venturing into a land where survival was dictated by cunning and swiftness with a gun, had given ground before a more reasonable but no less determined breed of men. And in this new scheme of things there seemed no room for those who looked backward, longing for the way it had been rather than the way it had become.

The most brutal awakening came with the realization
that the tenderloin was now extinct. Like the buffalo and the
wild mustang, it lived on in men's memories, but its turbulent wickedness was no more. Every crib, parlor house,
and dollar brothel along The Row had simply ceased to
exist after the long night of raids in which more than a
thousand whores were hauled off to jail. Most of the girls
were able to post bond, and the wise ones departed on the
next outbound train. Those who stayed behind for their
day in court were treated to a rude lesson in the art of reform politics. Maximum fines were imposed, and in no
uncertain terms they were warned that any further dalli-
ance in the world's oldest profession would net the offender
six months' free room and board. Courtesy of Denver's
House of Detention for wayward girls. Before the trials
some ray of hope, however slight, still existed among a
few. But afterward there were none who doubted that the
tenderloin's death knell had been sounded and whores fled
the city by the trainload.

The high rollers along Larimer Street were equally hard-
hit. Gambling was suddenly elevated to a cardinal sin, second only to prostitution, and the dives that had gleaned
millions of dollars in their heyday were padlocked for all
time. Dealers, shills, and gambling impresarios joined the
mass exodus from the once brightly lighted tenderloin, and
within a fortnight Larimer Street looked like a ghost town.

That left only the grifters, thimble-riggers, and bunco
artists, and the new order had already ceased to worry about
them. With the arrest of Lou Blomger the underworld got
the message in big, bold print, and they scampered for the
hills even before the former boss and his cohorts could be
arraigned. Some days later, Denver's crusading district attorney called a press conference to announce that Adolph
Duff, alias Kid Duffy, had turned state's evidence. With
Duff's testimony as corroboration, Vandever declared, there
wasn't a shred of doubt that Blomger would spend the better part of his remaining days behind prison walls. Right
about then people began to take the pompous, unsmiling

reformers very seriously indeed and the tenderloin emptied out as if a purgative had been sluiced through the district's bowels.

Through it all Handsome Jack had been Mattie's one source of strength. Like a rock he shielded her from the storm that raged around them, refusing to allow anyone to see her until after the funeral. Bringing Cort home in a rough pine box was like something out of a horror tale, and the next week had been the most dismal of Mattie's life. Sorrow alone would have brought a lesser woman to her knees, but for Mattie there was the added burden of deep self-recrimination. Pacing the floor night after night, unable to eat, she flayed herself for what had happened to Cort, certain she could have prevented it had she only taken him in hand sooner.

Through her ordeal, Handsome Jack had listened, consoled, forced her to eat even when the mere thought of food made her nauseous, and, in a roundabout manner, halfway convinced her that God himself couldn't have saved Cort. But above all he let her draw on his strength, somehow restoring her sapped spirit as if his own will was being transfused into the very marrow of her soul. Bend she might, but break she wouldn't, and by virtue of his sheer, dogged determination he made her stand erect and face life for what it was. Badgering, cajoling, sometimes taunting her for being a quitter, he slowly brought her around, and by the end of the third week she was well on the way to becoming herself once more. Not there by any means, but he had nudged her in the right direction, and from that point on it was only a matter of time.

Now, as she sat staring into the fire, it suddenly occurred to Mattie that a month was long enough for anyone to mope around, especially since she hadn't solved a damn thing for all her brooding and inner turmoil. She would just have to face up to the fact that most people lived out their lives in a no-man's land, where what they cherished or believed to be right was more often than not compromised by the harsh realities of life itself. Though the admission came hard, she was no different than anyone else. Just flesh and bone, and if she were rendered whole, not an ounce of saintliness would float to the top. She endured by making arrangements with herself, bartering bits and pieces of her soul in exchange for survival on her own terms. Like everyone else, she became corroded in the process, hooked on compromise as a means of dealing with life's demands, and thereby living to fight another day. Perhaps it wasn't something a person ever fully accepted, but then she hadn't made the rules. Life got dirty in the clinches, that's all there was to it. And by Christ, she wasn't about to lay down and die just because she'd gotten a bloody nose.

With the resolution to get up off her rump and get back to living, her mind turned to other things. Thoughts that had darted and flicked across her awareness whenever she could spare a moment from wallowing in her self-made puddle of misery. Intriguing thoughts that bore absolutely no connection to what had been or what was, but only to the road ahead and what it might be. The longer she thought about it, the more appealing it became, and from whatever angle she examined it, there seemed no reason for delay. Denver was finished, unless she wanted to join the ranks of retired madams and somehow she wasn't quite ready for the boneyard. Plump old dowagers with shady reputations were a dime a dozen, and she hadn't yet reached the point that she was willing to play second fiddle to anybody.

Just then the door shook under Handsome Jack's heavy knock. And as she called for him to enter she made another decision that had been roaming around in the back of her mind these last few days—one she should have made a long time ago.

"Evenin', Mattie. I brought you some supper." Standing in the doorway, balancing a tray, he glanced around the darkened room. "What do you say we light some lamps and drive the demons out of here?"

"Jack, let's forget about food for the moment. Come on over here and sit down. I want to talk to you about something."

The tone in her voice caused him to look at her a little closer. Maybe she wasn't dancing a jig, but this sure as hell wasn't the bereaved widow he'd been mollycoddling for the last month. Taking a chair across from her, he placed the tray on a table between them. "I sort of get the feeling you've come up for air."

"If I didn't know you better, I'd think you were a swami." Her soft lips curved into a teasing smile. "The fact of the matter is, I just got tired of feeling sorry for myself and decided to rejoin the human race."

"Mattie, that's damned good to hear. I've been wondering when you'd rear up on your hind legs and take another swipe at living."

"Right now, Jack. Starting tonight." She came forward on the edge of her chair, her eyes shiny-bright the way he remembered them from times past. "That's one of the things I wanted to tell you. It just came over me a little while ago, and it's still sort of fuzzy. But it's enough to start on, and I think it's part of what I've been searching for. The thing that came to me is that none of us are free, no matter how much we kid ourselves into thinking we are. Every solitary soul on this earth is in bondage to something or someone, and the problem comes when a person can't admit that to himself. Cort was a slave to his vanity. Blomger was hooked on power. Me? I had this thing about being important. I don't mean in the sense of being influential or powerful. That was just a coverup. I mean being important to someone, a certain person. Knowing that I'm needed by someone is what I'm really trying to say. Don't you see, Jack? We're all in bondage of one sort or another. It's just a matter of degree."

"Yeah, I reckon that makes sense, well enough." He mulled it over for a moment, then smiled slyly. "What about me? What am I bound to?"

"Oh, no, you're not going to fox me into a corner. That's one you'll have to figure out for yourself."

"And when I do? What then?"

"Why, I suppose you'll just have to work up enough gumption to do something about it."

Handsome Jack just studied her, with a curious twinkle in his eye. When he didn't say anything she decided to push on. "Jack, I've made up my mind to leave Denver. There's nothing left here for our kind of people, and it's time to move on. We weren't made for the dreary little lives that most folks seem to think represent progress. Perhaps we were born at the wrong time, or maybe we've just got to have the blood and thunder that goes along with frontier life. At any rate, I know now that Denver's not for me. The era I loved in this town is long gone. Dead as a doornail. But there'll always be some wild man set on opening up a new stretch of wilderness. And when he does I want to be there. That's where we'll find our kind of people, Jack, and if we're lucky maybe there'll be enough frontiers left to outlive us."

"Well, I can't say it'd trouble me any to move on." He spooned sugar into a mug of coffee, letting her wait for him to pose the question. "Just which frontier did you have in mind?"

"The Yukon, Jack. The Klondike!" Her voice tingled with excitement. "There's enough gold up there to make Colorado look like a busted flush. The paper says Soapy Smith is already bossing some town called Skagway, and as much as I hate the bastard, he must be raking in a fortune. But the biggest town is Dawson, right in the middle of the goldfields. And that's where I want to go. God, Jack, can't you imagine how we'll knock their eyes out when we waltz in there with eight or ten beautiful girls? It'll be like Christmas every night of the year!"

"What about your holdings here? You own considerable real estate just to pull up stakes and go traipsing off to the Yukon."

"Oh, hell, we'll sell it. Caruthers is a shrewd old devil and he'll get top price. Don't worry on that score." Mattie grinned with a sudden thought. "Jack, we'll sail into Dawson with enough money to build the damnedest parlor house this side of a sultan's palace."

"You keep saying we'll do this and we'll do that," Handsome Jack observed. "If I'm going along, I'd sort of like to know what my part in this deal is."

Mattie sank back in her chair, and a coy smile spread over her lips. "Well, Jack, I guess that gets back to what I said a minute ago. It all depends on how much gumption you've got."

Handsome Jack's eyes crinkled, and he grinned like a bear coming up out of a honey barrel. "Mattie, you've made me wait a long time, and you're going to have to come straight at me with it. Are you proposing what most folks call holy wedlock?"

"You big lug, can't you let a girl have a little pride?" She laughed, regarding him with a coquettish look. "I'll put it this way. I've gotten used to being an honest woman and I don't intend to hike off to the Yukon with any man that doesn't have a ring in his nose."

"Now there I draw the line!" Handsome Jack stood and grasped her arms, lifting her from the chair as he would a fragile doll. "There's only going to be one set of pants in this family, and by Christ, I'll wear 'em. The first time you try getting bossy, I'll hitch up your skirts and paddle your little bottom till it looks like a couple of ripe apples. That's my deal. Take it or leave it!"

"Jack, you're such a tease." Mattie snuggled against his chest, fluttering her eyelashes like a helpless fawn. "Besides, lover, if you paddled my bottom that hard it wouldn't be any good to either of us."

Handsome Jack's booming laugh rattled the window-panes. He didn't have a chance against her wiles, and he knew it. Mattie shoved him back into his chair and cuddled up in his lap. The soft glow of the fire played gently over her face, and she buried herself in his massive arms, home at last.